BURN, BABY, BURN

A Magical Romantic Comedy (with a body count)

RJ BLAIN

Bailey and Quinn are back!

Bailey Ember Gardener Quinn should've read the manual on caring for an incubus before marrying hers. The marriage license hadn't mentioned anything about their sexy, insatiable ways. If she doesn't get a single night of undisturbed rest soon, she'll snap—or go on a napalm bender.

Either would work.

Recruiting Tiffany "Perkette" Perkins to be her partner-in-crime isn't the best idea, but nothing says fun quite like a road trip, and Perkette the Misdemeanor Collecting Queen could teach the devil a thing or two about having a good time.

Add in a string of rabies cases, more puppies than she can count (or readily adopt,) a job promotion, and her very own incubus in disguise on the hunt for her, and Bailey's in for one hell of a ride.

Warning: this novel contains excessive humor, a unicorn on a napalm bender, Quinn on the hunt, and more shenanigans than you can shake a stick at. Proceed with caution.

This one is for all of you lovers of fire-breathing unicorns.

ONE

If I didn't get a full night of sleep soon, someone would die

---

APPROXIMATELY FOUR MONTHS FOLLOWING THE EVENTS OF PLAYING WITH FIRE...

BAILEY

I LOVED QUINN, but if I didn't get a full night of sleep soon, someone would die. I gave it even odds on which one of us would bite the bullet. I'd either expire from his drive to prove he was the perfect man, or I'd snap, pop a few transformatives, and shove my horn so far up his ass it would take a surgeon to separate us.

Come hell or high water, I'd enjoy a full eight hours of sleep. No, I'd enjoy twelve, not my current three to four. Not only would I enjoy my rest, I'd have a great time securing it, too.

Quinn loved the chase. It made him feel important, feeding his ego and adding extra spring in his step. The smug incubus-in-disguise didn't need any more damned spring in his step. He needed to be sedated, tucked into bed, and used as a quiet but sexy pillow.

Damn it. That was the entire issue.

Neither one of us had an off switch, and Quinn viewed it as his personal mission in life to fill my every craving. The months since our haphazard marriage had changed nothing.

When he walked into the room, my panties spontaneously combusted.

I checked out the bedroom window to make certain he'd taken his cruiser to work. He had.

Excellent.

The snow would screw with my plans for a while, but I'd make do. I wouldn't use my stash of transformatives until I reached somewhere a lot warmer and dryer. I'd eliminate Las Vegas from my bucket list first. If my tall, dark, and handsome failed to find me there, I'd head to California.

All I needed to do was confirm my partner-in-crime still wanted to haul ass across the United States. Using the day-old phone I'd purchased with cash, I called Tiffany.

She answered on the second ring. "Your man's cruising your block, and he's got mine in the car with him. If we want to bust out of this joint sometime today, you need to encourage them to leave. Why does he insist on prowling your block for twenty minutes every damned morning?"

"The same reason there are transformatives stashed in every room in the house, Perkette. It's also the same reason he ripped out a perfectly good fireplace and installed a new one. He's insane."

"Bailey, we've talked about this before. He's not insane. He loves you. Now, go text him on your other phone and give him the list of things we picked for clues. After you're done, we'll wait for your chief to pull over, read your message, and head to work. If all goes to plan, he'll be distracted by your requests and fail to notice anything amiss."

However much it pained me to admit it, Tiffany was right. Whenever I asked for anything, Quinn went overboard catering to me. I sighed. "He's worse than a puppy."

"It's so difficult handling a loving man. Mine needs some excitement in his life, too. That's what we're doing. We're giving them some excitement for Christmas."

"Or signing up for a divorce."

"The cretins need the time off anyway. If it takes them two weeks to find us, they obviously need to brush up on their detective skills. Have you sent him the list yet?"

"Working on it, working on it," I muttered, pulling up the note I'd meticulously typed out, copying it to a text message. "He's going to think I've lost my mind. Who asks for an indoor rose plant, not for eating? I had to specify, Perkette. If I don't, he gets too much. Last time, he bought three dozen roses, and he made certain they were food quality."

"You specified the color, right? That's important."

"Yes, yes. I specified eleven orange roses, not for eating, and I indicated I'd like to plant them outside eventually. I also asked for a single red rose, too. Also not for eating."

"You have to admit you have issues with his rose bushes, Bailey."

"I have issues, period."

"That, too."

I sighed. "Do you think he'll figure it out?"

"Maybe your man will need help, but mine is a mad scientist freak with a puzzle fetish. They'll be fine. Just make sure you're ready to roll and read from the script if he calls you on the house line."

I texted that I had work to do and would have my phone off for a while before I killed the device and tossed it under the couch for safekeeping. "I told him I had work."

His inability to reach me would drive him home right on time, which would begin the hunt, as he'd begin searching for me within five minutes of discovering I'd given him the slip.

I hoped he liked the effort I'd put into wrapping his first clue, an old Elvis vinyl and a record player for his enjoyment.

"Bailey?"

"Phone is off. I'm about to stage the box. Did Perky leave your car in the garage this morning?"

"I already parked it in the neighbor's garage and gave her the keys. Your man's baby will be safe. Don't forget the card or your bag."

"I won't."

"And definitely don't forget the saddle, bridle, or trans-formatives."

"I won't. Have they left yet?"

"No, but Mr. Police Chief just pulled into a driveway around the corner from your house. If he heads to work, we'll know he's taken the bait."

How had I let Perkette talk me into her special brand of insanity?

Oh, right. I missed sleep.

QUINN

MY PHONE BEEPED, and I glanced at the device. While Bailey often messaged me to reassure herself, she usually waited longer than ten minutes. Our morning routine hadn't changed; she'd crawled out of bed with the same general liveliness of a half-dead slug while I'd kept a close eye on her until she finished her shower. Rewarding her with kisses for restoring her base ability to function had earned me a hefty dose of her contentment.

All in all, she'd been more energetic than usual.

"You may as well pull over, Sam. I know that's Bailey's text tone. If you don't, you'll fret."

Some days, partnering with Perkins gave me a headache. "Why am I driving you to work again?"

"Tiffany wanted to move to Queens, I don't have a cruiser today, and she wanted the car. As you're so compassionate—and you didn't want me to be late getting to work—you agreed to drive me in. Just pull over before she calls—or decides to take the convertible for a joy ride and tail you today."

She would. She'd done it twice, and it amazed me that my car had survived. The third time, I'd endured her at her worst, running around a late fall Manhattan on four hooves, determined to make certain I stayed out of trouble. Cindercorns didn't handle cold weather well, and she'd about scared the life out of me after reversing back to human. It had taken hours for her to warm back up, and she'd suffered from symptoms of hypothermia for several days before recovering.

Her ability to attract catastrophe sent me to work early to do a sweep of the neighborhood. I never found any trouble, but I felt better for putting in the effort. Once I checked to make certain I couldn't see the house, I pulled into someone's driveway to check my phone.

A ten item wish list waited for me, and every request

puzzled me. "I love my wife, but she's a little weird sometimes, Perkins."

"A little? She turns into a fire-breathing unicorn with a meat fetish and views sunshine as a mode of transportation. She defines weird. What does she want? She's usually too shy to ask you for anything, leaving you to make guesses. Outside of a photo of you shirtless and wearing a suit for her, has she asked for anything for Christmas?"

"I think she just did? Maybe?"

"Hit me with it. What does she want?"

"Eleven orange rose bushes and one red one. She's made a note they're not for her consumption."

"*Orange* roses?" Perkins fetched his phone. "Well, symbolically, they might mean she either wants you in bed or she's enthusiastic about something. Oh, that's interesting. Eleven implies you're her treasure. That's surprisingly sweet coming from her. One red rose is easy. She loved you from the moment she saw you."

"Perkins, don't you have this backwards? She's asking me to give them to her."

"This is Bailey we're talking about here. She'd probably choke on her tongue trying to admit any of this out loud. I kept the picture of when she blurted she loved you at the station. Remember what happened? She locked herself in the bathroom for two hours. Amanda's positive she heard Bailey moaning about how her life was over and she'd made a mess of everything again."

I sighed. I loved my wife, but Perkins was right. She defined weird. "You think she's trying to tell me that this way?" I smiled, shook my head, and laughed. "All right. She would. We've only been married a few months. She'll figure it out soon."

I hoped. If she didn't, I might go insane.

"What else is on the list?"

"A trip to a car dealership to look around."

"Well, it's about time on that front. She drives the convertible like a little old lady afraid of the speed limit." Shaking his head, Perkins joined me in laughing. "Get her a big truck. She'll feel safe in it."

I checked her list, and the next item worried me. Sober, Bailey was a handful. When exposed to napalm, she turned into a building-wrecking menace. What would happen if I gave her alcohol? "The recipe for a rather large margarita is next on the list."

"Does she even drink?"

"Not often. Last time she had anything to drink, she was out with your wife and came home traumatized."

"My wife is very talented at traumatizing people and making them like it. I'm sorry Tiffany traumatized Bailey again. I'm impressed, though. She got Bailey to drink something?"

"Bailey said she needed the drink to take the edge off."

"Tiffany was probably committing a misdemeanor again."

"Probably. Maybe Bailey wants me to drink half of it with her?"

"Drinking half would be the gentlemanly thing to do and might save her from alcohol poisoning. What else is she after?"

"A new pillow, pajamas, a necklace as badass as she is—her words, for the record. I think she was running out of ideas, as the rest is new pieces of tack listed individually. She claims I feed her too much. As such, her old set is pinching."

"The tack will be hard to get in time for Christmas, but

the other stuff is feasible. Have you told her about the proposal yet?"

I grimaced. After I had married Bailey, the CDC had started looking into every option possible to unload my wife onto the NYPD, and the NYPD had taken to the idea with disturbing enthusiasm. "Not yet. I'm worried how she'll take her reclassification. She's convinced the CDC is going to poke her some more. The proposal to work for the NYPD might break her brain for a few weeks."

"Everyone at work already knows."

"I know." I sighed at her final message, which informed me she'd have her phone off for the rest of the day. "It looks like her asshole boss has her scheduled in for today, too."

"Do you think she'll make a good chief?"

I knew she would—if I could convince her to give the job a shot. "We're going to find out, and when she freaks out, I'm going to tell her it's her fault for tailing me at work while wearing her fur coat. I should be grateful she's figured out how to reverse the transformation on her own."

It had taken me tripping over my own feet and spraining my ankle to do it, but once her panic had worn off, something had clicked in her head, and with a little effort, she could force herself to change back to human. She still needed a transformative to become a full unicorn, but I'd caught her with a pair of horse ears once trying to gain full control over her shapeshifting abilities.

I, rather wisely in my opinion, hadn't told anyone she might be able to transform into a cindercorn without the help of transformatives.

Perkins sighed. "You have to give the commissioner credit; if she's partnered with you, it'll take an army to get near you. Say what you will about the Calamity Queen, but when it comes to you, she'll set the world on fire to keep you safe."

"Or a chunk of Wall Street."

"No one in Manhattan is stupid enough to piss her off after that."

I snorted, fighting my smile over my wife's antics. "She braided my grandfather's snakes last week because he wouldn't let us participate in an adoption match."

"As prospective parents?"

"Temporary foster, but she's got a soft heart for the kids. My grandfather thought Bailey would be too vicious, and if I join a match, everyone will back out because of my rank. It's unfair. Bailey also thinks it's unfair as she's eager and able to beat anyone who even thinks about hurting a kid. She hasn't said anything yet about wanting kids, but she's been eyeing her birth control in the morning. As far as I can tell, she's debating between lighting it on fire or tossing it in the trash can. I'm not even sure if she's using it right now at all. I try not to pry."

"She's something else. She really hasn't worked up the nerve to ask you about kids? She doesn't even need birth control with you. You can control your own fertility—and hers."

"She feels better about herself when she's responsible about when we become parents. She has so many self-esteem problems I can't undermine the work she's doing—and she's gaining confidence in that department, at least."

"Still. I'm worried about her. Maybe you need to make the first move?"

I shook my head. "It took her months to work up the nerve to ask for presents, Perkins. I've already gotten things for her, but she's mortified even asking me to pick up groceries. She'll get there. She's already improving, but it takes time for someone to get over what she's been through."

I suspected most of her hesitation involved old, buried trauma involving her asshole parents.

She'd spent her entire life believing nobody wanted her in the world, and she struggled to come to terms with how she was my everything.

Perkins snorted. "We need to work on her self-esteem issues."

"We?"

"You have met your wife, right? You're going to need all the help you can get. Did she include the measurements for her new tack?"

"She did."

"Since when has Bailey ever made things easy on you?"

"I'm definitely worried about that," I admitted, praying she hadn't found some new way to scare the life out of me.

BAILEY

I HAD TIME TO SECOND, triple, and quadruple guess our plan to escape life for a while before Perkette confirmed our husbands had abandoned their morning sweep to go to work.

"They talked for longer than I expected," Perky's wife muttered. "It's likely Arthur's fault. He's a thinker, and when he's done thinking, he starts talking."

"He has a name other than Perky?"

"When he's been bad or has to sign legal papers. Some

people even call him Officer Perkins so they lower their chances of being arrested."

"I'm still trying to figure out how a doctor became a cop," I admitted.

"The same way you married one of the hottest men in Manhattan. He sucked at being a doctor but makes one hell of a good cop."

"I don't see how him sucking at being a doctor relates to Quinn marrying me. I was a good barista, damn it!"

"You'd make a better cop, and no matter what people tell you, you're a shitty CDC contractor because you hate being a living janitor. You want something more, and we both know it. My man's a much better cop because he feels like he makes more of a difference."

Understanding stabbed me deep in the chest. "He lost patients."

Cops lost battles all the time. Sometimes, they arrived too late to the scene of the crime, stuck with solving a murder when they'd wanted nothing more than to prevent the death. Sometimes, there was just nothing they could do to change circumstances, but I respected their drive to make a real difference.

Doctors waged a daily battle, and they lost as often as they won. Doctors faced death far more frequently than cops did.

"The first time he lost a kid in the ER, I knew he wouldn't last long as a doctor. Part of his soul died that day. I saw an ad for forensics work, so I left it on his desk. He is who he is, so he went all in and became a cop. He didn't want to solve the mystery in a lab. He wanted to get his hands dirty trying to save the world. He's doing work he takes pride in now.

That's what you need, too. After you get some sleep and we force our men to join us on an adventure, of course."

Of course. I laughed so hard I struggled to breathe. "Me? A cop? They'd look at my magic rating and toss my app. While laughing at me."

"Your realistic magic rating is on par with your husband's. I don't know why the CDC hasn't upgraded you yet."

I understood why, and I shrugged. "Cheaper labor."

"Whatever you say, Mrs. Millionaire. Get your tack in the car, grab your bag, and pick me up already. I've reached my quota of lurking in the bushes spying on our spouses. I want a good head start before they figured out we bailed town. Move it, woman!"

As I didn't want Perkette to ram her foot up my ass, I shut up and did as told.

QUINN

A PILE OF PAPERWORK, which included my wife's employment file, her boss, and Commissioner Jack Dowry waited in my office. I regretted having spent the time doing my sweep when I could've stayed in bed with Bailey for a few extra minutes. I needed fortification when dealing with two doses of trouble.

"Commissioner Dowry, Mr. Clemmends," I greeted, determined to remain cordial despite my desire to shift and give my wife's boss a full dose of my gorgon powers. "What can I do for you this morning?"

With Mr. Clemmends in my office, I no longer wondered

why Bailey had her phone off for the rest of the day. She'd be lucky if they gave her time to breathe to ensure things remained quiet.

Commissioner Dowry claimed my couch and sat with a tired groan. "We want to move ahead with partnering you with your wife. Our research confirms our initial thoughts. She fits well with us and has the right skills for the job. The CDC can't push off elevating her rating, and frankly, it'll be cheaper for us to bump her to your pay scale with bonus hazard pay. With her abilities, you'll be a lot more effective in the field, too."

When my boss planned a speech like that, it wasn't up for discussion. I was expected to like the decision and make the most of the situation. However, I worried Bailey had somehow developed foresight. By the end of the day, I'd be more than happy to share her monster margarita with her. "What's the timeline for her promotion?"

"We're hoping for January, no later than the end of the month. We wanted your advice on how best to approach her about the situation. The CDC has already written the transfer contract. For the first six months, she'll be a liaison, after which the NYPD will move her to exclusive employment with a full salary and benefits."

Mr. Clemmends smirked but remained quiet.

It sank in they'd found a way to transfer Bailey without warning or recourse. When she found out, she'd blow a fuse. Not only would she blow a fuse, she'd have just cause to transform and scorch my ass over the situation. I'd accept the scorching as I should have told her the instant I'd heard the first rumblings of her impending promotion.

Shit. Shit. Shit.

"Please tell me she'll have a competitive salary." If I went home and told her she'd be forced to work with me on a lower salary, her fragile self-esteem would completely shatter, and I'd have to start all over again convincing her she was worth the air she breathed.

My boss chuckled. "She'll do quite well on the salary front. The NYPD has decided to treat her CDC education and experience as equivalent, which gave me grounds to propose a salary match with you. It was approved. Future raises will be performance based, but you can guide her on how to handle counter proposals and raise requests as needed. Honestly, I think you two will remain salary matched to keep the peace in the family. That leads me to the next bit of business."

I didn't want extra business. The promotion was too much business for me to deal with in one day. I sat behind my desk and wished I could beat myself into unconsciousness on the polished surface. "Go on."

"We need to try two other chief pairs; they arrived from out west yesterday. We're loaning them some of your officers until after Christmas. You're on full shift until the end of the day, then you're on paid leave until the second."

"Of January?" I blinked. "You're giving me three weeks of paid vacation?"

"Since Officer Perkins has been paired with you, he'll enjoy the same arrangement. Frankly, you both have been working too much, you need a breather, and you could use the time to prepare Bailey for her new work. While you're on leave, we'll be doing some construction and shuffling on this floor to give your wife a proper office here and make it easier for her to get around when transformed."

I foresaw a disaster of epic proportions, but I also saw an opportunity. "Bailey needs new tack. Hers is pinching. She's already given me the measurements, but she might fill out some more, so altering the design to include adjustable straps might be a good idea."

"She's a healthy weight now?"

"Close. A few more pounds in muscle and she'll be set." I smiled at the thought of her progress, her obsessive enjoyment of greasy fries, and how she'd lost her gaunt edge, which had been replaced with vibrant energy.

If I could convince her to stop feeling so embarrassed when I noticed her good moods, I'd be much happier. One day, she would understand I loved everything about her. I loved her when she shined. I loved her when she got lost in the dark, too.

She hated when I noticed or worried.

We made quite the pair.

"Good. Mr. Clemmends will be at the station all day if you have any questions. He's polling our offices to better evaluate what sorts of contractors he needs to have trained in the next batch of recruits."

I kept my mouth shut. If Bailey's boss wanted my opinion, he'd ask for it. He didn't. I made it through the mandatory small talk without succumbing to my desire to remind the man why it wasn't wise to toy with my wife.

It occurred to me I could dodge most of the blame in her promotion. When I told Bailey her boss had masterminded the entire situation, she'd forget my role in her promotion for at least ten minutes.

The two men left my office, and I waited for them to reach the elevator before barking an order for Perkins to join me for a talk.

TWO

This officially sucks.

BAILEY

THE UNIVERSE HATED ME. A light dusting of snow ensured the roads would be hell by the time we escaped New York. I barely eased Quinn's convertible to a halt before Perkette slid into the vehicle, wrinkling her nose. Since she knew I wouldn't even think about putting the vehicle into gear until she buckled up, she grabbed her seatbelt and clipped it into place.

"This officially sucks," she announced.

"Good thing we're headed to Vegas, then. Does Vegas ever get cold?" I hoped not. I already shivered, and I had the heat in the convertible blasting.

"Hell if I know. Think you can handle some snow as a unicorn?"

"Will it kill me? No. Will I kill you for making me? Very probably. Someone better be dying before I deal with snow as a unicorn."

"Point taken. We'll use our second plan, then."

I'd lost count of Perkette's plans. "Is that the one where we pay a cabbie a horrific amount of money to take us to a rental place?"

"Yes, it is. It's also the one where I get to drive because at this pace, we'll reach my house sometime next year. Sam isn't going to get upset with you even if you crash your convertible."

No matter how often Quinn—and everyone else—fed me the same line, I didn't believe it. One day, the bubble of my happiness would burst, and it would be my fault. "He really loves this car."

"He loves you more. You'll get used to it one of these days. A little time away will do you both some good. Don't worry about the car. Just get us to my house, Bailey. I said it once, I'm saying it again. Don't give our men a chance to ruin our plans."

If she wanted anything faster than ten below the speed limit when it was snowing, she was wrong and I wasn't going to listen to her bitch about it. Arrive alive was my motto when it came to driving, and she'd just have to cope with it.

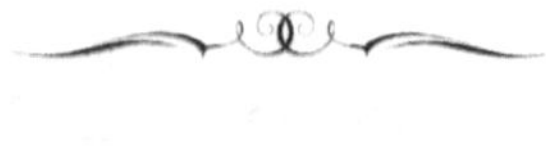

QUINN

WHAT COULD GO WRONG DID GO wrong, and for a rare change, Bailey had nothing to do with it. My cousin did. Murdering the asshole would land me in trouble with my family, but would anyone *really* blame me? He needed to return to Jersey where he belonged and stay out of my jurisdiction.

More importantly, he needed to stay the hell away from my wife.

"You can't petrify him," Perkins reminded me. "You'd have to transform in public to do that."

Why had I spilled my dirty shapeshifting secret to Perkins? Ah, right. I had done it so I wouldn't scare the life out of him if I needed to shift while on duty. One day, it would happen. When it did, it would create the kind of mess that might get me fired. Humans didn't like when the other species got too high up in the pecking order, and in reality, I was only human on paper.

I growled and wished I could shift just so I could lash my tail and hiss properly. "He's deep in the park. I can get away with it."

"No, Sam. I know you're still cranky he picked a fight with Bailey, but you're on official police business. Honestly, I usually wouldn't care, but I don't feel like getting caught in the crossfire of two gorgons duking it out today. Just think about it this way: we get three weeks of paid time off at Christmas."

I fully intended on enjoying Christmas with Bailey. "He wanted to pick her as his bride."

"I know. He ultimately picked a fight. Let it go. Anyway, you're so tightly bound to her thanks to your heritage you don't even need your magical ball and chain. No one else has a chance with her. Focus on that."

Logically, I knew he was right. Unfortunately, my demonic side felt a need to claim territory daily, my angelic side endured almost as many anxiety attacks as Bailey did on a bad day, and my gorgon side wanted to make a big family for me to coddle.

Add in the rest of my questionable genetics, and it was no

wonder Bailey woke up a tired mess in the morning. I'd never get enough of her.

I needed to work on that.

"Quinn, you're growling a little too much there."

I grunted, stopped growling, and curbed my desire to hiss at my partner out of spite. "I'm worried. Bailey was acting weird this morning. I was hoping to skip home over lunch to check on her. Instead, I'm headed into Central Park to scold my cousin for scaring the humans."

"Be grateful he hasn't petrified anyone yet. We could be done here in twenty minutes."

"But not in time for us to skip home and check on our ladies," I complained.

"You're being almost as absurd as Bailey. She's working. Let the woman work in peace. I know you're worried, but she can take care of herself most of the time."

"It's the rest of the time I'm worried about," I replied.

"While your concern is justified, she's been careful to stay out of trouble lately. She's even doing better on the self-esteem front, too. Think about it this way: she's made it clear you're her one and only. Don't worry so much. Frankly, I'm thinking I might get you both some counseling for Christmas. You're both suffering from extreme insecurities."

"I trust Bailey. It's everyone else driving Bailey batty I'm worried about." I shrugged and kept trudging across the park to where the calls claimed my cousin was making a menace of himself. "It's been quiet. Too quiet. When it gets too quiet, something bad happens to Bailey."

"Can we just get through this so we can get back to the station? I'm freezing my ass off. It's snowing."

"And why are you in a mood today, Perkins?"

"My wife will be less than pleased to learn I'm being reassigned. She hates when I get a new partner. I become an insufferable asshole for weeks."

"I'm pairing you with Nilman, unless you have a problem with that idea."

"I can live with that arrangement. Where will you put Cotsman?"

"I'm moving him into the domestic violence division. He wants to diversify, and with a kid on the way, he's motivated." As delaying wouldn't help matters for me, I picked up the pace, and Perkins matched my stride. "Thoughts?"

"Are we going to be backing you in the field?"

"Bailey likes you both, and it'll help ease her into her new position, so yes."

"This is going to be a disaster," he predicted.

While I agreed, I did believe Bailey would thrive working with me in the field. She had a lot of learning ahead of her, but she deserved to be more than a cleaner for the CDC. She'd still have to tackle the nasty jobs, but she'd enjoy a better base pay per incident *and* the hazard bonuses contractors didn't usually receive.

She wouldn't get any more excessive payouts like the one that had rocketed her straight into being a millionaire, but she'd be a lot happier.

I just needed to convince her that she could handle the job, somehow get her registered to take the critical police academy courses, and teach her how to be a cop in less than two months.

I needed to ask my grandfather for a miracle, as I worried one would be needed to prepare her on such short notice.

As reported, my cousin loitered in the heart of Central Park. "Darrel."

"I've got some intel for you. There's a New Jersey hive after your bride."

The world froze around me as the implication of his announcement sank in. I tensed, and I fought against the various facets of my genetics joining forces for the same cause: to protect what was ours.

Shifting would give me better weapons to accomplish that, but I resisted the desire to change shapes. "Who and why?"

I flexed my hands and clacked my teeth together.

"The Dover main hive needs a surrogate. A former police recruit, some idiot named John Winfield, tipped the male off about her immunities. They didn't research her much before putting in an offer, and they certainly didn't do any research on you. They have no idea they've bitten off more than they can chew. From what I can tell, they believe she's an easy grab. I'm not sure why they believe they can coerce her into being their hive's surrogate, however. Perhaps the male was raised by humans?"

It happened. Gorgon whelps sold for a fortune on the black market, and once they reached adulthood, some escaped and formed hives without understanding the intricacies of being a gorgon.

I remembered John Winfield, and the mention of the former cadet's name added to my irritation. "John Winfield was removed from the force following the 120 Wall Street incident due to behavior inappropriate for a police officer." I considered the rest of my cousin's statement. "Our marriage isn't exactly common knowledge. I didn't make a formal announcement, and Bailey isn't secure enough to be the one doing the announcing. She's still deciding if she wants a formal wedding."

Perkins scratched his head and sighed, shaking his head. "Your marriage may not be general knowledge for the public, but everyone in law enforcement is aware," Perkins corrected.

My day was looking a lot grimmer—and a great deal more annoying—than it had even ten minutes ago. "When did Dover's hive decide to stoop to kidnapping Bailey?"

My cousin shrugged. "Your guess is as good as mine, but it's pretty obvious that former recruit is out for revenge. Selling your bride out to a hive is foolish at best, but the hive's desperate and she's immune."

I tried to imagine what Bailey might do to an entire hive given ten minutes and a hit of transformatives. No, I needed to stop the hive before Bailey found out about the situation. She would wipe out all but the young and wallow in guilt over it for years, and she'd terrify a few years off my life in the process. "That poor hive. Are there any young?"

"Two whelps, a boy and a girl. Same hatching," my cousin replied. "Why?"

"Bailey's itching for a fight. If she finds out that hive wants to take her, it'll be a bloodbath—theirs. Once she's done killing the adults, she'll want to adopt the whelps."

"They do have the boy. If you start a hive, he'll make for a good trade."

"Darrel, we're talking about Bailey here. She will murder anyone who tries to trade for a whelp in her care. I *might* be able to sell her on fostering, but I expect I'll be saddled with both until adulthood. They can socialize in your hive if that's the case." The offer would please my entire family, and my cousin was in a position his hive could support another breeding male.

His serpents stirred, watching me with interest. "My hive

is large enough to support a young breeding male," he confirmed. "We could just wipe the hive out and take the whelps. They can be part of my hive's bride present for your wedding."

Sometimes, I hated gorgons. Other times, I loved everything about our twisted society.

Perkins snickered. "That's one way to handle this. Can you get proof that former cadet contacted this Dover hive?"

"I have sufficient evidence, Officer Perkins." My cousin smiled, and showed off his fangs. "For gorgon law."

I could make a few guesses, especially after evaluating witness reports of the cadet's treatment of my wife and his general attitude. "The idiot emailed the hive, didn't he?"

"Indeed. To make it worse, for him that is, the Dover hive's patriarch asked around about Bailey Gardener. I requested a copy of the offer. He sent it to me. He plans to offer five hundred thousand. I told him she was worth much more than that. I got the feeling that was all he had to offer. I also got the feeling he would pursue her without an accepted bride offer."

Kidnapping and coercion went against everything I'd been taught by my father and grandfather. It even went against what my cousin had been taught, although he'd suffered through a complete lapse of judgment following an alcoholic bender and exposure to an incubus.

The exposure to an incubus part of the equation had grudgingly won him my forgiveness.

He had gotten his ass handed to him by my wife, and I understood what demonic powers could do to someone. In part, it was why I always hesitated to reveal any of my demonic nature.

Unfortunately for me, Bailey could be very convincing,

and once she coaxed me into shapeshifting, she had a way of making my common sense dribble out of my ears.

We made quite the pair.

I sighed and shook my head. Considering how poorly Bailey had taken my cousin's multi-million dollar offer, she'd enter orbit over only being offered five hundred thousand. "Amanda's been teaching her self-defense. While I will do everything in my power to prevent another hive from even looking at her, I pity this patriarch should he manage to get near her."

Perkins snickered again, which grew into boisterous laughter. "She'll get so mad she might spontaneously combust. After she's done laying waste to the entire hive, I wish you luck convincing her she has value."

Bowing my head, I closed my eyes and sighed again. And again. I sighed a few extra times for good measure. "It'd be best if she doesn't find out about this. She's going to have enough trouble accepting she's going to be a Chief Quinn soon."

My cousin cackled. "She's going to turn the entire city upside down. Which jurisdiction is to be blessed with her?"

The sarcasm I expected from my cousin didn't come, and when I lifted my head, he watched me with open interest. "They're partnering her with me."

My cousin nodded, his expression satisfied. "Well, I'd like to see anyone get to you with her around. She's vicious. She sometimes flails, but she flails viciously. And I'll give her credit. She punches hard when mad."

I'd always treasure the memory of my wife beating my drunk cousin. "You deserved it."

"I did. I regret I didn't find her first."

I only regretted marrying Audrey before meeting Bailey. "Thank you for not finding her first."

"Who am I kidding? You two were made for each other. I know of no other capable of handling her fire without being burned." My cousin shrugged. "She'd burn the entire world to ash for your sake. That's what I want, for a woman to look at me like your bride looks at you. I doubt she's easy to love, but what you have will last. I don't typically believe in fate, but perhaps with you two, it was simply meant to be. How do you want me to handle the Dover hive?"

"Talk to your old man, and when you do, tell him my old man keeps telling Bailey she's too vicious to participate in the fostering matches. Should the Dover hive suffer from any unfortunate accidents pursuing my bride, she has first right to claim the whelps. I intend to back her on it, and I will fight for her if she's barred."

"While shifted?" My cousin's snakes hissed their opinion of that. "You'll scare off the competition."

"I'm all right with that. Bailey isn't. She's stuck on earning the fosters properly. I'm much lazier than she is."

I was also more ruthless, and if she wanted to foster children, I would end every fight as quickly as possible before accepting my beating as the victor.

"Whatever works. I'll try to defuse the Dover situation. What do you want me to do about that washed-out cadet? He's going to become a problem."

"Get what information you can on him. When I'm finished with him, he'll regret the day he thought he could touch my wife," I swore.

Bailey

AS I COULDN'T DRIVE worth a shit and Perkette wanted to reach Vegas sometime this year, I navigated. Navigation I could do. I didn't even need a map to guide her across the city to the mainland. After that, I informed my new, fancy phone I wanted to go to the Venetian in Las Vegas, and it dutifully relayed directions at the appropriate intervals.

I loved my new phone, and the next time my husband tried to coax me into accepting something a little shinier than the cheapest model available on the market, I'd listen to him. "Did you know Quinn believes he can't teach me how to use his laptop to save his life? The same goes for all tech. I've convinced him I'm completely and totally hopeless with all technology. In reality, I can use his phone like a boss. He just doesn't know that. According to him, it's a miracle I know how to text him. Am I a bad wife for liking when he does all the computer things for me because he likes it?" I held up my new phone. "He'll like this phone. He'll be delighted I picked it. It's the most expensive model of the brand he likes."

"You're not stupid, Bailey. Why are you playing dumb with your husband?"

"It confuses him," I admitted. "And he has this really cute expression when he gets flustered. Then he tries to help so much, so I feel bad when I can do something on my own, but he's so eager to help."

"You know how to use his laptop, don't you? And his phone. And all of the technological doodads in your house."

I loved that a scientist referred to technology as doodads. "Maybe a little."

"This is going to be so good. Describe your actual skill with his computer, please."

"I hate not knowing how to do something, so I looked it up online. Next thing I knew, I was upgrading his antivirus and basic protections because his are shit, but he doesn't know his are shit because I run mine in the background. And because I added extra programs, I may have taken his laptop to a store for a memory upgrade so he wouldn't notice. He hasn't. He's a very confused man sometimes. Well, I might sometimes tell him about weird porn to see what he'll do. He gets so embarrassed, Perkette. And the best part? He has no idea if I've actually watched any of it."

"Have you?"

"Hell no. Why would I? I'm married to an incubus. Well, that's not quite true. I tried watching one once because I was curious. The girl looked bored, and the guy looked like he wanted to be anywhere other than a studio filming porn. It wasn't sexy. At all. And they couldn't act worth a shit. I just browse for weird porn ideas in stealth mode and make a mental note of the interesting headlines to tease him."

"That must drive him crazy."

"I don't do it on purpose—usually. He just worries he isn't being husbandly enough, and then I try to tell him he's so much better than those weirdos who think watching each other pee is sexy."

"Don't you mean pee on each other?"

I snickered. "Quinn isn't sure, and it drives him insane. He's part angel, Perkette. Even the thought of checking porn for any reason freaks him out. All he'd have to do is ask what I'm doing. I'd tell him. While laughing. I can't help it. He makes the best expressions, and it's so hard to keep from laughing."

"And add in his obsession with making you laugh, and it's a recipe for disaster. One of these days, you're going to choke to death trying not to laugh, and he's going to have a heart attack from twisted porn. It's a good thing porn is legal or he'd already be halfway in his grave."

"It doesn't hurt—or help—that I sometimes spike dinner with pixie dust without telling him."

"You are half the reason you don't get enough sleep."

I grinned. "At least I'm honest about it."

"You know what? I can't blame you. If Arthur packed incubus genes, I'd be running on a lack of sleep and need an intervention, too. Trust me on this one, Bailey. Even vanilla human men like their sex plentiful."

"I'd say I know that, but then I'd be lying."

"I feel like I need to take you to some strip clubs when we're in Vegas. Your innocence isn't refreshing. It's downright terrifying."

"It's Quinn's fault," I announced. "It's all his fault. He walks in the room, and I forget other men exist. I've been told this is a good thing."

"For someone who is part angel like your chief? Yeah, it's a good thing."

"What do you think he'll do when hc finds out?"

"I don't know, Bailey," Perkette admitted. "Let's go find out. Have your phone take us to Atlantic City. We'll begin our reign of terror there."

We sneak out in thirty seconds and hit
the staircase at a run.

Quinn

THE DAY simply refused to end. Dealing with my cousin turned into one of the nicer parts of my shift. A dead political hopeful, a possible suicide but probable homicide, would keep the station busy until someone figured out the truth. My temporary replacements wouldn't appreciate the trouble I was about to dump on their laps.

Any other day, I would've cared more, but I had three uninterrupted weeks of time with Bailey ahead of me.

"Almost over," Perkins said, checking his watch. "You can survive for five more minutes."

I was done. Fuck the five minutes. My brand-new plan involved bolting for my cruiser and dragging Perkins along for the ride. "We sneak out in thirty seconds and hit the staircase at a run."

"We're on the eighth floor."

"So?"

"I've had a long day. I'm not going down eight flights of steps. We'll walk to the elevator without looking desperate. I'll even agree to do so early. That's more likely to work. Be realistic. It'll take us an hour to reach the elevator. Everyone knows they won't be able to reach you for three weeks."

I loved being a cop. I even loved being a chief, but some days, I wanted to quit so I could go home and mooch off my wife. At least once a week, she promised she'd let me model underwear for her. She'd tossed the idea of having me model for profit.

According to her and her insane budgeting abilities, we could live for at least a hundred years on what she had in the bank account. On interest alone.

Sometimes, I wondered about Bailey. I never suggested she should change her job field, however, despite the obvious staring me in the face. When she touched money, magic happened.

Her new stock accounts agreed with me. I'd set them up after talking her into a hundred thousand of seed investment, and I managed the account to her specifications. She told me when to buy and sell, what to buy and sell, and she'd more than quadrupled her money.

She had no idea she'd quadrupled it, however. She claimed she trusted me to do the evil technological stuff she didn't want to be bothered with, and that was that.

Perkins waved his hand in front of my face. "Earth to Sam. What did Bailey do now that has you off in la-la land?"

"She didn't do anything. Well, not really."

"Sam, you were staring off into space trying to figure your wife out again. I know that expression. Just spill it."

"I was thinking about her stock investments," I admitted.

"Her stock investments? She's playing the stock market?"

"Not exactly. More like she made a stock investment plan when she was bored one week. It was when we had the shooter at Grand Central. She was fretting, I told her she wasn't to come anywhere near the place until it was safe, and so she made a stock investment plan. She showed it to me, and I asked her if she minded if I implemented it on a hundred thousand dollar budget. It took some coaxing, but she agreed."

"That poor woman. I swear, she needs some serious therapy for her self-esteem issues."

I hadn't mentioned anything about her self-esteem, but at the heart of it, he was right. "She's been doing better."

"While true, she is terrified of disappointing you."

"Yep."

"So? How did it go?"

"I keep reinvesting that hundred thousand she finally agreed to, and I have her update her plan once a month. Right now, there's almost half a million in profit, after taxes, sitting in an account because I haven't figured out the best way to tell her she's a fucking genius."

"Don't tell her." Perkins shrugged. "She'll just freak out, and you can put that money into your retirement fund. She's good at the stock market?"

"She's better than good at it. She's amazing. She's had a few failures, but she's got a knack for it."

"Or a lot of time and an interest in market research?"

"I don't know how. She can barely use my laptop."

"She's tricking you," Perkins announced.

I narrowed my eyes. "What do you mean?"

"A woman that smart is not that stupid. She's probably convinced if you know she can handle things herself, you won't spend as much time with her."

I hated he was onto something. "She has a piece of shit phone that can barely make phone calls, she had a computer, but I ordered it to be napalmed and she never got another one."

"She just wants to use yours because it's yours."

Once again, I hated that Perkins was probably onto something. "I'm going to need time to think about that. Let's get out of this joint."

Perkins checked his watch. "Two minutes early. We could put a sheet over your head. That might work to get us out of here on time."

"No." I'd done the sheet walk once and only once for Bailey when she'd visited the station after a bad shift. She'd laughed so hard she'd crawled to the elevator, negating the sheet's effectiveness. As I'd already sacrificed my dignity for my wife, I'd enjoyed trying to startle the officers on the floor.

It had made her laugh harder.

I hadn't appreciated everyone calling me Casper for a week, but some prices were worth paying.

Gathering everything I needed for three glorious weeks off work, I decided on the bold approach, stepped out of my office, and announced, "If you don't see me in January, the future Chief Quinn didn't handle news of her promotion well. Wish me luck, have a great holidays, and I'm leaving. Ambush the stand-ins with any questions, and if you need anything from me, the answer is probably no. Expect to call the other Chief Quinn Chief Bailey, as I expect she'll look at me if you try to call her Chief Quinn."

Everyone laughed.

"We could just call her Chief Gardener," Perkins suggested.

"No." I'd won Bailey fair and square. "Chief Bailey will be

more comfortable for her. You'll have to use Quinn if we're near reporters or officials, but she'll need to be eased into it."

Amanda, who had a desk not far from my office, chuckled and grabbed her coat. "We've got a new batch of puppies, and they're looking promising. Any thoughts on if Bailey would make a good handler?"

Bailey teamed up with a police dog seemed like a disaster in the making. "If you can find a puppy capable of working with a fire-breathing unicorn, I'm game to try." I was always game to try something that might offer Bailey a few extra protections. "What breed?"

"We have a few Malinois, a German shepherd, a Tibetan mastiff, and a wolf-dog. She's half Egyptian, half Siberian husky."

"Who on Earth thought that was a good idea? What's an Egyptian wolf?"

"Think Anubis."

Perkins snickered, and I sighed. My family would just love it if Bailey worked with an Egyptian anything, but especially a dog that resembled one of my divine relatives. "Test the wolf-dog with the horses. If the puppy doesn't wash out, we can try it. If the puppy does wash out, why do I get the feeling someone is getting a puppy for Christmas? Keep me in the loop."

A wolf might be able to guard my wife.

"Sucker," Amanda muttered. "Break from Bailey's self-defense courses until February?"

"Good idea. Email me the contact details for the trainer and if there are any leads on a retiring or retired dog Bailey can work with. May as well make sure she's ready for handling if the puppy doesn't wash out."

"The wolf-dog puppy happens to be upstairs today," Amanda informed me.

I frowned. Why would the puppy be at *my* station? The puppies were typically trained at a compound on the mainland and brought to a facility on Long Island for additional training and partnering with one of my cops, after which they came to Manhattan to serve in the force. It wasn't the most efficient way to do it, but we didn't have the space needed for the intensive training.

It also saved me thousands of dollars a year. I did have a kennel and exercise room for the dogs in the building, but it was meant to keep dogs fresh on their skills, not train them from scratch.

I narrowed my eyes and stared at Amanda. She smiled.

"All right. I feel like I'm being set up."

Amanda shifted her gaze away from me.

I crossed my arms and arched a brow. "Spill, Amanda. Who wants Bailey to have this puppy and why?"

"Commissioner Dowry," she confessed. "He thinks the chief pairs should have at least one dog moving forward. Chief Bailey's the type."

"For what? Creating a calamity with her new canine sidekick?" I loved my wife, but she held the title of the Calamity Queen for a reason. Where she went, trouble followed.

Once again, everyone laughed.

"Come on, Chief. She loves babies. Baby animals especially. She also needs a dog who can keep up with her. Sure, wolf-dogs don't typically make great police dogs, but she'll be a great police dog for her."

"What's one more disaster in the making? Take me to this wolf-dog puppy, but you better have a really good sales pitch."

"Commissioner Dowry said so. That's all the sales pitch I need."

"On a puppy who will likely wash out? Come on, Amanda. The wolf-dog is part husky. Huskies are great dogs, but they're not great police dogs. They're exhausting."

"He found someone to help with the training."

"A husky wolf-dog," I repeated.

"Fine. So she's a little energetic."

Heaven help me. "Perkins?"

"Sir?"

"I don't own anything for a puppy, and I have a feeling Amanda is implying I'm taking a puppy home with me tonight. We're going to be late leaving."

"You accepted this rather quickly," he replied.

"Why waste my time or breath on the inevitable?" I sighed. "I don't even know if Bailey actually likes dogs beyond her shameless drive to rescue them from dumpsters."

Amanda chuckled and headed for the elevator. "We've the word of an angel that the wolf-dog will adore you both but will always be her dog."

"Angels are assholes."

Why did everyone have to laugh at my suffering?

"Come meet your new dog, Chief Quinn," Amanda ordered.

When she issued orders, she meant business, so I obeyed without further complaint. It wouldn't do any good to fight it.

I'd already lost the battle and the war, and everyone knew it.

Bailey

A BLEND of shit traffic and snow cost us three hours, but we arrived in Atlantic City without incident. After so long in New York, the quiet streets creeped me out.

"It's so empty," I whispered.

"Without the summer tourists, it becomes a ghost town," Perkette replied with a shrug. "The hotels and casinos are on a skeleton staff, the boardwalk is closed, but the strip clubs stay open year round. That leads me to a very important question: men, women, or both? Lap dances or no lap dances?"

What had I gotten myself into? "I have transformatives in my purse. And my pocket." And in my cleavage, but I wasn't going to tell her that. After my misadventure involving my kidnapping, an incubus, and a warehouse, I always kept a stash of pixie dust and transformatives in my cleavage. "If anyone other than Quinn tries to get onto my lap, I'm transforming and lighting him on fire."

"It could be a woman on your lap."

"I will light her on fire, too. I'm an equal opportunity pyromaniac."

"They don't touch you when they dance, and I won't take you to a brothel. There's a line, and brothels are not on the right side of the line. At least without our husbands. And your husband? Well, he'd probably faint before making it through the door. Angels and brothels don't get on too well."

"Unless a member of a triad is retrieving their demon from the brothel," I countered. Just three weeks ago, Quinn had gone to a brothel to retrieve the angel, the incubus, and their wife from a cranky succubus who'd wanted the incubus for herself. "He goes to brothels as needed for work."

Perkette shot me a glare. "If your man went to a brothel, that means my man went to a brothel, and that means my man went to a brothel without me."

"For work, Perkette. For work. He didn't work the brothel, I promise you!"

She cackled. "Well, maybe you're not *quite* as innocent as I feared."

Nope, I was really as innocent as she feared, and I knew it. Quinn knew it, too—and he enjoyed teasing me and driving me crazy every single day. Instead of answering her, I grunted.

"Come on, it'll be fun. They won't touch you unless you want them to."

"I will light the entire club on fire."

Perkette snickered. "Pose with a stripper for your chief? I'm sure we can find a lingerie store. His demonic side will adore it. His angelic side will have a freak fit, but those incubus genes will kick in and you'll have a great night."

That I would. Every night with Quinn was a great night. "No."

"Why not?"

"I'm not intentionally stripping in public." The first time Quinn had seen me naked, I'd been fresh off a napalm bender and collapsed against him. He still twitched if I even mentioned Wall Street.

He didn't need to tell me he loved me. All I had to do was mention the day he thought he'd sent me into a contaminated building to die. He told me anyway, as often as possible, to make it clear he meant it.

I wasn't as good at using my words, so I communicated with him the only way I knew how. Perkette was right. I was at least half the reason I didn't get enough sleep.

"No wonder it took an incubus in disguise to evict you from the virgin pool. Fine. You don't have to strip. How about a picture with a succubus?"

Narrowing my eyes, I considered her question. I'd been around enough succubi to be almost comfortable with them as long as they kept their kinky sex magic to themselves—and they usually did. My magical ball and chain helped with that. "But what if the succubus is related to Quinn?"

"It's even funnier that way. Come on. Live a little. It's a great prank. I'm not asking you to sleep with them. It's just a few pictures. What could possibly go wrong?"

I pointed at myself. "I'm called the Calamity Queen for a reason. We're somehow going to end up in jail. Again. Well, you are. I don't pull your stupid shit, so I just tag along to make sure you don't stay there."

"You can afford my bail."

"I like how you automatically assume you're going to jail."

"The last time I went to a strip club, I spanked a bouncer because I was drunk and he was hot." Perkette giggled. "I do stupid things when I'm drunk. By the way, you're driving tonight. I'm going to get so drunk we go to jail."

"Remember how I said there's no way anyone would make me a cop? This is why. You're going to get us thrown into jail before we get to Vegas."

"General holding until we sober up. Not an actual offense."

I'd almost learned how to tell Quinn no over the past few months. Almost. "No." It worked so well I tried again. "No."

"Come on, Bailey," Perkette whined. "Live a little."

Why had I thought sleep was so important? What had I been thinking, agreeing to travel with Perkette? Then again, our initial planning had lacked strippers and alcohol. "No."

"You'll have fun, I promise. You can record the entire night if you want. We won't do a single thing that'll show up on your permanent record."

I'd been around enough troublemakers to recognize one hard at work. "And what about *your* permanent record?"

"I enjoy community service and find general holding highly amusing."

"I can't believe I'm saying this, but you have more issues than I do."

"Thank you for noticing."

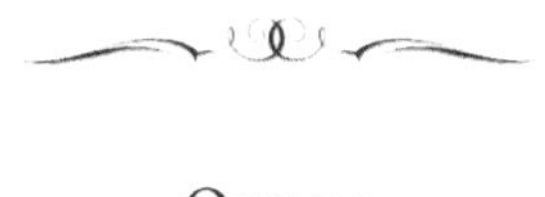

QUINN

I'D WORKED with enough lycanthropes to recognize a wolf when I saw one, and from the tip of her nose to the tip of her tail, the puppy was pure wolf. "Really, Amanda? A husky wolf-dog? Anything else you'd like to sell me along with some oceanfront property in Arizona?"

"How about a raise?"

"Depends on how good you are at selling me this 'husky' wolf-dog. This is a wolf. This is a very young wolf." The puppy sat on my foot and stared at me with adoring eyes. "And she's sitting on me."

Arnold Falhavert, the lead trainer of the precinct's dogs, laughed. Knowing him, he laughed in my face, well aware I'd be taking the puppy home with me. "It's a measure to counter Mrs. Chief Quinn's inexperience on the force. The puppy is a gift."

"From whom, exactly?"

"Me," my great-grandfather announced from right behind

me. "Her name is Sunny, and she's Bailey's wolf, but she'll give you plenty of love when you're feeling needy. Consider her a belated wedding gift. Mr. Falhavert agreed to help with training, but you'll find her a quick learner. Next year, her fur will shed to a lovely golden color."

"When a divine sneaks up on me and brings me a wolf, I worry. That the divine happens to be a relative worries me less but still worries me. Grandfather must be the angel in question?"

"The other dogs would be frightened of your bride, and she has enough issues."

While true, I considered taking a few swipes at my great-grandfather over it. I restrained myself. My great-grandfather always wielded the truth like the weapon it was, and fighting him over it wouldn't win me anything. "Mrs. Chief Quinn braided coral snakes together last week. She'd adore a chance to groom your fur."

"No."

"Anything I need to know about Sunny?"

"Of course. I'm sure you'll be kept busy figuring it out. Do say hello to your bride for me. Sunny already knows Bailey's scent in both of her forms."

Of course the wolf did. "How'd you manage that?"

"I cheated, of course."

Of course. "Thank you. Why now?"

My great-grandfather, with no care I was in the police station and supposed to be managing everyone present, ruffled my hair. "Your bride will inevitably need Sunny when she loses her way. It'll happen the first time. My present to you won't make much sense now, but I ask that you trust me. When your bride loses her way, don't fear. She'll return.

Some journeys she must travel alone, and for all your talents and magic, you can't hold living flame in your hand."

I tensed at the memory of Bailey igniting 120 Wall Street. Reconstruction had already begun, but I avoided the place, unable to forget the moment I'd almost lost her. "Again?"

"Again. She'll be fine. You'll panic, of course. That's what you do when it comes to your bride, but she'll be fine. Sunny will help her home."

"Are you trying to help or make me worry even more?" If my great-grandfather was trying to induce an anxiety attack, he was doing an admirable job. I didn't suffer from them often, but without fail, Bailey had *something* to do with them.

"A little of both."

"You're a terrible great-grandfather."

Anubis grinned and displayed his sharp teeth. "Sunny isn't truly a wolf, but she's not a golden jackal, either. You'll find her suited for Bailey, second only to you, so try not to become too jealous."

Sunny panted and nuzzled my leg. "I'm jealous she's getting a dog."

"Sunny will get jealous of most other dogs, although she'll accept a certain individual with no fuss. She can share, somewhat. How about a cat?"

"Will the cat like Bailey more than me?"

"Inevitably." My great-grandfather smiled. "You'll be fine."

"It'll still be my cat."

"Lion, tiger, panther, or other?"

"I can't keep a large predator in my house."

"I'll find you a small one."

Why was I even talking to my great-grandfather? All of my relatives were lunatics, especially the divines. Saying so had never done any good in the past, but I couldn't resist the urge to reply, "You're insane."

My great-grandfather chuckled. "You make this so much fun. Sunny might appreciate some company of the feline bent. I'll ask around the family."

What had I done? "I'm going to regret this, aren't I?"

"Of course. Do watch over young Samuel, Sunny. He'll be almost as much trouble as your ward. Do try to be patient with him. He's a most unreasonable human when it comes to his bride."

"I'm supposed to be unreasonable. She's my wife!"

"Yes, yes. We've heard this many times. Ah, Perky?"

Hah. Bailey had corrupted my great-grandfather. I'd have to reward her for that later.

"Sir?" Perkins asked.

"I took the liberty of calling in a prescription for a human-suitable chill pill for little Samuel here. Do pick it up after you acquire Sunny's things. He'll need it."

My great-grandfather vanished.

Everyone stared at me, Perkins included.

"It's only partially his fault I qualify to be your chief," I complained. "And if you could forget this happened, I would really appreciate it."

"No wonder Mrs. Chief Quinn blushes if I ask her if she had a good morning. You must be a beast in bed." Amanda smirked. "Enjoy your vacation, sir."

"You're a terrible woman, Amanda."

"But I'm a fantastic cop and a better self-defense instructor. Still. That explains a lot." Still smirking, Amanda wandered away, waving as she went. "Happy holidays."

I sighed, bent over, and picked up Bailey's new puppy,

who licked my hand and wagged her tail. "Happy holidays. Make sure everyone plays it safe while I'm gone."

"Always."

"Falhavert, email me with everything I need to care for Sunny, please."

"Of course, sir. I'll leave basic instructions for her initial training. We'll start the real work after you're back to work. For now, your job is to bond with her. I've been told she's already bonded with Mrs. Chief Quinn, so you need to work on your relationship with Sunny. It should be easy, as she already likes you. Keep a firm hand with her. She's going to be assertive and demanding, so you need to make certain she knows you're still the boss of the relationship. I suspect Mrs. Chief Quinn will have an easier time, as we've already established that Sunny is serving as her protector. You need to establish how your partnership will work. But, as long as you handle her correctly, she'll make an excellent companion and partner."

"How young is she?"

"Young enough she still gets some special milk with her raw meat. Honestly, she just likes it, but it's good for her. Her diet is more specialized than a regular dog's. You can wean her off at any time—or don't, as you choose. I'll have her basic supply list sent to you in a few minutes."

"This is going to cost me a fortune, isn't it? The instant you said raw meat, it became clear my great-grandfather staged a successful ambush of my wallet."

"You're doomed," the trainer confirmed.

"I'm trusting you with Bailey," I informed Sunny. "You have one job, so please don't screw it up."

Sunny licked my hand.

FOUR

Don't crush my dreams. I've always
wanted to be a stripper.

BAILEY

THE NEXT TIME I agreed to go anywhere with Perkette, I'd get drunk before leaving the house. Within five minutes of arriving at the strip club, the bouncers called the cops, and for once in my life, I bore zero responsibility for the turn of events.

"It's a strip club," Perkette protested. "I'm stripping."

To make it clear she wasn't stripping but had successfully stripped, she waved her shirt over her head.

I considered popping a transformative and braving the snow. "Perkette."

"What, Bailey? Don't crush my dreams. I've always wanted to be a stripper."

"Ma'am, would you please put your top back on?"

I gave the bouncer credit; he kept his tone professional and didn't stare at Perkette's lace-covered breasts. "Hey, Perkette?"

"What?"

"Where did you get that bra?"

"Victoria's Secret. And don't you even think about cracking that stupid joke. Can't you see I'm busy adding indecent exposure to my rap sheet?"

I'd have to pay bail, which would notify Quinn of our misdeeds in Atlantic City. "If this trip ends with my divorce, I'm taking you out with me in a blaze of glory."

"Burn, baby, burn!" Perkette whipped her shirt over her head again. "Live a little, Bailey."

"I haven't had enough alcohol for this." Or napalm. At the rate my night was going, only both would do.

"I need a count of indecent exposure. I already told you this."

"And I have to witness this why?"

"You'll take pictures and pay my bill."

The pictures would make good ammunition later, so I snapped a few with my new phone. "Why am I paying your bail?"

"You adore me. You're just too shy to admit it. I also take you out for good coffee. As your husband foolishly trusts me, he doesn't worry about you during our outings."

"You're a terrible, manipulative bitch."

A pair of cops strode in through the front doors, and Perkette tossed her shirt at me. Moments later, her bra landed on my head. "Good evening, gentlemen!"

The next time I needed sleep, I'd go to the doctor and request pills. It'd be more effective, a lot saner, and far cheaper than going on a road trip with Perkette.

I sighed. "I'm so sorry for her."

The bouncer laughed. "Don't worry about it, ma'am. This

happens every few weeks, and it's usually an officer's wife left alone for a little too long."

"Her officer works in Manhattan."

"The rush of freedom got to her, obviously." The bouncer stared at Perkette's breasts. "I think I need to get that bra for my wife."

I removed Perkette's bra from my head and read off the model number. "My suggestion? Get two or three and wait for a good sale."

"Are you going to snap and strip, too?"

"I haven't had enough alcohol for that." I wrinkled my nose. I hadn't had any alcohol at all.

"That's a pity. She's pretty, but you're in a league of your own."

I worried the poor bouncer had been dropped on his head as a baby. I still had a lot of scars on my face from a cell phone bomb, though they mostly resembled freckles. Quinn liked them. Then again, Quinn liked every part of me, and he wasn't afraid of proving it. "My officer is her officer's boss."

"Should you decide to snap, please come here."

Yippee. I had the attention of a man, and he wasn't my husband. Since popping a transformative and lighting the place on fire would cause everyone, especially Quinn, trouble, I kept my irritation to myself. I had to somehow deal with Perkette and her misdemeanor-collecting ways, which meant I needed to deal with the cops.

Again.

"Excuse me, officers?"

"Wow, Bailey. That's so polite."

"I hate you, Perkette."

The cops stared at me, exchanged glances, and the

younger one, who reminded me of the cadets who'd just gotten their badges, asked, "Ma'am?"

"Where's the station so I can bail her skank ass out?"

They humored me with smiles, and the young one said, "Would you like to follow us to the station, ma'am?"

"Yes, please. Thank you."

I needed a gold star. A few months of marriage to Quinn had transformed me into a functional adult. Miracles could happen, and with some investigative work, I could likely figure out which one of Quinn's relatives held responsibility.

QUINN

THE HOUSE WAS dark and quiet, and the instant I pulled into the driveway, I noticed the lack of warmth I associated with Bailey's presence. "She's not here."

Perkins, who'd offered to help me settle the puppy, frowned, fetched his phone, and tapped on the screen. "Huh. Tiffany isn't home, either. Give me a sec. I'll check the garage. She said she wanted the car for something today."

"I really need to monitor the house," I muttered.

"An alarm system might do Bailey some—" Perkins blinked. "Oh, shit."

"That's not what I want to hear, Perkins."

"Why is your car parked in my garage?"

My eyes widened. "You have got to be kidding me."

When Tiffany Perkins took my wife anywhere, trouble happened. Alone, my Calamity Queen could terrify years off my life. Tiffany collected misdemeanors for the fun of it, viewing community service hours as a way of getting out of the house for a good cause when she wasn't playing a mad scientist with a research fetish. "Please tell me Tiffany is still working on her book."

When Tiffany worked on a book, she took my wife out for coffee, which made everyone happy. She also limited her misdemeanors to minor mischief that made for good stories at the station.

"All three are with her publisher, her latest paper is out for peer review, and her next lecture isn't until late January."

Oh no. "If my car is in your garage, and our wives are not where we expect, what do you think that means?"

Perkins laughed, and it was a strained, tired sound. "We've been had, Sam. Your vixen of a wife tricked us both with her texts to keep us busy, and then they bailed out of town in my car."

I shook my head. "Oh, no. Tiffany's too smart for that. She ditched your car somewhere safe but hidden, likely with a neighbor. But, seeing as she's Tiffany, she forgot you have cameras in your garage." My wife playing me like a piano stunned me into silence. Anxious, blurt-things Bailey tiptoed around always afraid the tides of her good fortune would change. "Why did our wives skip town?"

"Why would two women skip town?"

We spent a long time thinking about it.

"Snow sucks?" I suggested.

"It's fucking cold," he agreed.

"Boredom."

Perkins's expression turned thoughtful. "Burnout or exhaustion."

I grimaced at that one. "Bailey's been really tired lately."

"Tiffany is easily bored, and she really likes Bailey. If Bailey's been tired, she'd want to cheer her up. Tiffany knows about the promotion, and she understands Bailey is going to be up to her eyeballs learning how to be a cop."

"And then add in that she's being dumped into a vat of boiling oil being partnered with me, and it's a recipe for disaster. And more exhaustion."

"There's the motive," Perkins announced.

"The list sent this morning. Do you think it's a distraction ploy, clues, or what?"

"Distraction ploy."

I thought about it, and I also thought about Bailey's insecurities, which left her incapable of doing something without her seeking my approval. "Clues," I countered. "Where in the United States would you get a monster margarita?"

I smiled at the most obvious answer.

"They ran to fucking Las Vegas?" Perkins groaned and bowed his head, running his hands through his hair. "This is a nightmare. Obviously, I was petrified by your cousin, and I'm trapped in a petrification-induced nightmare."

"Bailey's going to arrive at the strip, see the showgirls, and faint from mortification," I predicted. When she did, I'd be in position to catch her, and I'd enjoy carrying her off to do with as I pleased.

"They're not going to make it to Vegas because my idiot wife is going to realize how fucking innocent Bailey is, take her to the nearest dive, and get her ass arrested again. Again, Sam. You hear me? Again." Perkins groaned. "Last time, she put a full box of chocolates down her shirt and told the cashier to call her S'mores."

Coughing so I wouldn't laugh, I twisted in my seat to check on Sunny. Bailey's puppy slept on the back seat without a care in the world. "Bailey called me from the station in tears, Perkins. It took her twenty minutes to stop laughing long enough to explain she was paying Tiffany's bail. I still don't know if she had hysterics, found the whole thing funny, or didn't know how to handle the situation, thus becoming so frustrated she cried because killing people is illegal."

"There's no way Bailey would cry at a station unless she's laughing."

"Get her angry or frustrated enough, and she sobs." It made me a terrible husband, but I adored when her emotions got the better of her, good or bad. "But you're likely right. Tiffany would've been busy begging them not to let her off too lightly. That would make Bailey laugh."

"Chocolate was involved, too."

"The last thing Bailey needs is extra sugar. I've finally gotten her diet somewhat healthy."

"Monster margaritas have a lot of sugar. She's going to be a sight to behold."

"Where do you think our wives went first?"

Perkins snickered. "If Bailey is driving, nowhere fast."

"As I haven't gotten any calls about homicides, pyromaniac unicorns, or mass destruction, let's assume your wife is driving."

Perkins sucked in a breath, and he jerked his head up. "Oh, God. No. This can't be happening."

"Spill," I ordered.

He groaned. "Atlantic City. Tiffany would want to warm Bailey up for the insanity of Vegas. Bailey turns red if you're shirtless in public. Tiffany would take Bailey to Atlantic City to acclimate her and score a new misdemeanor on her rap sheet."

I gave that some thought, and I found I didn't mind the

situation nearly as much as I should have. "Think we should give them a head start? We can play dumb." I chuckled at the thought of Bailey storming Las Vegas. "While accidental, it's perfect timing. If Bailey and Tiffany are road tripping, it'll be a lot harder for the Dover hive to find them."

"It's good for our wives—and us—to get out of the house for a while."

"My car likes your garage. It just told me so. We should get a rental. We need a vacation. Right? We need a vacation, Arthur." Using his first name would indicate we were truly off duty, the kind of off duty where we wouldn't be fielding even emergency calls.

I'd view my rank as a police chief as temporary unemployment with a few perks if I needed to call in for some backup to protect my wife.

"Definitely. And since we're excellent husbands, we should pick up a few gifts for our wives on the way." Perkins grinned, and he rubbed his hands together. "We've obviously neglected them most cruelly, and thus they are in need of a reward."

I laughed. "This explains a lot. My great-grandfather must have known she was skipping town and wanted to fuck with me. He loves screwing with us mortals, especially the ones he helped bring into existence. It gives him an excuse to visit and create trouble."

"I'm rather surprised you're not panicking yet. I also understand why he got that prescription. You get edgy at the end of your shift when you haven't seen Bailey all day. After a few days, you're going to be an anxious mess."

"I'm not panicking yet because she's safest on the move," I admitted.

Perkins nodded. "Tiffany's with her. We'll have a call by

midnight about them, guaranteed. We'll be able to track them from law enforcement pulling Tiff's records—"

My phone rang, and when I didn't recognize the number, I answered, "Chief Quinn speaking."

"Quinn," my wife purred in my ear.

Normal humans couldn't purr, but my wife had developed a purring habit around the same time she'd started getting a better grasp on being a fire-breathing unicorn. I figured it had something to do with her special brand of magic, and I loved the sound.

When she purred, she was happy.

"Why hello there. Get arrested already?"

"No." Bailey stopped purring, but I heard a hint of her amusement in her faked sigh. "*I* didn't get arrested."

"Well, that's something. What has my beautiful wife been doing?"

"Watching Tiffany the Bitch Perkins bra whip a cop. Watching as in she's doing it. Right now. It's a bra from Victoria's Secret, and I want one."

Okay. I loved when my wife wanted new lingerie. She took me with her, and she kept staring at me with hopeful, innocent eyes every time she spotted one she liked, which roused my demonic side to an almost frightening degree.

She got whatever lingerie she wanted, and I had a great deal of fun destroying most of it.

I thought the sacrifices well worth the money.

However, she rarely admitted she wanted new lingerie, especially not when someone might hear her. "Have you been drinking?"

When my wife got drunk—or high off excessive sugar— trouble happened. So much trouble. She didn't need more than a sip or two for the trouble to start.

"No, not yet. I might if she doesn't stop whipping police officers with her bra." Bailey whimpered. "We were about to leave, but Tiffany remembered some law here letting her get only a misdemeanor for smacking a cop with her bra."

"Tiffany is assaulting a police officer with a *what*?"

Perkins's eyes widened.

"It's a brassault." My wife giggled. "And she's dancing on a table."

"On a table." I fought my urge to laugh and failed miserably. When I recovered enough to speak, I asked, "Do you need to be rescued?"

"No, not precisely. Yet."

"What do you need?" She wouldn't have called me unless she needed something—or wanted me to rescue her.

"A favor," she admitted.

Uh oh. Favors could mean anything. "What do you need?"

"Assurance this outing with Tiffany won't end with a divorce."

As always, whenever Bailey's insecurities got the best of her, she reduced me to an emotional mess of a man, and I wanted nothing more than to hold her and convince her everything was fine. I smiled, and I marveled I'd been able to breathe before she'd steamrolled her way into my life. "Bailey, you have nothing to worry about. Your man repellant is with you, and what happened the last time you met a rowdy incubus?"

"I stabbed him with my horn," she dutifully replied.

"Do you have your pills with you?" I knew she always carried a stash of pixie dust and transformatives in her bra, the best grade the CDC would legally allow her to cart around without additional permits.

We never spoke of that stash, and we pretended it didn't exist.

As such, my question was about the other stashes in the house, so numerous I'd stopped bothering to count them.

We had a special permit that covered the entire house for a wide assortment of controlled substances thanks to her special brand of magic.

"I stole the living room stashes."

"Stashes?" I tried to remember how many stashes we had kept in the living room. The last time I'd checked, she'd even put plastic baggies of pills inside the lamp shades. All of them.

"Well, I grabbed one, forgot I'd grabbed it, and then the next thing I knew, all of the stashes were in my purse of holding. Tiffany wanted to leave, and I didn't have time to put the extras back."

Every time I thought I couldn't love her any more than I already did, she opened her mouth and started babbling, often saying the first thing to pop into her pretty head. "You only need to take one pill unless it's an emergency, and try to limit it to no more than five if really needed, okay?"

After five pills, strange things started to happen around Bailey, and my grandfathers usually showed up to fix the resulting mess—or prevent a calamity.

"I'll be careful with them," she promised.

"Take pictures, have fun, and don't worry about the bail. If she can't negotiate her community service hours, or if either of you need legal advice, give me a call. When will you be home?"

"Uhm, about that."

"What is it, Bailey?"

"Merry Christmas!" She hung up.

I blinked and stared at my phone. "Hey, Perkins?"

"I'm not sure I want to know."

"Where in the United States is bra whipping a cop only a misdemeanor?"

"Atlantic City. Cops' wives, especially from here, head there when the going gets rough, and for some reason, someone thought it was a good idea to write it into the legal code so it'd be less of a hassle for their husbands in the aftermath. I'm pretty sure most of the married guys in our precinct have made a run to Atlantic City to retrieve their wives following such an incident. The local cops love it, and at most, she'll get a few hours of service."

I blinked, and upon thinking about it, realized he was right. Every few months, one of my cops did have to make an unexpected run to Atlantic City on personal business.

No one had told me why, however.

"Is this your wife's first time hitting Atlantic City?"

Perkins sighed. "She's bra whipping a cop in Atlantic City, isn't she?"

"While on a table. Bailey called it a brassault and wanted to be reassured."

"About what?"

"She wanted assurances her outing with Tiffany wouldn't end with a divorce." I laughed. "Then she wished me a merry Christmas and hung up."

"Do you want to head to Atlantic City tonight?"

"No. It can wait until morning. Let's let our ladies have their fun for tonight. We can pay the Dover hive a visit tomorrow before tailing them."

"We?" Perkins sighed. "Can I sit in the car?"

Considering how much Perkins hated petrification, it

impressed me he'd limited his request to just staying in the car. "Sure. Hey, do you like kids?"

"You're not wiping out that hive and taking the kids."

Perkins knew me well. Too well. "Why not?"

"It's wrong. That's why."

I scowled. "No. Threatening *my* bride is wrong."

"You're not wiping out that hive and taking the kids unless they go after Bailey or Tiffany first. Then and only then may you wipe out the hive and take the kids."

I could accept those terms. "Well shit, Perkins. How's that fair?"

"It's fair to them."

He presented a very good point. "Bailey's worth at least a hundred times their starting offer. At least. They deserve it for insulting her."

"I shouldn't have to tell you this, Quinn, but murder is bad."

"I'd kill them quickly. I should be given credit for being merciful. What do you think Bailey will do to them if she finds out about this?"

Perkins sighed and bowed his head. "I need to tell her that murder is bad, too."

I snickered. "I'll pay good money to watch you try to convince the pyromaniac, meat-eating unicorn of that."

"How is it that I became the adult supervision of this relationship?"

"That's a really good question."

The shoe fit a lot better than I'd anticipated.

BAILEY

WHAT HAD I DONE? Why had I called Quinn? I stared at my new phone, astonished I'd babbled so much without spilling the beans about our road trip. His reminder about our mystical ball and chain helped.

He knew I'd never betray him.

He just had no idea I'd run away from home for more than a few hours.

He'd forgive me. Probably. Hopefully. Maybe. At least he'd forgive me enough he wouldn't seek a divorce for running off with his cop's wife.

Perkette whipped her bra at the cops, and the idiots laughed. Granted, I couldn't blame them. I hadn't dubbed Perkette her name because of her breasts, but the shoe fit a lot better than I'd anticipated. I had no idea how her breasts defied gravity, but they did a damned good job of it.

I assumed magic was somehow involved.

Sighing, I considered how best to put an end to her behavior. "Perkette, you're married. You wouldn't cheat on Perky because you know I'd shove my horn up your ass. Put your damned clothes on and stop resisting arrest."

"I wouldn't call it resisting. I'm entertaining. Look! They're entertained." Perkette hopped off the table. "Heaven forbid you drive too late at night. All right, all right, I'll get dressed."

"Behave, Perkette. I mean it. You land anything other than a misdemeanor, and not only will I never make you coffee again, I won't renew my pixie dust license."

"You play dirty."

I smiled. "I've only just begun. Clothes back on, Perkette."

She even put her bra back on first, much to my amazement. While she dressed, I counted cops. After six, I figured they could spare one if I asked really nicely. "Excuse me, but I don't suppose one of you could accompany me? I've never been here before, and snails outrun me when I drive in the snow. Frankly, it'd probably be faster to walk."

"You can follow me, ma'am," the young cop who'd arrived to the scene first replied, and his eagerness confirmed my suspicion he was fresh from schooling and ready to prove he could handle any task.

The new cops were always so cute in their enthusiasm.

A cop ripe for retirement sighed, and I pegged him as the poor bastard saddled with keeping an eye on the green recruit.

"Thank you. Do you want to wait for them?" I glanced at Perkette, who was taking her time adjusting her clothes, meticulously checking her purse, and charming the other cops. If she'd been the type, she probably could've talked them all out of their clothes, too. Fortunately for everyone, she wasn't.

Perkette was a lot of things, but she worshipped the ground Perky walked on. She just would rather chew glass and rusty nails before admitting it. When I thought about it, we were birds of a feather.

The pair chuckled, and the young one shook his head. "No. We'll go ahead and meet them at the station. Don't drive often in the snow?"

"Not really. My husband is the one who usually drives, or I take a cab. He keeps threatening to make me take stunt car driver lessons." I shrugged. "I just don't want to be in an accident."

Both cops grinned, and the older one replied, "It's refreshing to meet a safe driver. Take your time. We'll wait if you fall behind. The roads should be quiet tonight."

I left Perkette to fend for herself, claiming the keys to the rental on my way out of the club. The snow had worsened, and I wondered how I'd make the drive without shaking to pieces or otherwise making an idiot of myself. Damn it, why couldn't I drive like a normal person?

My lack of experience driving in the snow took most of the blame while my fear of disappointing Quinn accounted for the rest. If I drove through the snow like a normal person without hitting anything, he'd be happy.

My husband really needed to raise his standards a little.

In what I could only classify as a miracle, I made it to the police station without incident. Snow drifted into absurd piles in the station's parking lot, promising we'd need the shovel the rental company had stashed in the trunk at Perkette's request if we lingered for too long. I took the spot near the dumpster, which was somewhat protected from the wind. Drawing a cleansing breath, I killed the engine and slid out of the vehicle.

Nearby, an animal whined, and as cats meowed and I didn't want to know what racoons sounded like, I assumed a dog had taken shelter near the bins. Stray dogs got me in trouble. Before Quinn, I'd hated myself for ignoring a dog in need. Quinn had changed everything.

Since marrying him, I'd been treated for rabies seven times, a city-wide record. Maybe if I stopped getting bitten or slobbered on by the strays I rescued, I wouldn't need to be treated for rabies so often. Quinn would mourn my lack of self-preservation skills, but I couldn't leave a dog to freeze in the snow.

Quinn would forgive me. He always did.

I checked around the dumpsters without locating the source of the whining.

Well, shit. I'd have to go dumpster diving again.

Yippee.

"Ma'am? Is everything okay?"

I gave it two months before the green recruit lost his enthusiasm, realizing he'd signed up for an exhausting job and that people like me, who courted trouble at every turn, existed. Since he'd hover if I didn't answer him, I replied, "There's a dog in the dumpster. It's too cold out here." I dropped my purse, jumped, and scrambled over the metal ledge to peek inside. A squirming, snow-covered bag guided me to the source of the whining. Fuckers. I hated people who dumped animals, especially in the sort of thick plastic bags they'd ultimately suffocate in without help. Teetering on the dumpster's edge, I stretched and snatched the bag.

It weighed a startling amount, heavy enough I strained to move it.

Why wasn't I allowed to transform and light animal abusers on fire? Wiggling out of the dumpster with my bag full of unhappy dog, I retrieved my purse and carried the wiggling plastic bag into the station. I claimed the nearest plastic chair in the lobby, set the animal on my lap, and freed it from its plastic prison.

A single white puppy cried its distress, staring at me with one pale blue eye and one emerald eye.

Perkette wouldn't mind the addition of a puppy on our road trip, would she?

"Another one?" the young cop sighed. "That's the fifth one dumped here this week."

Stupid, heartless animal abusers. I couldn't just add myself to the list of people who'd abandoned the poor thing. "How long does it take to book a brassaulter?"

The cops exchanged looks, and I bet they believed I'd lost my mind. I probably had.

"I'd like to take the puppy to a vet while you deal with her."

The older cop relaxed, and he grinned. "How long do you want us to keep her, ma'am?"

"Long enough for me to take my new puppy to the vet."

Both cops laughed, and the older one pointed at the door. "The 24-hour vet is next door. Turn right when you reach the sidewalk. The building looks just like ours, but they have the better sign. We figure whoever is dumping the unwanted pets here can't tell the difference between a police station and a veterinarian. I'll dispose of that bag for you."

"Thanks. Give Perkette a hard time for me, but I'd really appreciate if you kept her charges to misdemeanors."

They laughed, and I left the station to take the puppy to

the vet and learn if we needed to be treated for rabies. Quinn would love if I needed to be treated for rabies again.

Thanks to the invention of neutralizer, rabies treatments no longer involved a series of wretched needles. Guzzling an obscene amount of pink, sparkling fluid wasn't my idea of a good time, and I'd have to do the guzzling twice a day for a week, but I'd emerge hale and hearty—assuming the neutralizer didn't send my immune system packing again.

So far, it hadn't, but I wasn't going to hold my breath. Quinn could handle a lot, but he freaked if I contracted even a mild case of the sniffles. My hospitalization with every plague known to man and pneumonia had something to do with that.

Personally, I wouldn't mind a visit from the various Quinn models. I still hadn't gotten the sneaky bastard to wear a suit for me yet, but I'd caught him in his dress uniform a few times. The dress uniform caused us both problems. I developed a severe case of lust, and he developed a severe case of not wanting to leave for work.

The first three times I'd made him late for work because he'd been wearing his dress uniform had resulted in him leaving with his dress uniform in a bag so I wouldn't be tempted into stripping him out of it.

Sometimes, I was a bad wife.

The puppy handled the walk to the vet better than anticipated, although the poor thing shivered and kept trying to bury its head under my arm. "Don't worry, baby. You've got this easy. You get one treatment and you're done."

The storm ensured sane people stayed indoors, resulting in an empty clinic. The older man behind the front desk cocked a brow when I strode towards him.

"I found this puppy in a dumpster. I'm betting ten bucks

it's rabid, but half the dogs I've dug out of a dumpster in the past two months have been rabid, so if we could start with the rabies test and the neutralizer torture, that'd be great. I'm paying cash, and I'd like the full assortment of vaccines. Also, I'm going to need all the basics for a puppy, an idea of what its breed and gender are, and a really good excuse to give my husband."

"Rabies has been rampant lately. We'll assume a positive result and treat you both."

Score. Quinn would be so happy when I called him. "I've been treated before, and I'm CDC certified, so I can administer the treatment myself. I'll just buy the neutralizer supply from you. My license is in my purse."

"It's easy to treat a dog, and if you have the certification for human-level treatment, we can show you how it's done if you pick up any other strays you think might have rabies."

Double score. That would save me a lot of time and hassle. "That would be marvelous, thank you. What's this going to ding me?"

"The treatment for rabies takes an hour and costs six hundred. The first round of vaccinations will cost you seventy-five. The exam fee is waived since you're doing a rabies treatment."

Ouch. My wallet already whimpered, but there wasn't anything I could do about it. "Okay. How much for everything else? Do you sell collars and leashes?"

He chuckled. "We have everything you need, don't worry. For food and all the extras, it'll be a few hundred dollars. In good news, you're saving a few hours and one-fifty avoiding the rabies test."

"With my luck, it's definitely rabid."

"Four of five rescues lately have been. There's concern a

feral cat colony or dog pack is spreading the virus; domestic pets are all vaccinated, but the feral colonies can spread rabies horrifically quick, and there's just too many of them to vaccinate. So far, it doesn't seem to have hit the wild deer populations hard, but it's only a matter of time." The old man, with his salt and pepper hair falling into his eyes, reached for his phone and pressed a button. "Dr. Sennets to reception: we've got a probable rabies case."

"I should tell my husband I'll be frothing at the mouth within a month. Hey, do you do hooves and claws here?"

"Of course, ma'am. What animals would need to be groomed?"

"Me. I transform, and my claws and hooves could use a look. If you have a bored groomer…"

He laughed. "We do. Let's get your puppy treated first, and then we can take care of your hooves and claws. We need to decontaminate your clothing anyway, so if you transform, that'll give us a chance to make sure the virus doesn't spread."

"You're a lifesaver."

A startling young woman in a doctor's coat and armed with elbow-length gloves strode to the desk. Smiling, she took my puppy from my arms. "I'll bring your puppy back to you in an hour or two."

"Can I pay you extra for grooming?"

"That's already included in the price, ma'am. It's part of the rabies treatment. Austin, if you'd handle her clothing, please?"

"Before you go, do you know what breed it is?"

"He's a husky, ma'am. Possibly a purebred. I'd have run a DNA test to be certain, but those eyes scream husky, as does his build. He's probably around three months old, but I'll know more when I do a proper examination."

"How much for the DNA test?"

"Fifty. We have a basic machine here, and it doesn't take long to do the scan. It won't tell me more than if he's a purebred and base breed, but it's sensitive enough to identify a purebred. If he's a purebred, I can write up a certificate for you."

"Add it to my bill, please."

She nodded, smiled again, and walked away with my puppy.

"If you'll come with me, ma'am?" The receptionist rose from his seat. "We'll handle the required paperwork after we're certain you can't spread the virus."

I grinned. "I can't wait to tell my husband about this."

He'd be thrilled. Not. Unfortunately for him, when it came to puppies, dumpsters, and contracting rabies, I refused to be sorry.

QUINN

MOST OF THE TIME, very little of my wife's emotions bled through our bracelets, but a flash of anger caught my attention before it ebbed to soothing glee. Glee could mean many things. What, I wasn't sure.

No, I knew.

Trouble.

Glee plus Bailey equaled trouble, always.

I gave in to the inevitable and laughed.

"What's so funny?" Perkins eyed the package sitting on

the kitchen counter, a gift wrapped in red and green. He eyed me, lifted the box, and frowned. The way he carried it implied it had some heft to it, and he carried it to the living room before setting it down and resuming his circling.

As I found his odd investigation of my gift amusing, I let him examine it some more. I'd get to opening it eventually.

He sighed, nudging the box with his toe. "I don't have any idea what this could be. She gave you coal. That's my final guess."

She would just so I'd feed it to her. "Something annoyed Bailey, but now she's alarmingly happy. While I'm happy she's happy, she—"

My phone rang, and Bailey's new number greeted me. I grinned and answered, "Hello, my beautiful."

"I got rabies again!"

For fuck's sake. "Really?"

"And possibly tetanus, the black plague, and whatever else I can contract while dumpster diving. This time, you can't stop me."

My eyes widened. When Bailey went dumpster diving, she did so for one reason: a dog or cat needed her help. I twisted around to gape at Sunny, who slept on her new bed covered with Bailey's favorite throw blanket. No matter what I said, I lost. I could earn some affection, gratitude, and a dog's lifetime of work with one choice.

One choice that wasn't even a choice at all, not when she sounded so excited and had gathered the courage to be assertive.

Damnit.

I'd have to beg Falhavert to train a second dog.

"Okay. I love you. Please be properly treated for rabies

and any other disease you picked up while dumpster diving. What breed?"

"Rabid."

I sighed, wondering what good yet terrible deeds I'd done in some previous life to deserve Bailey. "Bailey."

"Soon to be not rabid."

"That's a little better," I conceded, although I worried about her reasons for evading my question.

"My puppy is white, and he has one blue eye and one green eye."

The husky commentary began to make alarming sense, as I was willing to bet one of my nosy relatives had been snooping into the future again. "All right. Since you're getting a puppy for Christmas, I have a favor to ask of you."

"A favor? From me? What do you need?"

"Your asshole boss is transferring you, I've known for too long, and I'm sorry I didn't tell you sooner."

Perkins sighed, shook his head, and shot me a look promising that I'd just created a disaster on par with my wife's troubles.

"I'm being transferred?"

"In good news, the transfer comes with a huge raise."

Bailey sucked in a breath. "I'm getting a raise?"

"You are," I purred to her, grateful I wasn't quite human. "You're also getting a good work schedule that will closely match mine." By closely I meant exactly, but I wasn't going to tell her that yet.

She squealed. "No more shit schedules where we don't see each other for days sometimes?"

"That's right."

"I can get eight hours of uninterrupted sleep?"

Ah-ha. Mystery solved. "Would my beautiful like some more sleep? Your wish is granted." I smirked. "Most nights."

"I won't be a mooch?"

I rolled my eyes at that. "You're not a mooch, Mrs. Millionaire. Really. But you'll find your salary rather comparable to mine."

Her squeal almost ruptured my eardrum. "Salary?!"

"You won't be working for the CDC anymore, but you'll still classify as a specialist and retain your certifications. Your bastard boss figured out how to transfer you without consulting you about it. I'm sorry. I should have told you sooner."

"But what will I do? I know how to make coffee and deal with toxic magical bullshit," she whispered.

"I have another confession," I admitted.

"What is it?"

"While I didn't get her from a dumpster, there's a puppy in our living room, and she's sleeping with your favorite throw. I'm bad at following instructions. I interpreted your list to mean 'I want a puppy.' So, when a puppy crossed my path, I surrendered without a fight. Her name is Sunny, and I've been told she'll always love you more than she loves me."

Bailey sucked in a breath. "But I got one, too."

"We can keep both," I promised. "You wanted one badly enough to risk rabies again, and I already broke the no-puppy rule, so we're even."

There was a long moment of silence, and then my wife whispered, "Can I get you a kitten if I can find one?"

When Bailey had discovered I loved cats, a secret passion I'd made certain no one knew about to avoid the ruthless teasing of my officers, she'd gotten a wistful expression on her face.

She loved animals.

I smiled. "Okay, Bailey. Why not? When are you coming home?"

"I don't know. I left Perkette to be booked for brassault. It'll take two hours for the vet to finish with my puppy, and they do hooves and claws here. I'm getting groomed!"

"Just make sure your new puppy can tolerate fire-breathing unicorns."

"I will."

"Call me if you have any problems," I ordered.

"What's my new job?"

"You'll find out when you come home, Mrs. Chief Quinn."

"A hint?"

I smirked, as I'd already given her one. "You'll find out soon, I'm sure. If you're not home by morning, I'm going to chase and catch you, and I'll enjoy every minute of it. Please run with your puppy."

Perkins choked on his laughter.

"Can you take a picture of Sunny for me, please?"

"Of course. Every day until you surrender and meet her," I replied. "Just be careful, okay? If any gorgons bother you, pop one of your pills, torch them, and claim their whelps."

"Quinn!"

"What?"

"That's illegal."

"Actually, it's not. You're *my* bride, and if any gorgon other than me tries to touch you, you're within your legal rights to torch them. And you get first crack at any whelps."

Her sigh implied she'd reached the end of her rope. "Quinn."

One more tug wouldn't hurt. "It's true. As you're my

bride, a queen as far as I'm concerned, should a gorgon try anything, self-defense is legal. Gorgon law states a threatened bride may defend herself. Death—theirs—is perfectly acceptable."

Bailey laughed. "You're a terrible cop."

"Sometimes." I relaxed for the first time since finding out the Dover hive had their sights on her. "So. I take it Tiffany's keeping you for the night."

"Maybe." She drawled out the word.

"Enjoy yourself, and know if you're not home by noon, I'll be coming for you. I fully intend to enjoy every minute of the chase. I don't have to go back to work until January, so I have all the time in the world." As I knew how much she enjoyed my growl, I catered to her. "Mrs. Quinn."

"Mr. Chief Quinn," she growled back. "Catch me if you can."

"Oh, I will," I promised. "You have until noon unless you wish to surrender now."

"Like hell I'll surrender," my wife hissed. "I'll call you tomorrow and mock your failure to catch me."

She hung up, and I laughed.

Perkins coughed. "Dare I ask?"

"She's going to call me tomorrow and mock me for failing to catch her."

He sighed. "She's getting carried away."

"Like we aren't?"

"Good point. What are we going to do until noon?"

"Sleep, then we'll get a rental in the morning and follow our wives. I'd like to keep them one step ahead of us, so if we're needed, we're close."

"With a wolf puppy in tow?"

"Well, she'll be used to car rides soon. It's training."

Shaking his head, my friend sighed again. "Whatever you say, Sam. How is it I became the bastion of sanity?"

"I'm more concerned you think you're a bastion of sanity. Your wife collects misdemeanors and community service hours when she gets bored."

"I really can't dispute that. We even had a proper wedding, and it was my idea."

"Think I should give Bailey a proper wedding for Christmas?"

"You got her a puppy. I think that's a sufficient Christmas present."

"It's really not. She deserves a proper wedding."

"In Vegas?" Perkins laughed. "That's hardly proper."

"The Venetian has a nice chapel."

"If it hasn't been booked."

In Vegas, everything could be purchased for a price, and a lot of people would work in the middle of the night for a nice paycheck. "Let's find out. Planning a wedding will keep us busy while we pretend we have no idea where our wives are."

"This is going to be a disaster," Perkins predicted.

"Well, yes. I'm married to the Calamity Queen. What were you expecting?"

"Caution."

I snorted. "Please. Where's your sense of adventure?"

"What did Bailey tell you the last time you asked that?"

"That it was hiding with her common sense."

"What she said."

BAILEY

I DOUBTED I'd ever understand Quinn. How had he translated my list to mean I wanted a puppy? Would he realize Perkette and I meant to go to Vegas? Had we not left enough clues? Shaking my head, I retreated to the nearest bathroom with a warning to spray down the tiles with neutralizer once I finished transforming. The grade of transformative I used wouldn't hurt anyone, but I played by all the rules, even the annoying ones.

Ten minutes later, I emerged from the bathroom with my clothes dangling from my mouth.

The groomer, an older gentleman armed with a utility belt loaded with combs, brushes, and clippers of various sizes, looked me over. "It's not every day I get to groom a cindercorn. Set your clothes down; a tech will be by to neutralize the bathroom and handle the rest of the cleaning. You want a standard trim?"

I set my clothes down and replied, "Puh-lease. Make mane pretty? Tail, too?"

"Braids over the top to thin your mane somewhat while leaving the rest long? It's too nice to hide."

"Some braids nice, puh-leash. Talk hard, sor-ree."

"That you can talk at all is impressive, ma'am. Please come with me."

He led me to a grooming room and retrieved a bottle of powder from a tall shelf. "Since your breed isn't tolerant of water, I'll use this instead. It'll clean your coat and add some shine. Don't ask how it works. I've been using it for years and still don't get it. It's expensive, but you'll like the results."

"Water bad, fire good. Pow-dur bet-ter than water."

"I'll admit, I never thought I'd get a chance to groom any sort of unicorn. We get a lot of centaurs, and some of the desert breeds hate the water, too. We're trained in most species. Zoos and rehab centers contact the emergency clinics if they get an exotic. It's free schooling for me, but I'm required to volunteer hours in emergency situations. As I'd do that anyway, it worked out great."

"That nice. They teach tooth clean-ing, too?"

"You open your mouth, I operate the toothbrush. Sentients are easy. Carnivore?"

"Yes. Very. Burn, eat. Eat ash and coal, too. And other things."

"Fuels? I can do a tooth check and brushing if you'd like. It'll only add five or ten minutes."

"Yes, puh-lease."

It took him over an hour to trim my fur, tend to my mane and tail, and do a full nose-to-hoof check. As promised, he even gave my teeth a good brushing. I passed the basic examination with flying colors, which would make Quinn happy.

Then, under the watchful eye of the veterinarian, I met my new puppy as a unicorn. He growled once, cast a doubtful glare at the vet, and then regarded me like a challenge to overcome, which beat him running away while yipping from terror. "He no run. This is good. Can work with this, yes?"

"He'll need training." The woman considered my puppy for a long moment, and then she smiled. "No, this is promising. I had the urge to run when I first saw your teeth."

Wise people did. My teeth could crunch through bone without much effort.

"Hus-band po-leese off-ee-sur. He know dog train-ers. I hire one."

"Oh! A police trainer would work nicely. I'll give you a sheet with his future vaccination schedule. I took the liberty of selecting the basics you'll need for his care. It's waiting for you in reception. If you have any questions, please ask. I've also prepared your first rabies treatment and had the rest packaged for you in individual dosages."

"Clothes clean?"

"Yes, ma'am. I'll bring them to the bathroom for you."

"Thank you."

Twenty painful minutes later and one rabies treatment down the hatch, I emerged from the bathroom so tired I shook. The aftermath of forcing myself to shift didn't help any, but I hadn't bled anywhere. I was proud of myself for that. The first time I'd shifted without waiting for the transformatives to wear off, I'd terrified a few years off Quinn's life and left a disturbingly large puddle of blood on the floor. Five minutes later, a thousand dollars in the hole, and armed with new supplies for my puppy, I left.

My puppy still regarded me warily, but he didn't growl. I carried him with his supplies hanging from my arms. At the station, I shouldered my way inside. "I'm sorry that took so long. We both needed to be treated for rabies."

I set my puppy on the floor and secured a hold on his leash. "Is Perkette booked and ready to go?"

The cop behind the counter grinned. "She's in general holding, rather miffed she's alone. You can take her."

"Please tell me she was only charged with misdemeanors."

"I wouldn't know, ma'am. How did your puppy do at the vet?"

I beamed. "He did great."

"Named him yet?"

"Not yet. He deserves a good name, so I'm going to think about it for a while."

"That he does. I'll call for your friend to be released, so feel free to take a seat. It won't be long."

SIX

No matter what we do, it's just not the
same.

QUINN

WITHOUT BAILEY AROUND, I didn't sleep well. My mixed
heritage let me get away with only a few hours of sleep each
night, but the little sleep I did get left me tired, sore, and
crabby. Perkins waited in my kitchen, engaging in a staring
contest with my wife's beloved monster of a coffee maker,
heaving sighs.

"It's just not the same. No matter what we do, it's just not
the same," he complained.

I smiled, still amazed she'd happily whipped out her bank
card and bought the same maker for the station but had hesitated to get one for herself. I'd gone behind her back, had it
ordered, and set it up in the kitchen. Her expression when
she spotted it had been worth every penny and then some.

Sometimes, I got a little jealous over how much she
adored the machine, but I tried my best to never let it show.
She loved coffee.

I gave the machine a fond pat. "I'm beginning to think it's magic. Since she doesn't use much magic often, it has to be bleeding off somehow. I think she makes magic coffee as a result."

"I don't know if I can deal with an idiot hive of gorgons without magic coffee."

"With luck, all I'll need to do is warn them off." I pushed Perkins aside and went to work making him a cup of coffee for the road. "My coffee isn't quite as good as Bailey's, but she keeps a stash of pixie dust in the kitchen, and she made me get certification to handle everything but the higher grades. She takes substance safety to the extremes."

"Well, she's a specialist. She really made you get certified for handling pixie dust?"

"A and lower. She keeps all grades of dust in the house, but the grades above A are locked in the biometrics safe the CDC sent over."

"They gave her a biometrics safe?" Perkins whistled. "Those things are wickedly expensive."

"Yeah. I have a code to get into part of the safe, too. It's ridiculous how many layers and doors are in that thing. If she wants to access the most secure section of the safe, it takes her half an hour just to open it. It's reinforced with magic, too. She, at the CDC's invitation, gave it all she had while a cindercorn. She couldn't even scuff it."

"That must have pissed her off."

"Just a bit. She tried to chew on the safe, which was when I lured her away from it and made her shift back."

"Lured? Do I even want to know?"

I snickered. "All I had to do was unbutton the top two buttons of my shirt. One of the CDC evaluators was a woman, and Bailey got territorial. She chased me all the way to our bedroom and wouldn't let me out until I buttoned my shirt."

"Bailey's unbelievable sometimes."

"She really is. That safe drives me nuts, though. Any time the CDC gets something they want secured, it goes into the safe until they're ready to transport it. They've got some samples of *something* in there, and they want Bailey in a hazmat suit if she comes anywhere near its compartment."

"Damn. There's a toxin that can actually affect Bailey?"

"I don't even know if it's a toxin or a disease sample or what, but the CDC is storing it in my basement in that safe."

"Think it'll stay put in the safe?"

"They promised even if someone lifted the safe and dropped it from space back down to Earth, that the compartment would hold and not spill a drop. I figured that should be safe enough, but I'm not sure I want her ever accessing the interior compartment again."

"I wouldn't, either. Will her job shift change that arrangement?"

"If they cart that safe off, I will be a happy man. So. What grade pixie dust would you like today, Perkins?"

"Give me a light dose of the good stuff. I'm going to need it if I have to deal with potential petrification today."

"A light dose of the good stuff it is." As Bailey would kill me if I got a hit of pixie dust without her around to enjoy the consequences, I took my time making his drink. I didn't wear the gloves or the face mask like she wanted, but I took my time giving his coffee a light hit of the good stuff. It would make his day more bearable, especially if he did get petrified. Perkins didn't take to petrification as well as others, and he'd be a miserable mess if he needed a neutralizer bath to revert him from a stone statue.

Worse, if someone *did* petrify Perkins, the hive would get me at my worst.

I didn't appreciate when another hive infringed on my territory, and Perkins—along with the rest of my cops—counted as my territory.

"You're tense. Dealing with a gorgon hive doesn't usually make you that tense," Perkins observed. "Even ones with their eye on Bailey. What else is bothering you?"

I wanted to protest, but I didn't waste my breath. He could read me better than an open book on a bad day. "It's that idiot ex-cadet I'm worried about. He's out for revenge. What will he do if his gorgon plan doesn't work?"

"He'll be sore out of luck if he tries any toxins on her. Not even ambrosia can take her out."

I scowled at the reminder of her last evaluation, which had involved enough ambrosia to summon a divine twice over. The CDC had wanted to test an exposure method. The method had worked; Bailey had become distant, but she'd been able to handle a world-record amount of ambrosia.

Some world records I didn't want my wife to hold, and surviving a ridiculous amount of ambrosia exposure ranked pretty high on the list.

"Sam?"

I sighed and handed Perkins his coffee. "It took over a week and exposure to rabies to get her back to normal."

"You never told me what the blood test showed."

"One of her grandparents is a divine, but the only time the damned scanner registers the DNA is when she's been exposed to ambrosia. And the rest of her genetics report back differently, too. When she's not exposed to ambrosia, she's a genetic match for her perfectly vanilla human parents. But once ambrosia is added? It's like she becomes a completely new person. And worse? The DNA scrambles the scanner, so while the CDC was able to register a grandparent was divine, they have no idea what the genetic makeup of anyone else in her line is."

"What does that even mean?" Perkins asked before taking a sip of his coffee. "I'd say you need one of these to get you through today, but we don't need you edgy because Bailey isn't around."

"I'm going to be taking a vial of low-grade pixie dust with us just in case. I figure that'll do an equal job to whatever the hell prescription my great-grandfather wrangled."

"Yeah. It's a serious prescription. I'll only force it down your throat if you really need it. I'm concerned he seemed so confident you'll need it, though."

"We're talking about Bailey, here. With her luck? I'm going to need it."

Perkins sighed and took another sip of coffee. "You know it's bad when the good stuff doesn't pack enough of a punch to stop worrying over one woman's bad luck."

"Well, as long as she's not exposed to ambrosia, she can handle just about anything on her own. However much it pains me to admit that, she can take care of herself. Usually."

Perkins raised his travel mug in salute. "A month ago, you would've been freaking out rather than admitting she does have some basic survival skills. Good job. I'm seconding you on the ambrosia thing, though. The last thing we need is Bailey contracting a severe case of divinity. Will we have time to swing by my place? I'm going to need clothes unless we're shopping on the way."

Sunny sat on my foot and stared at me. Right. I had a wolf, and I needed to feed her. "Take the cruiser, head to your place, pack, and then come back. I'll feed Sunny, get a rental reserved, and pack, too."

"Sounds like a plan. I should be back within an hour."

"Drive carefully," I ordered. Once he left, I began my sacred duty of feeding Bailey's new puppy and taking her on a walk. "Here's hoping you like road trips, Sunny. I have the feeling it's going to be a while until we come back home."

BAILEY

MY NEW PUPPY HATED PERKETTE, hiding behind me whenever possible. I found the whole situation hilarious. She didn't.

That made me laugh even harder, especially when the hotel gave Perkette a hard time for having a dog. The circumstances, the weather, and a bribe smoothed the way to keep the puppy in the room, but we wouldn't be able to maintain our plan of hitting the first hotel we liked anymore. We needed to find a hotel that would welcome a dog.

For that reason, Perkette hated me, too.

I still laughed despite having angered my friend.

"I still don't understand how my quest for misdemeanors resulted in yet another damned case of rabies and a puppy. That thing is a white devil."

The so-called white devil cowered behind my legs. "He is not."

"Yes, he is."

"Is not."

"Bailey, he's a ball of fluffy hatred and loathing."

"He's a traumatized puppy in need of love." I'd learned he

didn't appreciate sudden movements, a sign of abuse we'd need to address before Quinn noticed, flipped, and hunted for the abuser. While I'd love to see the abuser punished, my chief of police would take things too far.

He liked to pretend he didn't love animals as much as I did, but I was on to him.

"I'm not able to argue that point, but do you have to be the one to love that fluffy ball of hatred and loathing?"

Less than a year ago, I'd been a mess of hatred and loathing, too. "Yes."

"This is going to make our trip interesting. Do you even know how to take care of a puppy?"

"Not exactly. That's what the internet is for. Anyway, I need to learn. Quinn got me a puppy, Perkette."

"He got himself a guard dog and disguised it as a puppy. We both know he's going to train that puppy to protect you when you're more than five feet away from him."

He would. "My poor puppies. I'll have to protect them from Quinn."

"I wish you the best of luck with that."

"Is this a bad time to tell you that Quinn told me I could get him a cat?"

"Yes. You already have a puppy. We do not need a kitten on this road trip."

"I disagree. I need a kitten my new puppy likes. He needs a friend."

Perkette sighed. "We're supposed to be road tripping. Road tripping is not another word for pet shopping."

"We're not pet shopping. We're rescuing."

"Bailey. Cats aren't exactly renowned for their love of long car rides. How would we transport the cat?"

"Carefully. In a kitty and puppy play pen." I lifted my chin. "You can't stop me."

"Yes, I can."

I pointed at her. "Lying, misdemeanor collecting witch!"

Perkette laughed at me. "Be reasonable, Bailey."

"No. Quinn said I could."

"Chief Quinn has obviously been replaced by an alien."

Picking up my puppy, I hugged him. "He got me a puppy, so I'm getting him a kitten. I bet this beautiful baby will love Quinn. He doesn't mind me. He's probably a good police dog and doesn't like your misdemeanor collecting ways."

"I don't think they'll train him to be a police dog. He's a husky."

"You're mean."

"All right. Take your neutralizer, get your puppy's things packed up, and get ready to go. We'll go find Sam a damned kitten. But know that this is a terrible idea, and I am doing this under protest."

"This whole trip was a terrible idea. But it's not all bad. I got groomed when I took the puppy to the vet. I even got my teeth cleaned."

"Normal people would not be proud of that."

"If I were normal, would you even be friends with me?" I countered.

Perkette sighed. "It's all Arthur's fault. He said you needed a friend of female orientation before you became worse than a man."

"What is that supposed to mean?" I refused to be offended by her statement, as when I thought about it, she was probably right.

"Do you even own a dress?"

Crap. I had, for brief periods of time, owned dresses.

Quinn had a problem with dresses. They were fine until I put one on. At that point, their lifespan shortened considerably. "Well, no. I thought about getting a wedding dress once, but Quinn keeps breaking my dresses. I didn't want to waste more money on clothes. The dresses survive until I wear them, then all bets are off."

"Chief Quinn has almost as many issues as you do. All right. Here is the rule about any additional pets on this trip. One: no more dogs. Two: we do not shop. We adopt. Three: you must find and catch the kitten."

I scowled and set my puppy on the floor. "Those conditions won't make finding a kitten for Quinn easy."

"Exactly."

"Has anyone told you recently that you're evil?"

"Frequently. I enjoy it. You're so tolerant of my evil ways."

"Perky was basically right. You're the only woman I'm friends with who isn't a cop."

"There's a reason for that," my friend countered.

I thought about it. "Yeah. I'm an asshole."

"Not quite what I was going for, but you can be at times. No, you're happily married to Chief Quinn, and those who know you by reputation alone are so jealous they can't see straight. Personally, I think I need to send you a sympathy card. He's a handful."

"But he's a sexy handful."

"I feel this is a good time to remind you that you ran away from home so you could get some sleep."

Perkette existed to vex me, but damn it, she was right. "You suck, Perkette."

"Just get your shit packed up and ready to go before your man puts an end to our fun."

While I had no doubt Perky would chase his crazy wife to

the ends of the Earth, I kept my mouth shut for once in my life. I really could be an adult when I put in some effort. I waited a few moments to see if the world would end. It didn't.

Fancy that.

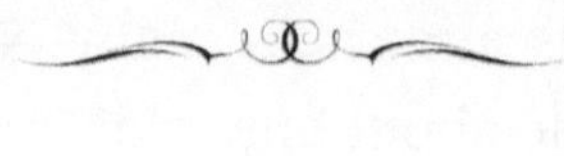

QUINN

ACCORDING TO THE CDC, the Dover hive lived in a former warehouse which had been converted into a mansion in Newark, New Jersey, which put his territory on the edge of my cousin's. I found that amusing, as my cousin typically handled territory disputes with the violence I expected from gorgons. I'd count his tipoff as all the bride gift he needed to offer to Bailey, as he could've taken care of the entire issue without coming to me at all.

As the Dover hive's turf didn't border mine, I lost several hours seeking official approval from the CDC to handle my business with the hive. No matter the outcome, I was covered legally.

Commissioner Dowry wouldn't be happy with me about it, especially since I'd ventured into a different state to handle the situation, but he'd cope.

No one threatened Bailey on my watch.

Once I was certain Bailey was safe, I needed to thank my family for the right to handle idiot gorgons threatening my bride with lethal force as necessary. If the Dover hive didn't roll over and make amends, I'd make an example out of them.

No sane gorgon in the country would look at my bride twice when I was finished.

The former cadet gunning for my wife would prove the most problematic element of the situation. Unlike with gorgon law, I couldn't just rip his head off, petrify his remains, and crush him to powder. I'd have to use the human legal system, which wouldn't have a satisfying enough punishment. It never did. Men still received preferential treatment over women, especially in violence cases, and I'd be lucky if he served more than a hundred hours of community service for attempting to sell my wife into slavery.

Then again, the same laws worked in my favor. If he made a move against Bailey and I witnessed it, few juries went against someone who came in defense of another.

The line was thin, but if necessary, I could walk it.

I would do anything to protect Bailey.

The former cadet's desire for revenge worried me, however. Revenge too often drove people to madness. I'd seen that with my ex-wife.

I'd hid the truth about Audrey through violence, leading my beautiful Bailey to believe I'd killed only to protect her. I had. I would as needed. But there was more to the story than she knew—than I or my grandfathers had been willing to tell her.

Audrey and her hive sisters had succumbed to madness *and* disease, and I wasn't convinced the madness hadn't been due to disease. Bailey still didn't know the one four-day nightmare shift had actually been me spending a round in a glass coffin to ensure I hadn't contracted the disease. My gorgon and incubus grandfathers had as well.

My angelic grandfather had returned to the High

Heavens and promised he would not be a carrier of any sort of disease.

Thanks to a puppy in a dumpster and a rabies treatment, I'd been able to spare my bride from a trip into the glass coffin, too. I'd seen her eyes after I'd finished burying Audrey.

Even the mention of a glass coffin terrified her.

It terrified me, too. I never wanted to see her clinging to life in a hospital again, her immune system reduced to ash thanks to overexposure to neutralizer.

Bailey also didn't know I'd taken representatives of the CDC to Audrey's body and exhumed her to confirm my initial belief they'd been infected with some disease.

The tests had confirmed they'd been ravaged from rabies, although the illness hadn't progressed to its final stages. It'd been too late to save them without extreme measures, but I'd left feeling a little better about what I'd done.

I'd given them a merciful end despite everything.

I regarded the warehouse with a sigh, wondering if I'd be facing yet another rabies situation. If so, treatment would be simple enough. I'd pull her trick, find a puppy in a dumpster, and call her to let her know I needed her to administer treatments. She wouldn't think twice about it, she'd come home, and everything would work out well.

Then again, I gave it two months before the NYPD implemented mandatory treatment of all officers once a month to prevent infection and spread of the rising disease. If rabies entered the civilian population as an epidemic, I doubted neutralizer could be produced in sufficient quantity to handle the demand. With so many medical treatments reliant on neutralizer, society would undergo an upheaval unlike anything seen since the emergence of magic.

"Quinn?" Perkins asked.

Woolgathering while outside of a rival hive's warehouse-turned-mansion made me look like an idiot of the worst sort. I sighed. "I had a thought."

"That's even more dangerous than this trip here. What's up?"

"What would happen if the neutralizer supply ran out?"

"Nothing good. A major disease outbreak for certain. A lot of deaths. Why?"

"Rabies," I answered.

"Ah. Tiffany wrote a paper about that."

Of course she had. "About rabies?"

"Epidemics and neutralizer supplies, actually. You're not the only one concerned. She got curious after the second time Bailey was exposed to rabies. She wrote the paper after running an experiment on the current rabies strain."

"Dare I ask?"

"It's so virulent Tiffany is worried it might become airborne with terrifying longevity outside of the body."

The idea of rabies mutating into a virulent, airborne catastrophe stunned me into silence.

"It probably won't. She pegged it at a ten percent chance."

"That's disturbingly high, Perkins."

"It really is. What got you worrying about rabies?"

"Bailey."

"Right. Dumb question. It might be worth keeping some extra stock of neutralizer around. Tiffany keeps a fifty pound bag locked in our basement."

A fifty pound bag could treat thousands of people of most ailments, rabies included. "That's excessive."

"Tiffany enjoys excess. What's really excessive is her basement lab."

Shit. She'd finally talked Perkins into a home lab? While I'd married the Calamity Queen, Perkins had married a mad scientist who might one day fight for my wife's title. "What were you thinking?"

My long-time friend sighed. "I wasn't. She's trying to create a new version of neutralizer with home-grown ingredients and common magic."

"Practitioner magic?"

"Yes. Her thought is if an outbreak does happen, she wants to be ready."

"I'm not sure I want to know how her experiments are going."

"Frighteningly well, actually. If we hurry up and get this over with already, I'll tell you more in the car."

Delaying would only make my plethora of problems worse, so I rang the doorbell.

A gorgon whelp, likely the male heir my cousin had mentioned, cracked open the door. A faint tingle of gorgon magic brushed against my skin, and I relaxed when Perkins showed none of the preliminary symptoms of petrification. "You're not Papa."

I showed the whelp my badge. "I'm Police Chief Samuel Quinn of the NYPD. Are any of your parents home?"

He deflated, and I tensed at the warning sign something was wrong. "He never came back."

Shit. *He*? What had happened to the hive's females? Gorgon whelps typically used 'they' or mentioned their mothers—however many they had. "May we come in?"

"Are you going to help us find him?"

Damn it, damn it, damn it. I couldn't tell him no, and I hadn't come ready to rescue the damned hive after my Bailey. "I'll do what I can," I promised. "Who is us?"

"Me and my sister. He left us home three days ago. He said he'd be back in a few hours."

Shit. Even if I wanted to brush off the whelp's concerns, when a gorgon male said a few hours, he meant it, which escalated the situation to something severely wrong.

No male would leave his whelps unattended for days.

I turned to Perkins. "Please contact my grandfather."

"On it." He strolled to our rental, his stride brisk without conveying any signs of panic.

"Your grandfather?" the whelp whispered.

"He's a former king, and he'll be able to help more than human law enforcement. Despite appearances, I'm a gorgon prince."

He pointed at me. "Shapeshifter!"

"Yes, I am."

His eyes widened. "That's so cool."

"Would you and your sister hood your serpents and put your glasses on, please? Officer Perkins isn't a gorgon."

"Yes, sir! Please come in? You can wait in the entry. We won't come into the entry until we're hooded and have our glasses." He held open the door, and the hope on his face hurt.

Poor kid. I followed him in, and I left the door cracked so Perkins could come inside. Careful to keep my expression neutral, I examined the foyer while he ran off to fetch his sister and prepare to interact with Perkins. The shoe racks, empty save for two pairs of children's shoes, worried me. My grandfather's hive had so many shoes that their entry often transformed into a maze. The coat rack told a similar story.

Where were the hive females? The hive females would have had spare shoes and coats for all seasons in the entry. A hive seeking a surrogate would have had evidence of females everywhere.

Perkins slipped into the entry, and he wore his sunglasses despite coming indoors. "Situation?"

"I'm concerned."

"Why?"

I pointed at the shoe racks. "The male left his young completely alone, and he didn't return for them." Gorgons were a lot of things, but they lived and died for their whelps, especially their sons, who were so rare. In the male's shoes, the only thing that would prevent me, my father, or his father before him from returning for his children, male or female, was death.

Within five minutes, the male whelp returned with his sister. The little girl, with the exception of her cobras, appeared to be human. She even had human hair flowing beneath her serpents, something so unusual I'd only seen it once before.

No wonder the Dover hive wanted Bailey. To have a son and a daughter like her in the same hatching, the hive's breeding male likely hoped his children might one day rule the gorgon world.

Between the two, they might, as the young male had eleven king cobras. If he didn't develop the Right to Rule, I'd be surprised.

"Before I ask any questions about your family, when was the last time you two ate?"

They stared at the floor, and in the following silence, two empty tummies gurgled.

"Officer Perkins, please bring Sunny inside. I'll arrange for their care."

"Sunny?" the little girl asked.

"My bride's new puppy. An early Christmas present. She'll become a police dog down the road. But first, let's get you two something to eat. Can you show me to the kitchen?"

Perkins shot me a salute, turned around, and ventured back outside.

The whelps led me to a house in dire need of cleaning, exactly what I expected from a pair of children left alone. Every step deeper into the house worried me more.

Once upon a time, the hive had had females; pictures decorated the walls, promising the mansion had once been a happy home. I worried all that remained of them were loving memories.

Disaster waited for me in the kitchen, the evidence the children had attempted to feed themselves with no luck. I could only assume the hive hadn't begun teaching them how to survive on their own—or the females had passed away recently enough the male hadn't been ready to rebuild his hive. I checked the freezer to discover several frozen pizzas, which would be the safest and easiest option for feeding them.

If I could tolerate cooking in the filthy kitchen. I gave it five minutes before my tolerance for the mess faded to nothing. I'd think about feeding them pizza to tide them over.

One choice was clear, though. I wouldn't be leaving without the whelps. "Until your hive is found, my hive, my father's hive, or my grandfather's hive will care for you. There'll be no adoption match scheduled yet; this is a temporary arrangement while we look for your family."

"Daddy wanted to find us a new mommy because our mommy died giving birth to us," the little girl whispered. "We're weird."

"Weird?" Their entire story was weird. Gorgons didn't become egg bound, and surrogates didn't carry eggs to term.

"We were live birthed. Our eggs broke in our mommy. It's not our fault," the girl assured me. "But we kept petrifying her, and she died after we were born. Our little sister didn't survive, but that wasn't our fault, either. Mommy loved us."

No wonder their father wanted Bailey. Broken eggs happened sometimes, but rarely in a case where the surrogate became pregnant with a human child at the same time. I'd never heard of any of the children surviving such a thing.

I beheld two miracles, the kind I doubted I'd ever see again. "Your mother must have loved you very much."

"But we're weird. We have big snakes. I'm the wrong color. I have to petrify people intentionally. It's tiring. My brother, too. It's *really* tiring. Daddy always worries someone will take us from him. But you're going to help us find our daddy, right?"

All the anger I'd carried over the hive's audacity of wanting my bride crumbled beneath the reality of their situation. I doubted their father still lived, and I didn't want to be the one to tell them. I'd have to, likely within a few days, but they stared at me with such hopeful eyes.

"I'm going to do everything I can to help you find your daddy," I promised. "What are your names?"

"I'm Beauty, because Mommy said I was beautiful before she died. My brother is Sylvester, because she told our daddy she liked the name."

My grandfather would love the boy because of his name alone. "It's a good name. What can you tell me about your daddy?"

Sylvester stared at his feet, and I recognized I'd have a lot of work ahead of me preparing him for life as a lead hive male.

"He's lonely," Beauty admitted.

"He is? Why?"

"Our other mommies got sick and died. Daddy took us to a fancy doctor, and we had to take a long nap, but we got better. Our mommies didn't."

Shit, shit, shit. Sometimes, I truly hated my job, and I hated myself for having to ask the pair more questions. "When did this happen?"

Both whelps sniffled, and I crouched in front of them, taking the time to stroke their cheeks and pay attention to their serpents, who nuzzled my hand in a heartbreaking bid for attention. "You can tell me when you're ready."

Their reactions cemented my new plan, one that involved taking them out for something nicer to eat and a change of environment.

"Did your daddy teach you how to make an evacuation bag?" The wise hives did. War between hives happened, and when angered, gorgons acted. Even I, who straddled several races, was guilty of a gorgon's base inclination for violence. It defined us all. It spoke of our history, heritage, and origin.

We'd learned, as a race, to temper our instincts with the necessities of modern times, but we remembered—even those of us born long after the first age of mythology and magic.

The children nodded.

"Go fetch your bags. Take a few minutes to gather a few things you feel are important. I can't promise when we'll return here, but I'll have my grandfather's hive handle tidying."

They ran, and I stared at the kitchen disaster. If their father had died, the children would inherit the place, and it would ultimately go to Sylvester for his future hive. Beauty would become the center of a chaotic bid war to have her. Every sane hive around the world would want her as its queen. If she carried the Right to Rule as I suspected, hives would wage literal war for her. Ironically, Beauty's father had been right to want Bailey.

There was no one better suited to protect the pair of young gorgons.

Sunny collided with my legs and sat on my feet, slapping her tail on the floor. "Thanks, Perkins."

"Your grandfathers will be here soon."

I sighed. "Which ones?"

"All of them. I snitched about Bailey. Any news?"

"It's bad. It looks like disease killed all but the children and the male, and to save the kids, I fear he had them put into glass coffins."

Perkins's brows shot up. "He put gorgon whelps into glass coffins?"

"Do or die. The girl is Beauty, the boy is Sylvester. We need to figure out who treated them and what they were sick with. I'll have my grandfather see about vaccinations for the uninfected hives."

"Rabies again?"

As I could see someone making a desperate gamble to cure late-stage rabies with a glass coffin, I shrugged. "It's possible. If he tried to treat late-stage rabies, I could see him paying out for the treatment. But it would have to be late-stage. Neither child seems mentally impaired."

"Unless he paid for a miracle. An angel could repair rabies damage."

A high medical bill to save his children would explain a

lot. "Call the CDC and inquire if the Dover hive requested any glass coffins. If so, call—"

My grandfathers, all three of them, appeared in a flash of golden light.

"—my father to get more information. Hello, Grandfathers."

For a being without a head, my angelic grandfather was unfortunately good at staring down his nose at me. "What have you done now?"

"Didn't peek?" I challenged.

"Not today."

"The little girl might have the Right to Rule, the females of the hive were wiped out by disease, and their father is missing."

My gorgon grandfather sighed. "Let me guess. You're giving Bailey two gorgon whelps for Christmas."

"I'm pitching it as temporary fostering until their father is found with the possibility of permanency."

"That's an upgrade from his original plan," Perkins muttered.

My grandfathers glared at me.

Damn it. "I was going for a peaceful resolution first."

"Also an upgrade from his original plan," Perkins announced.

All of my gorgon grandfather's serpents hissed at me.

"Thanks, Perkins."

"Glad to help. He's told the whelps to get their bags, so we should only have to be here for a few more minutes."

I shrugged. "They can't stay here alone, and I'm not going to let Beauty be thrown into the middle of a gorgon bid war. Forget it. Bailey's winning any fostering battles, and I'll pull out every stop to make sure it happens. They'll be safest with me for now."

My angelic grandfather sighed. "What was his original plan, Perky?"

"It involved legal violence and fostering."

"No," my grandfathers chorused.

Why couldn't I ever get a break? "It was only a little violence."

Perkins shot a glare my way. "And now it's no violence."

I gave up. "Fine. No violence, but he can't have Bailey. She's mine. The kids can come over and visit Bailey whenever they want after their father is found, and I won't even complain if he's in my territory, but Bailey is *mine*."

"We know, Sam. We know. After we find their father, you can scold him before helping him establish a new hive. That way, he's no longer a threat to Bailey." Perkins got in my face and prodded me in the chest. "But don't you even think of orphaning those kids because of jealousy."

I wouldn't, not without damned good cause. Sometimes, I wondered if Perkins had angelic genetics, too. Without fail, he never fucked up on the truly important decisions in life. Releasing my anger on a sigh, I nodded. "The whelps come first, always."

What makes no sense? The entirety of
your life?

BAILEY

MY NEW PUPPY howled whenever he needed a pit stop, which earned him Perkette's grudging tolerance. I searched around the SUV for evidence of divine busybodies influencing my puppy without luck.

"This makes no sense," I announced while we waited for my puppy to finish his business and investigate the falling snow.

"What makes no sense? The entirety of your life?"

Ouch. "Not quite, but yes." As the snow threatened to become a blizzard before we could escape the north, naming my new puppy after the weather seemed like a good idea to me. "Blizzard howls when he needs to go to the bathroom, and he's angelic the rest of the time. Who dumps such a good puppy?"

"A complete and total asshole." Perkette leaned against the SUV. "I'll give you credit, Bailey. When you decide to do something, you do it. I'm not sure it's possible for you to shower that puppy with more affection."

"His name is Blizzard."

"That's a foreboding name. I don't want to drive through a blizzard."

"Neither do I," I replied, waving my hand at the darkening sky and the thickening snow. "It seems probable."

"True. Has your husband told you any big news lately?"

I scowled at the reminder. "He mentioned something about a job transfer. He told me when I called him about Blizzard. I'm trying not to think about it," I admitted.

"Why not?"

"It sounded too good to be true. That means it probably is. He mentioned a salary." I sighed and watched Blizzard sniff at the snow skirting the road, and he didn't even pull at his leash. "What sort of job can *I* do that has a salary?"

"Police Chief of the NYPD, partnered with your husband."

I dropped Blizzard's leash, which Perkette stepped on before my puppy could make his escape. "What? Why would you even suggest *that*?"

For the past two months, the CDC had dumped me with the bomb squad, making me clean up explosives on top of my regular toxic substances. I still hadn't gotten the courage to admit my job description had expanded disturbingly into law enforcement.

"The CDC transferred your contract to the NYPD. They opted to partner you with your husband. They're renovating the eighth floor to give you an office. I have a spy feeding me intel. Sam's been worrying himself sick over how you'll react. He can be such a coward sometimes."

"Repeat that to me in smaller words I can easily understand."

"You're so badass you're now a cop."

I could list a hundred reasons why making me a cop was a terrible idea, including my lack of training, abrasive personality, lackluster appearance, and tendency to destroy buildings. "Someone's out of their fucking mind."

"While our menfolk have been incoherently flailing, I did some research."

Crap. When Perkette researched something, she emerged able to write a comprehensive and accurate book on the subject. Picking up Blizzard's leash, I herded him to the rental, toweled the snow out of his fur, and clipped him to his seatbelt leash. "Whoever proposed this is a nitwit."

"Your ex-boss."

"Which one? My regional contract supervisor?" My regional contract supervisor changed once a month, some-times once every other week. The position drove people to the brink of madness, and they tried to rotate it through qualified people so no one had to deal with me too much at one time.

Or so I liked to believe.

"The one in Washington."

Marshal Clemmends. "I regret not shoving my marriage certificate down his throat and lighting him on fire."

Perkette snickered and got behind the wheel, waiting for me to get settled in my seat and buckle up before starting the engine. "We all do. But being serious, it's a smart move."

"Before I call you out of your mind or batshit crazy, explain yourself."

"No one will be able to touch your husband while you're

on guard. You're practically indestructible unless you catch pneumonia or rabies."

Damned rabies. "I'm a walking catastrophe, Perkette."

"You're also a one-woman bomb squad. Got a bomb? You can eat the explosives. I've watched the tests. You can disarm most bombs through eating the payload. You only run into trouble when they have sensitive detonators. Even then, shrapnel-based bombs tear you up a bit, but you heal like a champ, and you ignore the concussive burst. Even the shrapnel doesn't hurt you that much. The assholes who shoot at you for screwing with their bombs have done more damage. The CDC has you playing on their bomb squads on live runs whenever the NYPD isn't around to snitch on them to Sam."

"Yeah. They don't want Quinn to know about that," I muttered. "He would not handle it well. At all."

"I only know that because you needed my help learning how to read a bomb schematic. Look, Bailey. If it's hazardous, you can handle it when a unicorn. You've been shot how many times now?"

I held up three fingers. The CDC had pulled out all the stops making the evidence disappear so Quinn wouldn't catch on to what they were doing—and paying me to do. "They weren't that bad. People get so offended when I eat their bombs for some reason."

"Your Sam is a lot of things, but he isn't indestructible. You know the rules and regs as well as most cops. You've been on crime scenes plenty, so you're familiar with basic procedure. Your record is so clean it squeaks when you rub it. Add in your budgeting brilliance, and they'd be stupid not to want you. With you, they get a motivated body-guard, a bomb squad, and emergency transportation. The puppy he got you is probably a police dog in training or a reject."

"Neither Sunny nor Blizzard are rejects."

"You got Blizzard out of a dumpster."

"This is me not caring."

"In good news, you're handling this a lot better than I thought you would."

"Salary," I blurted.

"What?"

"For the first time in my adult life, I'll have a salary."

"Seriously? *That's* what you're worried about? Having a salary?"

"I figured hoping for stable hours would be asking for too much."

Perkette laughed. "You never fail to amaze me, Bailey."

"I don't know how to be a cop," I whispered.

"Sam barely did, either. Now look at him. You're a quick study. You'll figure it out. Just think about it this way. You get more free education. I swear, if you thought you could get away with it, you'd be a lot like me, learning everything you could just because you can."

"I think I've had my fill of free education after all that bomb squad training. Quinn doesn't know I've been a bomb squad gopher for the CDC. Please don't tell him. He'll freak out."

"He's going to find out, probably around the same time the CDC clues in they sent their living cleanup crew to the NYPD permanently. In good news? Your ex-boss is going to get into a lot of shit for losing an important asset to the NYPD."

"He's basically at the top of the chain, Perkette."

"The politicians will eat him alive."

"Why would they even care?"

"Could you have some limits to your self-esteem issues, please?"

"I'm being realistic here. Clemmends won't even get a slap on the wrist for getting rid of me."

"He most certainly will the next time there's a major incident."

I scowled. "I've had my fill of major incidents for a lifetime."

"Me, too. Fine. You'll figure it out on your own eventually. I'm sick of driving through the snow. Develop magic that can fix this travesty."

"I will transform and poke you with my horn so you drive faster and complain less."

"It's rare I say this, but your threats don't actually need any work."

"I'm so glad I've earned your approval."

"Your sarcasm is in good form, too."

"Perkette, you're being evil again."

"I'll feed you some good napalm later. I have a recipe, and it only takes twenty minutes to make."

It occurred to me that adding a puppy to the mix ruined our plans to gallop across half the country. "I made a mess of our plan. I can't carry a rider and a puppy, and Blizzard can't run that far. He's just a puppy."

"Bailey, our plan had the general coherency of two drunks on a pixie dust high. Don't worry about it. Just tell your man we're going to the zoo to see if they have any lions or tigers up for adoption."

"We're not adopting a lion or tiger."

"You adopted a rabid puppy from a dumpster. A lion or tiger could happen."

"If I find a stray lion or tiger in a dumpster, I may change my mind," I admitted. "Or a panther, cheetah, leopard, or cougar. How about a lynx or bobcat? They're kinda cute."

Perkette giggled. "Let's make this trip fun."

"No." Fun, in Perkette's twisted world, landed me into trouble.

"Don't be a spoilsport. You need some fun in your life."

"We ran away because I was having too much fun."

"Wrong type of fun."

"Perkette, will you please be serious?"

"I am! You're a wayfinder. Use your magic to find the next little one destined to be adopted into your family."

"It doesn't work that way."

"What do you mean by that? Of course it works that way."

"Specific people, places, or things only."

"That's a pretty shitty limitation. What happens if you try for something unspecific?"

"Nothing happens."

"So there's no harm in trying, right?"

I sighed. Giving in to the inevitable would make my life easier. It wouldn't work, so what was the harm in indulging her? "Fine. I'm going to need a map, ink, some chalk, and a piece of paper. But don't complain later when nothing happens. I warned you."

QUINN

WHEN ASKED what they wanted to eat, Beauty and Sylvester stared at me with wide, hopeful eyes. I braced for the horror my life would become with their next words.

Gorgons could eat just about anything, and whelps often took their dietary adventurism to extremes.

"Nuggets?" they whispered in unison.

Somehow, I'd won the lottery of life.

"McDonald's, Wendy's, Burger King, or from somewhere else?"

The happy squeals in the back of the vehicle implied I'd mentioned their fast food joint of choice. It took several minutes for the whelps to calm down enough to tell me they'd do *anything* for McDonald's. Bailey would adore scheming with them for extra chances to eat all the nuggets she wanted, too. "McDonald's it is. All I ask is you take your time eating so you don't get sick."

If they'd been raised like most gorgons, they'd view my word as law, a painful enough thing to watch despite knowing their training was necessary. Gorgons who endangered humans rarely lived long lives. I'd have to enforce their obedient behavior, something Bailey would protest until I reminded her they needed to be disciplined if they wanted to survive through adulthood.

Then I'd have my hands full reining Bailey in, as she often struggled with the basic concept of moderation.

At McDonald's, Beauty seized my hand and attempted to meld with my leg while Sylvester latched onto the one being no sane mortal would test: his namesake. As angels loved children even more than gorgons, the whelp would be safe enough in his care.

Two joy-induced meltdowns and sixty nuggets later, I carried a sleeping Beauty to the SUV while my angelic grandfather coaxed her brother to walk under his own steam.

"I can't believe you fed them thirty nuggets each," my

gorgon grandfather complained, helping to settle Sylvester in and buckling his belt. "Have you considered calling Bailey and asking her to come home?"

"You know I won't do that. You also know why."

"I do, but I felt the need to remind you that it's a possibility. What do you want from us in the meantime?"

"I don't think a father who'd lost so much would risk his children like this." Like his sister, Sylvester passed out, and I sighed. "Find their father. If needed, I'll prepare Bailey for an adoption match."

My angelic grandfather's sigh didn't bode well. "Some mysteries shouldn't remain hidden in the dark. For their sake. You won't find him." The finality of his words made me wince. Angels couldn't lie, and when he said I wouldn't be finding their father, he meant it. I presumed it meant the gorgon had perished and his body had been destroyed.

The last thing I needed was another potent batch of gorgon dust making a mess of things, but I'd anticipate and expect it.

Gorgon males who disappeared without a trace usually ended up in a vat to become a batch of gorgon dust for some idiot's ambitions.

"That doesn't sound promising."

"It's not. I'm sorry. The how and why is the mystery you must solve, but there is no future with their father in it. I'm not permitted to look any further into the matter than that."

God worked in mysterious ways, as did *His* angels. "Per *His* will?"

"Per *His* will. *He* permitted me this much. Otherwise, I'd complain."

My incubus grandfather snickered. "*He* hates the whining."

How had my *gorgon* grandfather become a bastion of sanity? "Can you handle the legal matters for me and register Bailey as the primary match participant with me as her backup and partner?"

"You plan on fighting dirty for them, I see."

"They deserve only the best, and that's all Bailey knows how to do."

"While true, you as her partner sends an odd message."

"Does it? She rules my roost, and I'm okay with that. It's not my fault most gorgons have no real appreciation of a good woman. And Bailey, in case you were unaware, is the best of women."

"She's a walking disaster, little grandson. She's everything you need in a bride, but that doesn't change that she's a living, breathing, walking disaster waiting to happen. What sort of disaster will she create next? That's the real question."

"I wouldn't say she creates them," I protested.

"Samuel."

I sighed. "They just happen around her."

"She brought phoenixes to a gorgon fight and won."

"It's really not her fault the feathers became phoenixes."

"She planned on it."

She would. "She loves babies, so all incidents of rabies don't count."

My angelic grandfather laughed. "I peeked into the past. Yes, her new puppy was rabid, no, she didn't contract rabies rescuing him, and yes, she's doing the treatment anyway. Expect some form of illness."

My breath caught, and I shivered. "Her immune system is breaking down again?"

"It's nothing her friend can't handle, but she'll be miserable for a while."

Perkins sighed. "Tiffany has done so much damned medical research lately she could probably perform brain surgery and get away with it."

"No."

Everyone laughed at me, and my angelic grandfather ruffled my hair. "She won't need anything that drastic. It'll probably just be a cold."

"The last time she had a cold, she hallucinated hungry spiders in her hospital room and kept begging me to feed them." While her hallucinations had been hilarious, I had suffered from nightmares for weeks after, aware of how close to death Bailey had come. "You're sure it'll just be a cold?"

"Mostly."

"You know she'll get sick, but you don't know the specifics?"

"Precisely."

"Have I ever told you that angels are assholes?"

My grandfathers snickered.

"I've heard such a thing before."

"Well, it's worth repeating. Angels are assholes."

Perkins sighed, claimed the front passenger seat, and shook his head. "If I mouthed off to an angel like that, I'd be exploring the afterlife right now. You? You mouth off to an angel, and he laughs."

"There are perks to being the product of weird familial relations. They are few and far between, but they are there." I did a second check of the kids and their belts before closing the SUV's back door. "Is it a safe assumption you can't help with the rabies situation?"

"*He* has meddled enough in human affairs lately. When

men try to make themselves into gods, men must deal with the consequences on their own."

That didn't sound good. "Are you being literal? Please tell me someone isn't trying to become a god. Honestly? Being a police chief is a tough enough job. I don't want to deal with anyone with divine aspirations."

"No one sane does."

Perkins rolled down his window. "Not to interrupt, but I'd like to remind you that the bible does imply that things like intentionally spreading plague and so on is technically *His* domain."

"Not quite," my angelic grandfather replied. "That thought is close enough to serve a purpose in this discussion. The children of the divine are expected to do such things. That is their nature. However, men without divine blood are incapable of handling such power. All it will do is destroy them."

"Like ambrosia will." I wished I could forget Bailey's distant eyes whenever she was exposed to the divine essence. "Having divine ancestry isn't a guarantee."

My grandfathers laughed, and my angelic grandfather ruffled my hair again. "You think of your Bailey as always. She's safer than even you, Little Samuel, and you carry the blood of many divines. No, don't worry about her and ambrosia. When she dives into its golden depths, you'll understand why men fear the children—or grandchildren, or even the most distant of children—of the divine."

"I don't find that at all comforting."

"That's because you are wise. We must go now, and we will take care of the legalities. They will not find this a comfort now, but their parents loved them very much. Remind them of this often."

"I will," I promised, wondering how I'd tell Beauty and Sylvester the truth. Would they understand what an angel's word meant?

I'd find out soon enough.

BAILEY

BEFORE I EVEN ATTEMPTED TO DO THE magical equivalent of looking for a needle in a haystack, I needed to have a few words with one Police Chief Samuel Leviticus Quinn. I asked Perkette to pull over so I could step out of the vehicle and have the illusion of privacy while I spoke to him. I dialed his number and waited for him to answer.

He didn't, which meant he was likely driving. Tapping my foot, shivering in the cold, I waited.

Five freezing minutes later, my phone rang.

"Hey, Bailey. I was driving. How are you?"

I took a moment to enjoy Quinn's voice before I grinned and replied, "Perkette's trying to turn me into a bad girl, Mr. Police Chief Samuel Quinn."

"You have my attention, Mrs. Police Chief Bailey Quinn."

Before my talk with Perkette, I would've believed he was just playing over my use of his title. Knowing better, his clue amused me, a subtle warning of the sharp left turn my life was about to take. I had to give him credit. He was a sneaky, sneaky man when he wanted to be.

"Perkette has talked me into using my magic to attempt to locate you a kitten in a dumpster."

My husband's long-suffering sigh made me unreasonably happy. "Seriously, Bailey? You could just go to a shelter."

"I'm not going to find the breed I want in a shelter."

"Yet you believe you're going to find one in a dumpster?"

"Well, that's why I'm going to try and use my magic. If there *is* one in a dumpster, I'll find it!"

"Along with another case of rabies," he muttered.

In the background, I heard Perky laugh.

"I'll try to avoid another case of rabies, but no promises. I can't seem to resist rescuing rabid animals from dumpsters."

Quinn sighed. "There's a possibility someone is attempting to cause a major rabies outbreak. For my peace of mind, please get the largest bag of the best grade neutralizer you can get your hands on."

Damn it. Worse, I agreed with him. A spike in rabies cases in New York City among the feral cat and dog populations could happen, but I'd rescued my puppy from Atlantic City, too far away for it to be part of the same group of stray animals. "I'll do that. Will my new job let me put in the order, Mr. Police Chief Samuel Quinn?"

"Much to my relief, yes. You're not losing any of your CDC certifications with your new employment. Plus you get that salary you've always wanted. Please get the bag as soon as you can, and if you could resist the lure of the next dumpster to catch your attention, I'd appreciate it."

"No. I keep finding puppies and kittens in dumpsters. They need me to save them."

"Bailey, you're really going to contract rabies at this rate. You're a handful without being rabid. Have mercy."

"No!" I huffed. "Perkette said I could only adopt a kitten for you if I got it out of a dumpster and it met certain requirements."

"All right. Hold on a moment. I need to step out of the

car." I heard a door shut, and snow crunched. "There's an issue I need to talk to you about."

My eyes widened, and I stiffened. "What's wrong?"

"Remember Cadet John Winfield?"

I did. "From the 120 Wall Street incident? I thought about lighting him on fire and eating him."

"He tried to sell you to a gorgon hive. Well, several hives. My cousin notified me. I went to speak to the hive today."

Quinn dealt with threats from gorgons or other non-humans with violence, and if he had a legal option to indulge in violence in other circumstances, he would. He couldn't tolerate unknown gorgon males coming anywhere near me.

It always ended in a fight Quinn won, and Quinn usually let the other male escape. Usually.

I narrowed my eyes. "Speak?"

He sighed. "Speak. The hive females were wiped out due to disease, and my guess is that it was rabies. They have two kids. When we arrived, the male wasn't there. I asked Grandfather about it."

"Sylvester?"

"Yes. Well, he opted to have a look for me."

"And?"

"Dead or soon to be dead, and he says I won't be finding the body. The kids hadn't eaten for several days. They're asleep in the car. I've registered you as the primary contender for adoption, and I'll be your backup in the match. The girl's name is Beauty. The boy's name is Sylvester."

I loved that the boy's name was the same as Quinn's angelic asshole of a grandfather. Then his words sank in, and I sucked in a breath. "You registered us for a match?"

Every time I'd shown interest, everyone had provided a long—and accurate—reason why it wasn't a good idea, and it involved me shaming entire hives of gorgons and making more enemies.

"Technically, I'm registering you for a match. I'm going to watch unless you actually need me. I wouldn't want to spoil your fun. I'm going to give those gorgons a fair chance. You said I should be nice to other gorgons sometimes. This is me being nice."

"It'll be more fun if you help."

He chuckled. "I'll fight in a match or two so you can catch your breath. If you're on your own, you'll better show your determination. If we fight together, we'll crush them so thoroughly we won't be able to prove to the children how much we want them. It'll be an unfair fight unless my grandfather goes up against us."

I bounced on my toes. "Ask him to. I want to fight him. Please?"

"Bailey!"

"What? You won't let me fight him when we visit him."

"There's a reason for that. He's dangerous."

I snorted. "I'm dangerous, too. I eat napalm and breathe fire. And I can run really fast."

"You're also banned from eating napalm for a reason."

I smirked. "Perkette said—"

"No."

"But she—"

"Absolutely not."

My smirk widened to a grin. "Homemade—"

"No."

"Delicious—"

"Nope. Nope, nope, nope."

"Napalm," I crowed.

"Don't eat anything she gives you. She's a mad scientist. Why did I trust a mad scientist with you? What have I done?"

Giggling, I stomped my feet to help keep myself warm. "If you don't want me eating her latest fuel-based concoction made purely for my enjoyment, you better come apprehend me, Mr. Police Chief."

"You just want me to catch you."

"Yes, please."

"I have two kids, a puppy, and Perkins in the SUV."

I laughed until I hiccupped. "I'd say call me if you need any help with that, but I wouldn't know what to tell you."

"I'll be fine. I have more grandparents than I know what to do with willing to help."

In so many ways, I envied Quinn and his family. They were my family, too, when I could get beyond my wariness. "If my grandparents show up, petrify them."

"Have you even met your grandparents?"

"Only the ones on my father's side. They're assholes. Petrify them."

"If they threaten you or the kids, I will. I do have to keep it legal. So do you, so no napalm unless it's a dire emergency."

I still got a good laugh over how Quinn had managed to get them to overturn my ban on napalm to available in case of dire emergencies. The release of two phoenixes had something to do with the CDC's willingness to give me napalm if truly needed.

A drunk unicorn on a napalm bender did a hell of a lot less damage than two phoenixes on the loose enjoying their first taste of freedom in their new lives.

"I'll keep that in mind."

"Please be careful with Tiffany's experiments."

"I'd say I'm always careful, but I'm really not."

"Limit your disasters to ones I can rescue you from, okay?"

Typical Quinn. "You'd have to catch me for that to be an option."

"Already working on that. Are you having a good time?"

"Very, but I think Blizzard might actually be your puppy. He seems like the puppy of a big, manly police chief."

Quinn chuckled. "I'm going to enjoy myself a great deal when I get my hands on you, Mrs. Bailey Quinn. Run all you want, but you can't escape me."

I'd gotten rather fond of the predator in Quinn, especially when he felt he had something to prove. The real winner of the chase would be me. The faster I ran, the more enthusiastic he would become.

"I don't know, Quinn. I'm pretty good at slipping from your clutches. Can you really catch me?"

"Yes, I can. I'm merely being generous before I capture you."

'Capture' in Quinn's language might even include one of his ties, which he never wore to thwart my plans to see him in a suit. "Sure, sure. You say that now, but I don't see you here stalking me."

"When I catch you, I'll enjoy listening to you admit how wrong you are. I like it when you beg."

Whee. "Less talk, more chase. Drive safe, slowpoke!"

I hung up, did a little jig, and dove into the SUV. "Today is the best day."

"I feel this is a good time to remind you that we went on this road trip because you married an incubus."

"The faster I run, the better my reward. And damn straight I married my gorgon-incubus doohickey."

"Did you just call your husband a doohickey?"

"I called him the world's sexiest mutt once. It didn't go over well," I admitted.

"Poor Sam."

"He looked like he wanted to cry when I called him the sex toy model."

"You need to think before you speak just a little more."

I bit my lip. "Was it bad when I said I might be the only woman in Queens who has no need for a battery operated boyfriend?"

"No, surprisingly, that one is okay. You stroked his ego—and I don't want to know what else you were stroking."

"One of his cobras, actually. Francisco."

"You named his cobras?"

"Quinn hadn't, so I did it for him. Francisco gets nippy without attention."

"Has Francisco bitten you?"

"Several times. All those little bastards will nip if neglected."

"You're immune to them?"

I shrugged. "It stings a little."

"You know what? Nevermind. You talked to Sam for quite a while. What's up?"

"He registered us for an adoption match."

Perkette's brows shot up. "That's one hell of a Christmas present. Sam's notorious about avoiding them to spare the prides of the hopeful hives. He only let you two work the circuit for those unhatched whelps."

"He registered me as the primary contender."

She whistled. "I'll just say congratulations in advance, Mom."

"The females of the hive likely died of rabies. We're challenging for a boy and a girl. Quinn said their dad is gone, too."

"*Rabies?*"

"I'm worried, Tiffany."

"I am, too. It's one thing for it to be hitting the stray cats and dogs, but *gorgons?*"

"Quinn wants me to stock us with neutralizer. The best grade I can buy."

"Put in the call and get as much as you can. We'll do a supply run, look for a big cat kitten for Sam, and then do some investigating."

"What investigating?"

"Of the source of the rabies, of course."

"Are you mad?"

"Yes, I am. Two kids are orphaned now because of this. Enough is enough. Let's put your magic to the test for the good of everyone. If this keeps going, it's going to get out of hand. Let's stop it before it gets to that point."

"Okay. We'll get the neutralizer first. With my luck, Quinn's kitten will be rabid, too."

"Good thought."

EIGHT

She wants to fight you.

QUINN

I STOOD IN THE SNOW, staring at my phone for a long time. Bailey hadn't seriously attempted to use her wayfinder magic since the incident with Audrey, claiming she'd make a mess of her perfect life. I'd felt her fear, so I hadn't pushed her on the matter.

Most of her bravado masked her fears and uncertainties. I loved her a little more each and every time she overcame one of her inner demons, especially the ones that told her she didn't deserve me. The first time she'd hunted for my company in bed without me making the first move, I'd worried my heart might burst from love and pride.

She'd come so far, and most of the time, she didn't even realize it.

I worried what she would find with her magic—and what she'd do about it. Tapping my foot, I considered my options, which were few. Stocking up on neutralizer and notifying my grandfather the hives needed to treat and vaccinate would be the first step. Unlike humans, gorgons *could* be vaccinated.

Few opted for the treatment; it made them feel like animals. I'd hate myself for doing it, but spreading word of the Dover hive's fate might convince them.

I hoped.

I returned to the rental, got settled behind the wheel, and called my gorgon grandfather.

"What do you need, Samuel?"

"Get the hives started on treatments for rabies and vaccinations. Strongly suggest it, and tell them what happened to the Dover hive. I'm worried."

"Already on it. I figured you would suggest it. I'll also make certain they understand that Bailey is your bride and hive queen. I'll also make a note they should strongly discourage the former cadet creating problems for you and your bride."

I'd be very surprised if the idiot survived strong discouragement from angered gorgon males. I should've cared more, but I nodded. "Thank you." With him leading the charge, I could focus on tailing Bailey and taking care of the whelps. "I talked to Bailey."

"What did she say?"

"She wants to fight you."

"Of course she does. You're going to ask me to lose, aren't you?"

"No. I'm going to ask you to fight her like you mean it, even if it means she loses. Losing to you won't make her lose the bid for adoption. It'll prove her determination even more. I'm backing her, and should you defeat her, I'm confident I can beat you—and while I love my grandmother dearly, I win that fight with a look."

"Ah. I see. Yes, if your goal is to prove your determination to adopt, I'll make sure I'm overseeing the matches and will be your final opponent. Everyone knows I will not take it easy on you just because you're my grandson. No, if anything, they know I'll be harsher on you and your bride. You have to live up to the family name, after all. And should you win, losing to my grandson and bride is not a shame. Should she fairly beat me, it's a good thing. And as for your grandmother, she's used to being knocked out early. She'll forgive you for petrifying her."

"Bailey wouldn't forgive herself if Grandmother was hurt, so I'll end that fight before it really begins. I'll give Bailey a chance to tussle with you a little first, though. If Bailey needs a breather, well, I'll let Grandmother beat on me for a while first."

My grandfather laughed. "She'll enjoy that. She's going to try to spank you both if given a chance despite knowing she'll lose."

"You're in?"

"We're in. I'll claim the role of overseer of the match. You just worry about those whelps and your bride. I'll impress upon the hives you're planning on adopting them, so you two are there to endure a beating and fight. You need to control your temper, though. Bailey needs to prove her dedication to the whelps. Granted, I don't think it'll be much of a fight. Bailey wears her emotions on her sleeve. The whelps are smart. They'll see how much she wants to love them from the first match."

I nodded. "I know how it works. I'll keep my temper in check."

"You're unreasonable when it comes to your bride. Frankly, I'm amazed you haven't retrieved her yet."

"I'm regretting I haven't. She's about to create a great deal of trouble, I'm sure."

"Well, don't worry about the gorgon situation. I'm handling things. As your bride is always creating trouble, I feel I need to remind you that she's capable of handling the trouble she creates."

I sighed. "That's a stretch. Remember the hotel?"

"That's hardly her fault. She was sick and didn't know then she could go to you for help. That has changed."

A lot had changed. "I'm still worried."

"As am I. Be careful. I fear this will get much worse before it gets better."

Bailey

A SNOWY, empty parking lot at a long-dead strip mall made the ideal place to put my wayward wayfinding magic to the test. Blizzard appreciated the chance to stretch his legs and roll in the snow while I prepared the piddly ritual required to breathe a trail to life.

If I did find an abandoned big cat kitten for Quinn, I might have to put my magic in timeout until it developed a better sense of humor and some common sense on the side.

As I really didn't want to figure out how to keep a big predator from eating my dogs, my friends, me, or my husband, I flung the chalk and said, "Find me an orphaned big kitty kitten that won't eat me, my friends, my family, my pets, or my husband that actually wants to be adopted into my lunatic life—and it can't be infected with any disease, or illness, or virus."

There. I was guaranteed failure with those requirements.

The falling chalk erupted into golden, sparkling light and slithered over the snow to create a trail for me to follow.

"You have got to be fucking kidding me."

Perkette burst into helpless laughter.

"This is not funny, Perkette. This is the absolute opposite of funny."

"This is fucking hilarious. You tried so hard to fail. You left out the part about a dumpster, but you added a ridiculous number of other clauses, so I can't complain. It's fate, Bailey. Just accept it."

"Fate sucks. I'm inviting a predator capable of eating me into my home."

"It is what it is. You're driving." Perkette tossed me the keys. "It'll be good practice for you."

"How is it I end up driving myself to the next disaster whenever I use my magic?"

"Stop whining and start driving, Bailey. If you think this is bad, after we pick up Quinn's kitten, you get to drive us to the more serious disaster. I'll be nice and give you a break if you need one. In other news, we're going to need a lot more neutralizer."

I glanced at the fifty pound bag of the highest grade neutralizer on the market, which took up a horrendous amount of space in the back. "You have got to be kidding me. That bag cost me ten thousand dollars, Perkette."

"Get two or three more. We might need it."

"What the fuck am I going to do with that much neutralizer?"

"Save lives."

That shut me up, and I wondered just how major of an outbreak she expected; the fifty pound bag could potentially treat thousands to tens of thousands of people of the most dangerous ailments, rabies included.

If I went the risky treatment route, which had a one in five thousand chance of requiring a full set of vaccinations and general illness, a single pound of neutralizer could treat several thousand people. It didn't take much for internal treatments. Topical treatments took a great deal more neutralizer.

It only took a two pound bag to treat someone with a glass coffin.

I sighed. "I'm going to wipe out the stocks if I buy that much, Perkette. The only reason I was able to get a fifty pound bag is because the distributor just got a new batch in."

"Buy it in ten pound bags near expiration. When this goes down, my bet will be soon, and while the CDC won't sell or use it on the general public, they will sell it to you. If a major outbreak doesn't happen, no big deal. If it does, you'll be set."

"The SUV can't hold that much neutralizer, us, a dog, and a cat."

Perkette pointed at the SUV's tow hitch. "It can. We get a trailer. For now, we'll only get an extra hundred pounds. But if we think we need more, we pick up a trailer and we load it up with more neutralizer."

Quinn had rumbled about wanting a small trailer to go camping in so we could escape the city on the weekends. We'd have to exchange the SUV for a serious truck, but I thought we could get away with it. I could afford the transfer fee to get the SUV back to New York. If I got an extra hundred pounds of neutralizer before caving and getting a truck and a trailer, the entire back would be loaded with pink, sparkly powder. "Quinn's going to kill me when he finds out about this."

"He'll congratulate you on your wisdom."

"I willingly went on a road trip with you, Perkette. That's the exact opposite of wise. Is this going to prove I shouldn't be a police chief? It should."

"Relax, Bailey. Just follow the magical trail. Everything will be just fine."

QUINN

TO CATCH MY WIFE, I utilized every cheat at my disposal. First, I visited the nearest NY State Police station, showed them my badge, and requested a track on my wife's rental. Perkins helped, offering his officiated card from the CDC, which claimed his wife was a misdemeanor-collecting fiend who needed adult supervision. The card gave Perkins jurisdiction to conduct some police business in any state when the situation involved his wife.

The CDC viewed Tiffany Perkins as an invaluable menace, and they classified her brilliance as a national treasure, one that required my friend to be able to retrieve her as necessary.

That Tiffany kept her mischief to misdemeanors made all the difference in the world.

When I explained my wife was being promoted to be a police chief and classified as at risk, the state police joined my team and they got the ball rolling.

I gave it twenty-four hours before I got a card giving me Federal jurisdiction, too. I should've applied for one after my ex-wife had kidnapped Bailey and taken her to Vermont. Then again, the CDC had given me basic jurisdiction on the fly, which had limited my desire to fill out the forms.

Within two hours, the rental company hooked me up with their tracking software and gave me the vehicle's code along with a promise they'd give me the codes of any vehicles Bailey or Tiffany rented. To sweeten the deal in my favor, the state police got in touch with every other major rental company and had the women flagged.

If they rented a vehicle in the United States, I'd know about it within an hour.

Once I verified their location, I pulled up the weather map, as I liked knowing how bad the drive would be. Within a few minutes, I regretted being thorough. I bowed my head and sighed. "Hey, kids?"

Beauty and Sylvester stared at me with wide eyes, and I couldn't tell if they were overwhelmed they were in a police station or if they hadn't anticipated me asking them for their opinion.

"Do you like snow?"

They nodded.

"My bride and hive queen is about to drive right into a blizzard, and knowing her, she hasn't checked the forecast. We're going to go get some snow gear just in case and go to make sure she stays out of trouble."

"Is she hopeless?" Beauty asked.

I laughed. "Only when it comes to snow. Fire-breathing unicorns do not like the snow. She'll want to hibernate, and she gets grouchy."

"Unicorns aren't real," Sylvester announced with the confidence only a child possessed.

"I'm going to do you a favor and not tell Bailey you don't

believe in unicorns. She bites people who don't believe in her. Well, almost bites people."

Perkins snickered. "She snaps her teeth convincingly."

Very convincingly. I shook my head, smiled, and watched her rental's progress on my phone. "Only Bailey would drive right into the heart of an isolated blizzard."

"At least it's not a huge storm. It'll be fine." Then, Perkins laughed. "Who am I kidding? This is going to be a disaster. My wife will love it. In good news, Tiffany has done extreme weather research. She's crazy, but she won't intentionally put Bailey in danger."

I believed him. Tiffany was a lot of things, but beneath her drive to collect misdemeanors and her mad-scientist tendencies, she had a heart of gold. "Bailey will find a way to test Tiffany's skills."

"I'm trying not to think about how likely that is," Perkins confessed.

Knowing Bailey was driving right into the heart of some bad weather was going to make me a candidate for the prescription my great-grandfather had arranged. After months of adapting to having her around every day, I only had one method of controlling my worries: work. "I'm thinking we should've brought our work laptops with us."

"Our phones are fine. We're on vacation, Sam. That doesn't mean we work. If we really need to do something for work, we can head to the nearest station. Let's not waste extra time on unnecessary things." Perkins pointed at the mountain our wives drove towards. "Tiffany can make a viable shelter out of almost anything. Your wife breathes fire. They'll be fine."

"Bailey hibernates when it gets too cold and she isn't moving around a lot," I reminded him.

"I know. They'll be fine, Sam. Try to relax. We're tracking their vehicle, so even if something does go wrong, we can get to them. Right now, we're eight hours behind them accounting for the weather and traffic. We have the kids, so we'll have to stop more frequently, but we'll catch up."

I remembered what my great-grandfather had said. We'd catch up, but something would still happen to Bailey—and when a divine said something would happen, it would. Not knowing what would drive me insane. "We need to do some shopping for them, too. Books, toys, and games they can play in the car and hotel."

"E-book reader and access to a digital bookstore," he suggested.

Beauty tugged on my hand.

"Yes, sweetie?"

"We have readers."

I shouldn't have been surprised. Gorgon males did everything they could do for their children. I crouched in front of her and smiled. "I'm going to get you a new one so you can have two if the other needs to be charged or you want new books. Once we're home, we'll take you to the library so you can check out paperbacks, too—or to the bookstore so you can buy them if the books you want aren't available digitally. Bailey loves paper books." Like with most things, Bailey hadn't accepted she could buy as many books as she wanted.

Then again, if she ever figured that out, I'd have to remodel the entire house to make space for all the books she wanted.

I hoped Bailey never lost her sense of wonder. Everything was still a treasure to her.

Beauty's eyes widened, and her serpents stirred, lifting their heads. "Really?"

Uh oh. I recognized her expression. It was a perfect match for Bailey when she was about to goose me for something because I'd mentioned she could get something. "Really."

I didn't have the heart to tell her the real reason behind the new e-reader. I would have to muster my courage sooner than later, but how was I supposed to tell them their father wouldn't be coming back? I was still a stranger to them. I would have to, soon, but it could wait for a day or two.

Just because my grandfather hadn't seen a future with their father in it didn't mean us humans couldn't change the future. We could.

Maybe.

That was the problem with us mortals. We changed things.

But while mortals changed things, I didn't doubt my grandfather's word. Their father had likely already died.

Until I found the courage to tell them what we feared, I would buy the books they already had, fill their e-readers with the books they wanted, and prepare for when they learned the truth. "Why don't you and your brother make a list of books you'd like to read while I finish this?"

Beauty abandoned me, darting to her brother with a squeal.

Uh oh. I also recognized that level of excitement from Bailey. "I see I'm adopting a pair of book dragons."

"It could be worse."

Yes, it could be. "Since we're talking technology for them anyway, if they ask about phones, they will not be getting phones with data access. They're not to use our devices, either."

"All right. Basic at most?"

"Text messaging and calling only, and they'll have strict rules they need to follow. Gorgon whelps are often trafficking targets."

"But why?"

I shrugged. "They're exotic sentients, and they're very pliable when they're young, so they're stolen to become pets of the wealthy. They're almost to the age where they can better protect themselves, but not yet. Until they're eighteen, they'll be homeschooled or tutored. Some hives send their children to public school, but it's dangerous. For now, I'll bring them to the station on workdays with laptops. I'll ask my grandfather to set up the schooling software he uses for his hive."

"It takes a village to raise a child?"

"And an entire station of cops. It'll be interesting. They'll want to help."

"That sounds like a disaster in the making."

I laughed. "I hope not, but we'll see. If the station doesn't work out, I'll make arrangements with another hive. Beauty will be in demand."

"Bailey won't like that at all."

"No, she won't. But in good news, Beauty will have her choice of man when she's ready to join a hive."

Perkins snorted. "Bailey is going to need a very big stick until that girl's eighteen."

"I think Bailey will be fine." She didn't need a stick. She had a horn and breathed fire.

"I'm going to remember this later," Perkins promised.

He would. "She has claws, teeth, and a horn. She doesn't need a bat."

"I'm definitely going to remember that, too—especially when Bailey resumes her self-defense classes with Amanda."

"I can't win this, can I?"

Perkins grinned. "Not this time."

"All right, you win, but only because Bailey does have this bad habit of finding trouble."

"Where are we going to find e-readers for the kids, anyway?"

"Where else? The bookstore."

"You're going to take two book-starved kids to a bookstore?"

"Yes."

"We're never going to catch up to our wives."

"I'm sure it'll be fine. It's a bookstore, not a maze."

The look Perkins shot me informed me I was wrong. As he was probably right, I shrugged and hoped I'd be able to rein them in somehow.

Bailey

THE TRAIL LED us straight up a mountain into the heart of a blizzard. With ten foot visibility at best, by the time my glittery, glowing path veered off into the trees, I regretted everything.

"Well, your furry ass isn't going to like this. I'll stay in the car with Blizzard."

Sighing, I bowed my head. I would freeze, I'd want to hibernate, and I'd definitely catch a cold. With my luck, I'd come down with pneumonia again.

Shit, shit, shit.

"When I'm hallucinating in the hospital again, tell Quinn I did this because I love him that much."

"You'll be fine. I'll drive us down the mountain after, take you to a hotel, and make sure you get warmed up properly. You can handle a little cold."

I pulled over, turned on the hazard lights, and retrieved a transformative pill from my purse. The idea of standing naked in the snow didn't thrill me, but I had an orphaned kitten to rescue from a blizzard. "Its name is Avalanche."

"Can you please stop naming your pets after possible disasters?"

I snorted, threw my clothes at her, and got out of the SUV. As I didn't want to frighten Blizzard, I refrained from slamming the door.

Transforming in the snow hurt like hell. The cold stabbed through my fur and stung my nose. I snorted steam and cursed my dumbass self for thinking adopting some random, orphaned big cat was a good idea. Then again, I couldn't leave the poor thing to die.

Nature sucked, and I didn't like letting it run its course.

But first, I needed to eat a tree. The forest had plenty of old deadfall, and I tore into the nearest log, digging with my claws until I found some good, dry wood to fuel my flames. I ate until my coat steamed and I could snort flame instead of steam.

I'd have to assault several more trees to stay warm unless I got lucky and found Quinn's kitten nearby. I took off at a brisk walk so I wouldn't break my neck running around a snowy mountain—or trigger an avalanche.

Quinn would be proud until he realized I'd run around a snowy mountain on my own. Once he realized I'd done something stupid and dangerous, he'd scold me. I didn't mind scoldings from him. It took a single pout and sniffle to get him to back off my case, then he felt bad for yelling at me, no matter how much I deserved a scolding. When he felt bad for yelling at me, I got rewarded.

Yep, I was half the reason I didn't get enough sleep.

The trail led me across the mountain, down into a valley, and across a stream just starting to freeze. I jumped over it and snorted flame at the offensive water. The snow deepened, and I had to stop to eat several more trees until my magic guided me beneath an outcropping of stone hidden between scraggly bushes and a dying tree.

I smelled death before I spotted the wiggling, spotted kitten beside the frozen body of its mother and several other young kittens.

Nature truly sucked.

The kitten hissed at me, and I stuck my head into the hole, careful to avoid hitting anything with my horn. Careful to avoid snagging the poor thing with my sharper teeth, I seized it by the nape of its neck and lifted.

The poor thing weighed practically nothing.

Most days, I viewed my magic as a cranky, twisted entity out to ruin my life, but it took pity on me—or the kitten—for a change, and it backtracked towards the SUV. It followed the trail I'd blazed to reach the kitten.

As I didn't want it to freeze before I could get it to the SUV and the supplies we'd purchased for a young cat, I abandoned my brisk walk for a ground-eating lope. I stopped once to devour a tree, and I blasted the ground until it steamed to give the kitten a warm place to rest while I ate.

The kitten cried, but it didn't try to run away.

I picked the kitten up and bolted for the road and the warm safety of the SUV. When I arrived, I tapped on the window to catch Perkette's attention.

She opened her door and took the kitten out of my

mouth. "That was a lot faster than I expected. Get changed. I'll have a look at the kitten and give it some replacer milk." Ignoring the kitten's protesting squeaks, she flipped the kitten onto its back and poked between its hind legs. "It's a female. If my eyes aren't playing tricks on me, an ocelot. What in the hell is an ocelot doing *here*?"

I had no idea. I hadn't even known ocelots lived in the United States.

As freezing to death wasn't on my list of things to do, I circled the vehicle and began the process of shifting back to human. It went a lot better than expected; I got punted to my human form as though I'd offended my magic being a unicorn in a blizzard.

I understood. With chattering teeth, I climbed into the back of the SUV to warm up and change into my clothes. Blizzard licked my face.

"You okay?"

"Snow sucks."

Perkette laughed. "You're better off than I expected. Your lips aren't even blue this time. There's a blanket in the back. I'll switch seats with you, and you can take care of the kitten and get warmed up."

"Where do ocelots usually live?"

"Southwestern United States and down into Mexico. They are native to the United States, but this poor baby was probably someone's pet and dumped."

I shook my head. "Her mother and several other kittens were dead in their den."

"Maybe an illegal breeder lost a pregnant female? Odd time for her to have a kitten this young. Poor things. They really aren't suited for winter." Perkette held up the little kitten. "Aren't you a lucky little baby?"

"Avalanche is her name."

"That's such a terrible name for an ocelot."

"It's not! There easily could have been an avalanche."

"Not really. There hasn't been enough snowfall yet this year, and the peaks of this mountain aren't really steep enough to have avalanche conditions yet. Yeah, we're having a snowstorm here, but enough snow hasn't fallen yet. The drive is only bad because the wind is blowing everything around. Come get your kitten so I can get us out of this damned weather."

I spent a moment petting Blizzard before obeying Perkette, taking the kitten and the bottle of replacer milk she'd prepared while I'd been gone. After we got the milk into the kitten, we'd see if she wanted any of the meat we'd shredded not knowing how old Quinn's new kitten would be. "Any idea how old she is?"

"Not a clue. I was expecting a puma," she admitted. "Pumas are the only type of wild cat you might see here until you get into the magical species."

"Ocelots aren't magical, correct?"

"Correct. She's mundane. They're prized for their fur. She won't be too big. Fully grown, she'll only be twice the size of a house cat."

"That's not too bad!"

"She's technically a big cat species, but not by much. She's still a wild animal, so you'll have to be careful, but she won't be hunting your dogs for sport. Rabbits are more her speed."

That was something. "Think she'll adapt to captivity well?"

"You specifically asked for a big cat kitten that wanted to be adopted. I think you'll figure it out, but you might need to give her a habitat in your back yard to keep her happy. You'll definitely want to harness train her young. You can walk her along with your dogs!"

I rolled my eyes at that. "If you say so."

"I do say so."

As I knew just how sharp my teeth could be, I checked the back of the kitten's neck for any signs I'd cut her while carrying her. I spotted no sign of blood in her damp fur. "Quinn's going to kill me."

"No, he won't. Why would he kill you?"

"I invited a predator into our home, and she's adorable. I love her."

"Of course you do, Bailey. She's a baby. You love babies. How you aren't pregnant already, I have no idea. Then again, the last thing the world needs right now is you and a severe case of pregnancy hormones. At least you have a huge extended family, so if you do have kids, you have entire flocks of people willing to babysit. Gorgons are the best babysitters."

They truly were. Nothing was stupider than infringing on a gorgon's territory when children were involved. "I hadn't even considered Quinn's family as potential babysitters."

"For the record, you can totally be a police chief and a mother. Knowing you, you'd work right until you were ready to burst, then you'd be ready to go back to work the next day."

"No."

She laughed. "Okay, you're right. You'd want some time to pamper your little one."

"I'm not having kids yet!"

"Keyword: yet."

Perkette was impossible. Once she got something in her

head, she refused to let go of the idea. "I haven't even asked Quinn if he wants kids."

"Bailey. He's part gorgon, part incubus, part angel, part only-God-knows what. He wants kids. You could be constantly pregnant, and he'd be the happiest of men. He's genetically incapable of hating kids."

I blinked, tilted my head, and considered that. "Huh. You're right."

"I'm always right. If you want kids, ask. It's that simple."

I stared at the kitten on my lap before glancing at the puppy in the backseat. "Judging from my current actions, I totally want kids, don't I?"

"I thought you would have figured that out from your constant attempts to adopt gorgon whelps. Bailey, you're a treasure, but you're also an idiot."

I truly was. "Let me see if I survive three baby animals and two gorgon whelps first."

"Good thought. You'll be fine. Sure, you're a fire-breathing pain in the ass, but you mean well—and you truly love children. If you want kids ask Quinn. He'll be all in, so don't worry."

"But Perkette, I'm *really* good at worrying. It's my superpower."

My friend laughed. "You realize you shouldn't be proud of that, right?"

I snorted. "If I can't beat it, I may as well own it."

"You're something else."

NINE

Violence isn't a problem.

Quinn

TO MITIGATE the damage the two children could do to my wallet and sanity, I waited until two hours from closing to take them to a bookstore. With Sunny in tow, closer to closing time would help, too. Explaining to the staff that the puppy was a police dog in training would help, and someone had possessed the foresight to provide a training vest and harness for the puppy in several sizes.

As expected, the instant the employees heard Sunny would be a work dog, they fell for her furry charms, and as I had the attention of the employees anyway, I recruited them to help with my purchases. To do my duty as a book-providing parent, I needed to get them e-readers. As gorgon whelps tended to be more careful with possessions than human children, I asked the employees to recommend their best models, and I splurged on good cases for them. Once I paid for them, I took a few minutes to set each child up with an account and plugged in my credit card info.

"Perkins?"

"I have a feeling I'm not going to like what you're about to ask me to do."

I laughed and handed him Sylvester's new e-reader, which had a blue cover because he loved the color blue more than life itself. "Yep. I don't think I can operate two e-readers at one time. Can you watch Sunny, too?"

"Sure." Perkins claimed the leash, and the puppy obediently sat at my friend's feet. "Requirements for books?"

"If he wants to read it, get it for him. Just steer him away from the adult romance section."

"Violence?"

"Violence isn't a problem, and I'm capable of giving them the talk if there are adult-centric scenes."

"Right. Incubus."

I chuckled at that. "Yep. I had my first talk when I was two. I think I can handle giving it to them if it hasn't been done already."

Beauty tugged my hand. "Daddy doesn't let us read out of the girly section for mommies, but we can read anything else."

I translated 'girly section for mommies' as adult romance, and I fought my urge to laugh at their father's description of the genre. "We'll talk about why soon," I promised.

"We're too young."

"Ah, you are, but there's a reason why you're too young, and you should know. If you're old enough to ask the questions or be curious about it, you're old enough to hear the answer."

Both children stared at me with wide eyes. Smiling, I

shooed Sylvester off, and it only took a word from Perkins to get the boy running across the bookstore to begin his rampage.

"He likes Nancy Drew," Beauty whispered. "Daddy doesn't approve but lets him read it anyway."

"Hey, Perkins?" I called.

Perkins caught Sylvester's hand so he wouldn't lose him and turned. "What?"

"Get the entire Nancy Drew collection for him. That should keep him busy. Ask if he wants the Hardy Boys while you're at it."

"Do you know how many books that is?" Perkins complained.

"No, but my wallet can handle it, I promise."

He sighed, nodded, and resumed allowing Sylvester to drag him across the bookstore.

"We're never going to hear from my brother again. I'll miss him."

"It'll be fine, Beauty. What type of books do you like?"

She pointed at the horror section. "All of those."

Uh oh. "You like the books that have the most pages because they take longer to read, don't you?"

She nodded.

Book dragons. I'd somehow fallen prey to a pair of book dragons. Bailey would laugh herself sick once she found out. "Okay. Show me your favorites first, and I'll get those. Then you can show me the ones you've wanted to read but don't have yet."

"But that's all of them."

Beauty must have been somehow spending time with Bailey. "Humor me, please?"

She secured her hold on my hand and pulled me to the

horror section, where she proceeded to go to several authors, pointing at them and all of their books first. The thinnest book was over an inch thick, and I dutifully plugged in their names, purchasing every one of their titles I could while she waited patiently.

While on the shelf, the collections didn't seem too intimidating, but the first batch of books had over a hundred and fifty titles.

My poor wallet.

"How long does it take you to read one of these?"

"If I have quiet time, a day each or so, I guess. But I don't get a lot of quiet time."

Beauty would discover she'd get several hours of quiet time a day, as Bailey would love discovering she had book-crazed kids to keep her company. I enjoyed reading, too, but I found I was easily distracted whenever Bailey giggled at something she liked in her latest book.

I spent more time watching Bailey than reading.

I needed to work on that.

After she did her best to clean out my bank account in the horror section, she headed to the thriller section, targeted every spy book in the section, and ran back and forth trying to figure out which author to ask for first. Laughing, I observed until I was able to isolate several she kept going to, chucking all their books into the digital shopping cart to continue the sad destruction of my wallet. "Your top three favorites, please?"

She halted, and her serpents swayed while she tried to decide. I'd gotten two of her three choices right, and I added the third author's books.

According to my cart, I had an entire year's worth of books for her if she only read one a day. A wise tamer of book dragons, however, got a buffer. "Do you like science fiction and fantasy?"

She sucked in a breath, and she nodded so hard I worried she gave her poor snakes whiplash.

"I'll add my favorite authors for you, so we'll keep those ones a surprise for now. Do you enjoy children's books or young adult books?"

"Sometimes, but Daddy gets frustrated when I ask for them because I usually read big people books."

"You can read just about any book you want, and honestly, if you get a hold of a girly book meant for mommies, I can answer your questions and explain why they're meant for mommies."

"They're full of filth."

I rolled my eyes at that. Gorgons had a monopoly on the filth market; most of them disliked limiting themselves to threesomes, and they didn't discriminate gender when it came to their personal relationships.

One size fit all for them, and I found their special brand of love endearing despite the angelic genes that made it impossible for me to handle living in traditional gorgon society. "Not precisely, but you'll find out soon enough."

I was pretty certain at least one of the books I'd gotten for her had some borderline material.

"Okay. He didn't like our mommies reading them."

Ah-ha. Understanding why the gorgon male wouldn't approve of his wives reading romance novels made me laugh. "That's because he wants to make your mommies happy and he may have thought he wasn't doing that because they were reading those types of books. They're usually about women finding new love in their lives. That's not a bad thing, but gorgon males? We get jealous of our ladies easily. Bailey reads the tame ones because she likes it. I can ask her which ones are safe for you to read, because there are some that are a little too blunt about what happens between women and men in private."

"Oh! *That.*"

Right. That. "If you want some of those books, I'll talk to Bailey and find some suitable for you."

"Really?"

"Of course. Anything else you want to read?"

"Can we go into the non-fiction section?"

I nodded. "What kind of non-fiction do you want to read?"

"I want to learn how to cook."

Under no circumstances could I afford to laugh at her request. "I have some cookbooks at home, but you can get a few here. We'll get those as printed books. Printed books are better for cooking in the kitchen."

Her eyes widened. "*Printed* cookbooks?"

"Yep. We'll get them in print." I scanned the store, spotted the cookbook section, and guided her to it. "What type of food do you want to cook?"

"Chinese?"

Oh boy. I'd have my hands full trying to figure out how to cook Chinese food. I expected I'd have to get a gas stove installed in the kitchen, although I suspected Bailey would be game to breathe fire under a wok while we cooked outside.

She'd love it without reservation.

"All right. We'll get a Chinese cookbook. What else?"

"We don't like spicy food."

"Got nailed with some hot peppers?"

She nodded so hard I worried for her poor serpents

again. "I think I can work around that condition. How about barbecue?"

"It's too spicy."

"It doesn't have to be. It can be sweet."

"You mean it doesn't have to be red and catch my mouth on fire?"

Good God. What was their father putting on their barbecue? "I'll show you some pictures of good barbecue." It took me a few minutes to find a suitable cookbook, but when I showed her the pictures, she gasped. "Daddy's barbecue looks *nothing* like that. That looks yummy! Even that yellow stuff looks yummy."

I suspected her father had picked up a bottle of hot sauce, slathered it on, and called it barbecue. That happened in New York often enough. "That yellow stuff would be corn." I tucked the cookbook under my arm and pointed at a monster of a Chinese cookbook, which was over three inches thick and promised the secrets of Chinese cooking. "That one might work for your Chinese experiments."

Beauty snagged the book, grunting at its weight. "It's so big."

"Look inside. Does it have good instructions?"

She sat on the floor, set the book in front of her, and within twenty seconds, it held her undivided attention.

I kept a close eye on her, snagging a few more cookbooks by chefs Bailey liked watching on television sometimes. Once I had enough to get Beauty started on the basics, I set the pile down, gently took the book away, and put it on the pile. "You can continue reading it in the car, okay?"

"Okay!"

Setting her e-reader on the top of the stack, I headed for

the counter. "We'll buy these and go see how your brother is doing."

"He's probably on the floor reading the first book he saw. He does that."

After witnessing Beauty's abandonment of reality the instant she opened the cookbook, I had no doubt she told the truth. "Is there anything your brother would like that he's too absorbed in reading to pick up for himself?"

She pointed towards the toy section.

Of course.

Foolish me.

"All right. Pick two toys he'll like and two toys you want." Two each would somewhat limit the damage they could do to my wallet.

With a delighted squeal that proved I was, in actuality, caring for a child, Beauty ran for the toy section.

Yep. I was doomed.

Beauty went from dignified to boisterous and indecisive, which earned me the stares of the few parents on late-night outings with their children. I kept a close eye on her, and when one of the bolder children approached her, a toddler who insisted his fingers were edible, I kept a close eye on the pair and the adults watching.

The toddler grabbed a fluffy white unicorn from the rack of stuffed animals and announced, "Fluffy."

Oh boy. Of all the stuffed animals on the rack, which ranged from dragons to even gorgons, the toddler had to pick the unicorn.

Beauty stared at me, her eyes widening.

"It's okay," I promised. "If you're not sure you'll be okay without your glasses, put them on."

She did, and she giggled. "She's very fluffy."

The toddler nodded and hugged the unicorn before holding it out to Beauty. "Fluffy."

A rattled mother stepped to my side, her face a bright red. "I'm so sorry," she whispered. "He's always doing this. He still doesn't understand how money works, and I try to tell him he can't just give toys in a store to other kids."

"It's no problem."

Beauty took the unicorn and stared at me for guidance.

"If you want to buy the unicorn, you can buy the unicorn," I promised. Bailey would have a territory dispute with the fluffy white unicorn, but I'd cross that bridge when I got there. I glanced at the toddler's mother, and I almost chuckled at her harried expression. "Would he like a unicorn, too? There's two."

She stared at me as though I'd grown a second head. "You don't have to do that, really. I mean, he loves stuffed animals, but it's not necessary, but thank you."

I chuckled. "While it's not necessary, your son's quite brave and kind. That deserves recognition. Beauty, why don't you pick up the second unicorn for your new friend? We'll go to the cashier and buy them now, and then you can pick out another toy and toys for your brother later."

"That's really not necessary, I mean, you—"

"It's quite all right. She's still young, and young gorgons need to learn how to interact with others."

"Damien, introduce yourself," the mother suggested, and her expression relaxed.

The toddler stuffed his fingers in his mouth and mumbled something. Beauty picked up the second unicorn, and like he had to her, she offered it to him before she announced, "I'm Beauty."

Somehow, I managed to herd Beauty and the toddler to

the registers, although the woman had to scan Beauty's twice as the little boy refused to let go of his new fluffy white unicorn.

If all humans could be like little Damien, the world would be a better place. I only mourned for the reality of having to teach Beauty and her brother that not all people were as kind as the little toddler with more courage than most adults.

BAILEY

WHILE I COULDN'T CATCH a break, I could catch colds like a champ, and within an hour of my adventure across the snowy mountain, I began sniffling.

"Seriously, Bailey? Already? That's not how colds work. It takes a few days for a cold to incubate. You can't just go outside and develop a cold within an hour."

I sneezed, which startled Quinn's kitten into hissing. She looked me over, likely debating if she could eat me with her sharp kitten teeth, decided I wasn't satisfying enough prey, and went back to sleep, treating my lap like her throne. "It works like that for unicorns."

"Since when?"

"Since now."

"Bailey, that's not how colds work."

"I probably already had the cold, but my immune system likes camping out when I get too cold as a unicorn. Ask Quinn. And I've been taking so much neutralizer lately I will probably need another damned trip to the hospital. My immune system sucks."

"Neutralizer is a double-edged sword at times. Too much

of a good thing can easily become a bad thing. You still have to do the rabies treatment. Maybe it'll help with the cold."

I shook my head. "Stupid unicorn body. All extra neutralizer does is make it worse."

"That makes zero sense. Neutralizer can treat colds."

"Not my colds. My colds are awful, terrible, wretched little beasts."

"Are you sure they're colds?"

"What else would they be?"

"Divine punishment for being such a badass."

I shot a glare at Perkette. "No. They're demented colds."

"Maybe a strain neutralizer can't touch?"

"Or they're unicorn colds and neutralizer wasn't made for unicorns."

"That's actually a sound theory," she admitted. "Although I didn't know unicorns could get colds."

"I can, and I'm a unicorn."

"Only part of the time."

"At least you didn't say I'm not a real unicorn. That's what the CDC goons usually tell me."

"Anyone who can force a transformation back to human shape following a full dose of transformative is a real unicorn. I bet you could shapeshift to a unicorn without the need for a transformative. You just have to figure out how, just like you figured out how to shift back. And don't tell me that's impossible. Your husband wanders around looking like a human when he's a what, again?"

"He's my doohickey."

"Your doohickey has highly venomous snakes that bite. You can keep your doohickey. I value my life."

"They're not bad. It just stings a little."

"Bailey, if one of Sam's cobras bit me, without the right

antivenin, I would be dead within thirty minutes. Faster depending on the toxicity of his cobras—and gorgon venom tends to be potent. For his bites to only sting a little? That immunity alone ranks you high enough to deserve your new job."

I didn't want to think about my unexpected promotion to police chief. "Fine. My immunities are a little ridiculous. The CDC stopped making me do toxicity evaluations after their last ambrosia test. Quinn flipped."

"Bailey, you were on an entirely different planet for a week after that test. It took a dumpster, another case of rabies, and a round of neutralizer to snap you out of it. Of course he flipped. Everyone who knows you was flipping. You were awake but nobody was home."

I barely remembered anything about the testing, and unable to argue with her, I shrugged. "If I can become a unicorn without transformatives, I have no idea how to do it."

"We could experiment."

"No."

"That was a rather immediate and harsh no. I'm hurt."

I snorted at that. "You have feelings?"

"I feel like you have been learning from Arthur. This is entirely unfair."

"Perkette, you're a mad scientist. When it comes to things of scientific interest, you're evil. Pure evil. Frankly, I'm astonished Quinn doesn't mind when I run away with you."

"No one screws with a mad scientist. I might build a lair, attach lasers to sharks, and take over the world while seeking revenge."

My eyes widened. She would. With the right resources, she'd try. "That's terrifying."

"It really is. All right. Do we have reception yet? You need to report your kitten to the CDC and make arrangements for a permit. While she's not a lion, tiger, or other really big cat, she's an uncommon large cat species. She's not an endangered species, but they're not exactly common, either."

"That's something. I'm not sure I could handle getting the permit needed for an actual endangered species."

"I'd like to remind you that you're an endangered species."

Technically, cindercorns were endangered—critically so. There weren't many places left in the world they could thrive, and humans encroached on where they could live, transforming active volcanoes and deserts into tourist attractions. The conflict between the large predators and mankind ensured the black and red unicorns dwindled each year.

Hawaii and Iceland both had cindercorn populations, but both groups dwindled a little more each year.

If the current projections were accurate, I'd be the last one within ten years, and I wasn't a true cindercorn. I sighed. "Critically endangered, at that."

"It makes me wonder if unicorns have been right under our noses the whole time, but like you, they're only found when exposed to the right drug. Could it be cindercorns aren't as endangered as we believe, but that, like you, they are only discovered in the right circumstances?"

"According to the general DNA tests, I am, unfortunately, my parents' child."

Perkette snorted. "And when you're under the influence of ambrosia, nobody knows who the hell your parents are, except you have *a* grandparent who is a divine. I remember you ranting over how you think the test results are stupid and wrong."

"It's biologically impossible for someone to be two people at one time. Ambrosia completely rewrites my DNA."

"Well, ambrosia *is* the essence of a divine, Bailey. Perhaps it's showing us who you actually are."

"My mother was most certainly pregnant with me, and my father? Don't get me started on my father's opinion of me. These are people who dumped me with gorgons hoping I'd become a garden statue and forever disappear."

"Arthur told me all about your encounter with them when you married Sam. They're assholes. No one is disputing that."

"So, they're unfortunately my parents."

"View them as annoying hosts."

"Are you calling me a parasite?"

Perkette thought about that for long enough I was tempted to throttle her. I kept my hands to myself so she wouldn't crash the SUV. "Beneficial for you, not beneficial for them, so I guess I am. I'd be sorry about that, but I like you and I don't like them. Sure. You're a most excellent parasite."

Scientists were assholes. So were angels. Gorgons could definitely be assholes, and while incubi could also be assholes, I loved my angelic-gorgon-incubus asshole. Somehow, I'd surrounded myself with assholes. "I'm telling Quinn you think I'm a most excellent parasite."

"He'll just say you have a symbiotic relationship with him and claim you're not a parasite."

"You should listen to him."

"Where's the fun in that?" Perkette giggled. "Do you have reception yet?"

I checked my phone, and I sighed at the presence of

several bars, ensuring I'd be able to conduct a conversation with someone. "I wish I didn't."

"It's not that bad, Bailey. Just tell them you found an ocelot in West Virginia, tell them the mother and other kittens were dead, and that you rescued it."

"We're in West Virginia?"

"Yes, we're in West Virginia."

"Huh. I didn't know West Virginia had mountains."

"Have you never looked at a map of the United States, Bailey?"

"Why bother with geography when you know you're never going anywhere because of no money and a shitty family?"

Perkette drummed her fingers on the steering wheel. "Yeah. Okay. I got nothing. I can't say I would blame you for that if I were in your shoes. I get it. Why dream about places you know you can't go?"

"Exactly."

"But what if you *could*? It's okay to think about it now, Bailey. If you say you want to go walk the entire length of the Great Wall of China, Sam will make it happen. He'd give you the entire world if he could."

Calling the CDC seemed like a better option than dealing with Perkette and her flights of fantasy, so I called the primary switchboard, asked to speak to someone in wildlife conservation, and began the tedious process of pleading my case to become the permanent caretaker of an ocelot kitten destined to become my Quinn's beloved guard cat.

QUINN

IT TOOK until the store closed to convince Beauty and Sylvester we really needed to leave. They would 'five more minutes, please?' me to death, and Bailey would laugh, as she pulled the same stunt in bookstores and got away with it. Perkins kept snickering at me, helping to haul the ridiculous number of books I'd gotten for the pair despite having loaded their new e-readers up with every book they wanted.

"You're a sucker," my friend informed me while he settled Sunny in the back between the whelps, who fidgeted while we got their hoard packed in.

I was. "If Bailey finds out about this, she's never going to let me live it down."

"She won't, but she'll accept it as inevitable, as she's determined to make sure no child suffers through the type of childhood she endured. Offer her a back rub. She'll forget about why she was annoyed within five minutes."

"I hate how right you are." Once I finished loading the books into the back of the SUV, I picked out a cookbook for Beauty to read in the car, the book lights I'd gotten so they could read in the dark, and the first volume of the encyclopedia on paleontology Sylvester insisted he needed to read immediately if not sooner. "Bailey is never going to forgive me when she realizes I'm accidentally raising a pair of mad scientists."

"I'm not sure Beauty's collection of cookbooks is a starter kit for becoming a mad scientist. I'm not going to argue about Sylvester, though. He's definitely a mad scientist in the making. Also, I hate you. It took me an hour to get every damned Nancy Drew and Hardy Boys book onto that e-reader. He looked like he wanted to cry when I told him he needed to put the book he was reading away so he could pick something else."

"It could be worse. Book dragons are easy to manage. If you provide them with books, they will read."

"You will regret this when Sylvester becomes a mad scientist. I know this. I married a mad scientist."

"And she's a phenomenal woman despite being slightly deranged."

"Slightly?"

I laughed. "Okay, maybe more than slightly. Still. Tiffany is a wonderful woman despite her mad scientist tendencies."

"Beauty is going to take over your kitchen and experiment if you're not careful."

"If that's what she wants to do, I don't have a problem with it. I will make certain it's what she wants to do, however—not what she's been taught she should do because she's a young gorgon."

"Well, considering there's no such thing as a gorgon scientist until this point, I think it's safe to say they weren't brought up traditionally. Gorgons can be very intelligent, but they tend to focus on being, well, dragons. You know, making a horde, caring for nests of eggs? They're like very small dragons with a snake problem." Perkins shrugged. "If you drive, I'll do some research and give the CDC a call about it. But I'm pretty sure they're unusual."

"Everything about them is unusual," I replied, careful to keep quiet. I handed the whelps their books of choice and their lights so they could read. I reached over Beauty to stroke Sunny, who didn't even stir from her hard-earned nap. I chuckled and gave the whelps my full attention.

The instant they got their books opened, they no longer noticed my presence—or remembered I was there. I suspected there could be an explosion beside them and they wouldn't notice a thing. I let them be, closing the door so they could read undisturbed. "I'm impressed with their base education. Most gorgons their age can't read yet."

"How old are they?"

"I'd guess somewhere between six and eight. My grandfather will get their birth certificates eventually. It doesn't matter."

"When do gorgons typically learn to read?"

"My grandfather waits until his whelps are twelve or thirteen. My father learned earlier because he's more like me, generally human. Their early education primarily focuses on controlling their powers as much as possible and teaching good habits for when they interact with humans. I'm a little worried they're behind the curve on interspecies interactions, but if they have the Right to Rule, it'll be easier on them. I'll have to do some tests with them once we've retrieved our brides and the current situation settles down."

"I never asked. Can your father shapeshift?"

I shook my head. "No. Dad lacks the right genes."

"Ah. The demonic genes let you shapeshift?"

"I guess. It could be one of many genes that let me do it. My great-grandmother's a master at shifting."

"Well, she's the Sphinx. That makes sense. And can't Anubis shift if he wants to?"

"I think so. There are a lot of shapeshifters, especially on my mother's side of the family."

"Your mother's side of the family is even crazier than your father's side of the family."

"Yeah. I'm a certified freak."

Perkins chuckled and claimed the front passenger seat as his. "Yeah, but you're Bailey's freak, and she likes you just as you are, so you're just going to have to deal with it."

"Siding with Bailey now, are you?"

"She needs a few people in her court."

"She has people in her court."

"Sam, this is Bailey we're talking about here. You can tell her that until you're blue in the face and she's ready to light you on fire, and she won't believe it. I figure if I tell you I'm in her court, you will believe me."

I got behind the wheel, started the SUV, and heaved a sigh. "You're right. However much it pains me, you're right. Maybe we do need therapy."

"I married a mad scientist. I married a mad scientist who calls *me* a mad scientist with a puzzle fetish. You're not the only one in need of therapy. Worse, I encouraged my mad scientist to befriend a fire-breathing unicorn."

"How much trouble do you think a mad scientist and a fire-breathing unicorn can cause?"

"Depends. Do they have access to a lab?"

I shuddered. "I hope not."

My phone rang, and I checked the display, smiling when I recognized Bailey's number. I answered, "Hello, my beautiful."

"Do you like spotted kittens?"

"I like kittens of all stripes and spots," I replied, trying to think of what species of cat had spots. I knew leopards had spots, as did cheetahs. Were there other spotted cat species? "Why?"

"I just spent two hours on the phone with the CDC, but I am now a proud permit holder for endangered feline species native to North America. Also, for once in her life, Perkette was wrong about something. Your new kitten *is* on the endangered species list, but they're a very recent addition, so it's not really her fault her knowledge was slightly dated."

In the background, I heard Perkins's wife heave a sigh.

"All right. What sort of kitten did you find?"

"She's an ocelot, and her name is Avalanche."

Ocelot? I'd heard of the breed, but I couldn't recall ever seeing one. Her name, however, worried me. "Please tell me there wasn't an avalanche."

"There wasn't. I did have to go on a run—" Bailey sneezed. "Fuckshit."

All right. Bailey had a cold. Again. Colds happened whenever she shifted and was exposed to cold temperatures. I could handle Bailey being sick with a cold. Tiffany was with her. I could get through the conversation without panicking.

Once I got through the conversation, I'd let Perkins drive and fret about Bailey being ill.

I drew a slow and calming breath. "Caught a cold?"

If she had pneumonia, I'd need one of the little pills my great-grandfather had acquired for me.

"Perkette has a theory."

Mad scientist. Fire-breathing unicorn. I knew where that combination was headed: straight for trouble.

I gulped. "What theory?"

"She thinks I'm a parasite, ruthlessly used my mother as a host, and I might be something *really* badass. And that ambrosia just shows that I'm actually a parasite out to take over the world."

"That is *not* what I said," Tiffany protested, loud enough I could hear her despite her not being the one on the phone.

"It's close enough," Bailey replied.

"You didn't do a very good job of being a parasite. Both of your wretched parents survived." I grunted, shaking my head over how Bailey's parents had treated her. I hadn't seen them after meeting them at the courthouse, and I hoped to never again. I'd done enough reading about them to confirm my initial feelings about them.

They were truly awful people.

"Quinn!" my wife wailed.

"What? It's true. You're not a very good parasite, but you're the perfect wife."

"You're impossible."

I smiled at that. "Where did you find an ocelot?"

"Her mother and the rest of the litter had died because of the storm."

No matter how many times I told Bailey her wayfinding magic was a blessing in disguise, she never believed me. She always focused on the tragedies surrounding her magic, not the good her magic did in the wake of disaster.

She always showed up during the aftermath, but she interpreted that to mean she was the cause of the disasters rather than a saving grace. She struggled with my ex-wife's death, the loss of so many whelps, and the utter destruction she'd wrought using a pair of phoenix feathers.

She lost sight of the other consequences of her actions, the good ones that ensured the gorgon dust could never be used again.

I worried the gorgon dust had been nothing more than a precursor to the rabies outbreak, the next step taken to accomplish some wretched goal to lower humanity's numbers.

Or, perhaps, the rabies had been the first step taken. I wouldn't know until I found out when the Dover hive's females had perished.

I sighed. "I'm sorry about the other cats."

"They were gone before I got there. There wasn't

anything I could do to help them, even if I had gotten there sooner. It wasn't my fault."

I blinked. Usually, Bailey blamed herself for every failure, even when she couldn't have done anything to prevent it. "Are you all right?"

"Beyond this stupid cold, yes. I'm all right. I'm worried."

"About the rabies situation?"

"Especially about that. How are the children?"

"It seems we're welcoming a pair of voracious book dragons into our home, and we will need to convert a room into a proper library, have an addition built, or convert the basement into living space."

She sucked in a breath. "They like to read?"

"When you check the bank account statement, please don't worry. I know I spent a lot at the bookstore."

"I'm okay with that. Reading is good for them! I like the idea of adding a proper library to the house." Bailey giggled. "Our current storage method for books is a little sad."

"Anywhere a book can fit is sad, I do agree. We'll make it a Christmas present to each other, figure out a plan, and have the work done soon. Sound good?"

"That does sound good. Hey, Quinn?"

"What is it?"

"Do you think we should maybe stop playing our game right now? Postpone it, maybe? This situation…"

While well aware Bailey enjoyed the chase as much as I did, I hated the worry and fear in her tone. "If things become dangerous, we can team up."

"I think they're already dangerous. Perkette talked me into using my magic to find the source."

I froze. "She did?"

"I think it's a good idea."

Part of encouraging Bailey to trust herself more and trust her judgment meant I needed to let her use her judgment—and make decisions for herself even when I wanted to wrap her in a blanket and keep her safe from all harm.

I couldn't undermine her efforts.

"All right. If you think it's a good idea, I trust you. Please be careful, and if you have any reason to believe you've bitten off more than you can chew, call me."

"I can do that. But I can chew a lot."

Yes, she could. I'd seen her devour an entire tree before. It had fallen into the road near our house and no one could remove it, and one of the neighbors couldn't get to her kids, which had not set well with Bailey.

Bailey's solution to the problem had been simple; she'd eaten the tree. It'd taken her less than an hour to devour it, leaving a hole in her wake, as the trunk and the upper roots had been, in her words, the best part.

"You can," I conceded.

"I bought the neutralizer like you wanted."

"Good. Listen to Tiffany about your cold, okay? She's qualified to help with it." I hoped. I might even pray a little.

I'd do a little more than hope and pray. As soon as I was off the phone with Bailey, I would give the faery doctors who'd treated Bailey when she'd been hospitalized a call.

"Okay. I will. How is my puppy?"

"She's asleep between the kids in the back. She's had a very long day wrangling young gorgons."

"She needs a raise and a lot of cuddles. Blizzard is a good puppy. He's taking a nap, too."

"Take a picture of my kitten and send it to me."

"After we get her to a hotel and cleaned up. She's had a rough day and needs some care. I'm not looking forward to giving her a bath, but it's a necessary evil. You'll get upset if I show you a picture right now. She'll be fine. The CDC told me everything I need to do to take care of her, and they're going to send me a list of vets who are qualified to examine her. But they also said I can be trained to administer her vaccinations, too. They're going to put me in touch with someone about it."

I clenched my teeth at the CDC's offer—which they'd use, as always, for their benefit. "If you want to do the training, I'm all right with that."

Sometimes, I was such a liar, and I was grateful I didn't have a complete aversion to falsehoods like true angels.

"I'll only take enough courses to know how to help take care of her. I'm volunteering you for the same courses. She's your kitten. I already put in the request for you to get the permit to keep her. The courses are mandatory for the permit."

I relaxed. "Ah. So it's not a standard certification?"

"It's mandatory for the permit, and there are two levels we can choose from. The more extensive certification would let us rescue any big cat. The other one would require us to get additional certifications for other exotic cats. The extensive certification also requires a few hours of volunteer time a year with a rescue or zoo."

"Okay. Pick whichever one you like best. I'm happy to go volunteer with you if you'd like."

"Really?" she whispered.

Yep, my beautiful Bailey had a serious obsession with helping animals in need, and I was powerless against her enthusiasm. "Yes, really. Consider it an early Christmas present."

As I knew my wife well enough to predict her reaction, I

removed my phone from my ear, held it away, and waited for her squeals to quiet.

Perkins snickered and shook his head.

"There's even a wolf rehab program we can work with, if we want to work with other predatory exotics. The CDC rep mentioned it. There was an asshole who had entire packs of wolves in cages, and they all need a lot of work because they were so mistreated and ill."

"Ill?"

"He didn't tell me what they were ill with, but it was treatable, and they only had to put a few of the wolves down. They had so many they might be able to restore the wild wolf populations in the United States if they can get enough people helping with their rehabilitation!"

I was about to get goosed by my own wife, and I'd end up with an entire pack of wolves in addition to large cats. Poor Blizzard would be the only normal animal in our household, and I hoped the poor husky was adaptable.

Then again, a husky was like a hyperactive wolf with a preference for cold temperatures. With the right training and patience, they could make excellent work dogs.

I'd have my hands full.

"I'll look into that."

"Really?" Bailey inhaled, and I jerked my phone away from my ear in time to dodge her squeal. In the background, my new puppy warbled a complaint. "Sorry, Blizzard!"

I laughed. "All right, Bailey. You keep on running. I'm going to find a place for the night and get the children settled. They've had a long day. Make sure you get plenty of sleep. I need you well rested for when I get my hands on you."

"Promises, promises," she muttered before hanging up.

Still laughing, I shook my head and put my phone away. "You up for driving, Perkins? I need to make some phone calls."

"Are you going to need your medication?"

"That depends on what the doctor says when I give him a call about Bailey."

"I heard something about her and a cold. What happened?"

"She used her wayfinding magic and found an ocelot kitten. The rest of the litter and its mother were dead. She retrieved the kitten as a unicorn."

"In that blizzard?"

"Yep."

"Right. Going to call the twins?"

"Sure am."

"I'll get the medications, check the instructions, and find a hotel if you're okay with that. Otherwise, we'll drive through the night, and I'll take a breather after your chill pill wears off."

"We'll get a hotel. Let's give the kids some stability. We'll save mad dashes across the country for if it's really needed."

Tonight, I'd hope and pray it wouldn't be needed while preparing for the worst.

Hopes and prayers did jack shit in the long run, an illusion with potential power if the divine felt benevolent and happened to be listening in.

I had enough trouble without any divines listening in, so I'd just stick to the hope part of my night and skip the prayers. Maybe that might mitigate the mayhem.

Then again, I had a prescription for chill pills courtesy of my divine great-grandfather. No matter what I did, I was probably screwed, so maybe I'd indulge in a little prayer after all.

It couldn't really hurt, could it?

Bailey

TO GIVE us a better idea of where we needed to go to move forward with our plan to put an end to the rabies threat, I attempted to use my magic again. Instead of a trail of glittery light to follow, I took an unscheduled nap.

In the snow.

Tiffany would've been justified to leave my ass out in the cold to freeze to death, but she took pity on me, shoved me into the rental, and slapped me back to consciousness.

I made a note to never underestimate the strength of a mad scientist again.

"We're going to a hotel, I'm going to take care of your demon kitten and puppy, and you're going to sleep," she announced. "And we will never speak of this to anyone. If Sam finds out I let you push yourself to the point you fell over in the snow, he'll begin his career as a biologist and dissect me."

He would. "Sorry."

"It's my fault. I forgot you have a tendency to push yourself beyond your limits because you have no sense of self-preservation."

I couldn't argue with her, so I didn't. "I'll take care of Avalanche and Blizzard."

"No, you won't. You will go into the room, take a warm shower, and go to bed. I will take care of the animals. I'm also going to feed you warm soup and get you medication so you don't expire from the plague. I'm just glad Sam didn't clue in something was wrong. I swear, that man has a sixth sense when it comes to you."

Since even I recognized arguing with her wouldn't accomplish anything, I nodded. To remind her he had less of a sixth sense and the help of a magical ball and chain, I lifted my arm and showed her my bracelet. "It's probably this thing and not a sixth sense."

"Oh. Right. Still. I'm surprised he didn't call."

"Well, he does know I have a cold."

"True. Blast the heat as high as you need it and stay warm until we get to the hotel. Tomorrow, if you're not perking up, I'll whip you up a small batch of napalm, drive you somewhere remote, and let you go to town."

"That sounds like a very bad idea."

"It sounds like a great idea. You can cook the virus out of you."

"I'm pretty sure that's a really bad idea, Perkette. Anyway, I'm banned from having napalm."

"It won't be napalm, specifically. It'll be a thick variant of gasoline with a few special ingredients."

"Which is also known as napalm."

"If you get really sick, I'm shoving transformatives down your throat, and I will hold your furry ass down and make you eat the napalm."

Damn. When Perkette started issuing threats, she meant business, and I had no doubt she'd live up to her ultimatum. Calling Quinn and begging for help might save me—maybe. Then again, Perkette might find some way to torture my husband, too. "Fine, but only if I get really, really sick—like in the hospital addressing people as models sick."

"You only addressed Sam as a model of any sort, which is probably a good thing. He's the jealous type."

"He really is."

"So are you."

I stared at her. "Have you met the man?"

"Surprisingly, yes."

"Maybe you can explain why me. I can't figure it out."

Perkette sighed. "You're you. That's why. Just roll with it."

I blinked. "Have you met me?"

"Surprisingly, yes."

"I'm a walking disaster."

"He appreciates a good challenge."

That he did. "Anything else we shouldn't tell Quinn?"

"If you get seriously sick, he'll freak. And by freak, I mean he'll have a meltdown. A really bad one. In fact, I'm going to make certain you don't have to go to the hospital at all, because if you do, he'll lose his mind."

"Are you running for an understatement of the year award?"

"No, but I really should," Perkette replied. "Get some rest. I'll take care of the hotel and the pets. And no, don't argue with me. If you get really sick, our fun trip—and our chance to put an end to this idiot rabies outbreak—goes up in smoke."

TEN

I'm not giving this crap to you again.

QUINN

IF GIVEN THEIR WAY, the whelps would stay up all night reading. I waited until I'd gotten Sunny settled before insisting the pair take a bath and get ready for bed. The tiny pill Perkins had given me did a good job of numbing me to the reality of the situation, although I found I needed to concentrate to get through the basics.

I disliked how the medication made it difficult to focus on any one thing for more than a few minutes, but Perkins nudged me back in the right direction. Sunny helped, pawing at my leg when I stared off into the distance like an idiot without setting down her dish of food.

I got my act together enough to play a parent properly, confiscating the whelps' e-readers and print books, stacking them on the computer desk and promising they would get them back in the morning.

If they were raised like most gorgon children, the stack of

books and readers would remain undisturbed during the night.

The children engaged in a brief but fierce war over who got to bathe first, which Beauty won after a brief display of her cobras' hoods and a few hisses. Perkins watched with interest, and I expected I'd get an earful later over the insanity of sharing a room with me, two gorgon whelps, and a wolf.

Finding a suite with three beds that would allow me to bring Sunny inside had been a challenge, but my rank and Sunny's status as a training police dog helped. As the master bedroom was easier to defend, the children shared the king-sized bed, leaving Perkins and me to share the second bedroom. At least it had a pair of double beds.

I drew the line at sharing a bed with him, something we'd both agreed on without discussion. If our wives found out we'd shared a bed, they'd never let us live it down. Bailey would spearhead the relentless chain of jokes, and as she loved discovering my limits, she'd recruit Tiffany to join in.

"I'm not giving this crap to you again unless you're actively having a freak out," Perkins announced, giving the prescription bottle a rattle. "Go to bed. I'll make sure the kids are settled."

I'd meant to protest, but the instant I flopped onto the closest bed, I clocked out. I woke to wolf breath, and Sunny pawed at my shoulder until I groaned and rolled over. Hitting the floor did a good job of restoring coherency, and I sighed.

Perkins snickered. "Good morning, Sam. The kids are still asleep, we have two hours until checkout, and if we can roll out within an hour, we can get some breakfast downstairs before we hit the road. Sunny would like you to take her for a walk. She's already been fed."

"She woke you?"

"No, I woke up naturally, which was a nice change. Get dressed and attend to your puppy duties. I'm going to get a shower. Then you can wake the kids up. I figure I'll dodge potential petrification today."

"Good idea. They might wake up confused." I sighed. Neither child would be able to petrify me, but in time, they might give even me trouble. Unlike Perkins, I'd reverse petrification without any outside interference. Stifling yawns, I trudged to the bathroom, got changed, and walked Bailey's puppy. My phone rang while the wolf sniffed around the thin stretch of woods separating the hotel from an office complex next door.

I checked the display, which showed an unknown number. I hated unknown numbers. While telemarketers were barred from calling the number and scammers had figured out it belonged to a law enforcement officer, too many pests could—and did—call me. "Chief Quinn speaking," I answered.

"It's been a while, Samuel," a nasally voice greeted. It took me a moment to recognize the man as the lead gorgon male from Orlando's main hive. "The word on the wire is that you're challenging for a pair of whelps. Congratulations in advance. Only a fool would challenge against you, and no sane whelp would reject a chance to be in your hive."

It was too early in the morning for posturing, and I considered chucking my phone at the nearest tree. "Good morning, Thomas. What can I do for you?"

"Several things. First, in light of what your grandfather sent yesterday, I'd like to report that my hive was approached about a lead on your bride. I have not rejected the offer, as I thought I'd give you a chance to deal with the human yourself."

John Winfield again, I bet. After confirming no one watched me, I indulged in a low hiss. "Winfield?"

"Yes, that was his name. A rather insolent little human. I considered petrifying him as a risk to the general IQ of the entire Orlando area. I proposed a meeting for tomorrow to discuss his offer."

"Petrify him, notify the CDC, and present all evidence of his attempt to traffic my wife," I suggested. "And I will be pleased to offer you compensation for the work."

"Rather than traditional monetary compensation, I thought I'd offer something potentially beneficial to both of us."

Great. I'd have a rap sheet of gorgon-created sins so long Bailey would try to kill me herself when she got her hands on me. "What's your offer?"

"As I'm aware you're busy and don't follow gorgon gossip, a smart move most days, if I do say so myself, I was blessed with a second son. He's seven, around the age of your new daughter. I'd like to plan an introduction, and if you're game, potentially arrange for you to foster him over the summer. It's time he learned to interact with other hives—and with humans—and your household would be an ideal place for him to adapt to human society. Should your new daughter and my son form a friendship, I would be interested in making an offer for her."

Thomas was many things, but he toed the line well; the arrangement wouldn't offend Bailey, would give Beauty a choice in the matter, and would help Thomas's cause and potentially establish his second son as a contender for leading a strong hive. "I'm not necessarily against this idea, especially as they're close in age. Do you have a daughter of the same whelping?"

"I do. I had two daughters and one son that year."

"While I need to discuss the issue with my bride and make arrangements with the NYPD, I'm open to discussing fostering all three of them over the summer. That will give Beauty and Sylvester a chance to socialize with other young gorgons. They were the hive's only whelps."

"Those poor whelps. Is the situation as serious as Archambault claims?"

"It's probably worse," I admitted. "If you haven't vaccinated your hive, do so. As soon as you can. Also contact the CDC about a small stock of neutralizer. Vaccinations should protect you, but you may need to treat your bride."

"I've scheduled us for the vaccinations today. I dislike it, but after hearing about the Dover hive's fate, I would rather be treated like some animal than lose my bride and wives."

"That's my thought on the matter, too. If I could vaccinate, I would. I'm too human to qualify." I sighed at that, shaking my head. "I've had my bride treated for rabies so many times now it's a way of life here, but you'll find the treatments for your bride annoying at best. Simplistic enough, but annoying. Inquire with the CDC about training so you can administer it yourself."

"How has your bride contracted rabies so many times?"

"Dumpster diving to rescue stray animals."

Thomas choked on his laughter. "Your bride is a jewel among women."

"She is. If you can work on convincing hesitant hives to vaccinate, it would be appreciated. Seeing one hive wiped out is one too many."

"Despite their interest in your bride?"

I wrinkled my nose at that. "I would have corrected the hive male with appropriate amounts of violence, and I would've left him alive if he showed remorse for interfering with my bride. I wouldn't like leaving him alive, of course, but I dislike orphaning children without good reason. A hive without whelps would be a different matter."

It would have tested my restraint, but I would've left the hive male alive—barely.

"I appreciate your candor."

I bet he did. "Let me know if you manage to catch Winfield. It's best if I do not come to Florida personally."

"Yes, it would not go over well if one of your former cadets happened to be petrified and crushed into a fine powder at your hands, no matter how strong of a case you would have in the human courts for the threat to your bride. We will handle this matter, and we will try to get information on any accomplices. I believe he has them."

"Care to share why you think that?"

"He spoke in plural."

That would do it. "It might not go amiss if you were to suggest to other hives if they're willing to attempt to sell a bride off to another hive, their brides might be targeted next."

Thomas chuckled. "You're devious, Samuel. I'll do this just for the fun of watching our kind join forces for a rare change against humans who are too foolish to understand what they do. And your thought is not amiss; I wondered the same, and I've asked my bride to stay close to the hive for the time being. I don't like when my bride worries."

It never failed to amaze me how strange gorgon society could be—or how loyal gorgons could be to their surrogates, who were as much the heart of the hive as the hive's gorgon females. I could never see eye-to-eye with my kin; I only had room for Bailey. In some ways, however, few species had the sheer capacity of love as a gorgon despite the species' inherent flaws.

"Thank you, Thomas. Call me when you have more information, and as soon as I'm certain my bride's safety is secured, we'll discuss fostering in the summer."

"I look forward to it, as does my son. It will be his first time fostering outside of the hive."

I wondered if I should warn Thomas or his son my Bailey would turn their world upside down within minutes of meeting her. I decided against it. Some things took seeing to believe, and I'd yet been able to convince a male gorgon my bride would happily take them on and win.

They foolishly believed I was the true threat in our hive of two.

"I look forward to hearing from you soon, Thomas." I hung up and shook my head. Sunny watched me, her head canted to the side. "I've invited a mouse to a dinner date with the cat, but the mouse believes he's a lion, and the cat? Well, she's a stubborn fire-breathing unicorn lacking a sense of self-preservation and a temper. This summer is going to be interesting."

Sunny showed her teeth in a canine grin.

BAILEY

THE LAST TIME I'd been so sick I viewed pouring a can of soup down my throat as a viable option, I'd been hospitalized and kept in the ICU for longer than I cared to think about. With my morning already shot to hell thanks to a relentless cough, I thought I was being practical wanting to just go back to bed, chug whatever fluids were required to keep me alive, and sleep it off.

Perkette didn't agree with me, and her first act as an evil dictator involved me taking a hot soak in the hotel tub and sipping warm soup from a mug. I appreciated the soup; it beat my first plan, which involved a can and a complete disregard for my taste buds.

Blizzard and Avalanche kept me company in the bathroom, although I suspected both of the furry monsters wanted me to feed them. They stared at me, I stared at them, and I lost the staring contest each and every time I coughed or sneezed.

"Kill me, Perkette," I whined.

Perky's wife poked her head into the bathroom. "You have a cold. You're not dying. And no, I refuse to feed you cold soup out of a can. That is the most disgusting and vile thing I have ever heard of in my life."

"It works!"

"No, it doesn't. Yes, it provides basic hydration, but it is not suitable for sick individuals. I'm going to call Sam, tell him I'm keeping an eye on you, and that you probably won't call him until the evening as you'll be sleeping off your cold while I drive. And yes, I already fed both monsters, and Blizzard already had his walk. You should be happy your pets like you."

I was, but it didn't explain why both were staring at me. "You're mean."

"I'm mean for refusing to kill you?"

I nodded.

"That's not how this works, Bailey. First, Sam would kill me if I killed you, and I like living. Second, your pets would be sad, even that soul-sucking ocelot."

I stared at the soul-sucking ocelot, who found the tip of Blizzard's tail to be absolutely fascinating, doing her best to pounce despite being wobbly on her paws. "Avalanche isn't very menacing right now. She's a lot sleeker than I expected. And those spots, Perkette. Look at those spots. How can you say such mean things about a kitten with such cute spots?"

"There's a reason ocelots are prized for their pelts. I think she's stunted, but she should start growing like a weed with the right care. She's a very lucky kitten to have a fire-breathing unicorn trudge out in a snowstorm to save her. So, you can't reach your expiration date. You have to take care of the spotted kitten so you can give her to Sam for Christmas. But I'm pretty sure she's your kitten. Kittens can bond with their mothers, and with her mother gone, you're now next in line. But I'm sure Sam will love the challenge of convincing his kitten to love him, too."

"I'm a terrible wife, stealing my husband's kitten." I sneezed, which startled both animals, and they glared at me. "Sorry."

"You're a fantastic wife. Sam adores you, and you're everything he needs. Despite what you may believe, you're a good friend, too. Crazy but good. Okay, there's a whole lot of crazy packed into that tiny body of yours, but whatever. I prefer crazy over boring."

"You're a mad scientist married to a mad scientist with a puzzle fetish. Are you capable of doing boring?"

"Lab experiments can be very boring. You have to do the same thing hundreds of times with minor changes to see what happens. But the results are worth the boring. I just try to do a lot of interesting experiments between the long stretches of boring experiments. Anyway, my mad scientist with a puzzle fetish prefers being a cop, but I've caught him poking around my lab a few times."

"For some reason, the idea of Perky in a lab scares me."

"Despite the bullshit you like to spout, that's because you're smart. Yeah, he can be scary if you put him in a lab. He'd be a god in a forensics lab, but he loves the beat too much."

"I'm surrounded by weirdos."

"And you're our queen. No one does weirdo quite as well as you do."

I splashed at the bubbles in the tub. "Are you really sure you can't put me out of my misery?"

"I'm sure. Don't let the water get cold and soak until I say you can come out. You always have a hard time getting your core body temperature up, and that's not helping. I'll bring more broth for you in a few minutes. I will expect you to drink it all. We clear?"

As Perkette redefined stubborn, I gave up without a fight. She'd win, and we both knew it. "Okay."

"Good girl. You'll be fine. I'll give your man a call and make sure he doesn't freak out. The last thing we need is him freaking out and raining on our parade right now. If he thinks he needs to rescue you from your cold, he's going to show up after breaking every speed limit between where he's at and us."

He would. "I'm sorry I'm sick."

Perkette rolled her eyes. "You'll only be sorry if you don't keep that water warm and drink your soup."

QUINN

DODGING an excited puppy and two whelps, I did a final check of the room while Perkins handled charting our route to chase after our wives. My phone rang, and I glanced at the display, recognizing Tiffany's number. Narrowing my eyes, I answered, "Good morning, Tiffany."

"Not fair, using your Caller ID to identify me. I was hoping you'd answer as a smug police chief."

What had I been thinking encouraging Bailey to befriend the mad scientist? Ah, right. Tiffany was a wonderful woman even when a pain in the ass. "You're in a good mood. What can I do for you?"

"Your woman's soaking in the tub, whining because she has a cold. Don't listen to her whining. She's fine. I'm keeping an eye on her. I'm calling you because until she's able to communicate in something other than raspy coughs and sneezes, I'm limiting her phone time. Right now, she has a puppy and a kitten watching her. I know she got the kitten for you, but it's her kitten. I'm pretty sure the poor thing is bonding with her. Avalanche was trying to nurse on her knuckle last night while she was sleeping. And yes, I fed the kitten milk, but she's all over your woman."

"I figured that would happen," I admitted. "How bad is she? I'm going to contact the specialists in Texas after I'm off the phone with you."

"So far, so good. If you can get a detail sheet for their work, I'd like a copy emailed to me. I'll try to figure out what makes her tick so we can avoid another reboot of her immune system. Right now, I'm focusing on keeping her core temperature up. We're headed south to get out of this cold weather."

"Can you go west more first, please?"

"West? Why?"

"I'd prefer if Bailey went nowhere near Florida at this point in time."

"Why?"

If I hid anything from Tiffany, she'd go to Arthur, and once she went to Arthur, it would be game over anyway. "Remember Janet's old cadet she booted for behavior inappropriate for a member of the force? Anyway, he's causing problems in Florida."

"Janet? Oh, that hot number of a brunette you use as a spokesperson when you don't want to deal with the media?"

I sighed. "That 'hot number of a brunette' has almost as many degrees as you."

Tiffany laughed. "I know, she attends my lectures sometimes. You should be encouraging Bailey to hang out with Janet. They're a good match. And you need to toss Janet in Amanda's self-defense courses. She's weak on her right side."

Rubbing at a temple, I observed the tangle of children and puppy at my feet. Sunny beat my leg with her tail, and the children wrapped themselves around my ankles, which made doing my sweep of the room a challenge. "All right. I've been thinking about having Janet transferred to my building and direct management anyway."

Perkins looked up from his work. "Please do."

"And your husband seems to like this idea."

"Partner her with him. They get along."

I considered that. "Hey, Perkins? You game to test out a trio with Janet and Nilman? If you two have to put up with me and Bailey, a third might not be a bad idea. We haven't tried a trio yet, and when I'm called out, we typically need numbers anyway."

"I'm game. Bailey will love it, too. She likes Janet. Janet likes her, too."

I arched a brow. "How do you know that?"

"She said so at the Wall Street incident. Janet filled me in. It didn't occur to me to mention it because Janet works at a different precinct."

"I'm going to request for her, especially if she gets on with Bailey out of the gate."

"I can get in touch with Dowry for you if you want to start the ball rolling on that," he offered.

"Do it." I decided to stay still and let the kids and puppy play while I talked to Tiffany. "Sorry about that, Tiffany. When the mad scientist gives me a good idea, I'd be a fool not to pursue it."

"I knew there was a reason I tolerated you. So, Bailey will be fine, but she's probably going to be sick for a few days. If she gets sick enough I want you hovering, I will notify you of this, so if you can control your overprotective maleness, please do so."

"My overprotective maleness?"

Perkins burst into laughter, bowing his head and shoving his chair from the computer desk. The chair slid on the mat and dumped him on the floor, where he continued to laugh.

"And your husband is literally on the floor laughing."

"Was he near any electronics at the time?"

"Actually, yes."

"He sometimes spits coffee on the computers when laughing. He didn't want to damage it."

"Well, his phone was on the desk. Or a tablet. Actually, I don't know what he was using, but we didn't bring our laptops."

"Same difference. Screens and liquids. He has problems

with them. How is he handling his separation anxiety from my most glorious majesty?"

I snickered. "I think he's handling it just fine."

"I'm so sad right now."

"I'm sure you are. So, how did your brassault booking go?"

"Five days of community service in a women's shelter. I'm happy with this. They made me do some heavy negotiating, too. Your wicked wife told them to keep me amused while she went to the vet, so they were trying to hit me with everything they had, and just because they thought it was funny, they actually called a judge to confirm the hours."

"Nice. You won't have to go back to Atlantic City for a hearing?"

"That factored into their decision to call the judge. They didn't want to give me an excuse to earn more misdemeanors in their jurisdiction. One of the cops asked Bailey to come to Atlantic City if she decided to snap. She's got a lot of fans for a woman who is convinced she's uglier than sin."

I snorted at that. "She's not ugly."

"She's quietly gorgeous and doesn't know it, and her scars are adorable. She oozes cute, but she'll never be a super model."

"If I wanted a super model, that would be a problem. But yes, I agree. She's perfection."

"I feel like this whole conversation is wasted because we're holding it where she can't hear. I'm in the other room, and I'm fairly sure she has tinnitus."

"Tinnitus?"

"Ringing in the ears, common when there's an ear or sinus infection, of which she likely has both. She's talking louder than normal, and I have to raise my voice if I want her to hear me. And since she's focused on her sore throat, sneezing, and coughing, she isn't paying attention to her ears. She hasn't realized it yet, and I'm keeping it that way. Once again, don't worry. I'm keeping an eye on her."

"I'm going to worry. This is a fact."

"Right. Because you're Police Chief Worrywart. I can work with you worrying, but I can't work with you knocking on the hotel room in the middle of the night because you're having a freak out. We clear?"

"Perkins, your wife is bossy."

"She's always like that. Just give her what she wants. Otherwise, she'll take hostages," Perkins replied between fits of laughter.

"Your husband says I should just let you have what you want."

"Tell him I'm counting that as one of his Christmas presents to me this year. But, being serious. I'm going to keep a close eye on Bailey, but I don't want you rampaging and ruining our road trip. Do you need an instruction guide to where we're going?"

"The Venetian in Las Vegas."

Tiffany fell silent. "The Venetian?"

I found it amusing she lowered her voice to a whisper.

"If you don't already have a room booked at the Venetian, I will be booking one for you."

"We have two rooms booked at the Venetian," she confessed. "The goal is to force our wayward husbands to catch us, and as there are some things we refuse to share, we have a room each."

"I'm going to have to upgrade one of the rooms to a multi-bedroom suite. Two dogs, a cat, two adults, and two whelps is a lot to fit into a regular room."

"Hold on. I'll give you the reservation number for Bailey's room." Tiffany was quiet for a few minutes before reading off a number. "I'll text it to you as soon as we're off the phone, too."

"Good. You planned this pretty well, didn't you?"

"The ideas were all Bailey's, I just helped refine them. Well, the list of contingency plans were all me. If I let Bailey plan the whole thing, we would've just gotten on a plane like sane people. The road trip idea was initially wishful thinking, but then I reminded Bailey you love chasing her. We got carried away."

"I'm okay with you getting carried away, just keep her safe. I won't even ask you keep her healthy, although I do ask you try to get her a little healthier or take her to the hospital if her condition worsens."

"Did Arthur give you drugs? You have to be on something like alprazolam for you to be saying shit like that. This is not the conversation of a lucid Police Chief Samuel Quinn."

"I had a divine-prescribed chill pill last night, but I don't like taking them, and I will probably fight the next person who recommends I take one," I muttered.

"Made you dull-witted and numb?"

"Yeah."

"Try buspirone. It's friendlier on the side-effects and while it takes longer to kick in, it's less likely to screw with you quite as much. Photograph your prescription bottle. I'll give the doctor who prescribed it a call."

"Anubis arranged it."

"I'm okay with telling a god he picked a shit drug and to give you a different prescription. I can also send you some reference materials for meditations and other methods that can help prevent you needing to take it as often. If your separation anxiety worsens, we can meet up for a temporary visit before we run away again."

"Why aren't you a medical doctor?"

"Too many restraints, not enough flexibility to research. Rules suck. I like the research I can do without needing a bunch of annoying sentients complaining they're test subjects. Also, most patients suck, and the last time I had to do a medical evaluation for some random idiot, telling them their diet was shit and that they're the reason they're sick didn't go over well. It didn't matter I was right on my evaluation. That said, some hospitals will call me in for help on weird cases."

"I'm afraid to ask what classifies as weird to you."

"There was an infant with Hutchinson-Gilford progeria. That's a scary one, but really rare. It's accelerated aging. The doctors couldn't figure it out, but they knew there was something seriously wrong shortly after birth. With progeria, you need to act quick even with magic helping. Took me two labs and three days with the poor baby to figure it out. Usually, babies with the syndrome show signs after a year old, not so soon after birth. She's doing okay. Not great, but okay. She'll die in her thirties, but it beats the initial prognosis. Before, she would've died of old age by thirteen."

"That poor kid. Still, it amazes me sometimes. I look at you, and I don't really think you're a mad scientist. You look normal. But you go into your basement and change the world. Or other doctors contact you because they're stumped and you're amazing at finding obscure things."

"Don't respect me too much, Chief Samuel Quinn. I have your wife, and I'm out to corrupt her."

I laughed. "Just try to keep your corruptions manageable.

If you could get her to ask for more things, that would be nice."

"Now you're just asking for a miracle."

"I really am. Still, thank you for keeping an eye on her. If you need anything at all, let me know."

"Hey, I have a question for you."

"Yes?"

"A truck and one of those nice camper trailer things to go with it? Yay or nay?"

"Yay, keep the trailer below twenty-two feet and make sure the engine in the truck can handle it. With the truck, I want performance and longevity. The bigger the better. I can give you the bank wire details or call the dealership myself. Your husband helped me translate her request to mean she wants a trip to the dealership to purchase a truck."

"Brand?"

"Whatever Bailey sees and falls in love with that has good performance and longevity. If you call in the order to a Las Vegas dealership, it can be ready for pickup by the time you arrive."

"How about New Mexico and we pick it up on the way there? It'll take us a few days to get there with her sick. I'm going to take her to some touristy things, maybe take her to a zoo to have a checkup done on her ocelot, and otherwise take it easy. She wants to find the source of the rabies, but her magic failed last night."

Uh oh. "Failed?"

"I think she was too tired to get a trail started. I'm going to delay her from trying again for three days just to be safe."

"Keep me in the loop," I ordered.

"Let me know what the twins say. It's time for me to feed

her some more soup, make sure the pets are okay, and check her temperature. Text me with updates."

"Will do. Drive safe, and thanks." I hung up. "Perkins? I can't tell if your wife is a devil or an angel."

"A bit of both, really. Why?"

"She's on a mission to corrupt my wife, who is sick enough Tiffany felt a need to call me and tell me she'd let me know if it got really serious, but was interested in knowing what the twins have to say about Bailey's condition."

Perkins sighed. "All right. And?"

"I need a different prescription for a chill pill, but she'll take care of it, apparently."

"Yeah. She's good at that. She'd make a damned good doctor if being a doctor didn't annoy the hell out of her."

"Not everyone can be a good doctor, and really, she's a better mad scientist, I think. She gets the groundwork on some good breakthroughs in motion, dumps it on the lap of someone ambitious enough to want the credit and the fame, and quietly gloats when she's right."

Perkins chuckled. "And most of the scientists give her credit for the groundwork, too. It's only polite."

"Then she not-so-quietly gloats, but I can't really blame her for that. It works. Although, if she does anything weird to Bailey in her basement lab, I make no promises the lab will survive. Also, how did you even afford a lab? I've seen the bills we've gotten for basic medical equipment for the forensics guys. That stuff is not cheap."

"I stopped asking, Sam. I'm worried she might have robbed an actual bank for it, and some things I just don't want to know about. That's one of them."

I couldn't blame him for that. "All right. You give Dowry a

call and inquire about Janet and a possible transfer, I'll get on the phone with the twins, and then we'll hit the road."

ELEVEN

He had a chill pill yesterday.

A LONG DRIVE while sick sucked. At one point, I unbuckled my seat belt and did my best to curl up on the floorboard so the heat keeping our feet warm might somehow permeate the rest of my body. By some miracle, I fit, although my feet ended up on the seat.

Perkette pulled over long enough to move the seat back to give me more space and dump a blanket on me. Somehow, she managed to stuff a pillow into my new nest for my enjoyment. "That's one of the most ridiculous things I've ever seen you do, and that's saying a lot. If you were cold, you could've just asked me to turn the heat up."

"You would've started gagging because it's too hot in the car," I mumbled.

"While true, I would've done it. Don't suffocate down there, okay? And if you feel up for it, you can give your husband a call. He's probably not driving."

"He's not? Why? He usually drives."

"He had a chill pill yesterday because he's an anxious man. Think of him like one of those puppies who whines when separated from its owner."

I patted around for my phone and found it crammed in a pocket, and I relocated it to the seat. "This SUV is surprisingly spacious."

"That it is. So, your husband has sent me on a mission to acquire a Christmas present for you. Ironically, we'd already decided to do this on our own. First, we're headed south. Probably New Mexico, possibly Texas. I'm to take you to two dealerships. First, we're to find you the biggest, manliest truck Sam's money can buy."

"Nope."

"Nope?"

"I want to see his face when I pick the truck."

Perkette laughed. "But I can't haul one of those camper trailer things with this SUV."

"Nope. Same reason."

"I need a travel lab, Bailey."

"Rent a trailer. Put it in that. Rent a truck if it's not one of those box trailers. I want him to take me. Non-negotiable."

"I'm not sure I can stomach much more of the disgusting sweetness levels you two produce. I'm setting your kitten up on the seat, and Blizzard is taking a hard-earned nap. I do believe he was on guard duty last night. I'm proud of you, Bailey. You managed to charm both of your husband's pets."

"He'll walk into the room and they'll forget I exist," I muttered.

"And you'll walk into the room and he'll forget they exist. It all works out, so don't worry about it. If you're not going to let me take you to a car dealership—"

"I didn't say that."

Perkette was quiet for a moment. "But you don't want a truck or a trailer."

I smiled, and while I considered myself to be a very bad wife, I knew what Quinn liked, and it was red and it currently sat in Perkette's garage. "I never said you couldn't talk me into going to a car dealership to pick out something for *him*."

"You're going to buy him a new convertible, aren't you? Bailey, I swear, I love how you can just go with the flow, but there should be limits on how flighty you can be. You were all over the truck and trailer idea yesterday. Granted, you said you thought he'd kill you for it, but you were all into the idea. Now we're on to buying him a convertible?"

"One I'm not scared of driving. If I buy it, I won't be afraid of driving it. The red one has *history*."

"Right. And he's going to abandon it the instant you give him his new one. I'm just warning you that is what will happen. And it will."

"No. He will keep it, and he can give it to one of the whelps when they're older."

"Now that's what I'm calling thinking ahead. You're going to need a bigger house with extra garage spots. You're also going to need to get a second convertible for the other whelp, of a similar make and model as the red one."

"Truck can sit in the driveway. It's a big, manly truck. Cruiser can sit in the driveway, too. Convertibles go into the garage," I announced. The only flaw in my plan was the lack of a third spot, but I supposed we could get the second convertible for the second child when they were older.

"Okay. We'll go convertible shopping, and once you pick

one you like, we can have it made and delivered to New York. That still leaves me with the problem of the lab."

"Vegas."

"Vegas?"

"We're having Christmas in Vegas. Do we have time to get to Vegas and get the car ordered?"

"We could just blitz straight to Vegas," Tiffany said. "I could turn a hotel room into a lab. I've never tried to make a compact lab before. If we stop only to sleep and walk the pets, we can be there in two days. You can sleep it off at our hotel. I'll have to get our reservation changed. We'd given ourselves until right before Christmas to get there, as we don't know your true endurance as a unicorn."

"We'll hotel crawl. That's a Vegas thing, right? We just go hotel to hotel?"

"I'm not even going to ask how you know that, but yes. We can do that until our check-in date at the Venetian. That still leaves me the problem of my lab, Bailey."

As Perkette was a mad scientist, I had faith she could figure out how to handle her lab with her new restrictions, so I ignored the issue. "I'm not completely ignorant about the perversions of Vegas."

"I'm turning you into a Vegas showgirl for Quinn's amusement. This is revenge for you thwarting my lab plans. Consider yourself warned."

I thought about that. "But only in private, and you have to watch the kids and pets."

"Deal." Perkette got back behind the wheel where she belonged. "I'd say fasten your seatbelt, but if you feel better there, I won't tell if you don't."

Quinn

"WHAT DO you mean Janet is missing?" I demanded, and everyone in the room froze, including Sunny and the whelps.

Perkins recovered first, and he sighed, setting his phone on the desk.

We were within five minutes of leaving, but what should have been a standard inquiry had turned my already hectic morning upside down. If I hadn't known about John Winfield's behavior—and his grudge—I would've stuck to the protocols.

But I knew, and knowledge was power as much as it was a dangerous weapon.

"She didn't show up for work yesterday, and no one has been able to get a hold of her. She was scheduled for work this morning, too. Commissioner Dowry had been informed right before I called him. Once she's found, he's going to approve the transfer, however."

My brows rose at that. "He doesn't even know why she's missing."

"He's not a uniformed cop anymore, but he knows his business—and he knows Janet. He suspects foul play. And he has more than just some suspicions. He thinks he knows who. Janet filed an official complaint a week ago."

I tensed. "Against?"

"Her chief. She was scheduled for a transfer. Dowry was going to ask you about her, ironically. Because of Bailey."

Right. "I don't believe in coincidences like this. What was the complaint about?"

"He didn't tell me."

I forced myself to relax. "All right. I need you to call your wife about that prescription, because by the end of the day, I have a feeling I'm going to need it." Even admitting that pissed me off, but I recognized when too much was too much, and I'd need something to calm me down without Bailey nearby.

Bailey liked telling me how I was utterly incapable of handling threats to my people. She was right.

Maybe Janet didn't work in my station *yet,* but she was still mine. She'd been mine from the moment she'd gone up with Bailey into that wretched building on Wall Street. I smothered my territorial instincts, but I'd been considering raiding the Hamptons for several officers, and Janet topped my list.

"All right. I'll call her, and I'll make sure we swing by a pharmacy. I'll ask her for non-medicinal recommendations, too."

"She's going to make me drink tea again, isn't she?" I complained.

Perkins laughed. "Probably. She's good at that, and you have to admit, her tea blends help."

"She was probably spiking them with chill pills," I grumbled. Once I had better control over my temper, I gave myself a shake and resumed herding the whelps out the door. "We're getting laptops, we're swinging by a station to get into the networks, and I'm going to ask Bailey for a favor."

"To find Janet?"

"Yes."

"Even when she's sick?"

"If Winfield has anything to do with Janet's disappearance, waiting for her to get better might be a lethal mistake."

Perkins cursed. "You're right. Let's get this show on the road. Dowry is expecting you to call him later."

"You drive, we'll get laptops, and I'll talk to him." I turned to the whelps and crouched so I was at their level. "All right, kids. Things are going to be busy for a while, so I'm going to need you to read while we work. Is that going to be a problem?"

Sylvester shook his head, and Beauty's eyes widened. She hesitated, but then she asked, "Can we help?"

Her offer startled me, and I considered her question. How had their father and hive raised them? Most gorgon children often became self-absorbed, focused on making sure they didn't incur parental wrath—or break any of the rules. For all gorgons could give humans a run for their money in the humanity department, it was a *learned* trait, not a natural one.

Her question made me wonder about them—and about the man who'd been so desperate for a surrogate he'd go beyond the limits of the sane for his children.

I was beginning to wonder if I'd made a severe error of judgment about how I thought of their father.

"If I can think of some way you can help, I will ask you for help," I promised.

"We know how to use computers, we can read maps, and we can do basic research," Beauty announced.

With their love of books, I bet they could research like champions. "I'll keep that in mind. For now, I have to do basic footwork, which is something only a police officer can do. I also need to get jurisdiction permissions, another thing only I can do. But if you can help, I'll ask you."

Beauty smiled. "Okay."

I thought about it, and then I grinned as an idea did occur to me, one that was open to public records—and would give me a better idea of how much data someone with a grudge and an internet connection could acquire. "Actually, kids, there *is* something you can help me with, but I'll need to get you computers first. If research is what you like to do, I have a project for you."

Perkins narrowed his eyes. "What are you up to, Sam?"

"I'm going to find out just how much information a pair of determined children can find on the internet. If *they* can find it, anyone can, and that can help us figure out just how compromised our security is—and how easy it would be for Winfield to accomplish what he's been doing."

"You're trying to recreate the crime."

"Something like that."

"I can't tell if you're just ruthless, brilliant, or both," my friend muttered.

"Go with both. I think it's time we do a public audit, and who better to audit than a pair of determined children with a love of research?"

"I'm not going to argue with that, but I'm not sure what good it will do. Winfield had access to our systems."

"Only for a while. So he'd have an edge on the kids, that's true—but what I don't know is how easy it would be for him to get information about specific members of the force outside of the system, and we're quick to cut off access once someone is being fired. So, it's a safe assumption that while he knows our infrastructure, his knowledge wasn't as strong as a full officer's, and he was restricted. He'd have to do a lot of research in the public system. The kids can work on building a profile while we work with our intel. They might find something we'll miss."

Perkins sighed. "Maybe. Let's get this show on the road. I have the feeling this just got a lot messier and a great deal more complicated."

I worried he was right.

Bailey

MY PHONE RANG, and I checked the display to see Quinn's number. I groaned but answered, "I'm not dead yet."

"For which I'm grateful. How are you feeling?"

"I'm not dead yet."

"I'm sorry to bother you, but there's a situation."

Uh oh. "Situation? What situation?"

"Do you remember Janet?"

How could I forget Janet? Janet was the queen of badasses, and I wanted to be like her if I ever grew up. "Yes, of course."

"She's missing, and I'm worried there's a connection to the other issues we're having. I want you to try to find her with your magic. I know you're sick, but I think we need to locate her as soon as possible."

I sucked in a breath. "Perkette? Pull over. There's a problem." While I loathed leaving my warm nest, I uncurled from my position on the floorboard and slithered onto the seat, gently moving Avalanche, who didn't even stir from her nap. "What happened?"

"I was going to request for Janet to be transferred to the station, but she didn't show up for work yesterday or this morning. We suspect foul play."

I coughed, wrapped the blanket around myself, and narrowed my eyes. "For the record, if Janet was kidnapped, I will use lethal force as necessary to recover her alive. This is not negotiable."

"I was hoping you'd say that," my husband replied, his tone darkening. "If she has been kidnapped, especially by gorgons, I want you to ask Tiffany to give you one of her homemade concoctions. I want what you did to Audrey's hive to pale in comparison to what you'll do to anyone threatening Janet."

"Is that legal?"

"If Janet has been kidnapped, lethal force is permitted during rescue operations. You need to confirm, witnessed by an angel, that there were hostiles and that you acted in Janet's interests."

Death in defense of another was a thin, narrow line shrouded in darkness, but as long as I could confirm to an angel and did it to recover a police officer in peril, I'd walk without a mark on my record. It wouldn't even count as a premeditated murder despite going in knowing and willing to kill to secure Janet's safety. "Noted."

"How are you feeling?"

"Angry."

Quinn's chuckle had a dark, sinister edge to it. "Good. So am I. When you get a trail on Janet, I want a direction, okay?"

"Okay." I eyed the roadside, which had an unfortunate amount of snow on it. "Tiffany? I need the map and chalk and other junk. I need to find Janet."

"On it," she replied, killing the engine and getting out of the SUV to dig the supplies out of the back.

"Here is how this is going to work, Bailey. Every time you cross a state line, I need you to let me know. I'm going to have every state you're in added to your jurisdiction."

"My boss is a dick, I'm going to be a terrible cop, and I don't even know why some idiot thought I'd be a good police chief."

Quinn sighed. "You were born for this kind of work. I wish I could ease you into this, but there's just no time, not with Janet missing. I'll be able to get you jurisdiction rights, but you'll have to work with the local chiefs and captains—and the feds—on the case. Your job is to find her. If the situation looks critical, retrieve her. You can handle just about anything, but I'm going to worry anyway."

Huh. What happened to the Quinn who wanted to wrap me in a bubble so I wouldn't even get a scratch?

"I can handle anything from sticks of TNT to plastics. I could probably even handle a dirty bomb," I announced, not bothering to smother my pride.

"Please don't eat a nuke."

"I can disarm them traditionally."

Silence.

I smiled.

"Could you repeat that?"

"I can disarm them traditionally."

"You don't mean eat the payload, do you?"

The worry in his voice bothered me, but as he'd held my promotion close to heart, it was time I got a little of my own back. Being sick made me a bitch, but I'd teach him a thing or two about clandestine actions. "I've been working with the bomb squad behind your back because if something goes wrong and the bomb detonates, I don't explode. I've been formally trained in the disarming of most bomb types. Tiffany helped me learn how to read the schematics, too."

My husband groaned. "I'm begging you, please tell me you're not serious."

"I think we're now even on the secrets score."

"You're really serious. They had you on the bomb squad?"

"If I couldn't disarm it traditionally, I ate the payload.

Also, we've learned I have accelerated regeneration when transforming between unicorn to human when I don't reverse naturally."

"You were hurt?"

I smirked. "You can't kill the bastards. They're already dead."

"Did you kill them?" he growled.

"No. That honor went to the bomb squad backups. I would've been delighted to light them on fire, but bullets are faster than my flames as a general rule. Did you know the CDC has some damned good snipers? They usually sent one or two out with me when I had sketchy jobs. Also, we should recruit their snipers. I bet we could lure one or two to our team. The CDC pays for shit by incident, and they're not salaried, either."

"Yes, I was aware the CDC had snipers. No, I wasn't aware they were contractors without salaries. If you like them, I'm willing to bribe them away from the CDC. Who put you on the fucking bomb squad?"

"The asshole in Washington, of course. Who else? The fucker probably wishes I'd fall over dead."

"Well, you don't have to worry about him anymore," my husband promised. "Your contract belongs to the NYPD now."

"Your tone suggests that I belong to you and the NYPD can suck it," I replied, smiling despite feeling worse than shit.

"You would be correct."

Perkette got back into the SUV with the required supplies for me to work my magic. "All right. I have the stuff I need to try to find Janet. I'm going to give the phone to Perkette and get to work. Neither one of us are responsible for any shit my magic does to me, because I'm not waiting to get better to try to pick up her trail."

"I'm aware of the risks, I do not like it, and I'll talk to Tiffany about what to do if things sour on us. I will even take a chill pill if she orders me to."

"Who are you and what have you done with my husband?" I snarled. The harshness of my tone triggered a coughing fit, and I cursed at myself for getting sick, at the cold for making a mess of things, and I slung a few at Quinn for being a pain in my ass.

"I just recognize when freaking out would be detrimental, and I'm fairly certain Tiffany's diagnosis of separation anxiety is correct."

Poor Quinn. He hated when I was far from him for too long. I hated being separated from him, too, although I still believed a little separation did us both some good—at least for my ability to get a full night's sleep. "Okay. I'll get a lead on Janet, and you can chase me to her, and we'll join forces, make sure she's all right, and then have a spectacular fight."

"You want a spectacular fight?"

"I like making up," I admitted.

Perkette snorted. "I told you you're the reason you don't get enough sleep."

I flipped my middle finger at my friend.

"As do I, but we could just skip the fight and go straight to making up." While humans lacked the ability to purr, my human-gorgon-incubus doohickey pulled it off with lust-inducing grace. "You just worry about finding Janet and making sure she's safe."

"I will," I promised. "I'm giving Perkette the phone."

She took my phone and put it to her ear. "Hey, Sam. Despite her whining, she's doing much better. She curled up on the floorboard by the heater in a nest. It looks like the trick is to get her core body temperature up. Half an hour after she got tucked down there, her symptoms started to ease up, so you don't have to worry about that. I'm keeping an eye on her."

I was about to undo all the good the heater had done, but Janet came first. I could land my stubborn ass in the ER for all I cared, but I was going to find out what had happened to Janet and why. If my magic knew what was good for it, it'd cooperate without a fuss. Getting out of the car, I slapped the map, blank paper, and jar of ink onto the hood. I popped off the cap, picked out a stick of chalk, and took my temper out on it. It crunched in my hand.

I didn't even need to vocalize my request; the instant the chalk left my hand, it erupted in a burst of golden light and formed a sparkling trail for us to follow. When it first appeared, it pointed due west, but then it altered its path to follow the road, which headed south. I frowned.

As always, my magic seemed to opt for the most direct route, but it'd taken the slightest detour to inform me which way we were really headed.

Huh. Maybe my magic had taken my unspoken threats seriously.

Why was the trail headed *west* when Janet worked in New York? I got back into the SUV. "You're driving, Perkette. Tell Quinn she's somewhere west of us."

"West?" Perkette frowned. "But why would she be *west* of us?"

"That's what I want to know." I snatched my phone out of Perkette's hand. "She's west of us."

"You just told me to tell him," Perkette muttered.

"I'm indecisive and incapable of following through with my initial plans," I replied. "Catch that, Quinn?"

"I did. What's due west of you?"

"Give me your phone, Perkette." I held out my hand and wiggled my fingers until she obeyed. I pulled up her map app and zoomed it out, tracing a line directly west of us. My brows rose. "Well, it's not *exactly* due west, but possibly close enough for our purposes, and probably because we're on a mostly westbound road, but I'd say Las Vegas."

"Probably something smaller between where you're at and Vegas," my husband replied. "But anything's possible if she was taken by plane."

"Wouldn't it be hard to kidnap someone and fly them somewhere?"

"Yes. Or they have multiple drivers and are going without stopping."

Shit. I hadn't thought of that. "What do you want me to do, Quinn?"

"Find Janet and stay safe. No unnecessary risks. Please be careful."

"I'll be careful," I promised. "You be careful, too."

"I will. Get yourself a laptop if you don't have one, go to a police station, and introduce yourself as Police Chief Bailey Quinn of the NYPD. They'll get you set up with everything you need, and I'll be able to reach you on our internal network with files, permits, and everything you need. I'll get on the phone with the FBI and start processing jurisdiction expansion."

"Can we even do that?"

"It's one of the perks of being a police chief, my beautiful. We have a shit job, but there are limited numbers of us who can do our level of work because of the rating requirements.

And when it comes to one of our own? Yeah. They're going to give us jurisdiction. They'll probably assign us agents to assist, too. If they offer you one, accept."

"Only if they're babysitting my puppy and kitten," I muttered.

"I'm sure arrangements can be made. And Bailey?"

"What?"

"I owe you a spanking for working on the bomb squad without telling me. I'm so mad at you."

His tone promised I would enjoy my punishment. "I was shot three times and demand additional punishment."

His laughter warmed me even better than the brightest sunny day. "Consider your wish granted."

He hung up, and I pointed at the trail of glowing, sparkling light. "We're on the clock, Perkette. First, to the nearest store with laptops, and then we have to go to a police station. We have work to do."

TWELVE

My grandfather? Also an incubus.

QUINN

NOTHING MADE SENSE ANYMORE.

While finding Bailey had turned my world upside down, I'd viewed my life as relatively normal. Well, as normal as someone with my heritage could get. I loved my family, but I'd grown up with a rather skewed perspective on life.

Having a rather untraditional number of grandparents ensured that, although I was grateful I had the traditional number of parents. I'd seen my mother's birth certificate. It redefined complicated.

Leaving the hotel with two children wrapped around my legs and a wolf puppy who wanted to prove she loved me, too, once again turned my world upside down. I'd seen fathers with their families, but I hadn't truly understood their expressions until trying to check out while juggling Beauty and Sylvester and a wolf puppy, all in need of tender loving care from me.

Perkins rescued me from Sunny, taking her leash. "You've already mastered the harried look of a man whose wife is not around to help with the kids. Well done!"

"The day you and Tiffany have a child, I will be present, and I will be smiling," I promised.

"Tiffany's barren."

Well, shit. My brows rose at that. "That's not what I expected to hear today."

"I think it's part of why she became a mad scientist. She couldn't become a mother, so she went for the next best thing."

I stared at him, and when he didn't read my mind and figure out he was talking to someone with a higher than normal percentage of demonic genes, I asked, "You realize I'm part incubus, right?"

Perkins blinked. "Well, yes."

"My grandfather? Also an incubus."

"And?"

"Merry Christmas." I chuckled at that, shaking my head over how simple it was for me—or my grandfather—to solve a problem I hadn't known existed. "If you want kids, I can take care of the problem."

"It's not that simple, Sam," he hissed. "She doesn't have eggs. Her ovaries are a complete bust."

"Still not a problem," I promised. "Sure, it's a little harder to do the work, and I might have to ask my grandfather for help, but it's not a problem. He's been teaching me so we won't have kids unless Bailey's ready for them. It's the same principle but reversed. While demons come bundled with all sorts of problems, they aren't without redeeming qualities. She could have a complete hysterectomy and my grandfather could reverse it."

Perkins sucked in a breath, and he stared at me with wide eyes while I handled turning in our room keys and paying the parking fee. Once I had the hotel room sorted, I untangled the children from my legs, gave them one of the wheeled suitcases so they could help while not being too burdened, and gathered the rest of our bags.

"I'm not joking, Arthur. I wouldn't do that to you. I just had no idea she's barren. I don't snoop all the time like most incubi. If you're not comfortable with an incubus, I can inquire for a succubus. Either can do what needs done. If she's not producing hormones properly, she'll need a few sessions with one possibly. That happens sometimes, but even if she needs daily boosters throughout the pregnancy, it's not an issue."

"I think she became a scientist trying to discover if she could fix herself. Turns out medical science can do a lot, but it can't make something from nothing," he replied.

A lifetime of anguish burdened his tone, and I wondered how long he'd been carrying that deep, dark secret around with him.

"You have several options, I think. One is a permanent fix, which will throw her for a complete loop. Her body will have to adapt to the changes. The other option is temporary, although she'll have to adapt for the duration of the pregnancy until she's done nursing. Miracle kids, if you will—and yes, incubi and succubi can control the number of kids. We can even determine gender, but I think you'd prefer that to be a surprise, right? We can also ensure the pregnancy goes well from start to finish. That's the one thing humans forget. Sex demons aren't just about the sex. They're about the children, too. Right up until birth is their domain. My grandfather's probably a better choice, but if she needs some basic regulation, I can take care of that. Bailey had some issues, too. She didn't know about it, but I took care of it."

"Issues?"

"Hormonal irregularities. It happens in a lot of women. She wasn't producing enough estrogen and needed a boost." I grimaced. "Don't tell any ladies in the office this, but I'm a bit of a meddler at the station. I just never saw Tiffany with any obvious symptoms when I was checking in on everyone around me. If I had noticed, I would've talked to you about this sooner."

"You've been meddling with the women at the station?"

"Their health is my concern," I growled. "To be fair, I check in on the men, too."

"While I understand that—wait. You've been fixing our sexual health issues?"

"Basically. I've been doing it the entire time I've been a chief. Dowry knows," I confessed. "I told him he could screw himself with a stick if he thought I wasn't going to meddle when some of the women were in crippling pain while on the job. Some of the men were having heightened testosterone production, too, which was impairing them to some degree. I fix the actual problems and let the doctors do the rest. I am also the one who'll tip off doctors if I think there's a health problem I can't fix."

Perkins's eyes widened. "Amanda. She'd be practically green sometimes, and that eased up after a while. I haven't seen her turn green in ages."

"She had endometriosis. In that case, I asked my grandfather to meddle with it when he was in the station. He did a permanent fix because I couldn't. I've learned how to since, but I figured with a problem that severe, she was better off in the hands of an experienced incubus. And not literal hands.

He didn't even have to touch her to meddle. She could never get a correct diagnosis; I had her medical record pulled last year because it was harming her performance and concentration. That made it my jurisdiction."

"I can't tell if she'd thank you or kill you for meddling," he admitted. "Secret's safe with me. You can really…?"

"Help you and Tiffany have kids? Definitely. As soon as we catch up with our wives, if you'd like. Or even on Christmas. It's looking more and more like we'll be spending Christmas in Vegas. You'll have to get her to stop drinking, though."

"Unless I tell her, good luck with that," he muttered.

"I can have my other grandfather meddle. He'd probably do it."

"Which one?"

"The angel."

"Okay, this I have to hear. Just how could he pull *that* off?"

"Simple. He can use an aversion. Anything alcoholic will turn her stomach." I grimaced. "That is one of his favorite punishments for disobedient children and grandchildren. Misbehave? Favorite food rights are revoked until you're ready to behave."

Perkins snickered. "That's brilliant. Do you think he'd be willing to do that until she figures out she's pregnant?"

"I'll ask."

"We were talking about adopting."

"You can still do that and have one of your own, you know." I led the way to the rental. "Once we get this mess settled, I'll take care of the details. I'm thinking I'll recruit the grandfathers to watch the kids while we're in Vegas, too. Start getting them socialized with hives and keep them busy.

They'll love it, and they're old enough to start making new friends."

"You really think…?"

"I wouldn't do that to you, Arthur. Really. Yes, it's possible, yes, I can make the arrangements by Christmas, and yes, we can keep an eye on her for the entire pregnancy. My kind? We're walking fertility clinics. In case you didn't know, most? Would do it if you asked. No payment needed. Most humans don't ask, though."

"Seriously? Why not?"

I shrugged. "Ask my grandfather. He'll give you an entire historic breakdown of the prejudices of humanity. Haven't you ever thought about why triads happen?"

"I just figured an angel really wanted to get it on with a human."

"It's much more than that. *He* loves triads, did you know that?"

That got Perkins's attention. "Really? I thought he'd hate anything to do with one of *His* angels consorting with a demon."

"A being of love can't begrudge love, Perkins. And ultimately, *He* is a being of love. That's not how it works. A triad is a true expression of the purest love. For a triad to successfully have a child, all three must have nothing but love for each other and the child they're bringing into the world."

"Huh. I never would have guessed."

"Most don't. It takes a special human to be part of a triad. That's why triads are so rare."

"You'd figure the demons would cut and run the instant the child is born."

"With great love comes great sacrifice. Angels tend to

suffer, too. They stay on the mortal coil as long as possible, their power significantly weakened for however long the triad lasts. *He* will call his triad angels back if *He* feels their health is suffering too much, but angels and demons alike pay a high price for their children. The human of the triad has it much easier, although they make sacrifices, too."

"Well, I learned something new today. Let's get this show on the road. Do you think Bailey will be able to get to Janet?"

"It depends on if she gets upset enough to call and ask for pet sitters. If she does, that woman has rockets strapped to her ass when she wants, and they've been making good time. Considering Bailey took her saddle with her, the saucy wenches were going to make a literal run for it."

"Shit, Sam. Get Bailey on the phone, ask your grandfathers to watch the pets, and set Bailey loose. We've clocked her at over two hundred miles an hour, and the woman just doesn't tire. If she's out on a sunny day? She could cross the country in a day. We've tested some, and as long as she's at a full gallop when she jumps, it doesn't even bother her rider much."

I blinked. "I see she's been doing a lot of testing behind my back."

"Don't feel bad about it, Sam. I was the guinea pig because she knew how sick I got the first time she took me on a trip. We've figured out it has to do with inertia; as long as she's at top speed when she jumps, her riders don't really suffer from the jumps. We knew you were resilient to her jumping, so it was pointless testing with you. And she gets distracted when you're riding her. Her focus snaps to making sure you stay perfectly safe. She's willing to dump my ass off her back because I'm not you."

While I didn't like it, I acknowledged his point with a nod. "All right." I got the kids into the SUV before digging out my phone and calling Bailey's number.

"You again?" my wife answered, her tone amused. While her voice was still rough, she did sound better than earlier.

"Me again. Do you trust one of my pesky relatives to watch the pets? Perkins had an idea."

"Shoot."

"Transform, get saddled up, and take Tiffany to Janet. You could make it to Vegas by nightfall if you haul ass."

"But we have the rental…"

"One of my pesky relatives can take care of the rental and the pets. They can't meddle, but there's nothing in the rule book saying they can't follow you while *you* meddle." I smiled. "We need to get to Janet as quickly as possible, and you're the only one I can think of who can do it."

"I'm in. It'll suck, but I'm in. The SUV is loaded with neutralizer, too. In case there's an outbreak."

"Good. I'll ask my grandfathers to make sure it follows after you while you do the heavy lifting. I'll call them and call you back. Sound good?"

"I'll talk to Tiffany about the details. We might need to use the n word."

Napalm. The thought of my wife rampaging across the United States while on a napalm bender terrified the hell out of me, but there was no better fuel for her. "Ask Tiffany if she can make her blend with store-bought supplies."

The sound clicked off Bailey's phone, indicating she'd muted her line while she talked to Tiffany. I found that amusing, and while I waited, I considered how best to ask my grandfathers to care for the husky and ocelot.

They would be less than thrilled with me, but I couldn't

think of another way to make Bailey willing to leave them for any period of time.

"Okay. She says we can. Apparently, one of the ingredients is neutralizer, and we've got the best of the best in the back. She says the ignition point is even higher than the ridiculous stuff the CDC uses, so it should be good for me for a long run."

"Okay, listen to me carefully, Bailey."

"I'm listening."

"Go to the nearest police station and ask for a temporary badge; tell them you were on vacation. Tell them to patch in through the FBI for the badge. Get a firearm exemption for Tiffany, and tell them to pull her records. Have them arm her with the best firearm they can. Tiffany's good with a gun, and I want you to have backup, okay? Also, tell them you're going in after one of your kidnapped officers; Dowry's already confirmed the transfer, so Janet is ours."

"Got it. Should I just go straight to an FBI building?"

"If you can find one. Do not go to the CDC."

"Why not?"

"I trust the FBI more right now," I replied, allowing my tone to darken. "They can handle your badge situation, too. They can also care for the pets until my grandfathers arrive. They'll guard your rental and supplies as needed. The FBI and the NYPD have a good relationship."

"But we're not in New York."

"Doesn't matter. You're a cop, and the FBI gets cops. We have friendly feuds, but at the end of the day, when a cop is in trouble, the FBI is who we turn to."

"All right. We'll be heading to the nearest FBI building. How are the kids?"

I smiled at the breathless quality of my wife's voice.

"They're good. They're going to help us do research work. They're sweet, and I think you'll like them."

"Like them?" My wife's laughter soothed me as nothing else. "I already love the little brats, and I'll rip the snakes off anyone who tries to come between me and those poor babies."

Bailey never did anything in half measures, and if I loved her any more, my heart would surely burst. "We are supposed to withstand a beating for them, Bailey. That doesn't mean beat the competition into full submission."

"I can beat the competition into submission before accepting a beating. Grudgingly."

The grudgingly part worried me. "The kids do get to decide."

"I'm very bad at charming people," Bailey whined. "But I'm good in a fight! They'll understand that, right?"

I smiled at the two kids, who were already lost in their books. "You fight, I'll charm."

"Deal! And you screwed the pooch this time, Police Chief Samuel Quinn!" my wife crowed. "You're letting me do the fighting while you're doing the charming, *so you can't stop me this time!* I get to fight!"

Shit. I laughed despite knowing I had made a basic mistake and removed my ability to protest her participation in the fight. "You win. Get to the FBI station, get your badge taken care of, and go find Janet. We'll be hot on your heels. I'll be there as soon as I can. I'll need you to update us with your position. Once your rental is gone, we won't be able to track you anymore."

"We'll be talking about you tracking the rental, you sneaky man."

She'd find I would be a willing participant in whatever punishment she had in mind. "Noted."

"Good. We'll call you with updates as we have them," my wife promised before hanging up. I took a deep breath, sighed, and called my angelic grandfather.

One day, I'd figure out how an angel kept a cell phone, but by the second ring, he answered, "How can I be of service, little grandson?"

"I know you're not allowed to meddle in this situation, but is watching a husky puppy and an ocelot kitten meddling? And perhaps driving a rental car to Las Vegas along with a very expensive stash of high-grade neutralizer?"

"An arrangement could be made," my grandfather replied.

I sighed again, this time out of relief. "Thank you. Bailey is going after Janet, and I don't want her worrying about the pets. We're going to blitz—"

"Take a plane, my little grandson. It will be much faster and beneficial for you to do so."

I blinked, wondering how I could have possibly failed to consider the option of taking a flight out west. "Huh. You're a fountain of wisdom."

My grandfather chuckled. "You have something else you want to ask."

"Think you and grandfather can help Tiffany? A child for Christmas. I already told Arthur I'd try to help."

"That's the sort of meddling we can help with, yes. Has he asked?"

I held the phone out to Perkins. "Ask for a child for Christmas, Arthur."

Perkins's eyes widened, but he took the phone. "Uh, hello? Oh! Sylvester. I, uh… I don't suppose it's possible for us to have a child? At Christmas? She's…"

I smothered my desire to laugh at my friend's perplexed expression. He wouldn't understand I'd laugh out of happiness for him rather than mockery at his nervousness. A moment later, he handed the phone back, and I pretended I didn't notice the sheen of tears in his eyes.

"Nervous, that one," my grandfather said as soon as I had the phone near my ear. "However embarrassing that may have been for him to say, it needed to be said."

"I told him about the need to ask."

"I know. I will take a moment to check in with your bride when I go to care for your pets. Your worries for her are more potent than usual."

"She's sick from being out in the cold as a unicorn."

"She'll be fine. She'll be plenty warm enough soon, so don't worry."

"That reminds me. I need a new prescription for a chill pill. Tiffany said the one I have is wrong."

"I'll take care of it and have the details sent to your phone along with where you can pick up the prescription in Las Vegas. It's so much fun when mortals tell the divine they're doing their job wrong. I look forward to seeing Anubis's face when I tell him a mortal has better sense than he does."

I bet he would. "Thank you for taking care of Bailey."

"Always, my little grandson. Always. And you should be proud of yourself."

"Why?"

"It takes a lot of courage for a man like you to let your bride find her strength and truly fly. We're proud of you both."

My grandfather hung up, and I stared at the display for a long time, my brows furrowing as I considered his words.

"Everything okay, Sam?"

I pocketed my phone and smiled, and some of the tightness in my chest eased. "Yeah, Perkins. Everything's going to be just fine."

We'd make everything fine one way or the other.

THIRTEEN

This is going to be a disaster.

BAILEY

TIFFANY RAIDED a gas station for several gallons of diesel, mixed it with neutralizer and a bunch of other ingredients she'd gotten at a grocery store and a hardware store, and stirred it together in a bucket while whistling a merry tune. After sealing the concoction in the bucket, she then drove me to the nearest FBI resident agency, located in Little Rock, Arkansas.

"This is going to be a disaster," I predicted. "Shouldn't we have gone to the police station first? We have a sealed container of napalm in the trunk. We're going to die from gas fumes."

"We're not going to die from gas fumes. I used a practitioner trick to seal the bucket. It'll be fine. Anyway, the FBI will confirm your rank and get any badges you need here. This is a major agency. I could've taken you to a closer agency, but this one will have the ability to give you a

Federal badge until we can get your NYPD badge shipped in. And since they're giving you a broad jurisdiction, running you with an FBI badge makes sense. Of course, they might just ask a cop to run a police badge over, but it'd be for the wrong state. If you're really lucky, they'll ask an angel or demon to teleport to New York to fetch your real badge."

I stared at the building while Perkette drove up to the gate. The guard watched us with interest while she leaned through the window to speak to him. "I'm Tiffany Perkins, and this is Police Chief Bailey Quinn of the NYPD. We need to see someone about a badge replacement and a jurisdiction issue. It's about a missing police officer taken out of state."

I had to give Perkette credit; she sounded like she meant business, and her tone implied she wouldn't be accepting no for an answer.

"Any weapons in the vehicle?"

"No, sir. We have two animals, a husky and an ocelot. Chief Quinn has a temporary permit issued through the CDC while waiting for an official card."

While I thought a bucket of napalm counted as a weapon, I kept my mouth shut. Technically, it wasn't a weapon, and it wouldn't even ignite without a lot of help. Then the reality of Perkette's statement punched me in the gut.

I doubted I'd ever get used to anyone calling *me* Chief Quinn. I fought the urge to twist in my seat to look for Quinn despite knowing he wasn't with us.

The guard pointed at a nearby lot. "Park there, go inside the building, and speak to the security desk."

Perkette saluted the guard, waited for the gate to lift, and parked where told. "See? It's easy to get through when you know what to say and you have the right rank. And the FBI takes badge replacements seriously. Toss in a missing officer, and they'll be dancing to your tune in minutes."

"More like dancing to your tune," I muttered, gathering up Avalanche and making sure she was swaddled in her new blanket. The kitten yawned and resumed her nap. Perkette grabbed Blizzard's leash, and while the puppy preferred me, he wagged his tail and heeled like I'd been trying to teach him whenever I got to take him on a walk. "Good boy!"

He beat Perkette's leg with his tail.

The gate guard must have called security about us, as the two men behind the huge desk in the lobby watched us like hawks from the moment we stepped through the doors until we reached them. I set my kitten on the ledge, grabbed my wallet, and tossed my license onto the polished surface. "I'm Bailey Quinn, and I need to get a temporary badge issued. I also need to work with the FBI about a missing officer."

The older man, with gray streaking at his temples and a name tag that declared his name to be Eric, picked up my license. "Rank?"

"NYPD Police Chief," I replied, wondering how the hell I'd become my husband's equal.

"I've heard of a Chief Quinn, but he's a man," the guard said, taking my license and looking it over. "No disrespect meant, ma'am, but you're not a man."

"That Police Chief Quinn is my husband. I'm not offended. I'm the Police Chief Quinn who transforms into a fire-breathing unicorn."

Both guards stopped what they were doing to stare at me.

"You're the cindercorn from the 120 Wall Street incident," Eric said.

Damn it. Had everyone heard about that? I sighed. "That's me."

"You weren't a uniformed officer during that incident. Welcome to the force, Chief Quinn. Former CDC specialist?"

I sighed. "Thank you, I think. And yes. I worked for the CDC, and the NYPD somehow hoodwinked them out of my contract."

"I'd say the NYPD made out like bandits to get someone like you batting for them. All right. You're going to need some special handling; you have clearance flags most chiefs lack, so you need a special badge issued. There is one already made for you in New York, so we may be able to send a teleporter to retrieve it. Please come with me." Eric stood and gestured towards the bank of elevators behind him. "Have you been evaluated before?"

"Through the CDC."

"What's your rating?"

"I'm sure one day they'll bother to tell me rather than filing shit on my behalf," I muttered.

Eric chuckled. "The FBI has a history of doing that to us, too. Sometimes, they don't tell us we're cleared because we don't need to know. We find out when they think we need to know."

"If I need to know, I'm sure someone will tell me. I suspect I have whatever rating is the minimum for working as a chief. They haven't removed my vanilla rating from my licenses yet."

"Vanilla? They called someone who can transform into a cindercorn vanilla?"

"Cheaper labor that way."

"Ouch. And I thought the FBI could be ruthless at times. That's just harsh."

I nodded my agreement. To my dismay, Eric swiped his security pass inside the elevator and pressed the button for the top floor before leaving Tiffany and I to fend for ourselves. "Someone will meet you in reception," he said, and the doors closed before I had a chance to thank him.

"I feel like I've been invited to dinner, and the host is a cat." I sighed. "And I can't transform because I'll drop my kitten."

"You don't need to be a unicorn for this, Bailey. You'll be fine. They're not arresting you. They're helping you."

The elevator dinged, and the door opened. I stepped out, and flash of golden light startled me into spinning around. I sucked in a breath as I almost crashed right into Quinn's grandfather. "Devil angel," I hissed, clutching my kitten closer. "We meet again."

He hooked a finger into the blanket to reveal Avalanche. "When you get something into your pretty head, you go in all the way, I see. You found a lovely ocelot." He stroked the kitten's head, and she nuzzled the angel. "You've done well by her. A little malnourished still, but otherwise healthy. I thought you would like to know."

Relief washed through me. "Thank you, Sylvester. I got a cold rescuing her, too. What are you doing here?"

"I am your pet sitter, and I'm also volunteering to teleport to fetch your badge, as you will need it, and getting a new one made would cost you valuable hours."

"I would hug you, but I'm holding the kitten." I bounced and nodded at Blizzard. "That's Blizzard, and he's Quinn's puppy."

"Hello, Blizzard," my angelic grandfather-in-law greeted.

Blizzard sat and held out his paw to shake. The angel chuckled but obeyed the puppy's wishes while Tiffany snapped pictures with her phone.

"Excuse me," the receptionist said. He was an older

gentleman in a suit with a badge hanging from his neck proclaiming him to be a member of the FBI. "Which one of you is Chief Quinn?"

As my grandfather-in-law had already been hired as a pet sitter, I handed him Avalanche. "Defend her with your immortal life," I ordered before strolling to the desk, arming myself with my driver's license. "I'm Bailey Quinn. Sorry to be a bother, sir."

"It's no bother. It's admirable you're coming out of vacation to join the search for your missing officer. We need to do some paperwork for your badge retrieval, although I see we have already acquired an angel. That'll simplify things."

"He's an in-law, and I'm abusing my granddaughter-in-law privileges. I'm a wayfinder, so the sooner I can get the paperwork filed and jurisdiction issues settled, the faster I'm on the road."

"Yes, I have a note here I'm to have you fill out jurisdiction forms for the entirety of the United States excluding Hawaii, Alaska, and territories. If you need to go to Hawaii or Alaska, come to any FBI building to fill out the forms. I've a note I'm to issue you a firearm as well."

"Are all secretaries as badass as you are?" Had I missed a better calling? The FBI secretary seemed like he could probably kick my ass given any justification.

Sylvester laughed, and as always, I relaxed despite knowing the angel found me and my thoughts amusing.

"I'm actually in management, and since you were on the way, I let the actual secretary go take a break. She'll be back in a few minutes. If you'd follow me, I'll take you to the conference room, and we'll get this show on the road. I'm Alfred, and no, I'm not a butler, nor do I have access to a cave full of special gadgets and crime-fighting tools."

"But is your last name Pennyworth?"

"Much to my eternal shame, anguish, and dismay, yes."

Poor bastard. "Are you English?"

"I was born here, but my father's British. My mother's American," he replied, guiding us through a maze of hallways to a spacious conference room with a massive table. A tall stack of papers waited.

"That's a lot of paperwork." If it was anything like the CDC's forms, I'd be hard at work filling it out for hours.

"You have to read it, you don't have to fill it out. Someone is printing the real forms now. It'll take a few minutes, but we're digitally populating the fields from what we have in your file. You just need to know what your jurisdiction rights are for every state."

"I'm going to need a digital cheat sheet," I muttered.

"Conveniently for you, we have one of those. Still, it's protocol, so bear with it. We'll be done in no time. It looks like a lot, but we can churn through this in an hour. That's about how long it'll take to get your firearm issued."

Damn it. There was another secret about to fly right out of the window and strut its stuff for the world to see. I hadn't told anyone I'd been practicing at the range at the start of most shifts. Perkette only knew about my bomb work because I'd needed her help with the schematics.

Perkette grabbed a seat and raised her hand. "I'll need a firearm and carry permits."

"You need tossed into the nearest jail, too," Alfred muttered, taking a seat across the table from the stack of papers.

"So you've seen my file."

"The first thing I did when security notified me was to

check your files. You hold the record in the United States for most unique misdemeanors collected."

"Have I hit the world record for them yet? I have ambitions. What sort of interesting misdemeanors could I collect here?"

"All crimes committed in an FBI building typically classify as a felony," he replied.

"You're ruining my fun," Perkette complained. "I'm going to need a firearm. Don't give the fire-breathing unicorn one. She's useless with a gun. Her husband is going to have fun sharpening her skills. She's really not a chief because she's handy with firearms. She's great at demolition and explosives, though. If you have a bomb you need defused, she's your woman. She's also an excellent bodyguard for the other Chief Quinn."

I sighed and bowed my head. Once we were back in New York, I'd need to drag Perkette to the range and kick her ass in a marksmanship contest. She could shoot a gun; Perky had taught her. I'd been practicing for at least three days a week for an hour a session, and I'd come prepackaged with, according to my instructors, a freakish amount of natural talent with a firearm. "Please ignore everything she's saying."

"You've probably never touched a gun in your life, Bailey. It's okay to be useless with a gun, but they're dangerous if you don't know what you're doing."

I was *not* useless with a gun. I could hit the target every time on a full clip. I understood why she had the opinion she did, however. I tended to glare at Quinn's gun when he came home because mine usually made my hands and ears hurt after an hour of practicing at the range.

She likely assumed my general dislike for guns meant I couldn't use one.

"I was unaware Chief Quinn needed a body guard." Alfred checked his phone. "He has a very low number of incidents where it was deemed his life was at risk."

"His predecessor was murdered, and the NYPD is targeted at a higher rate than typical law enforcement," Perkette replied. She pulled out her phone to tap at the screen, and a few moments later, she slid the device across the table. "Statistics from your own agency's website."

"You're an insufferable know-it-all, aren't you?"

Sylvester set Avalanche on the table and sat beside her. I didn't blame him for sitting on the table, as I doubted he enjoyed cramming his wings against the back of a chair. The angel chuckled and gestured to Perkette's phone. "She is a fountain of wisdom should you choose to listen to her. While she has opinions about Chief Quinn's experience with a firearm, one should still be issued to her. Her officer might find it useful."

Sneaky, tricky angel. I admired how he said nothing but the truth but allowed Perkette to maintain her beliefs.

"Noted. Can you handle the acquisition of her badge?"

"I will handle the acquisition of the badge and attire for her missing officer. I will return shortly." Sylvester vanished in a flash of golden light.

"But I haven't..." Alfred sighed. "Angels."

"Angels are assholes," I agreed. "He'll do what needs done, and then he'll return and be annoyingly smug over it. That's what angels do. Let's get through this, shall we? What specific jurisdiction issues will I have to worry about?"

"Due to your special circumstances, you'll be considered a liaison between the FBI, police, and the CDC. Your CDC ranking and certifications qualify you, and considering the nature of your situation, it's best if you have joint jurisdiction in case there's any destruction of property. You, ma'am, are a master at destroying property. Your jurisdiction allowances will let us avoid liability issues."

I groaned. "Burn down a building just once, and no one forgets it. It was a sanctioned destruction!"

"It was also exceptionally effective and minimized cleanup. Should we require a demolition due to gorgon dust or another toxin of its scale, we intend to repeat that method of demolition. The CDC has already begun attempts to negotiate with wild cindercorns. The plan is to offer suitable housing and environmental care for their species in exchange for igniting the highest grades of napalms. Phoenixes are far more inclined for mass destruction than cindercorns. It might even save them from extinction."

"You mean they can't fly and have to limit what they can reach by hoof," I muttered. As I was well aware cindercorns were on a collision course with extinction, I kept my opinions on the downsides of bringing cindercorns among humans to myself.

They likely viewed humans as dinner.

"Precisely," Alfred replied.

I regarded the man with narrowed eyes. "Okay. I'll bite. How do you know about this?"

"I teleported in from Washington. This isn't my agency building. I'm a visitor like you. Security called Washington, as is protocol on your file."

Well, shit.

"If you're in cahoots with Clemmends, I may be tempted to transform and light you on fire."

He chuckled. "It's also mentioned in your file that you have a rather turbulent relationship with your supervisor."

"Which is why he sold my contract to the NYPD."

"Yes, I expect he will be unhappy about this decision soon enough. The CDC is displeased they lost a key resource. The FBI wishes to play nice with you in hopes you'll consider an official liaison position."

I scowled. "For the first time in my life, I have a job with a salary and the same hours as my husband."

"Translate to mean she will transform and incinerate anyone who screws with her ability to work with her husband and have her salary," Perkette announced.

"How did you get here so quickly?" I considered how long we'd been at the security desk, which wouldn't have been more than five or ten minutes.

"We have a devil in our employ, and he will teleport staff between agencies as needed. He brought me here."

I sniffed for any signs of sulfur, the typical giveaway a devil had teleported into the area. "I don't smell a devil."

"He cleaned up after himself. Some humans have allergies to brimstone. I see you have an education on devils."

If it could start a fire, I'd had information on it drilled into me. I shrugged. "The CDC invested in my education."

"And then dumped you with the NYPD."

"I never said my supervisor was smart or wise," I countered.

"This is true. So, let's start with Arkansas, shall we?"

I grabbed the stack and plucked the first two sheets off the pile, which were clipped together and had a sticky note with the state's name. After working with the CDC for so long, the form didn't bother me as much as the list of special rules for law enforcement in the state. One of the entries startled me. "Law enforcement officers must wear pants with their uniforms?"

"Yes."

"What about shorts? Doesn't it get hotter than hell here in the summer?"

"It's not a law many appreciate, but some men made a fuss because women were wearing skirts to work and they weren't allowed to wear shorts, so all uniformed law enforcement must wear pants. As a result, no one is happy now."

Damn. "Perkette, remind me never to move to Arkansas unless that dress code changes. I'd also like an undercover rating for this state."

Alfred chuckled. "As a chief, you can decide when you're undercover."

Score. "I don't wear anything other than pants and I don't even have a uniform right now, so I'm undercover effective now. Got a pen?"

The FBI agent slid one to me across the table, and I made a note on the form about having to declare my status as undercover. The rest of the rules seemed simple enough, and I tossed Arkansas's aside and picked up the next form, scanning over it. When it seemed sensible enough, I put a checkmark on it and tossed it onto the pile.

"Effective," Alfred said, watching me work. "You're no stranger to paperwork."

"The CDC just loves its red tape." I went through most states before halting at Nevada. "Nevada has a flat out ban against law enforcement marrying each other on the state level?"

"Yes."

"That's stupid. I'm married to a cop, and I refuse to be unmarried to my cop. Exemption or Nevada can take its jurisdiction and shove it up its ass."

"An exemption will be made. You just can't actively marry a law enforcement officer in the state."

"Exemption."

"Pardon?"

"Ex-emp-tion." I lifted the form and waved it in his face. "If my husband comes anywhere near Las Vegas, I'm paying an Elvis impersonator and renewing my vows. That counts as marrying take two, right?"

He laughed. "I'll make a note in the file that you have plans to renew your vows while in Vegas. Figure you may as well enjoy the experience?"

"We had a courthouse wedding," I admitted.

"Your marriage and vow renewal plans are safe. Exemptions are made for this one all the time. We have a special form for it. I'll make sure you sign it before you leave, and your husband will also be required to sign. We need the form any time our liaisons are married to cops, which is somewhat frequent. Liaisons can't seem to keep their hands off the local law enforcement."

"Cops are hot," I informed him. I pointed at Perkette. "Just ask her."

"Cops are hot," she agreed.

"I see where you ladies stand. We'll make sure your marriage isn't hampered by Nevada's rules, Chief Quinn."

"I'm going to need to either go by Gardener or add something to the front or use my full name, or everyone will look for my husband," I complained.

"Sam will not be happy if you go by Gardener. He's a bit territorial," Perkette announced.

I snorted. "A bit? And anyway, I think he secretly misses growling Gardener at me."

"He would. He's almost as hopeless as you are."

As I lacked a sufficient rebuttal, I rolled up Nevada's form and smacked her with it before making a note about the exemption and tossing it into the pile. I blitzed through the rest of the forms and slid the stack across the table to Alfred. "What else do I need to do?"

"Sign the actual forms and fill out the exemption forms as needed. I'll send you a copy of the list, issue your firearms, and obtain—"

Sylvester popped into the room with a flash of golden light and set a pile of blue uniforms and a box on the table. "I have two sets of your uniform, Bailey, your badge and firearms, and some other permits the NYPD printed out for you."

Alfred sighed. "Firearms is plural."

"My grandson has more issues than sense. It seems he has picked three firearms for his lovely bride. They are, rather like him, ridiculous." Sylvester removed a holster from the box and offered it to me. "This is a Beretta M9, and it is your primary firearm."

I took the gun, and as I was annoyed everyone felt I was completely useless with weapons, I put on a show of checking the chamber, ejecting the magazine and checking the clip, and doing a full inspection of the weapon. "For the record, for the assholes at this table who presume I've never handled a firearm, the CDC made me qualify as part of my bomb squad activities. Apparently, they somehow assumed I would be capable of operating a firearm while sporting hooves. I'm proficient."

"You should compete," Alfred replied. "Your qualification results are in your file. You could use some work in motion, but if you're standing still, you don't miss." Alfred checked his phone again. "And your adjustments for environmental conditions are excellent."

"The qualification test was a bear, I hated it, and I wanted to light the ranges on fire, especially the outdoor range."

"Chief Quinn, you qualified for a full Federal license. That qualification test is much more difficult than the one standard law enforcement use."

I blinked. "What? I didn't take the standard test?"

"No. You took the Federal test."

I slumped in my seat. "The CDC played me *again*?"

Perkette blinked. "She qualified for a Federal permit?"

"Yes. The note here says her handler made the request for additional education with firearms and explosives."

I wanted to find out who that handler was and shove my M9 right up his ass crosswise. "Which handler?"

"Marshal Clemmends. He seems to have taken an unusual interest in your safety."

"In my *safety*? He tries to blow me up several times a week, and then he transferred me to the NYPD!" I hesitated. "I'm not complaining about the transfer."

Alfred humored me with a smile. "I figured as much. It's a compliment, really. Marshal Clemmends has a reputation."

"As what? An asshole?"

"That, but he does work to ensure his staff is equipped for everything they need. Looking over your supplementary training, he's been planning to move you into law enforcement for a while. The contract also seems to indicate an intent to transfer you."

I frowned. "Really?"

"I'll be back. I'll print something for you to review that may help clarify the matter. I'll also make a note about the serial numbers of your weapons, if you could give them to me?"

I read off the serial number of my M9 and Sylvester read off the numbers for a Glock and a SIG.

Alfred frowned. "That's not a Glock 18, is it?"

"It's a Glock 18. Do not ask me why the NYPD wants her to have a fully automatic gun. I'm just delivering the packages."

I perked up. "My baby!" Setting the Beretta aside, I grabbed the Glock and set it on the table in front of me, stroking its sleek, lethal lines. "I got to use this one at the range. I had to qualify with fully automatics in the entire range. I like this one even more than the Browning."

"Browning?" Perkette's eyes widened. "You don't mean a machine gun, do you?"

"Yes. They brought out a military trainer for one week of my range lessons, and I had to use a bunch of different weapons."

"She's gotten a very extensive weapons education through the CDC. As I said, Marshal Clemmends took special interest in your general education. There's a note you'll particularly like. Excuse me for a few minutes, and you'll understand when you see it." Alfred left with the serial numbers and forms.

I frowned. "This is so weird. This is more than just weird, it's freaky. Clemmends *hates* me."

"Don't judge him so readily, Bailey," Sylvester scolded. "Certainly, he holds a certain amount of dislike for you, but he doesn't willfully endanger those he's responsible for. While he certainly views getting rid of you to the NYPD as directly beneficial to him, he takes his job seriously, and that means preparing you for the work. Did it not occur to you that you have a far more extensive education than basic CDC contractors?"

"Well, no. It hadn't. I mean, sure, I know some rules and regulations, but I need to know them for my work. All contractors know the regulations associated with their work. We need to stay legal."

"Bailey." The angel sighed. "Once again, you underestimate yourself and your education."

"I do not!"

Perkette jabbed me with her elbow. "You learned how to fluently read bomb schematics in a week."

"I didn't want to be turned into unicorn goop."

"A week, Bailey."

"I *really* didn't want to be turned into unicorn goop."

"It's typically a two year Master's degree program, Bailey. You picked it up in a week."

"Really. Didn't. Want. To. Be. Turned. Into. Unicorn. Goop."

"Yes, we heard you the first two times. What we're saying is you have a ridiculous capacity for learning, and once you've digested the basics of a subject, you assimilate it. You learned a complicated schematic in a week. Not only did you learn a singular schematic, you were then able to apply what you learned to other bombs. It's only when you find a new type that you get confused and fall to the urge to just eat the fucking payload rather than disarming it properly! *With your fucking claws.*"

"I don't understand why you're upset over this issue."

"You disarm bombs with your claws and teeth."

"What else am I supposed to use? I don't have the option of using my hands! I'm not impervious to bombs when a human." I pointed at my face. "See? See these little scars?

These little scars say I'm not impervious to bombs when I'm a human."

"You should just have those removed," Perkette grumbled.

"Quinn likes them."

"He likes that you're his because of them. He doesn't actually like that you were hurt by his ex-wife. It reminds him of that every time he sees them."

I turned to my grandfather-in-law and pointed at my scars. "Can you remove these for me for Christmas?"

"I could remove them for you right now. There's no need to wait until Christmas."

"Would you please remove them now? If Sam doesn't like them, I don't want them. I thought he liked them. I could get the creams, but those take weeks to work."

Perkette's eyes widened. "You called him Sam."

"I call him Sam!" I scowled.

"You usually call him Quinn."

"She saves Sam for the special occasions because my little grandson loves when she calls him Sam or Samuel that much," the traitor angel announced.

Asshole angel. "That," I admitted, as there was no point in trying to hide the truth with a pesky angel around.

Perkette grinned. "You're absolutely unbelievable, Bailey."

I sighed. "No matter what I say, I just can't win, can I?"

"Nope," she replied. "You really can't."

FOURTEEN

Sometimes, the simplest solutions
worked the best.

QUINN

IT OCCURRED to me I could beat Bailey to Vegas in one simple way, and it wouldn't even cost me anything. Over the years, I'd accumulated various favors from angels, devils, and demons alike, smoothing things over with local law enforcement or simply helping them because I could. If I called in some of those favors, I could have everyone teleported to Vegas within a few hours, which would put me in position to reach Bailey if she needed me.

Taking a pair of young gorgons on a public flight was a recipe for disaster and mayhem, and while I'd be entertained, the effort would delay us long enough that driving might be more efficient.

Sometimes, the simplest solutions worked the best.

My first step was to call the FBI and process a jurisdiction request for Nevada. When I finally got a hold of someone, I discovered I'd been granted country-wide jurisdiction for the purposes of recovering Janet—and that my sneaky wife had made a few requests regarding the rules and marriage in Nevada.

Once I resolved the jurisdiction issue, dealing with Perkins was next on my list. He wouldn't be happy when I told him about my plan, but I needed to make sure he'd be okay with it before forcing him to teleport across half the country. After his experiences teleporting with Bailey, I worried he would take my idea poorly.

I sighed and glanced at him. "I have an idea."

"Those are the scariest damned words you could possibly say to me right now. Ideas are dangerous things. The only thing more dangerous than you having an idea is your wife having an idea—or my wife having one."

Damn, my friend wasn't pulling his punches. "How does teleporting to Vegas sound to you?"

"You are permitted to have a single idea today, and that is the idea you're permitted to have."

I laughed. "You're in a mood."

"I've been socially engineered to be incapable of expressing gratitude in gracious ways, so I'm resorting to mockery, sarcasm, and generally being an asshole to express my gratitude."

I raised my brows at that. "You're welcome."

"Right. I was supposed to say thank you. Thank you."

"You're welcome," I repeated, directing my attention back to my phone. "Take us to the nearest FBI building. We can use that as a staging point, get them to deal with our rental, and prepare. I'll call in a few extra favors to have our firearms and uniforms retrieved and make arrangements for a babysitter when we can't watch the kids personally."

"Gorgons?"

"I was thinking angels or a divine."

"Has it occurred to you that you may be taking the over-protective parent thing a little too far?"

"Absolutely not."

"Sam, you can't ask a divine to babysit the kids."

"Like hell I can't. And I will. The Sphinx adores kids, and she's the best protector I can think of, and she's immune to petrification. My grandfather's a good choice, too. I'd like to see someone get to them with either of them on guard."

"You're serious."

"Sure am. I mean, I'm going to be calling in favors from demons, devils, and angels to get us to Vegas in a hurry—and get us everything we need to be able to act once Bailey finds Janet. I don't want to be halfway across the country when she might need us. Our wives, too. But Janet's going to need the most help."

Perkins stared at me, his eyes wide. "Did you just admit someone might need more help than Bailey?"

"Yes. Actually, I'm more concerned about what Janet will do if she's able to escape. That woman has backbone."

"I'm worried Janet hasn't set herself free. If she could, she would."

"Petrification. I'm hoping not with gorgon dust, but my bets are on petrification. This makes me wonder if that ex-cadet was involved with the 120 Wall Street incident, too." I growled, remembered we had kids in the car, and fell quiet. "I'm worried this is more extensive of a plot than mere revenge."

"We need to figure out who his accomplices are. He has to have them."

"That's what Thomas thought, too." I frowned.

"Thomas?"

"He's a gorgon from Florida. Winfield had contacted him, and he tipped me off about Bailey. He's definitely in league with gorgons; he's been able to contact multiple hives. I just don't know which hive he's working with."

"And it's not that bitch's hive, either."

I wrinkled my nose but didn't argue with him or his choice of terms.

"That's a bad word," Beauty announced. "Say you're sorry."

Perkins sighed while I grinned.

"I'm sorry, Beauty. She was a very bad person who'd done very bad things to your foster parents. She earned the title."

"She's a dog?"

"Basically," Perkins replied. "But you're right. It wasn't a nice thing to say."

"What mean things did she do?"

"She targeted your foster mother with a bomb, and when that didn't work, she kidnapped her." Perkins grunted. "She emotionally abused your foster father, too."

As he said nothing but the truth, I kept my mouth shut despite wanting to protest his choice of words.

"That bitch!" Beauty blurted.

My annoyance over my ex-wife's actions faded. I fought my laughter over Beauty's reaction, but it escaped, and choking it back only made things worse. "We'll just call that even," I gasped out between fits of laughter. "She's dead now, so we really shouldn't be saying bad things about her even though they're true."

Sylvester giggled and leaned between the seats. "We're not in trouble?"

"Not at all," I assured him. "But let's not say mean things moving forward." I worried Bailey would also help expand their vocabulary, but the realist in me recognized raising two gorgon children in New York around a bunch of cops at the station would result in colorful language and a certain hardened view of the world.

Gorgons needed a hardened view of the world.

Perkins pulled over long enough to input a new address into the navigation system, and he sighed at the hour-long drive ahead of us. "It could be worse, I guess," he muttered.

"It could be. We could have to run to Vegas. Bailey's going to be wiped."

"Hey, just think about it this way, Sam. You're always worried she's not getting enough exercise. I think she's covered for a while."

"Your silver linings need work, Arthur."

"Yeah, they're a bit tarnished, aren't they?"

Despite everything, I laughed.

BAILEY

WHILE WE'D ESCAPED the snow and the worst of the cold, I didn't appreciate transforming at all. I emerged from the bathroom with a little help from Perkette, who held the door open enough that I could squeeze through.

Curious FBI agents observed from the hallway, and to make it clear I could burn and eat them, I bared my teeth, showed off my fangs, and snorted fire.

"Chief Quinn gets pissy when it's cold outside, but I have her favorite treat in the car."

Alfred's brows rose. "Favorite treat?"

"Napalm. I made it myself." She beamed at the FBI agent.

"It's made with store bought ingredients with the exception of high-grade neutralizer, which Chief Quinn provided upon request. You can't even hit me with a misdemeanor for it."

"I better file the forms sanctioning napalm consumption," he muttered, fetching his phone and tapping on the screen.

I pricked my ears forward at that. "You auth-or-ize nay-palm for me?"

"Yes, I will. The situation warrants it. Please try to avoid any severe incidents. Will you need additional napalm?"

"Yes," Perkette replied. "She will. Any flammable fluids will work, but napalm gives her the most energy and lasts the longest. I'm not sure how long my bucket will last."

"Most agencies have a small supply on hand in case of emergency, but we measure it in cups."

"Cup works," I said, licking my lips. "Cup get me far. Bucket get me far-ther. But can work with cup. Po-leese keep gas. For gen-ur-ay-tors?"

"They should. You can run on gas?"

"Can. Not as good. Go gas station if need some."

"I never thought I'd see the day a deputized civilian might need to gas up her unicorn during a cross-country sprint," Alfred admitted. "How long do you think it will take you to get to Vegas?"

I flicked an ear back. "Two hour? Maybe three? Depends on fuel. I fast. No dep-u-tize Per-kette. She take over. Rule world. Bad idea."

"Too late, Bailey. I got my papers. It's okay, though. I don't get to actually do anything other than accompany you on official business. It's lame. Well, and carry a firearm. That part's important. Anyway, I've clocked her in at over two hundred miles per hour at a full gallop, and I suspect her jumps are around light speed."

"Light speed?" Alfred blurted.

I lifted a hoof, and aware I could destroy the floor, set it back down with a faint click. "I ride sunlight. It fun. Got-ten bet-ter at taking rider. Per-kette test often. She used to jumps. She no get sick. Sor-ry, hard to talk like this."

"I'm having no problems understanding you, so you're fine, Chief Quinn. You can travel at light speed?"

I turned my ears back and snorted flame. "No ex-per-i-ment on me. Can take one rider. Rider Per-kette. Or Sam. Sam can—"

Perkette clamped her hands around my muzzle and held my mouth closed. "You would regret saying that. Please don't burn me."

I didn't burn her, but I thought about it. I waited for her to release me before I said, "Sam can accept offers of tran-spor-tay-shun whenever he want."

"Good girl," Perkette said, giving my shoulder a slap. "You stay here and keep Alfred company while I get your saddle and napalm out of the SUV, grab some neutralizer, and call the rental company to transfer the keys to Sylvester."

My grandfather-in-law popped into existence, and I whinnied my laughter. "I took care of the rental company already, Tiffany. I thought you'd appreciate getting on the road faster. Go with her and get saddled outside, little one. I can handle the rest of the matters here. Let's not bring the napalm into the building."

I bobbed my head, careful to avoid stabbing anyone with my horn. "Pets okay?"

"Both are taking a nap in the upstairs conference room. Archambault is watching them."

I lifted my head, pricking my ears forward. "He here?"

"He is. You want to see him don't you?"

I whinnied again. "I fight him! For babies."

Sylvester laughed. "You will later, little one. Don't worry about that. Go rescue your friend. He'll hold his word and let you fight him for them."

I tilted my head and regarded the angel curiously. "You talk better now. Not so for-mal. Good angel. You do good." As I could be as much of an asshole as an angel, I took a few steps back, reared, and patted his shoulder with a hoof, careful not to claw him. "Good angel," I repeated.

"You're something else," the angel complained.

Pleased I'd finally won a round against the angel, I dropped to all four hooves and trotted after Perkette, my head lifted high.

QUINN

SOME DAYS, everything went right to plan. Others, the Lord of Hell showed up at the FBI building instead of the devil I'd actually called, not that I was actually able to reach Edwin. The Devil chose to make his appearance as a dark-skinned incubus with a pair of horns. I had no idea what type of suit he wore, but it worked so well with his wings and tail I almost forgot I stood in the presence of a divine.

"It's a custom," Satan announced, giving his cuffs a tug. "I'll have my tailor make you one. You have plans to properly marry your wife, do you not?"

Devils, like angels, existed to drive me insane, and the Devil did just as good a job as any of the full divines in my family. I sighed. "How much?"

"Already paid in full," he replied. "I owe you interest for a favor one of my devils owes you but is no longer able to repay."

That drew me up short. "Pardon?"

"He disobeyed, so he's in time-out right now. As he cannot repay a debt owed, I am paying it for you in his stead. It's that simple. A bargain is a bargain, and while I'm annoyed you won the bargain against one of my devils, it is my role to ensure all bargains are rightfully paid. Your end of the bargain is worth more than merely teleporting you and your children and your friend somewhere on the mortal coil, so here we are."

Perkins coughed at my side, and Beauty and Sylvester hugged my friend's legs, staring at Satan with wide eyes.

"Devils take their debts seriously," I informed Perkins. "And Edwin owed me a rather large favor for cleaning up a complicated mess."

"That's a gentle way of putting it," the Devil replied. "I'm a rather nosy fellow, so I've taken the liberty of snooping to find out what you're about. You won't need to call in any additional favors for what you need, and a suit for you and a dress for your wife will help even the scales. Babysitting your children will also help even the scales. My wife adores the little ones, so she'll keep them safe. I've also made room arrangements you'll find rather pleasing."

The Devil turned his attention to Perkins, and I tensed at his unrepentant grin. "As Chief Quinn was owed a rather substantial favor, I offer a contribution to your Christmas activities with your wife. A lovely woman, your Tiffany. Delightfully chaotic, disgustingly good-natured."

Perkins's eyes widened. "Thank you."

The Devil's attention returned to me. "I like him. You're right to keep him underfoot. This is still insufficient, so I will pay off the remainder of the owed bargain with knowledge. You won't even have to guess what the knowledge is—that's what will make this valuable enough to fully even the scales."

"Honestly, I have no idea why angels don't like you," I admitted. "You're strangely likeable."

"Oh, angels love me. They just hate admitting it. Your grandfather absolutely adores me."

I couldn't tell if he was lying or not, but I decided it didn't matter. "Any ammunition I can use against my grandfather that won't cost me in a bargain?"

"Of course. Tell him his big brother sends him a hug and kisses. And pretend to kiss him on the cheek for me."

A laugh burst out of me. Some requests were easy to fulfill, and I'd enjoy watching my grandfather's reaction. "I'll do that."

"As a special bonus, just so your grandfather knows I was toying with his precious little grandson," the Devil said before giving me a peck on the cheek. "Do pass that along for me, Samuel."

Perkins choked, but before I could worry something was wrong, he laughed so hard he cried. "This is amazing. *The* Devil just kissed you. I can't wait to tell Bailey about this."

Bailey would spend hours trying to purify my cheek, and I'd enjoy every minute of it. "Please do."

The Devil laughed. "If only you were a little less balanced. You'd make a glorious incubus. Alas, I'll have to be satisfied with the mayhem that trails behind you and your bride. Here is the knowledge you need to know but that your relatives have been hesitant to inform you. First, I'm technically one of your grand uncles—or great uncle, depending on which way you like it. Your grandfather is one of my brothers, which is why that little kiss will drive him wild."

Knowledge was power, and my brows shot up at the Devil bothering to claim a relationship with *me*. "I can't tell if that's interesting or terrifying, but I'm going to invite you over for dinner on Easter because I can."

Satan tossed his head back and laughter boomed out of him. "I do love when I get to toy with my brothers, and so many of them are flitting around the mortal coil right now. This is related to your heritage as well. I know your grandfather has a rather secretive side to him. Sylvester, he calls himself now?"

"Yes, that's right."

"Well, you'll like this. Your 'incubus' grandfather? He's only technically an incubus. I converted him from a devil to a demon at his request, which is partially why you're so well balanced. You're part demon and part devil, which is why you have your particular form. I figured your grandfather would appreciate a slight edge. A Christmas present he doesn't know about."

"He doesn't know?"

"Not even archangels are completely infallible, and it's difficult enough when they're stuck on the mortal coil for so long. Also, a devil turned demon is better able to withstand angelic influence—and be better equipped to handle life in a triad. Despite appearances, I *do* like my brothers, even the annoying ones."

Something clicked, and I sucked in a breath. "Are you saying my grandfather is an archangel?"

"Why, yes, I may be saying something like that. He's Sariel. Christianity and the other religions have a slightly confused view of him. They like to say he has fallen. He has not. I suppose being a member of a triad might classify as fallen in their petty views, but *he* doesn't feel that way. It's the one thing we agree on. Triads are special—and the children of triads are even more special because they do not fall into either of our plans."

"They're what humans were meant to be," I said, thinking about my mother and how my grandfathers treated her. "And my grandmother was a special woman. It's more unusual two parts of the triad remained beyond her death, isn't it?"

"It wouldn't surprise me if Sariel and Agares form another triad should the right woman come along. Despite themselves, they enjoy being parents. Some are just like that. But I doubt that will happen until your mother's death. They really enjoy being parents, and they don't want your mother to experience the loss of a parent again."

Family, as always, was complicated. "Agares is not a minor devil."

"I see your education is not lacking," the Devil replied, his tone pleased. "He's not. And he still has his portfolio. He's just enjoying his time on the mortal coil. It's rare for the angelic and demonic—or even devilish—sides to be such close friends. But that's how triads should be. Some are more chaotic than others, of course."

I tried to imagine my grandfathers seriously fighting but couldn't. They bickered, but they did so with a certain amount of glee. "Of course. It's like putting a cat and a dog who hate each other on base principle in the same room together. Except in the case of my grandfathers, they like each other."

"They're known to cuddle up on the couch together when feeling sorry for themselves because their wife is gone. They'll get over it eventually."

"Are you saying I should invite them over for Easter, too?"

"I'd like that."

"Consider it done. Bring your wife, too."

"She'll like that. Thank you."

Perkins laughed. "This is the most bizarre conversation I've heard in my life, and that's an accomplishment because I know Bailey."

"So, with that out of the way, the next piece of information is about your wife."

I tensed. "Is something wrong with Bailey?"

"No, no. Not at all. She's just going to be more attuned to her divinity than before, and she'll need a conduit back. Anubis provided this already, but I'm going to give *you* the ability to be a conduit for her. I have been snooping on Anubis on this matter." The Devil's gaze fell on Sunny, who wagged her tail. He smiled, and the gentleness of his expression startled me. "You're a most excellent conduit, but two paths back is better than one, and he has the appropriate heritage as well. Anubis is simply too kind to be willing to discomfort his descendant. I've no scruples about torturing my nephew a little for his benefit."

"I'm against torture as a general rule, but if it will help Bailey, I'll do whatever is necessary."

"Excellent. I'll also work with Sunny as well, as this is my domain as much as it is your wife's. Fire is our element—although hers is different."

I sucked in a breath. "Hers is the fire of the sun. Yours is the fire of Hell."

"I love when my brothers produce smart children—and in her way, your mother is just as clever as you. She's figured out a lot of this on her own, although she's not sure which angel her father is. Her last guesses were Gabriel and Michael, and she met both with her father in the same room, so she's delightfully confused. She's a splendid little niece."

"Should I just call you my uncle?"

"Keeping track of the greats and the grands is so tedious."

I agreed; my family tree confused me on a good day. "Why does Bailey need a conduit?"

"When pushed too far, she'll transcend temporarily. Transcending involves abandoning the mortal coil for a period of time. However, because hers is temporary and will always be temporary, she needs to figure out a path to return here. She can only teleport where the sun shines. Your sun is not the same sun as the one that shines beyond the mortal coil."

"Amun-Ra. The sun god. She's one of his children, isn't she?"

"She's broken the rules, yes. She's one of his children," the Devil replied.

"So that mortal fucking asshole is Amun-Ra?"

"Not exactly."

I narrowed my eyes. "Is she the product of a triad?"

"It's more of a quartet, and a very odd one. Amun-Ra, who does prefer to be called Ra, if you please, gets bored. But he's a being of sunlight and fire; he never was all that good at manifesting on Earth, so he took over a human for a while. Her human father. This is where it gets complicated."

"So, Ra possessed Bailey's mortal asshole of a father?"

"Yes."

"Let me guess. Someone possessed Bailey's asshole of a mother, too."

"You're such a smart little nephew."

I groaned and bowed my head. Bailey's odd genetics

began making a sickening amount of sense. "And Ra is the product of other divines, isn't he?"

"So, so smart. And her divine mother is likewise the product of divines." The Devil grinned. "She's a first. A double possession so two naughty divines could indulge in each other. They forgot their actions could have consequences. It's entirely possible neither realize Bailey was born. When they learn, your wife will find herself the subject of doting parents. Perhaps for Christmas?"

My eyes widened. "Her mortal parents are not ideal people. She's having trouble accepting people could care for her."

"I'll make arrangements for Christmas and bring them along with your attire for your special day. She deserves a little joy, and I do enjoy tweaking *His* nose whenever I can. As for her mortal parents? No, they aren't ideal. There is a special place in my hell for them, as I do not appreciate when anyone mistreats members of my family—which she is thanks to marriage to you. That arrangement has already been made, and there is insufficient compassion in their darkened hearts to earn *His* mercy."

After what had happened at the courthouse, my grandfather had likely indulged in an angelic temper tantrum, aiding in the loss of two souls from the heavens.

The Devil smiled.

"Who is her mother?"

"A Cahuilla divine representative of the moon, Menily. That's why they did as they did. Their admiration for each other blurred some lines."

"Cahuilla?"

"A Native American tribe. Menily is a quiet divine, and as is the way of things, opposites attract. She is a good tempered and sweet divine of the night, a rather misunderstood guardian. Ra is of the day. They met in the middle, possessing a pair of amorous humans for their tryst. They would have conceived your wife without interference, but their magic infused the newly conceived child. Hers was a rather unique conception, really."

"Unique is one way to put it. Why does Bailey become a unicorn, then?"

"That would be the fault of one of her grandmothers," the Devil replied. "Epona. You should invite her, too. When you expose Epona's divinity to Ra's, it's sensible for the result to be a mix of the two. Cindercorns are the closest the mortal coil has to such a being, so that is what she became. It's even more complicated than that, truth be told, but I don't think there's sufficient paper to even attempt to draw that tangled family tree. Yours is bad enough, little nephew."

That it was. "And her immunities?"

"Her grandfather on her mother's side—her divine mother's side. Februus. He was, in the time of the Etruscans, a god of purification, death, wealth, and the underworld. She strongly inherited his purification magics. You should thank him for her resistance to death, too."

"I'm not sure how to invite them over for Easter or Christmas," I admitted. "I would."

"I can help you with that. I'll have to make arrangements for your wedding, anyway. I'll issue both invitations at once. I will enjoy informing Ra and Menily they produced a daughter. Tormenting them over their ignorance will be so very enjoyable. Ra will be rather put out with Anubis. It's going to be a delightful wedding."

"Wait. He'll be put out with Anubis?"

The Devil snickered and gestured to Sunny. "He knows,

of course. He figured it out when he saw her magics. There are limited divines who could create a child like Bailey. He's known from the first time he saw her in the courthouse, that Ra had brought forth a child into the mortal coil, and she carried with her the matured powers of all her line. Her inheritance from Ra is minor compared to the rest."

"Breathing fire and teleporting through sunlight is hardly minor!"

"Compared to the rest of what she can do? She has but an echo of her father's powers. But that is for the best. Otherwise, you would love living flame and be left with nothing to hold." The Devil patted my shoulder. "Come along, little nephew. Arthur, do watch over his little children for a while. They would be distressed should they witness what is required for my nephew to become a proper conduit for his wife."

Before I could protest leaving the children, the Devil seized my arm and silvery light enveloped me.

FIFTEEN

There's hope for you after all.

BAILEY

PERKETTE OFFERED me the bucket of napalm, which I devoured while she sorted my tack. I stopped eating long enough for her to strap my bridle into place before she went to work on the saddle. I ignored her work, eager to devour the spicy gel before someone came to their senses and decided to take it away from me.

My grandfather-in-law stood nearby, the kitten cradled in his arm while Blizzard sat on his foot. "Tiffany, as you are far less durable than my little granddaughter, do make sure you take care. Let her be the one to run head-long into danger while you stay back and cover her back."

"When an angel says I should mind my own business, even I'm smart enough to listen," my friend muttered.

"There's hope for you after all."

Tiffany sighed. "You're right, Bailey. Angels are assholes."

I paused long enough to whinny a laugh before chomping at my napalm.

"No one is going to take your napalm, little granddaughter. You can take your time with it and enjoy your treat."

I loved how the angel understood I chowed down on my life's true ambrosia.

"She loves napalm second only to her Samuel," the angel announced.

I swished my tail at that.

Tiffany chuckled and tightened the cinch. "Yes she does. And Sam loves all of his cops, even the pain in the ass ones, so even if Bailey wasn't already the founding member of Janet's fan club, she'd be itching to retrieve her personally. Janet's all right for now?"

"For now. I'm not allowed to interfere beyond that. Helping you watch the furry children doesn't count as interfering, either. Nor does dealing with the transportation of your vehicle." The angel glared at the SUV. "I'm quite tempted to teleport it to Las Vegas, as I rather do dislike cramming my wings into one of those... things."

I whinnied a laugh and licked the bucket clean. "No care how you get to Vay-gus. Just no hurt kit-ten and puppers."

"The kitten and puppy will be safe with me, as will your neutralizer stash." Sylvester shook out his wings. "Your rather impressive and perhaps unnecessary stash."

"We were worried about a rabies outbreak," Tiffany mumbled. "It could happen."

"But it won't. That is already written in the stars, and is a matter of the past. I am allowed to say that much. It will come in useful, but you didn't need that much. I recommend five pounds."

"I was bringing ten. I can make her another batch of napalm with the five extra pounds."

"That would be one way to handle the situation. Perhaps you should take fifteen pounds in case she needs a larger napalm snack. She does so enjoy her napalm snacks."

I pawed the bucket in search of even a drop of napalm, and I whined my disappointment when my search proved futile. "No more nay-palm. Is all gone. Why is it all gone?"

"It's gone because you ate it, little granddaughter. You have the weapons, Tiffany?" Sylvester asked, his tone amused.

My friend hesitated before replying, "I could use a pocket knife, a box cutter, and a sharpie."

Sylvester held out his hand and the three requested items appeared, landing on his palm with a soft thump. "By pocket knife, I assumed you meant one with extra gadgets. This one has thirty gadgets for your enjoyment."

"So cool," I whispered, flicking my ears forward. "What we need those for, Per-kette?"

"It's your bomb defusing kit."

I flattened my ears. "No need. Claws. Teeth. Eat payload."

"I need them if I have to draw for you to figure out what you can cut and eat, Bailey."

"I tell Perky you go play with bombs," I threatened, daring to be the one to bring my psycho-but-lovable friend back into line.

"That's cheating."

"No cheat. Im-por-tant. You no play with bombs this time."

Sylvester snickered. "The day has come, at long last, where my little granddaughter is the one being sensible. May all the angels of *His* heavens rejoice."

"Syl-ves-tur mean," I complained. "Asshole angel."

He laughed harder. "Go on your run, little granddaughter. I'm sure my little grandson will appropriately reward you for your good deeds."

I liked when Quinn rewarded me. Quinn liked his rewards sexy with a side dish of extra sexy. If he was particularly pleased with me, he'd shift, and I'd get to play with his serpents before he rewarded me.

Their bites only made everything better.

"You have to do the good deeds first before you're rewarded," the angel reminded me.

Asshole angel. I snorted, flattened my ears, and shot a thin stream of flame in his direction, careful to keep from singeing him or my pets. "You take care of my pets."

"They'll be perfectly safe," he promised. "I will even take your little kitten to a mortal vet for a checkup and any care she might need while you are off rescuing your cop."

"Okay." I tossed my head and presented my back to Perkette. "You mount. Hold tight. We run fast."

"What about your trail? We need that."

Oh, right. The trail. We'd gone off the path, but I hadn't ended the spell, either. Resetting the path wasn't too difficult. I just needed to concentrate, throw the equivalent of a magical temper tantrum, and stomp my hooves a few times to reset it. The real work had already been done.

I stomped a hoof on the asphalt, concentrated, and snorted flame, which burst into a shower of pink, sparkling light that condensed into a trail I could follow. It didn't follow the road as my magic typically did.

I supposed my magic understood I didn't need to follow a road.

"I'm pretty sure that's cheating," Perkette muttered.

"Less whine, more ride. We ride fast."

"Have a safe trip," Sylvester said, stepping forward and giving my nose a brisk rub. "When things get dicey, don't worry much. Where you go, my little grandson will always follow, even when you think it's impossible."

I turned my ears back at that. "You know something I don't."

"As always. There are reasons I'm not permitted to interfere this time. Had someone else not already interfered, I might've been inclined to exercise my free will more than *He* likes, but I'm confident the matter is in competent hands. Honestly, I'm having the time of my life right now. This is so gloriously convoluted."

I tilted my head and bumped my nose against the angel's hand, lipping at his fingers before asking, "But not good hands? Just comp-eh-tent ones?"

"Good hands wouldn't do the job quite as well. But while I would not say the hands are good, they're fair and competent. That's all I would ask for in this situation. You should hurry."

Perkette mounted, and her weight slammed onto my back. I grunted, waited until she relaxed and was confident of her seat, and bolted west in search of Janet. I hit top speed in several strides, a trick I only did when Perkette rode me, caught a beam of light, and chased the sun west.

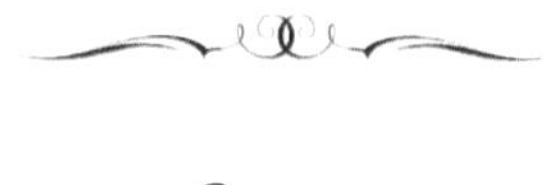

QUINN

IN THE FUTURE, I'd think twice before telling someone to go to hell. All in all, the Lord of Lies had a pretty nice home, although I found the temperature far colder than I liked. The long hallway of dark granite with painted, vaulted ceilings, reminded me of a full cathedral, and I held my breath while taking in the artwork overhead.

"It's like the Sistine Chapel," I whispered.

"What can I say? I'm a masochist."

I shot the Devil a look. "I fail to see how you receive sexual gratification from a painting."

The Devil laughed. "I don't, but it's so much fun toying with my mortal guests. Michelangelo spent time here for his sins, but rather than inflict the purest of miseries on him, I struck a bargain with him. He would paint the ceilings of my home before I gifted him with a second chance of life. I'm an asshole like that."

He was? I admired the ceiling even more, noting how instead of mortal man, *He* reached out to touch the Devil instead, depicted as a flaming incubus who shed golden light in his wake. "Is that your true form?"

"No, not quite. I'm an angel, Sam. Should he have seen my true form, it would have destroyed his soul. I can create a likeness without this risk, but my form is not for mortal eyes. It's as close as a mortal can stand—for how I am now. For all I'm considered fallen, my true form is still that of an angel." The Devil regarded me with a smirk. "You'd be able to withstand most of it, but it would leave you changed."

"Pass," I replied.

He laughed.

"Still, I'm definitely putting in some second thoughts about telling someone to go to hell."

"You should, especially once I've finished with you. Your word will hold more sway than you anticipate," the Devil replied. "And anyway, if you think this is chilly, you should try the heavens sometime. The crystal road? It's ice. Heaven is a cold place despite mortals portraying it as a paradise," my uncle replied, grinning at me and releasing my arm. "As for my home? It's called air conditioning, Sam. I enjoy it almost as much as my wife, who likes to view the entire house as her personal freezer. While my flames can rival that of even a star, hell isn't all fire and brimstone. It's personal for every soul I claim. And despite what most believe, the punishments always fit the crimes. For some, my hells are eternal misery. For others, it's a mere blip before they've done their time and are given the choice to try life again, like Michelangelo. Eternity isn't as long as some like to think, and for all I think my father can be an annoying dick, *He's* not always an asshole."

Sometimes, I questioned the relationship of God and Satan. "Isn't the general belief system that you two are the first creations? That there can't be one of you without the other?"

"That's right. But he's still, technically, my father. I exist only because *He* exists. It's one of those annoying universal laws. And while I am the Lord of Lies, you'll find I'm a disgustingly honest fellow."

I could work with disgustingly honest and cheerfully sleazy.

The Devil laughed. "Now, before I worry your friend too much, it's time to attune you to the flames. Your bride would become a little too hot to handle if I didn't give you some of my ancestry properly. As I said before, your heritage is what allowed your angelic side to have some dominance—a necessity for you to exist as you do. I'm going to adjust the scales a little so you're a little more devil and a little less demon, but you'll still be more angel than both. I'm sure your grandfather is going to love this. It's like a Christmas present to myself."

"Should I be worried?"

"I'm about to put you through hell. So yes, you should be."

I sighed. "And this will let me become a conduit for Bailey?"

"And let you cuddle with her even when she's a unicorn snorting flame. You'll be immune to her fires. Or, more accurately, you'll be attuned with them, so they won't hurt you. Someone dumping a bucket of napalm on you and lighting it on fire would still hurt. I can only do so much with what I have to work with, but as my brother so helpfully bound you to her, I have more leeway than usual. For once, I'm so glad I had to spank one of my devils. I don't usually, you know. Fulfilling their bargains is a pain in the ass. But you held the only outstanding bargain, which made it worth my while. Otherwise, I would've just left him hanging for a while."

"And here I thought my family was confusing before I added you to it." Shaking my head, I wondered just how crazy my family tree truly was.

"It's complicated."

I laughed. "Which part? That I have two grandfathers on my mother's side? That my father's side is essentially the same? I still don't know if I have any of my gorgon grandmother's DNA."

"You do. Gorgon reproduction isn't far off from a triad, and the magic that makes a gorgon egg become fertile helped with your father's conception. While he wasn't born from a gorgon's egg, your gorgon grandmother's magic did help make your father. For the record, it was Emilie's magic. She's since gone on to stay with *Him* for a while."

For some reason, I found that knowledge comforting. "And Beauty and Sylvester?"

"They told you the truth. Their eggs broke within their mother."

I sighed. "Are you allowed to tell me the state of their mother's soul?"

"She was reincarnated and her seed of life was given to a mother who would've otherwise lost her child. A rainbow baby, if you will. I sent one of my succubi to resolve the infant's physical problems, and I provided her soul so the child could survive. I'm gentler with reincarnations than *He* is. For all *He* is the Heavenly Father, I'm the Sun in Glory, the Lord of the Morning—and new dawns are my specialty."

"Yet you're the Father of Sin, the Lord of Lies, and the Shepherd of Lost Souls."

"I'm misunderstood," the Devil replied with a grin. "Their father's soul was likewise shepherded. They'll meet again. Some things are written in the stars, and *He* is still new to *His* profile, so *His* heart is still soft. When *He* asks for a favor shepherding souls, I do tend to go along with it. *He* does loathe asking me, and sometimes, heaven isn't a destination but a second chance to live life with a true love. They earned their heaven, however much it disgusts me to admit it. That's a good way to earn *His* favor, in case you didn't know. A selfless sacrifice always catches *His* attention."

I sucked in a breath. "So their father is dead."

"You already knew that." The Devil smirked. "I like how mortals shut down and ignore what they can't readily understand. I've told you *He* is not a static being, and that a mortal ultimately takes the place of another mortal to wear *His* shoes for a while, and you just ignore it." The Devil snapped his fingers. "Humans are so entertaining."

While I had ignored it, I'd done so because I'd already known. I arched a brow at the Devil, well aware he was reading my mind, and kept the subject on the gorgon male. "I hadn't known for certain."

"*He* is a compassionate soul, and *He* rewards those who are deserving. Instead of an eternal heaven, they were given new life. *He* thought a second chance for their happiness was their due. As I said, *He* doesn't ask me for favors often."

"Yet you'll battle until the end of days."

"Ours is a dysfunctional family."

I blinked, and it sank in that if the Devil was my great uncle, that meant *He* was also a direct relation. "My family tree is fucked up."

The Devil laughed. "Indeed it is. And you're correct. Technically, you are a child of the Heavenly Host. It's amusing, really. Your Bailey is everything you are not. That's why you work so well together. And to put your mind at ease, you two have no relation to each other."

I arched a brow at that. "Knowing my lineage, I find that difficult to believe."

The Devil smiled. "From the beginning of time, never have your lines met until now. That is part of what makes you—and her—so interesting. Your children will change the world, just as you two have already changed the world."

I raised a brow at that. "We have?"

"You have," the Devil answered, and he gestured for me to follow him. "The rebirth of two phoenixes alone is enough to change the world, Sam. That act was the work of you both. That's a great deal of magic released on the mortal coil, which in turns wakens other older things. Your wife will change the world again when she puts that idiot who wishes to become a god into his place. And she will. That's written in the stars. The how of it is still to be decided, and I look forward to the show. Your Bailey? She is so creative. That's her nature. She blasts right beyond the obvious solutions to problems without any realization there's an easier way to go about her business."

I grimaced. I'd been around my family enough to understand some events would happen no matter what mortals did to stop it, and I disliked the idea that my bride was in the center of one of those events.

I definitely disliked the idea she'd blast right by the easier, simpler, and ultimately safer solution. "I'm going to go gray before Christmas," I groaned.

"Your hair is safe," my uncle said with laughter in his voice. "Bailey raising two phoenixes was also written in the stars. It would have happened, perhaps at a different time and a different date than when you foolishly faced your ex-wife alone, but it would have happened one way or another. The first time she laid a hand on them, they would've risen. And with her field of work? It was inevitable."

Sometimes, I truly hated the divine. Sighing, I followed the Devil through his palace of dark granite stone, pausing every now and then to admire the classical paintings on the ceilings.

Michelangelo had created true masterpieces for the Devil's enjoyment, and the images would haunt me for a long time to come, as he rewrote the entire bible from something closer to the Devil's perspective.

I halted at a depiction of Noah's flood, pointing at the shores of an icy island. "Is that a cindercorn?"

"Sharp eye. This isn't from my perspective on this one, by the way. This is the true history. When the world fell to the floods, the last remnants of humanity fled to the mountains.

This is the history of a vampiric family who survived along with some mortals and the last herd of cindercorns." The Devil joined me and smiled at the painting, pointing at a pale figure. "Do you see the pale woman there?"

"Yes, I do."

"She is another unicorn, and the cindercorns took her in and kept her safe until she could find others of her kind. Bailey is a descendant of her and the stallion there."

My eyes widened. "I thought you said she was descended from Epona."

"Her, too. Remember, most divines are born from mortal children who inherit the profile. The mortals who become divine still possess their mortality as an echo. Those echoes are within Bailey."

"Are they still alive? Her relatives in that painting?"

The Devil shook his head. "They died long ago. I believe one of her great-great grandmothers is still alive. A standard unicorn. She's the last of her line for the cindercorns. And while her genetics are rather extensive, your genetics will lead to interesting children. For better or worse, they'll take after one of you more strongly than the other, but I wouldn't be surprised if you produce a winged cindercorn or variants of yourself with a few extra abilities. Either way, you'll have your hands full, especially with the other children."

"I'm going to need a bigger house," I predicted.

"You're probably right." The Devil halted and opened a door, gesturing me to walk inside. I raised a brow at the massive bathroom, which was large enough to fit the entirety of my living room inside. "This is the best place for this work, as I don't want to disturb my wife with your screaming."

Great. I just loved when someone informed me I'd be screaming. "This is going to hurt that much?"

"It sure is. There's only one way to attune you to her magic and make you a conduit, and that involves a lot of exposure to her type of magic. Fortunately for you, I'm the Devil. Little is beyond my power. It's just going to hurt a lot. I recommend the tub, as it'll make the cleanup much easier. Go on, strip. Wouldn't want to incinerate your clothes or get blood all over them."

"You know how I was thinking hell wasn't all that bad?"

The Devil chuckled. "I did find that rather amusing."

"I was wrong."

BAILEY

NOTHING AMUSED me quite as much as trotting up to a gas station to get a hit of diesel. Perkette headed inside armed with the FBI clearance sheet allowing any gas station in the continental United States to feed me diesel, and once she got through the paperwork, she filled a bucket so I could have a drink. It lacked the punch of napalm, but it did a good job of keeping me toasty warm in preparation for the rest of the run west.

At our current pace, I expected we'd arrive in Las Vegas before sunset, with a total transit time of three and a half hours.

"You doing okay?" Perkette asked, waiting until I slurped up the contents of the bucket and refilling it before putting the nozzle away.

"Not much tired," I replied before returning to my sacred

duty of consuming as much diesel as possible. "You have enough for more nay-palm after we find Janet?"

Whoever had taken Janet would experience me at my finest, hopped up on my favorite fuel and ready for a party. I'd make the party so memorable nobody with a single grain of sense would touch one of my cops ever again. I hadn't even had my first shift as an officer, and I was already as bad as Quinn.

He'd be proud.

"I can make one small batch, yes. Thank your grandfather for that; the extra five pounds I bought will give you a nice batch of napalm. If we really need more, I can get the FBI to dish out for the supplies. Unlike the CDC, they're willing to work with your napalm habit. Banning it outright is typical CDC stupidity. If the situation requires it, why keep it out of your arsenal? Those bastards were willing to expose you to a damned *nuke*. Fuckers."

"I said no on that one, re-mem-bur?"

"I was very proud of your restraint. I was too stunned to say a word when they said what they wanted to test."

"For two whole min-utes. Then you mad, very mad, ask if they were trying to make Quinn rampage and rip their hearts from their chests."

"You've really improved with your English, Bailey. Well done. Drink up so I can give the bucket back and we can get this show on the road. I don't suppose you have any idea how far away Janet is?"

I shook my head. "May-be if have map can tell?"

Perkette skipped into the gas station and returned several minutes later with a road atlas, which she opened. "Try Nevada first?"

I bobbed my head before drinking more diesel.

Once she had the page open to Nevada, I concentrated on the map and tapped the paper with my claw. Ever since the incident with Quinn's ex-wife, I'd found my magic more cooperative. I couldn't tell if ambrosia exposure had done the trick, but I didn't need any supplies to make a map show some of its secrets.

A pink, swirling light appeared a short distance east of Las Vegas, smack dab in the middle of nowhere. "What here? There road?" I asked.

Perkette checked her phone, referencing the map. "A gypsum mine."

"Why Janet at gyp-sum mine?"

"That's a very good question." Perkette tapped at her screen, and her brows rose. "Apparently, it's closed. Abandoned."

I read between the lines: it was the perfect place to stash a cop and perform all sorts of illegal activities—or start a new gorgon hive without humans getting in the way. I'd learned all about that from Quinn's ex-wife.

Starting gorgon hives just loved taking over abandoned buildings so they could expand their numbers before legitimizing themselves. I flattened my ears, guzzled the rest of my gas, and restrained my urge to snort fire at the thought of having to deal with more gorgons. "Gor-gons?"

"It's entirely possible. That's totally the type of place a hive would move into."

I turned my head and regarded Perkette's collection of firearms, which also included mine. "May need more guns."

"And more napalm. We could rescue Janet and burn the whole place down."

"Can get you more in-gree-dee-ants. For nay-palm."

"You just want to burn an entire mine down."

"I like fire."

"I know you do, but don't you think that's excessive? It's a pretty big place."

"They take Janet, they deserve fire."

"While I'm not disputing that, shouldn't our first line of offense be something other than burn the whole thing down?"

"Res-cue Janet, then burn whole thing down. Get order right. Res-cue first. Then burn. Burn, baby, burn!"

"This isn't going to end well," Perkette predicted.

"This end great. We res-cue Janet, burn mine down, diss-ee-pline gor-gons. Take kids. If they have kids, they now my kids."

"You can't just kill a gorgon hive and take the children, Bailey."

"Can, too!"

"You really can't."

"They take Janet. They no good par-rents. I bet-ter par-rent."

Perkette sighed. "But Sam already adopted two children, Bailey! And you have two dogs and a cat now. You can't add more."

"If they have kids, I take kids. And Janet. Kids need bet-ter par-rents. Quinn good par-rent! May-be ask for more kids for Christmas? Yes? He like that? Me like that!"

"I'm just going to hope they don't have any kids, because I don't know what I'm going to tell Sam if you add to the mayhem. More than you already are. And yes, he'd love having kids of his own because he's Sam and loves children."

"You tell Quinn I want kids. Quinn okay because he like kids. Stop com-plain-ing. We run. Take buc-ket back."

Perkette sighed, returned the bucket to the gas station

attendant, and mounted. "This is going to blow up in our faces, isn't it?"

"No, no. It blow up in my face while I have fun with nay-palm. You stay safe distance with Janet. Will be good."

"If you ask me to hold your beer, I'm sedating you," Perkette warned.

"Me no drink beer. You can hold my empty bucket of nay-palm instead."

"Heaven help us all."

I whinnied my laughter, waited until Perkette settled in the saddle, and headed west, catching a ray of sunshine the instant I reached top speed.

SIXTEEN

Your grandfather's a pain in my ass.

QUINN

THE DEVIL PINNED me in the bath tub, shoved a pill down my throat, and said, "This is going to hurt."

Great. I opened my mouth to ask what he'd given me when fire swept through my body. Instead of questioning the Devil, I yelped.

As promised, it hurt, but the pain faded after a brief but intense flash. The next thing I knew, the tub had become a great deal more crowded. My visual perspective had changed, granting me a broader field of vision than I expected, but colors seemed somehow muted and less vibrant.

"Oh, that's unexpected. I guess it's easier to shift when you're already used to transformations. Well, that's something. Memorize this form, nephew. It's a good trick in your incubus arsenal when your wife is being stubborn and doesn't want to shift back to human. When you stand, be aware you have four hooves instead of hands and feet."

How was I supposed to memorize a form?

"Your grandfather's a pain in my ass," the Devil complained. "Not teaching you all of your incubus tricks. You need to remember the feel of it. Concentrate. Focus on the part of you that feels the oddest. That's usually a good way to remember the feel."

Wait. *Hooves?* I blinked, lifted my head, and looked down. After seeing my wife as a cindercorn so many times, I recognized the black and red mottling in my fur and the tips of the retractable claws peeking out of my hooves. I snorted, and flame burst out of my nose. The flame's color captured my attention, bright and vibrant compared to everything else.

"Best class of transformative money and magic can create," the Devil announced. "And because you're already a shapeshifter, you can get back to your human form unlike most. Now, I did meddle a little to ensure you became a cindercorn; if left to your own devices, you would've become a rather impressive serpent of the dragon variety."

Dragon? I lifted my head to stare at the Devil with wide eyes. I loved Bailey, and I loved when she pranced around as a unicorn, but I could be a *dragon?* Because of my gorgon heritage, I'd skipped out on the transformative tests, as nobody knew what would happen. The CDC had gone along with it, as they weren't sure what would happen, either.

I'd need to find out if I could pop transformatives like Bailey and shift back at my whim.

"As a matter of fact, yes. It's one of the perks of being a shapeshifter. The CDC hasn't clued in to that anomaly yet; lycanthropes, shapeshifters, and most demons can be influenced by transformatives, but thanks to their genetics, can transform back to human even with the potent drugs. You'll be able to do that parlor trick one of these days, but when you do, it'll really piss your wife off. Dragons are slightly more impressive than cindercorns. Unlike her, you're not a natural cindercorn. I'm just taking advantage of your devilish and demonic ancestry to allow you to shift into her form. Of the appropriate gender, of course. You were aware incubi can shift into any species they want, yes?"

I nodded.

"The transformative is just paving the way with a few nudges from me. You were supposed to be in agonizing pain for at least twenty minutes. Unfair, dodging the first of your torture sessions."

The Devil had a wicked sense of humor. Aware I could poke holes in his tub with my claws, I rolled and got to my hooves, mimicking how Bailey rose when she lounged about on her favorite rug. I opened my mouth and experimented with my equine lips, which didn't form the shapes I needed to speak very well.

"That part I can't help you with. It's unlikely you'll be mastering English anytime soon. Honestly, it's impressive your bride can at all."

Being told I couldn't lit a fire under my ass, and I twisted my ears back. "Can."

The Devil sighed. "You're definitely my nephew. You must drive my brother absolutely wild. Keep doing it. I approve. I'm going to be your favorite uncle in no time. Just think the questions you want to ask. It'll be faster that way."

I wanted to know why he switched between bride and wife when discussing Bailey, and I stared at him while waiting for an answer.

"Blame our family for that one. They can't decide how to

address her, either. You're just as bad, too. You like wife when you're being particularly possessive, and you prefer bride when you want to be romantic or she's wrapped you around her finger even more than usual. That's not hard. She just has to smile for that. You're hopeless."

I was. Careful to avoid destroying the tub, I stepped out onto the bathroom tiles, keeping an eye on my hooves and retractable claws.

"So, now that you won't be immediately incinerated due to exposure to hellfire, shall we move on to the next portion of the process? This part will hurt quite a bit, but you'll find it worth the price. Mostly. As you can't teleport without help, when you become a conduit, you won't relocate yourself to another plane; that's your bride's problem. She can teleport, so once she uses her magic to its full potential, she'll transport herself to a different plane. Her controlled teleportation is limited. Her real range goes beyond what she can control, thus the need for a conduit. What a conduit is, in this case, is a beacon she can teleport to. So, once you're properly attuned, all you or your Sunny will have to do is create a beam of light for her to catch. That's actually simpler than it sounds—at least it will be once I'm finished with you."

The Devil pointed at my left leg, and I looked down to discover my grandfather's bracelet glowing through my fur.

I lifted my leg for a closer look; I'd never poked much at Bailey's left foreleg while she was a unicorn looking for the mark; I'd assumed it was still present in some form or another.

"That's the key to this working, truth be told, so you'll have to thank my brother for that later. Once you've been exposed sufficiently to fire, you'll just need to concentrate on your binding. That will reflect to your bride's, and will open the conduit. Once again, after I finish forging the connection between you two. Now, follow along. We're on a schedule."

For someone who thought he was on a schedule, the Devil strolled along without a care in the world, leading me through the high-vaulted hallways until he reached a door leading outside. Lakes of fire and brimstone merrily burned and bubbled away, with the nearest geysers of flame bursting towards the black sky close enough I could stretch my neck and touch them if I really wanted. Some form of magic kept its heat from me, and I appreciated the Devil's air conditioning system once I realized how close the flames came to his home.

"It is pretty impressive, isn't it?"

I bobbed my head.

"All right, little nephew. In you go!" The Devil pressed his hands to my hindquarters and shoved me into the nearest molten pool. "Have fun. I'll be back for you in an hour. Try not to burn the house down."

BAILEY

PERKETTE MADE me go to every damned FBI building in the state of Nevada for napalm before deciding I might have enough, including her homemade batch, to cause trouble at the gypsum mine. I disliked having to carry buckets of fluid on my back, as they tended to bounce into my ribs where they hung from my saddle.

I also wanted to gobble them down, as I was tired, cranky, and ready for a nap.

"You can't nap," Perkette informed me while triple-checking our guns. In the distance, the mine loomed, and the large, central dome gleamed in the setting sunlight. "We have to go rescue Janet."

According to my trail, I'd find her within the domed structure. Amusingly, my magic had common sense; it ended at the fence surrounding the compound, as though afraid it would expose my rescue attempt if it proceeded any farther.

"Re-move sad-dle, re-move bri-dle," I said, giving my mane a shake. "Need bag of neutralizer around neck. May need for Janet. You shoot people not me or Janet, yes?"

"Shooting people is a bigger crime than a misdemeanor," Perkette complained.

"Death in de-fense of an-other is no crime. You no get re-cord. Any-one who chase us bad person who kid-nap Janet. Unless Quinn show up. Or Perky. Don't shoot them. Or chil-dren. Unless they're evil children?"

"How am I supposed to tell if they're evil children?"

"If try to kill Janet they evil and only look like children. Like mini demon devil things."

"You realize you married someone who is part demon, right?"

"But he sex demon, not kill Janet demon," I replied in my most solemn voice. "Very sexy sex demon. Very."

Perkette snickered. "I love your brain so much. Are you sure you don't want me to go in with you?"

"You no im-mune to pet-ri-fi-cation. I im-mune to pet-ri-fi-cation. I look forward to stomping bad gor-gons."

"This is true." Perkette sighed. "Please don't get into any trouble. Please don't burn down the entire mine."

"But what if I want to? They kid-nap Janet!"

"Bailey. It's an entire mine! You can't burn it down with the amount of napalm you have." Perkette slid off my back, removed both buckets of napalm from my saddle, and set them on the ground in front of me. "Two little buckets. That's not enough napalm for you to burn it all down."

"I make it be enough," I replied.

"You're insane, aren't you?"

"You just fi-gure this out? Silly Per-kette."

"You're right. It was obvious. Are you sure you want to go in there alone?"

"I be stealthy like ninja. Res-cue Janet. Then find out who and why and burn them!"

"Shouldn't you try to arrest them?"

"No?"

"Bailey."

"What? They kid-nap Janet. Burn them!"

"You can't just burn people you don't like, Bailey."

"Why the fuck not? They take Janet!"

"Death is too quick and easy of a punishment."

I thought about that for a few minutes. "May-be?"

"Not maybe. Definitely. You can't just burn them, Bailey."

"Why not? They take Janet."

"You are a one-track mind hellbent on death, doom, and destruction."

"No, I like fire. Not same."

"With you, it is the same. You like fire so much you create death, doom, and destruction in your wake."

"More doom and de-struc-shun. Less death."

"That's true. Fine. Do what you want." Perkette opened up the first bucket of napalm and offered it to me. "Just be careful. I'd hate to have to explain how I let you get yourself killed."

"Let is strong word. How you stop me?"

"I'm using this argument in my defense," my friend announced.

I gave the napalm my full attention. Sometimes, the only way to handle Perkette's brand of crazy was to ignore it.

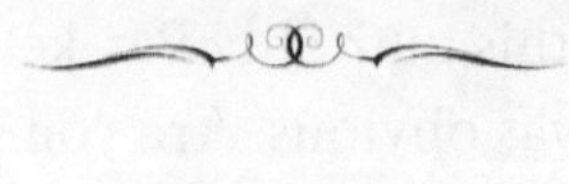

QUINN

THE LORD of Lies needed an attitude adjustment, and I contemplated shoving my horn right up his ass for locking me outside. No matter where I stepped, I encountered flame of some sort. Sometimes, it burst from the ground in plumes of steam. The lava had a tendency to follow me around like a puppy, which was disconcerting enough, especially when it liked to wrap around my hooves and legs.

That hurt enough I bolted without fail, often uncovering more of the Devil's trickery and handiwork.

I lost count of the times I'd plunged into lakes of fire, pockets of steam and superheated gases, and lava tubes. Nothing ruined my day quite like being dunked head to hoof in molten stone.

Sometime after I lost count of how many times I'd gone for a fiery swim, the Devil took pity on me and provided a solid patch of ground. He stepped through a shimmering curtain of flame and laughed at me.

I'd put in plenty of thought on how best to stab my bastard of an uncle, but I hurt too much to follow through. I hadn't known it'd been possible for horns to hurt, but mine did.

"It's just a little pain, and now your tolerance for the flames is much stronger. You did just fine," he announced.

I flattened my ears and snorted flame, waiting for him to get on with the conduit portion of the torture session.

"Sorry, little nephew. You get at least another hour playing outside before you can be a good conduit." The devil planted his foot against my rump and shoved me into the nearest puddle of flame. "Okay, I'm lying. You don't need another hour. I just wanted to push you into the fire because anyone else would start screaming and whine about how cruel I am to them. I'm the Devil. I'm supposed to be cruel. You're just slightly miffed I'm inconveniencing you, and it's delightful—except for the first time you were fully submerged. That was appropriately the fiery pits of hell. It's delightful, isn't it?"

I stepped out of the flaming puddle and shook my head. No, it was not delightful.

My horn was not supposed to hurt, and I had a much better understanding of why Bailey had complained after ramming a steel door while escaping my ex-wife's incubus.

"So, the conduit part. It's rather simple, actually. You have to teleport to her once and establish the connection. As I'm a terrible cheater, I will do this for you. Once the connection is forged, you can do whatever it is cindercorns do when performing rescue missions, as that's the whole point of this, is it not? To rescue your little cop. She's a delight, too, but you really should leash her—or give her to your bride as a Christmas present. I am pleased you decided to adopt her into your station, though. That'll make it easier to keep track of her." My uncle paused, and then he laughed. "You're such an incubus, surrounding yourself with difficult women."

I flicked an ear back at that and glared at my uncle. While true, did he have to say it? Once Bailey started coming to the station daily, it would be glorious mayhem married to overprotective zeal and wrapped in a beautiful package of determination. Amanda would join forces with Bailey, and in no time, the women would completely take over.

Then again, knowing Amanda, I'd have some of the best trained officers in the world, especially once news of Janet's kidnapping spread to everyone in the station. Janet would be attending self-defense courses with Bailey, I'd be attending them because our schedules would finally align, and if I attended them, most of my officers would be squeezing time in their schedules to go to lessons, too.

And if *they* went to lessons in self-defense, I foresaw their wives and children attending, too.

All in all, my station had issues.

"But you'll have issues while being exceptionally well-trained. Anyway, your bride is currently consuming napalm and is planning on attempting a rescue mission on her own. As I have missed quite a few of your birthdays and other holidays, I thought I'd be nice and help you forge said conduit so you can join her. It'll be more fun that way. You can storm the place together. Alas, the delightful young Tiffany didn't bring enough napalm to allow your bride to go on a true bender. I, in the utter goodness of my heart, am able and willing to assist you in this matter."

Bailey plus napalm equaled mass destruction.

"This is true." The Devil snickered. "You and Bailey plus napalm will be even greater destruction, and there's nothing I like more than good old-fashioned destruction. That, plus it would be useful if you're covering her back while she's getting into trouble. Also, your great-grandfather is most correct. You're going to panic delightfully. His attempts to appease you with a chill pill, however, will be a complete and total failure. You'll just have to cope in other fashions. In this case, it involves a lot of fire and defending your turf and your cop. Oh, and Tiffany. Her, too. As a bonus, you'll have ready access to napalm. You and your wife can indulge together."

The more the Devil talked, the less I liked what he had to say, and I heaved a sigh. No matter what I did, I couldn't catch a break. Then again, two cindercorns on a napalm bender could be interesting.

For someone.

I weighed the advantages of going on a napalm bender against the resulting hangover, narrowing my eyes.

"You can't catch a break, but you can get a good rush from the best napalm ever made. You're going to need a full tank to keep up with your bride. Admit it, nephew. You like the idea of keeping up with her for a change. Now, hurry it up. You have napalm to eat and a swift kick in the ass to endure so the connection between you two is fully opened. Also, I am not at all responsible for anything you say or do while under the influence of napalm. Just be happy I'm giving it to you. Your bride is on napalm limitations. You're not. Yet."

Yet. I hung my head low and groaned.

Nowhere in any of my plans had I considered going on a napalm bender.

"Don't worry. You won't be quite as bad as she is. I don't really care about anyone else, but I'll be entertained."

The next time I accepted help from the Devil, I would remember he had a wicked sense of humor, no boundaries, and a love for chaos and mayhem—and I'd also remember he was the Devil.

My uncle patted my shoulder. "It's okay. I forgive you. It's just everyone else you have to worry about."

If it meant being able to help Bailey later, I'd deal with the consequences of dealing with the Devil, and I'd invite the whole family over to my house for Easter with a smile.

The Devil chuckled. "Don't forget about the wedding. Invite everyone to that, too. Now, come along. You have a long evening ahead of you."

I was beginning to believe a miracle
would be required.

BAILEY

WHILE THE FBI hadn't barred me from napalm, I had no realistic way of pulling another 120 Wall Street stunt on the gypsum mine. Without a tanker, or the magic required to transform water into napalm, the best I could do was light everything I could on fire and let it burn.

First, I needed to get Janet out of the building before I burned it, which would be an interesting endeavor. I excelled at blowing things up—or stopping things from blowing up.

I needed a few classes on hostage recovery, stat.

I suspected Quinn would be dragging me to classes to make sure I wasn't an incompetent Chief of Police starting the instant we made our way home. One day, preferably before I died of old age, I would stop attending classes of some sort. Maybe. If I asked my grandfather-in-law, could he arrange for a miracle?

I was beginning to believe a miracle would be required to turn my life into something almost sane.

As requested, Perkette tied a bag of neutralizer around my neck so I could treat Janet if she was petrified as I suspected. Once she was mobile, getting her out would be simple enough.

I could run really, really fast despite the lack of sunlight offering me a quick and easy lift. Not only could I run fast, I could stab obstructions with my horn and claw them into submission. Janet could ride, mostly. I hoped she'd be able to ride without a saddle or bridle.

They'd get in the way, and if I had to start burning things in earnest, they'd fry. I didn't have another saddle or bridle if I broke mine.

I really needed a new set—and a spare.

As the sunset light had grown too dim to ride, I jumped over the fence and crept towards the dome. I took my time, hoping the darkness would mask my presence from anyone watching. Then again, would anyone truly be looking?

Nobody expected a fire-breathing unicorn to show up in the middle of the desert, far enough away from civilization to be inconvenient. I checked over my shoulder to make sure Perkette had remained behind.

She had.

I took a few more steps, double checked the mad scientist with a fetish for causing trouble hadn't followed, and plowed into something large and warm. I snorted, scrambled back, tripped over my own hooves, and crashed to the hard-packed ground.

Ouch.

I'd seen enough incubi to recognize one, although I'd

never seen one in a suit sheathed in flame before. I scrambled upright to discover he wasn't alone.

Where had an incubus gotten a very large cindercorn? I flattened my ears and bared my teeth over how much larger the stallion was compared to me. He braced his legs and shook his head, and heat radiated from his fur.

"I stole him," the incubus replied, and I snorted over his reading of my thoughts. "Yes, I am. Also, I'm not an incubus. I'm your uncle."

I blinked. I had an uncle who was an incubus who didn't believe he was an incubus?

The incubus-whatsit pointed at the cindercorn. "Merry Christmas. That's your incubus, and I helped him learn how to be more useful to you in the future."

What the hell was going on? I flicked an ear forward, as there was only one incubus I considered to be mine. "Quinn? That Quinn? Quinn cin-der-corn? Not gor-gon in-cu-bus whats-it doo-hickey?"

"He is. And as he's my little nephew, you're my little niece, so you get to call me your uncle. You're welcome. Oh, don't mind him. He's not used to teleporting, so he'll need a few moments to regain his bearings. Do have fun rescuing your cop, try not to get too excited until after you get her to safety, and try not to cause too much trouble. I mean, you're going to cause trouble. That's inevitable. You're involved. Also, I fed him a rather ridiculous amount of potent napalm, so if you need something to be lit on fire, he can do it."

I had an uncle? I sucked in a breath at that. What was I supposed to do with an uncle? How did uncles even work? Were uncles like crazy versions of parents? While I liked Quinn's parents, mine needed a trip straight to hell. "But who you? Which crazy family member you brother of? Why you bring Quinn? Quinn babysit!"

The incubus-whatsit cackled his laughter. "You'll find out soon enough. To begin with, your children are perfectly safe, so don't you worry about that."

"Puppy, too?"

"Your puppy is safe, too," the incubus-whatsit replied. "And I'm not a whatsit. I'm the Devil."

First, Quinn had a gorgon for a grandfather, an incubus for a grandfather, an angel for a grandfather, divines for great-grandparents, and now I had to deal with *the* Devil?

Wait. Could the Devil send my parents straight to hell?

The Devil snickered. "It won't be a straight trip to hell. There will be some memorable detours, one of which will occur near Christmas. I'm a fan of just desserts, and this one will be particularly delicious. Like chocolate but better. I have a special place prepared for them."

I shot Quinn an accusing look. "You very bad. Bad Quinn. You no tell me the Devil part of your crazy family."

The way the cindercorn lowered his head, flopped his ears to the sides, and heaved a pained sigh did a good job of convincing me he was my Quinn. "I didn't know," he mumbled. "I'm sorry, my beautiful."

What didn't look like Quinn but acted like Quinn and sounded like Quinn was very probably Quinn, and I had no complaints with having Quinn accessible as a stallion for my future enjoyments—and for lighting things on fire. "Oh! You talk good. You be able to do cin-der-corn more later? We have fun. Lots fun. And fire. You stick head in fire-place, too. I like this. Fire-place big enough for even you. You big." I spent a few moments admiring him. "You very big. You really Quinn, yes? Proof."

"For the record, she's very ready to accept you're you, but she's trying to be a responsible adult for once in her life. It's rather endearing," the Devil said, the tip of his tail twitching. "Also, I'm the brother of your angelic grandfather-in-law."

I knew just enough about Christianity to understand the Devil only claimed kinship with a very select group of angels, whom humanity wisely viewed with a mix of fear and awe.

Sylvester was an archangel? I snorted, my eyes widening. "Noooooo. Angels assholes. Archangels extra assholes." It explained so much. Only an archangel would chase me around, plow me over with his magic, and make me his bitch. I moaned and joined Quinn in hanging my head. "Not fair."

"I know. It's terrible." The Devil patted my shoulder. "I've cloaked our presence here for the moment so you aren't discovered prematurely. I thought you would enjoy staging a rescue with your husband, and I owed him as part of a bargain."

Fury swept through me, and I whipped my head around and bit Quinn's shoulder. As a cindercorn, he could handle a few bites, even if I caught him with my teeth. "Bad! No bargain with Devil. You *bad*."

The Devil snickered. "Technically, he bargained with a lesser devil."

"That even *worse*," I snapped, giving my husband another bite. Quinn tasted deliciously of sulfur and napalm, and I switched from biting to licking. "Oh. You tasty. Dipped in nay-palm for my enjoyment."

Quinn sighed. "I didn't bargain on *purpose*. I did a devil a favor. It wasn't really a bargain. Well, okay. It was a bargain. It was more of an open-ended favor I held over that devil's head.

It was a good bargain for me because that devil needed my help. And I wasn't dipped in napalm, but I now have a rather disturbing understanding of why you enjoy it so much."

What the hell? Quinn could talk better than I could as a cindercorn. "Not. Fair. Why you talk so good?"

Quinn blinked, and despite the darkness, I could make out him trying to stare down his own nose in the general direction of his mouth. "Huh."

"I helped," the Devil announced, his tone smug.

"You help me, too, or I bite you!" I darted forward and snapped my teeth at Satan. "Want to talk nice, too. And no bar-gain. You do it be-cause I niece and you have to spoil me. That how being niece works, right? Never been a real niece before. Have not met Quinn's father's brother or sister people, either. You should do it because angels assholes and archangels extra assholes. You no be asshole."

Quinn laughed and intervened, pushing me backwards so I couldn't bite the Devil. "I'd be sorry for her, but I'm really not."

"I will consider rewarding you for good behavior with making communicating easier on you, should you rescue your cop without major mishap. I've interfered enough, so you two have fun storming the castle." The Devil vanished.

"I like that movie," I admitted. "We watch it when we get home with chil-dren?"

Quinn laughed and brushed his muzzle against mine. "Whatever you want, my beautiful. This hadn't been part of my plan, but I like it far more than sending you in against this… whatever it is… on your own."

"Prob-ah-bull gor-gon hive. Old gyp-sum mine. We near Las Vay-gus. Janet inside." Careful of my horn, I snuggled close to Quinn and basked in the warmth of his presence. "Why you cin-der-corn?"

"It's just as the Devil said. He is repaying a bargain on behalf of a devil, and the rest of what he's done wasn't quite enough to be equivalent value. So, here I am. He thought it'd be nice if I'd be able to use my incubus genes in your favor, it seems."

I buried my nose into his thick fur and breathed in deep. "You smell like nay-palm. You taste like nay-palm. Want to eat you up."

Quinn chuckled. "Later," he promised. "After we rescue Janet and get to the bottom of this once and for all."

That sounded like the best plan I'd ever heard in my life, and I pointed my nose at the dome. "Janet in there."

Quinn bobbed his head, and his ears twisted back. "If anyone even looks at you wrong, I look forward to tearing them into pieces."

I considered my husband and struggled with my urge to whinny my laughter. "Just no eat them, how-ever tempt-ing. Eating sen-ti-ents is bad."

"I wonder if I can petrify someone in this form."

I snorted. "Let's go find out."

"Let's."

QUINN

I'D ALWAYS WONDERED how Bailey moved so easily as a cindercorn, and I ultimately came to the conclusion some form of magic handled the basics. I should've had trouble coordinating four hooves, a horn, retractable claws, and my large mass around. In reality, I barely thought about it.

Instead, I contemplated the many ways I could warm up and light the building on fire. When I snorted, trails of flame escaped my nose.

"No fire yet," Bailey scolded. "I know look well."

I bet she did, as I was usually the one telling her not to light things on fire without a good reason. "In the future, I'm going to be more considerate about your interest in committing acts of arson."

"Lies," she muttered, and she bumped against me and rubbed her nose beneath my chin. "You still scold when I make fire."

"But I'll be much more understanding and considerate about your general compulsion to burn things. I really find this entire building offensive."

"That be-cause Janet inside and your terr-i-tory vi-o-lated."

As she spoke nothing but the truth, I didn't argue with her. I eyed the central dome of the mine complex. "Can I burn it after we help Janet?"

"That is idea," my wife replied, her tone amused. "How much nay-palm Devil give you?"

"A lot."

"How much a lot?"

"Several bathtubs filled," I confessed.

"You be so hung-over later. Me take mercy, get you orange pills. You feel drunk?"

"Not yet."

"Yet key-word. Soon. Take time. Once you make fire, it fun! I jealous."

Of course she was, and she would be until she remembered just how bad her hangovers got. "If I don't burn too much I won't get drunk or hungover?"

"No know. Not try? We try later?"

The CDC wouldn't like that experiment at all, and for that reason alone, I'd see about finding some way to try it. Maybe the Devil would invite us to his house and let us hit up his napalm supply and go on a real rampage. What was a little more fire in hell? "I'll think about it."

"Today best day ever."

I refrained from laughing, as I'd heard Bailey's laughter as a cindercorn often enough to understand we'd inform everyone inside we were here if I whinnied in earnest. "So, Janet is in the dome?"

"Trail end at dome. Must be?" Bailey lifted a hoof, and I assumed she tried to point at the bag of neutralizer hanging around her neck. "Prob-ably pet-ri-fied. I fix that. You can fix, too. You gor-gon."

If my newfound uncle was to be believed, Bailey would find her, go on a rampage, and trigger whatever magic destined to drive me insane, worry me, and require me to be a conduit so she could find her way home. The how of it worried me almost as much as the reality of it happening. Too many of my divine relatives all agreed.

It would happen.

I wanted to take her home to prevent it, but it wouldn't work out. We needed to help Janet.

"It's easier with neutralizer, but yes. I can help reverse the petrification," I replied. I would need to be very careful until I transformed to a different shape. Fire and statues didn't mix well. "When you snort, is it hot enough to melt stone?"

"No worry about Janet. Must do on purpose to hurt statue. Snort no hurt unless you snort too hard. It okay,

Quinn. I show you how to be good uni-corn. You big, handsome uni-corn. I play much with you later."

I loved my wife, but she had a one-track mind at times, although I fully intended to indulge her at the earliest opportunity. I suspected the Devil had fiddled beyond his claims, as under any other situation, I would've been inclined to indulge *before* rescuing Janet. I needed to figure out the trick to that.

When Bailey was around, I often thought about indulging.

On second thought, I needed to figure out how we'd be able to work together without our breaks involving inappropriate behavior while at work.

Hmm.

"Where do you think we should look first?" I asked, careful to keep my voice quiet so we wouldn't draw attention early.

"Into dome. If we find someone, try to petrify?"

I nodded. I could petrify someone while human, but it was harder; I hoped the same applied as a cindercorn. Then again, if push came to shove, I could transform and join Bailey's rampage as her personal gorgon-incubus doohickey.

The thought made me unreasonably happy, and I nipped her shoulder. "Lead the way," I ordered. "Sooner we done, sooner I take you." I flicked an ear and eyed her. "Home."

"You can take me any-where, thank you," she replied in her most solemn voice. Lifting her head high, she eased into a ground-eating trot, heading for the dimly illuminated dome. "Try not fall behind, Quinn. No be slow."

BAILEY

A STEEL DOOR barred me from entering the dome, and I glared at the obstruction. "Doors dumb."

Quinn backed away from the door, eyed one of the nearby windows, and continued to back up, his ears turning back.

"Too small," I warned him, as his beautiful but large body would have trouble enough getting even through the door. While cindercorns were remarkably durable, he'd have to contort and pancake himself to fit through the window. I might make it through if I jumped just right—or waited until dawn.

I had no intentions of waiting until dawn to rescue Janet.

Quinn ignored me, snorted flame, and charged towards the building. He jumped and plowed through the window, taking out a large chunk of the wall with him. The hole smoked, and I expected the building would catch fire without my husband having to breathe flame. Inside, I heard a rather loud thump, likely from my husband smacking into another wall and the wall winning.

That would hurt later.

Without much other choice, I followed him in, careful to pick my target and jump with much greater accuracy and less force.

Inside, I discovered my husband had rammed his head directly into a wall, resulting in his horn becoming stuck.

"I love you, but you idiot," I informed him. "You drunk idiot."

"Maybe," my husband conceded. He lifted a hoof, pressed it to the wall, and yanked. After several tries, he popped free and fell over. "Okay, definitely."

As he credited me when I did something right for a rare change, I nuzzled his neck. "But we inside. You good but cray-zee, Quinn. You just drunk. Would say go home, but two is bet-ter than one, and Janet need help. Cray-zee, drunk Quinn."

"Says the woman who went on a napalm bender and torched a skyscraper. I'm just following your example."

As I'd done my fair share of ramming my head through doors, walls, and windows, I couldn't judge him too harshly. "Don't think you ate enough nay-palm for good bender. Sor-ree. Need much more, and need the infused stuff. It go where it want. It extra tasty. More punch. But stuff we have make hyper, yes? Hyper!"

Quinn got to his feet, shook his head, and sighed. "Bailey, darling. Have you ever seen me hyper?"

"Maaaaayyy-be," I replied, refusing to look him in the eyes. "At night. In bed. Hyper there!"

He sighed, and I loved the patience-worn sound. "You're incredible."

I was. "I uni-corn. I in-cred-uh-ble by de-fault. Still not fair you talk good."

"I'll make it up to you later," he promised. "Can you make us a path to Janet?"

"No map or ink or stuff. Sor-ree."

"Then let's get moving before someone checks out why the window broke."

"They see Quinn-sized hole and know you do it. You make very big hole. I del-i-cate flower, no make very big hole."

While soft, he whinnied his laughter. "Right. Nobody is going to expect fire-breathing unicorns, Bailey."

"They expect me. I like Janet. They not stupid. Well, they stupid for taking Janet. Why else take Janet?"

"I don't think they're expecting you. I think they're expecting a gorgon hive to kidnap you. Again. Because the person I think might be responsible for Janet's disappearance has been trying to sell you to gorgon hives." Quinn's ears flattened, and he snorted flame. "I will enjoy tearing him to pieces."

I assumed a napalm bender resulted in Quinn indulging in the more violent tendencies of his heritage. "Wait to fight until Janet safe. Then you fight. Not before."

He sighed.

I suspected I was getting a taste of what he felt like when I ran around on four hooves. "Go be-fore we found," I ordered, poking him in the rump with my horn. "Go, go!"

Quinn picked his way along the hallway, which curved along the dome's façade. Glass doors led into abandoned offices. Once upon a time, some of the offices had been converted into bedrooms, but those too had grown dusty from disuse. All remained quiet, but something on the other side of the building creaked.

"Think that some-one?" I whispered.

Quinn focused on the nearest office, which had been converted to a bedroom. "I think this dive is about to crumble around their damned ears. We'll be doing them a favor torching the damned thing."

Yep. Quinn cruised on a napalm high. "Later." I bumped his shoulder with mine and pointed my nose at the office. "Gor-gon?"

"A female's solitary nest—or had been." Quinn pushed his nose to the door, and it opened. He pawed at the bedding crammed into the corner. "Most females share rooms or suites but have personal spaces for privacy. This would've been one of the women's personal spaces." He narrowed his eyes. "I had no idea you could see so well in the dark, Bailey."

"See good. Uni-corns best."

Quinn explored the office. "Her things are still here. Jewelry, and so on." Quinn lifted his hoof and snagged a necklace off the desk shoved up against the wall with a claw. "See? She probably died, and the hive male left her quarters intact. It's part of how gorgons grieve. At first, they don't touch anything that belonged to their lost wife. Then, over time, they begin taking items away, donating them, or giving them to other wives or sisters in the hive as they accept her death."

"That sweet. Sad but sweet."

"Gorgons are often misunderstood. Their capacity for ruin comes second only to their capacity for love. Most only see how good they are at death and destruction." Quinn's ears turned back, and he returned the necklace to the desk. "I wonder if the hive was also infected with rabies."

"And left only male?" I asked, sighing at the reminder of how Quinn and I had somehow become candidates for parenthood.

"A very desperate male. Perhaps Winfield sold Janet to this hive to get his revenge on you both. That would make sense. The male—or males—were likely vaccinated for rabies but his females weren't. Most gorgons won't get vaccinations without a good reason, and you know how expensive treatments for rabies can get."

"Ver-ry ex-pen-sive," I conceded. "I spend all your money on rabies cure."

Quinn nuzzled my shoulder. "If they tried to use Janet as

a surrogate, we'll take care of her—and we'll give her the option of co-parenting with us. She likes children."

"Janet good person. That why. But this trauma."

"Janet's tough. We'll take care of her no matter what her circumstances. But this is concerning. Are the gorgons participating victims, too?"

"Even if victim, they take cop. You know law," I reminded Quinn. "If let gor-gons break law be-cause threat-ened, they make dust, make more gor-gons, make more problems. Can't let slide, Quinn."

He heaved a sigh. "I think I understand why you like fire so much. It's so much simpler just to burn it all down, isn't it?"

"That the nay-palm talking. It talk loud and like fire. You be okay."

"Why do I have a feeling this is going to be an unmiti-gated disaster?"

"I in-volv-ed, you smart. That why."

The look Quinn shot at me made me laugh.

EIGHTEEN

Bailey was a force of nature.

Quinn

THE EXTERIOR CIRCUIT of the dome revealed bedrooms enough for twenty females, which made it a strong enough hive to worry even me—or a collaboration of several hives. While males were often territorial, family units would stick together.

Had my father been born a gorgon rather than a human, he would've shared territory with my grandfather. Had I been born a gorgon rather than human, I would've shared territory with both of them.

It would've been glorious chaos.

My grandfather, at last check, had one bride, sixteen wives, and more children than I could readily count or remember. While my father wasn't a gorgon, he competed with the rest of the family in terms of number of children.

My mother refused to share my father, and not even gorgons were willing to cross her.

I needed to introduce Bailey to my sisters. All fourteen of them. I also needed to warn Bailey that my mother didn't seem ready to slow down having kids quite yet despite her age. I blamed my grandparents for that.

The children of triads found some way to break the rules, and my mother seemed to view aging as optional.

With the outer ring of the dome explored, that left us with four hallways leading deeper into the complex. After not-so-careful consideration, I picked the hallway farthest from where we'd broken into the place. While tempted to torch the bedding in the offices to smoke anyone out, I couldn't afford to light any fires until we made certain Janet was safe.

If the situation allowed, I would also make sure Bailey didn't fulfill any damned prophecies involving her taking a trip to another plane because she went loco without the benefit of a napalm bender. I couldn't figure out what might cause her to lose control of her magic, but if I could avoid it, I would.

Even with the Devil's precautions and magic, I prayed I wouldn't have to serve as a conduit. As was often the nature of prayer, it would be futile, but I did it anyway. *He* worked in mysterious ways, and I didn't ask for much.

Though, when I thought about it, I found myself praying a hell of a lot more than normal when Bailey was involved. Could anyone blame me?

My beautiful Bailey was a force of nature.

And the daughter of the divine.

I didn't look forward to that conversation.

"Oh! Big mine room," Bailey whispered, trotting ahead to peer over a railing, which was illuminated with a dim overhead light, barely enough to see by. "Ew. That gross."

When Bailey found something to be gross, I worried. I trotted to her and peered over the steel railing.

When gorgons died, most hives petrified their lost loved ones and buried them in stone walls to make sure their bodies weren't used to create gorgon dust or other potent substances. Either the males had died, too, or they'd lost their bloody minds.

They'd left the deceased gorgon females to rot on the concrete floor.

"That awful," Bailey said, and her coat steamed.

Shit. Bailey wouldn't need napalm or anything spurring her on to start the kind of fire that would rival the one she'd ignited at 120 Wall Street

Her temper already burned hot enough to light her fur on fire.

"Yes," I agreed, sighing at the inevitable work I'd have to do to help lay the women to rest and prevent their bodies from being used to manufacture gorgon dust.

Bailey lifted a hoof. "A young one. Child. Whelp." Bailey's fur blazed, and a golden glow filled the central part of the dome. "They killed a child."

Yep. Bailey was t-minus five seconds from a meltdown, and I'd be very appreciative of the Devil making certain she wouldn't incinerate me by the time she finished rampaging.

Snakes hissed, drawing my attention to the curved wall below. A male with black snakes stood, looking up at us. Not far away, I spotted the gray stone of a petrified human.

Janet.

"You're not supposed to be here!" John Winfield announced, stepping out of the shadows. I remembered his voice from 120 Wall Street. "You bitch."

I dug my claws into the tiles, and they broke.

In the months we'd been married, Bailey had made so much progress, but some things never changed. The instant the word 'bitch' left Winfield's mouth, she snapped. With no care we were on the second story, Bailey jumped, and the entire building shook from the force of her landing on the floor below.

I recognized her pawing at the floor as her preparing for a charge, the kind that would end Winfield's life the instant her flaming bulk crashed into him. She'd probably crush a hole through the wall behind him while she was at it. Then she'd light the whole building on fire.

I needed to get the neutralizer away from her before she took her temper out on Winfield. I followed, landing with a pained grunt. I grabbed the leather band securing the neutralizer bag and tugged. I gave up after the second tug and gnawed through the material.

John Winfield pulled out a dart gun, and I recognized the glowing golden fluid inside the clear shaft as ambrosia. "See this, bitch? This is what revenge looks like."

I tensed, and my eyes widened. Most people wisely believed ambrosia was a good way to die with a bang—a very destructive bang. In my case—and Bailey's case—things could go wrong in entirely different ways.

I found it ironic the Devil had made me into a conduit for Bailey and that ambrosia could turn us into conduits for any divine with an interest in paying the mortal coil a visit.

"Stupid," Bailey announced, and she tossed her head. "All this because you stupid? You kid-nap cop? Are you *mad?*"

"Shut up, bitch. I haven't killed the cop yet. She deserves it for siding with you, though. I didn't think there were two of you, though. I'd heard you could find anything. I guess they were right. I would've preferred selling you into slavery.

That would've been a lot more profit for me on top of a hefty dose of revenge."

"You idiot," my wife announced.

I loved my wife, but I really wished she would stop antagonizing crazy people. If I opened my mouth, Winfield might recognize my voice, and I wasn't sure how he'd react to that. While I could petrify him, I wouldn't be able to petrify him fast enough to prevent him from shooting his dart.

"Petrify the large unicorn," Winfield ordered.

The gorgon male sighed and focused his attention on me. The tingle I associated with an attempted petrification swept over me, far too weak to do anything to me. I flattened my ears, lowered my head, and set the bag of neutralizer on the ground.

All right. If the gorgon wanted to play, I'd play. The Devil hadn't said I couldn't transform after finding my wife. And if, for whatever reason, I needed to be a cindercorn to serve as a conduit for Bailey, I could contact Perkins and get Sunny's help. I dug my claws into the concrete floor and snorted flame.

Then I embraced my true nature. Heat washed over me, and fire sheathed me before my body contorted, transforming from unicorn to gorgon.

"In-cu-bus gor-gon doo-hickey!" my wife squealed.

John Winfield's mouth dropped open.

The gorgon male's snakes reared back and hissed. "You."

The flames sheathed me much as they had with the Devil in his hell, and while I found fire disconcerting to wear as clothes, Bailey hated when anyone other than her could admire my physique. I stretched my wings and rolled my shoulders. My snakes, save for Bailey's beloved Francisco, hissed at the rival gorgon male.

Francisco wanted his owed attention, and Bailey stretched her head to nuzzle the scarlet hooded cobra.

I really needed to teach Francisco he needed to wait for cuddles when I had a gorgon male to deal with.

"What the fuck are you?" John Winfield demanded, and he pointed the dart gun at me.

Bailey's body erupted into flame and she charged towards the former cadet. "No! *Bad.*"

Everything made sense, and as the inevitable loomed, I lifted my hand, pinched the bridge of my nose, and sighed. Of course. At the first sign of trouble pointed in my direction, Bailey would be Bailey. She'd dive headlong into danger and get herself shot with a huge ampoule of ambrosia, something that would kill most people.

Fortunately for me and my blood pressure, Bailey wasn't most people.

The concussive bang of the gun discharging confirmed my fears, but the cadet hadn't fired in time; once Bailey decided to do something, she did it. A moment later, six hundred plus pounds of unicorn crashed into the former cadet, and she, as expected, plowed right into the wall.

I grimaced at the wet crunch.

Then I turned my attention to the rival male. "You have a choice, gorgon. Surrender to the Quinn family or join your women in death."

I thought I was being generous. The gorgon disagreed. He turned towards Janet, and his movement drew Bailey's attention. Golden flames burst off her coat until she resembled the flaring surface of the sun.

"No," she said, and her voice hissed and crackled from flame. She dipped her head, grabbed the end of the dart that had embedded in her chest, and tossed it aside.

The glass cracked, but it didn't matter. It had emptied into my wife.

I regretted I didn't have my prescription chill pills with me. I'd need them in a few minutes.

The gorgon recoiled, and his eyes widened. "What are you?"

"Your worst night-mare," Bailey replied, taking a step towards the gorgon. "You take Janet with that thing."

I leaned to the side to get a look at the fallen human. Upon closer inspection, 'thing' was an apt description. His body hadn't handled the impact of six hundred plus pounds of angry flaming unicorn all that well.

Gross.

"That was the deal. I petrified and transported the woman, and he will rebuild my hive. He has a lead on a good breeder."

Bailey snorted flame, and her glow intensified. "Die, rapist asshole."

I opened my mouth to remind Bailey she had no proof he was a rapist, but the gorgon erupted into a column of flame. In the time it took me to blink, Bailey reduced him to ash.

"Worse than asshole angels," she announced. Bailey's body turned translucent, and I tensed as the fires surrounding her intensified. She glanced at the bodies of the dead gorgons, and they, too, erupted into flame.

Within moments, nothing remained of the gorgon females beyond a few blackened smears on the concrete and some ash.

Then, like the smoke wafting upwards, Bailey disappeared.

I HAD TWO REALISTIC CHOICES. I could do what I typically did when Bailey got herself in trouble and panic, or I could grab the bag of neutralizer, reverse Janet's petrification, get her out of the building, and then panic.

Either way, panicking would be on my agenda. I was just delaying the inevitable. Despite having been warned *something* would happen, it'd happened in a way I hadn't been able to prevent.

I could petrify just about anyone, but even if I had started petrifying Winfield immediately, I wouldn't have been able to prevent him from shooting the dart, nor would I have been able to stop my wife from plowing into him. Knowing her, she would've gotten herself dosed with ambrosia anyway.

Even understanding she was the daughter of two divines and the granddaughter of more divines, and the great-grand-daughter of even more divines, I worried.

Janet first, then I could panic properly.

I grabbed the bag of neutralizer, hoped the powder without water would be sufficient to reverse petrification, and stepped to the officer's side. According to her attire, she must have left work right before being kidnapped, as she was in her standard uniform. As typical with petrification victims, her clothing hadn't turned to stone, which made it easy to disarm her.

I discovered a half-filled water bottle hooked to her belt, which would make my life a lot easier. Cracking it open, I tore into the bag, dumped in the pink, sparkling powder, and shook it.

I started with her head, and once I'd coated her head and hair with the fluid, I narrowed my eyes and began unraveling the magic binding her flesh to stone.

To my disgust, the gorgon barely had the strength needed to petrify a human, and the gray eased from Janet's flesh. I tensed while observing the reversal of petrification, giving her water bottle another shake.

When she began to breathe again, I tipped the neutralizer-infused water into her mouth. "Drink," I ordered.

I couldn't tell if she obeyed because of instinct or recognized I was helping her. It didn't matter. She drank, which helped speed the reversal process. I supported her back as her body softened and she slumped. She blinked, and her stunned gaze fell on me.

Then her eyes widened, and she looked me over.

Right.

Janet had never seen me in my true form before.

Groaning, I bowed my head and sighed. "If I told you to pretend you hadn't seen this, would you listen?

"While I want to know what the hell happened, I thought you should know I now totally understand why Bailey has the hots for you."

I considered going outside and burying my head in the sand. "Thanks, Janet."

"Anytime. What the hell happened?"

"You got kidnapped by a gorgon." I pointed at the smear that used to be the gorgon. "That's what's left of him after Bailey got a hold of him."

Janet leaned forward enough to look at the pile. "What did she do to him?"

"Mrs. Police Chief Quinn of the NYPD took serious offense that he stole one of her cops."

Janet's eyes widened. "Mrs. *Police Chief* Quinn? As in she's a chief now?"

"Yes."

"But she's been working the bomb squad circuit."

I sucked in a breath. How many people knew about Bailey's bomb squad activities? "Seriously?"

We stared at each other with wide eyes, and Janet covered her mouth with her hands. "Shit. You didn't know?"

"I found out recently," I replied, my tone wry. "Nevermind. She's my partner now, so I don't care if she was playing with bombs. Since she loves C4, I'm not going to even complain. Are you all right?"

"My eyeballs itch."

"That happens with petrification sometimes," I replied, rising to my feet and offering her a hand. She hesitated before accepting my help. Once certain she could stay on her feet, I retrieved her firearm, returned it to her holster, and spent a few minutes checking over her gear and making sure she hadn't had anything taken from her during her kidnapping.

They'd even left her phone in her pocket, which no longer had a charge.

"What are you?" she whispered.

"Part gorgon, part incubus, part angel, part devil, part demon, part human, and a part of a lot of other things all mixed together. There's a lot of gorgon in my heritage, as my shapeshifting is rather unique."

"You're dressed in fire."

"That would be the devil or demon in me, I suppose." It could also have been from swimming in lava and brimstone in hell for a while, too. "It's better than being naked. Transforming is hard on clothes."

Janet looked me over again, her brows rising. "You must spend a fortune on clothes, especially if Bailey talks you into tearing out of your clothes. Can't say I blame her. And here I just thought you were shy, Chief."

Shy was one way to put it. I sighed. Determined to change the subject, I said, "You've been transferred to my station, which is why I'm here."

"Damn, really?"

"Really."

"This day just turned around, because Chief Morriston? He's a dick."

Considering Chief Morriston liked men like Winfield, I had no grounds to argue with her. "Well, he's not your problem anymore. If you think you can handle a walk, we need to get out of here before this whole place catches on fire."

"How? Spontaneously?"

I gestured to my flaming attire. "More like I'll brush up against a wall and torch the place."

"Right. Where you go, Bailey's rarely far. Where is she? Is she all right?"

I gave it less than five minutes before the unsettled feeling in my chest grew teeth and made a mess of my day. "Winfield hit her with an ambrosia dart."

Janet sucked in a breath. "Oh no. She's…?"

"No. She's like me. She's the descendant of divines. But it was an entire ampoule and I don't know what that's going to do to her."

I hated lying, but unlike my grandfather, I could lie when the need was great enough. Like everything else in my mortal life, I somehow found myself having to make difficult choices for the greater good. I knew exactly what the ambrosia was going to do to her—had done to her. It had taken her somewhere I couldn't follow.

I really wanted to indulge in that panic attack, find a nice hole, hide in it, and chew my nails until Bailey returned.

"She'll be all right?"

All right was a stretch, but I nodded, once again bending to the greater good. "She should be."

There. That was the truth. Should was a powerful and terrifying word.

Janet relaxed and smiled. "Don't worry about it, Chief. We're talking about Bailey here. This is the woman who reduced a skyscraper to rubble because she wanted to make sure you were safe. She'll be just fine, but she might be a little pissy when she's done doing whatever it is crazy unicorns do after being shot with ambrosia."

"Running amok," I muttered.

"Precisely." Janet scratched her head. "Hey, Chief?"

"Yes?"

"Where are we?"

"Somewhere in Nevada."

"Nevada? You mean like Vegas?"

I nodded.

"Well, damn. Why would anyone bring me *here*?"

I regarded John Winfield's body with a wrinkled nose. "I have no idea, and I have no idea how to find out. And that pisses me off."

"In your shoes, I'd ask Chief Morriston."

"I would? Why?"

Janet arched a brow. "You didn't know? Winfield is his ex-son-in-law, and they're birds of a feather. That little asshole couldn't take a piss without the chief knowing about it."

And just like that, things had gone from bad to worse.

"You're just as bad as Bailey at creating problems, Janet. I just thought you should know this."

The woman snorted but shrugged. "Can't say you're wrong. What's next? A sweep? Blow this joint?" She hesitated, staring at my flame-sheathed body. "Not literally blowing the joint."

"Yet." I had the feeling when Bailey found her way home, she'd want something to blow up. "Let's get out of here, get to a phone, and place some calls. I can't guarantee there's no gorgon dust in here, so blowing this joint is for the best."

And, for a rare change, I knew exactly how to get what I wanted, and I'd enjoy getting my chance to level a building with the help of some napalm. If all went well, I'd invite Bailey along for the ride. I'd call it an early Christmas present and follow up with a monster margarita at the Venetian.

We could call it a date.

I just needed to figure out how to get her home first.

NINETEEN

I no die, right?

BAILEY

I DISSOLVED INTO GLORIOUS FLAME. I remembered the sensation; I'd been the purest fire when I'd torched 120 Wall Street. The thrill of life without a body filled me, and I basked in the joy of leaving everything behind and existing as nothing more than a thought.

The world was mine to burn.

"Most people would call charging someone armed with so much ambrosia foolish," my great-grandfather-in-law, Anubis said, his tone amused.

I whirled to face the divine, and I snorted flame, which ignited the grasses at my feet. Instead of charring to black, the green turned to brilliant golden sand, which wafted away on a cleansing breeze.

The grass regrew.

"That odd," I said, pointing to the grass with a disturbingly insubstantial hoof. "I no die, right?"

"No, little one. You didn't die. Why do you always jump to such strange conclusions? You just went on a little trip. My great-grandson is handling this better than I anticipated. I thought you would appreciate knowing he's caring for your cop while waiting for you to cool your temper and burn off the ambrosia."

Ugh. Ambrosia. No wonder I felt twitchy. "I do. Thank you. But why are you here? I smooshed stupid cadet. But he shot me. With ambrosia. Stupid cadet."

"Yes, that was a rather foolish move, pointing his little dart at my little great-grandson. I'm impressed all you did was run him into the wall. As for why I'm here, I'm here because this is my home. Well, somewhat. My home isn't here specifically, but it is on this plane of existence."

I regarded the blue skies and brilliant sun skeptically. "This does seem much brighter than where you from, right? Is that right? You from underworld. That like hell, right? Not sunny place."

"I do have this tendency to poke my nose in the underworld often. It's fun watching the dead toil in the afterlife." Anubis regarded me with an ear twisted back. "It is not like hell, though. Wrong pantheon."

"But it's e-quiv-a-lent?"

"Somewhat but not precisely."

"You suck," I muttered. "Be con-fusing on purpose."

Anubis laughed. "It's one of my joys in life. No, I'm just a meddling relative, and I have fewer rules I have to follow compared to many other divines. Or, more accurately, I have fewer scruples about breaking unimportant rules. I'll be scolded by my wife later, I'm sure."

"Uni-ver-sal rule. Men be scolded by women for doing

annoying things. Quinn need scolding. He bargain with Devil!"

"He didn't bargain with the Devil. He bargained with a lesser devil."

"This even worse! Worse! Worse! Bargain with best if bargain at all. He bargain with *lesser* devil? Then he show up cin-der-corn! Not in-cu-bus gor-gon whatsit doo-hickey. But he very nice stallion. Very nice. *Very* nice."

"He's back to being his gorgon-incubus-whatsit doohickey self. Helping your cop was easier with hands."

"So sad," I whined. "All gone? No stallion?"

"He'll be able to become a cindercorn again for you, I'm sure. It'll just take him practice to master shapeshifting to other forms. I'm sure you can criticize him if he's not the perfect cindercorn."

"Yes. Can do. Can do him."

Anubis sighed. "Yes, I'm aware. If we could not discuss my grandson like that, I'd appreciate that."

"Great. You forget great."

"It's too much of a hassle to add it. It simplifies things."

"Okay. So you grand-father." I flicked an ear. "Can skip in-law?"

"If you'd like. No one will mind."

I bobbed my head. "This good! Now why here? This not there."

"You got pissed off after being injected with ambrosia. This activated some of your latent genetics, and as a result, you took a little trip to here. It has to do with your heritage."

"Right. Divine grandparent."

"That's… not exactly accurate."

"Explain. D-N-A test say grandparent. That not right?"

"Your mother, your father, all of your grandparents, a few more of your relatives, actually, you're just one big ball of mortal divinity," Anubis announced. "But you're still mortal and not a divine because..." Anubis frowned and his second ear twitched back. "I'm not really sure why, when I'm truthful about the situation. I was volunteered to keep you company."

"Who volunteer you?"

"Me, myself, and I. And my wife. Mostly my wife. You two would get into a fight because you're two predators who get easily bored."

I stared at him, trying to comprehend how someone could be even crazier than me. "You need help."

"Despite your belief, I'm not crazy. It's true. You're a predator, and my wife is most definitely a predator. The instant you both got bored, you'd fight. You do want to save your energy for the adoption match, right?"

I pranced and tossed my head. "I win that fight, yes. I kick gorgons! I bite gorgons! They can't petrify me! I win fight. Children mine!" I paused. "Quinn's, too."

"You have to fight them while human, Bailey."

"Can still bite and kick."

"You would. Sometimes, I question my grandson's life choices, but then again, he's proven himself to be quite sensible. I suppose good partnerships in life must balance."

"I am sensible!"

Anubis glared at me. "Your solution to dealing with a human who threatened Samuel was to charge him and crash the entirety of your bulk into him. You crushed him against a wall. You popped him like a grape under foot."

"Well, yes. He pointed gun at *my* Samuel. He's mine. My Quinn. My Samuel Quinn. He deserve popped like stupid grape."

"I'm relieved to discover you do, indeed, know your husband's name. But I'm concerned you have zero remorse for popping someone like a grape."

"If he hadn't pointed gun at Sam, no pop like grape."

"It disturbs me this logic is rather sensible."

"Samuel Leviticus Quinn is also known as mine," I announced in a solemn tone. "He pointed ambrosia dart at him. This off-en-sive."

"Yes, it is offensive. I can't fault you there. Still, you could have just lit him on fire."

I thought about that. "No. Hit hard better. Squish him like grape. Faster to squish than snort big fire."

"I can't argue with that. Rather than arguing over the merits of squishing threats to Samuel like grapes, I should give you your Christmas gift."

I perked my ears forward. "I like presents."

"First, your wolf, Sunny. While you haven't met her yet, her purpose is to help you find your way back to Earth when you accidentally teleport yourself here. This will happen when your magic becomes too strong. You took a rather large dose of ambrosia. When enough of the ambrosia has worn off, she'll come help you get home if you can't figure out how to get home yourself. There's more than one way for you to return to where you belong, but Sunny is working her way here and will guide you back to Earth. Do try to avoid overexposure to ambrosia in the future."

"Full ampoule," I replied. "Way too much. Not good. So it brought me here?"

"Yes. You have a strong affinity with the Egyptian pantheon, although your line and my line never met, which is a good thing."

"My line?"

"Your father."

"My father vanilla human. He suck. Want to squish him like grape."

"Please don't squish your human father like a grape. If you want to make him miserable, I recommend you invite him to your proper wedding and show him how deliriously happy you are. That will upset him, as he is a firm believer in shared misery."

"No squish like grape?" I blinked. "Wait. Proper wedding?"

"And no lighting him on fire, biting him, kicking him, sitting on him, or otherwise ending his life prematurely. The same goes to your human mother. And yes, there will be a proper wedding."

"You suck. I like idea of wedding, but I no have pretty dress."

"A pretty dress will be provided."

"I like sound of this. What is present?"

"What I'm about to tell you should make things a little better. Your father was possessed by a divine when you were conceived, and your mother was likewise possessed by a divine when you were conceived. Technically, you have four parents. My Christmas present to you is the opportunity to have all four of your parents in the same room together at the same time. It will be delightfully chaotic."

I bowed my head and groaned. "My family crazier than Quinn family? That not fair! Not fair at all!" I flopped onto the grass, rolled onto my back, and kicked my hooves. "Not fair! I was *normal*! Normal compared to crazy Quinn family!"

"Bailey, you transform into a fire-breathing unicorn. Did you really believe you were, at any stage of your life, actually normal? You view light as a mode of transportation. You deliberately goad one of my grandson's snakes into biting you because you like it. You're not normal."

"So mean."

"But honest. Aren't you curious about why you shapeshift into a cindercorn?"

"Maybe little."

"It's because one of your great-great-great-great grand-parents—add a few extra greats in there for good measure—was a cindercorn."

"That weird. How get feet instead of hooves? Weird!"

"Cindercorns are inherently shapeshifters. So are standard white unicorns. Add in your divine relations, and you have a very high percentage of shapeshifter DNA. Transformatives don't really bother natural shapeshifters. They can just shift back at their whim. You should feed Samuel a good transformative sometime. You'll get to see something truly special."

"It won't hurt him?"

"He'll be able to shapeshift back as he wants."

"Neat! And cindercorn stallion? He so pretty as stallion."

"Thanks to his incubus heritage, he can shapeshift to any form he's been before, and he can be nudged in the right direction by properly motivated divines. He was a cinder-corn because the Devil nudged him along. Ironically, a Christmas present to you."

"The Devil likes me!"

"Most people would not be excited to know the Devil likes them, Bailey."

"Better than Devil not liking me. That would be bad. May go to hell if he no like me. Much better this way."

"Your logic sometimes terrifies me."

"Only some-times?"

"Yes. Also, sometimes, I wonder about you."

"Only some-times?"

Anubis bowed his head and sighed.

QUINN

I FOUND Tiffany pacing along the fence, and she gaped at me while I rubbed my temples and debated how to survive through the rest of the night. All things considered, getting straight to the chase would work best. "I need you to call the CDC and request a napalm tanker, please."

Tiffany hung her head and sighed. "I sent Bailey in there, and you come out? This is not normal. Where's Bailey?"

"Cruising an ambrosia high somewhere. Winfield got a hold of an entire ampoule of ambrosia. Because Bailey was involved, of course she got dosed with the ambrosia. What can go wrong does go wrong, and I, being the fool I am, left my medications with your husband."

Tiffany's brows shot up. "That was stupid of him. Is she inside going on a bender? If you need the medication, I can get it for you, so don't worry yourself about that. And if needed, I can insert my foot in your ass and deliver a dose that way."

She would. I opted to ignore the threat; if she needed to insert her foot in my ass, it was because I deserved it. "I don't know where Bailey is, precisely," I replied, unable to keep my tone neutral. "And Janet has the name of a potential conspirator."

"Shit. Who?"

"Chief Morriston," Janet replied, stepping to my side. "Hey, Tiffers."

"You look like hell, Jan-Jan. You all right?"

I foresaw a lot of trouble in my future, as I had not expected Tiffany to be close enough friends with Janet to warrant cutesy nicknames. When Tiffany used cutesy nicknames, it meant trouble was surely on the horizon.

Tiffany plus Bailey plus Janet might give me a full head of gray hair and a complex.

"I think so." Janet pointed at me. "Do you see this?"

"As a matter of fact, yes. I do. He's part incubus and part gorgon, and his genetics created quite an interesting secondary form. He won't let me experiment with him. It's no wonder Bailey gets so flustered about him. She knows exactly what goods he's packing, and she's one of the most jealous women I've ever met. In a good way, of course."

Janet nodded.

"The napalm, Tiffany?" I begged.

"Hold your horses, Chief. We won't have a way to reliably light it. I'm trying to figure that part out. What excuse am I giving them for the tanker?"

I sighed. "An entire hive of gorgons died in there, and I have no way of knowing if there's any dust or if there's dust in production. The entire structure has to go. It's also possible the bodies are a rabies vector."

"How long have they been dead?"

I shrugged. "No idea. Gorgons don't decay quite the same way humans do. It's been long enough I'm worried their ashes will convert to dust if left alone."

"We'll need containment mages, then. And Bailey to light it. Any idea on her ETA?"

"No idea, but I can take care of lighting the napalm."

"How?"

"I called in a favor and got a lesson in shapeshifting to a cindercorn," I admitted.

"Damn, Sam. Bailey's going to go nuts when she learns you're an on-demand stallion for her amusement." Tiffany snickered.

I wished triplets on her as a special form of revenge, and I'd have to have that little Christmas present of hers contain some extra bite. Maybe quadruplets. Arthur and Tiffany definitely deserved quadruplets. "I'm so glad you're enjoying yourself, Tiffany. Anyway, she already knows."

"When it's at your expense? Always."

"Can you please just call for a tanker, Tiffany? I don't have my phone."

Tiffany handed me hers. "You can call. If I ask, they'll laugh at me and accuse me of wanting to feed it to the crazy unicorn. Just don't tell them you're going to be the crazy unicorn tonight."

I hated she was right, and sighing, I looked up the number for the primary CDC switchboard and placed the call. It took over twenty minutes of snarling at idiots to be put through to the last man on Earth I wanted to deal with, Marshal Clemmends.

"What do you need, Chief Quinn?"

"There's an old gypsum mine in Nevada, and I need a napalm tanker, a containment team, and pyros to light it up. There are a lot of dead gorgons inside, and it should be flagged as a high risk of becoming contaminated with gorgon dust."

"Why must you insist on toying with gorgons, Chief Quinn?"

"I didn't toy with any gorgons this time. They kidnapped

a police officer. She's been safely recovered, but she'll require treatment for rabies, as it's unknown if she was exposed. It's probable the gorgons were rabid, and it's unknown if the virus will spread."

"If I hadn't already had several documented cases of gorgons infected with rabies hit my desk this week, I would say you were screwing with me, Chief Quinn. I just have one question. Will your wife be on hand for this napalming?"

"Unknown. She's currently not at the site, but if the techs are incapable of lighting the napalm, I can handle it."

"You can? How?"

"Through a careful application of fire," I replied, careful to keep my tone neutral. "You were aware of my unique ancestry, correct?"

"Yes. Unfortunately. Very well. If you say you can get it lit, I'll trust you. How big of a site is it?"

"It's an old gypsum mining operation that seems to have been abandoned. It's miles from civilization, so there's no chance of the fires spreading to any buildings nearby."

"Got an address?"

I turned to Tiffany. "What's the address of this place?"

"Hell if I know. It's a gypsum mine east of Vegas. There's only one of them just east of Vegas."

One day, I would retire, life would become normal, and I meant to enjoy it. "It's a gypsum mine just east of Vegas," I informed my wife's ex-boss. "There's only one of them."

"You have no idea where you're at, do you?"

"I teleported to the site."

"Ah. I see. I'm sure I can find it. I'll authorize the tanker. Is there water accessible?"

"Doubtful."

"I'll send two napalm tankers and several water tankers to make certain there's sufficient volume. What grade?"

"Use the same stuff used on 120 Wall Street."

Clemmends sighed. "I was hoping you wouldn't say that. Very well. I'm only authorizing this because it's a remote site and you'll be in charge of the operation." There was a long moment of silence. "Actually, scratch that. I'm going to authorize your wife to help ignite the napalm should she show up. I may as well earn some good favor with her for a change."

"That will make up for assigning her to work with the bomb squad."

"Found out about that, did you?"

"Not from her. Someone snitched." I arched a brow in Janet's direction, one of several snitchers.

The woman grinned and waved at me.

"It was good developmental training for her new job. I had her trained in the traditional disarming of most devices. She's also been trained to handle nuclear weaponry, although we did no live testing. She tests quite high on working with schematics. She's wasted in the CDC as a contractor."

My brows shot up at that. "Was that a compliment I heard, Clemmends?"

"Don't have a heart attack. Despite my lack of a functional relationship with your wife, I do respect her learning capacity and general skills. She's miserable in the CDC, and while I recognize she's excessively well-trained, she's in a better position to be productive with you in the NYPD."

"And here I thought you were just trying to get rid of her."

"That, too."

"What's the CDC's jurisdiction in dust cases and potential

involvement with the kidnapping of a law enforcement officer?"

"I can get jurisdiction joint with the FBI. Why?"

"John Winfield, a former cadet of the NYPD, was behind the kidnapping. He is the ex-son-in-law of Chief Morriston."

"Morriston?"

"He's the kidnapped officer's chief. He oversees the Hamptons."

Bailey's ex-boss mulled over that in silence, and I waited, aware of Janet glaring at me. Finally, the man sighed. "And her chief would have access to her schedule and be able to make arrangements for such a kidnapping in a way where no one would be aware of the officer's disappearance—which is exactly what happened until she was scheduled to show up for her shift. While her chief isn't specifically named in this file, there was an accusation of abandoning her duty. That was overturned when it was exposed she had likely been a kidnapping victim."

I could see a vindictive ex-cadet attempting to frame his target, and the NYPD took such accusations seriously. "You're aware of the situation?"

"The documentation hit my desk because of your country-wide jurisdiction. Let me guess: you'd like to be involved with Morriston's questioning."

"I certainly wouldn't mind being the arresting officer along with my wife."

"You know full well why that won't be happening, Chief Quinn."

I grumbled curses over standard protocols. "I'd like to file the official request for angelic verification in the case, especially as there are ties with Winfield's attempt to sell my wife into slavery."

"Now that is a request I can meet. I'll keep you in the loop, and I'll notify the FBI about your interest in being involved. If he puts up a fight, I expect you'll be given the nod to deal with him. And if he runs, we'd be involving your wife anyway. How did the napalm experiment go?"

"Tiffany? What napalm experiment?"

"Gassing a unicorn up on napalm before a long run. It worked great. The second leg of the trip, I gassed her up on diesel. That wasn't as efficient, but she broke records. Hell, she beat most planes."

I relayed the information.

"Excellent. I'll mark on her file to allow access to small amounts of napalm for when she needs to make a run. I'm still barring access to large quantities of napalm, however."

"Wise. How long do you think it'll take to get a tanker here?"

"Call it three hours; we'll have to make a batch of napalm in Vegas. Can I call you back on this number?"

"Yes. It belongs to Tiffany Perkins."

"More trouble," Clemmends muttered.

I laughed because it was true. "Indeed."

"I'll notify you when Morriston is dealt with. Stay accessible," Clemmends ordered before hanging up on me.

Shaking my head, I gave Tiffany her phone. "Three hours. I'm going to see about shifting to a unicorn and doing a sweep of the building."

"While a unicorn?"

"Easier to prevent spread of rabies and possibly gorgon dust. If I become contaminated, I'll burn it off with the napalm. Just have them flood the entire complex with napalm when they arrive. I'll take care of the rest."

BAILEY

THE NEXT TIME Anubis suggested I play twenty questions with him, I'd just stab him with my horn. Death at his hands seemed a great deal more merciful than trying to figure out how the hell I could possibly have four parents, who my other two parents were, and how I'd gone for so long believing a lunatic like me had come from a pair of vanilla assholes.

In retrospect, it'd been rather obvious *something* had been very, very fishy about my ancestry.

"This game suck," I announced, stomping a hoof. "I never guess right."

"Try again," Anubis replied, mocking me with his canine grin. "I'll pretend I didn't give you several tries already. Your mythology can't be *this* bad."

"Can be. Divines suck. It hard enough to keep track of crazy Quinn family," I complained. "Why you make me guess parents? You mean."

"It's keeping you busy while waiting for the ambrosia to wear off, and you can't return to Earth until it does. It will only take another hour or two unless you burn off a lot of magic."

I perked my ears forward. "Map, chalk, ink, paper? I make trail! That burn magic, yes?"

"Yes, I suppose it would."

"Give!"

Anubis grumbled something in another language, swept out his hand, and snapped his fingers. The items I asked for manifested on the ground.

Whinnying, I snatched the map in my teeth, which depicted the entire United States, and I shook it out, spreading it over the grass. "Open ink, please."

Anubis chuckled but did as asked. "I'll be very curious to see if you can open a pathway back to Samuel."

"Oh, that good idea. I was going to try for mystery mother or father, but I like that idea better."

"You would." Shaking his head, my grandfather set the paper in front of me and picked up the piece of chalk. "Would you like me to powder this for you?"

"Please." I concentrated on the map, and since I already knew where my Quinn was, I tapped the spot with a claw. Put there once powder."

The chalk didn't stand a chance, and the Egyptian wolf god dumped the powder onto the map as directed.

I engaged in a staring contest with the map and the pile of chalk. "Path to Quinn. No toy with me, magic. To Quinn."

The divine howled his laughter, fell over onto his side, and writhed.

The only appropriate response was to claw and bite him into submission, but before I could act on the impulse, the chalk erupted into golden light, and a trail formed leading across the sunlit, grassy plain. "Oh, path. I kick and bite you later," I promised.

"Must you?"

I snorted flame, lifted my head, and trotted after the glowing trail. "Yes. You earn no kick or bite with bribes."

"You're ruthless."

I swished my tail, pleased with the divine's complaints. "I try. Now, hurry. You no fall behind. You slow."

"Sane people are afraid of me, you know."

"Sane people not your grand-daugh-ter. You like me, no

lie. Have to be a little insane to deal with crazy Quinn family," I muttered. "Be happy I little insane."

"I'm getting you a dictionary for Christmas, and we're going to sit together and learn new words. None of those words mean what you think they mean. For example, you are not a little insane. You are a lot insane. Also, our family is not that crazy."

"While you get me dic-shun-air-ee, I get you mental help. You need."

Anubis sighed.

Your confidence is going to get you bit
one of these days.

Quinn

IT TOOK me several tries to figure out how to shift back to being a cindercorn, and when I did, the urge to light something—anything—on fire surged through me. When I snorted, flames roiled from my nostrils, which only strengthened the need to torch anything unfortunate enough to cross my path.

I pawed at the hard ground, tearing at it with my claws until the urge passed.

"Damn, you're pretty," Tiffany announced.

I whipped my head around, flattened my ears, and displayed my teeth.

"You won't eat me, so don't even posture, Mr. Samuel Quinn. Bailey would get mad if you did that, and you're certainly not going to eat Janet, either."

"Your confidence is going to get you bit one of these days," I predicted.

"Hot damn. Your English is good. Poor Bailey struggles. How'd you pull that off?"

"I had help," I confessed.

"Okay, that's fair enough. Your transformations are much smoother than Bailey's, too. I wonder if you can help her with them. It didn't look like it hurt you at all?"

"It hurts some, but I'm used to it. I've been shapeshifting for a long time." I shook my head and quelled the urge to snort more fire and try to ignite the dirt. "Janet, do you remember when you were petrified?"

Judging from her attire, she'd been taken—and petrified —shortly after leaving work. I couldn't sense any of the warmth I associated with a pregnant woman, either, much to my relief.

Janet huffed. "I'd just made it home from work. I was getting out of my cruiser in my own damned driveway; I'd worked a longer-than-normal shift, and my driveway was dark when I got home. Two gorgons caught me by surprise."

"Males?"

"One male, one female, but I didn't get a good look at either one."

"Bailey torched the male. There isn't much left of him."

Janet raised a brow. "She did?"

"She reduced him to a pile of ash right before I reversed your petrification. She lost her temper."

"Damn. I wanted a piece of him. And I can't get a piece of Winfield, either. I mean, I guess I could go in and shoot his body a few times, but that's not exactly satisfying. Also illegal. I still haven't figured out what happened to him."

"He got rammed by six hundred plus pounds of angry unicorn."

"That's gross. Bailey got a hold of him, too?"

"He pointed a gun at me."

"Death by stupidity. Only an idiot would point a weapon at you with her around. With both of you working the Manhattan circuit, you're going to be untouchable."

"That was the CDC's angle when pitching her transfer to the NYPD." I flicked an ear back. "It makes me wonder if Clemmends knows something I don't. I've never needed strong security before."

Thanks to my magic, I made my own security, and when I was in the field, I was usually with several pairs of officers. Accidents could happen to anyone. While my predecessor had been murdered, and while I often became a target of the vengeful, I'd never really considered any of the situations I faced to be particularly dangerous.

My heritage helped with that. I hadn't even needed to use any of my natural defenses to protect myself. When my gun didn't suffice, someone nearby handled the situation before I had to rely on petrifying someone.

I had no doubt I'd one day have to petrify someone while on duty, but I'd enjoy playing at being human until then. Once the secret was out, I'd have to reveal the entirety of my DNA test to prove I was mostly human with an odd smattering of other species. Some vanillas, like Bailey's parents, would pitch a fit about it.

I'd enjoy reminding them that they were at the mercy of people like me to keep them safe as they had few ways of protecting themselves. The laws favored vanilla humans, but the laws only went so far.

If I really wanted, I could give the Gardeners a taste of their own medicine. Unless they did something to Bailey, I wouldn't, but I'd enjoy thinking about it.

My worries over my wife intensified, and I took my

agitation out on the fence, melting the nearest section to a smoking puddle.

Janet whistled. "Remind me never to piss off a unicorn."

Tiffany laughed. "Bailey's worse. She cusses while lighting things on fire. Sam's just anxious because Bailey's not here right now. Go do your sweep of the building, Sam. I'll keep an eye out for the tankers and whistle when we're ready to get this show on the road."

I stepped over the molten steel and trudged to the dome to start there. In the time I'd taken Janet to Tiffany and called the CDC, nothing had changed. Aware of the possibility of disease and gorgon dust in the building, I checked John Winfield's body, removed his possessions, and dumped them near the fence.

"Janet, when the tanker arrives, have someone scan these for contaminates. They're from John Winfield's body, and they might have evidence on them."

"You slobbered on the evidence," she complained.

I glared at her. "The evidence will survive, and it's not like we need fingerprints from the corpse's possessions. We know exactly what killed him, we know he was involved, and there might be intel from his stuff. It's not like I can drag his body out here."

"Why not?"

"I don't think he'd stay intact," I admitted. "That plus he might be contaminated."

"That's disgusting."

"That's what happens when a large and angry unicorn crashes into a human at full throttle. Honestly, I'm impressed she didn't go through the wall."

"Don't tell Bailey I said this, but the next time I have a questionable shift, I want her to be my partner."

"I'm thinking about partnering you with Perkins and Nilman. That's not quite as good as Bailey, but they'll take care of you."

"Chief, that would be three of us working together. What happened to us working in pairs?"

"You'd have to work with Bailey and I directly, so having three of you makes sense. If you three are used to working together, we won't have issues in the field."

"Sounds good to me. Manhattan is a major upgrade to the Hamptons. Hell, truth be told, that's enough motive alone for me to think Morriston's being a dick."

"I really hope Morriston is not that idiotic. There aren't enough people with the right ranking to lose a chief to blatant stupidity."

"With Bailey working directly with you, Manhattan could absorb the Hamptons' turf with no difficulties."

"Except location, location, location," I reminded her. "That's a hell of a long drive. And Long Island doesn't have enough chiefs in the first place. I am not up for managing Manhattan *and* Long Island, Janet."

"Nonsense. You'd handle it with grace and dignity. It's not like the Hamptons are a hotbed of magical crime. It's mostly mundane shit and the overly wealthy crying that they *might* be targeted by someone who isn't as well off as they are." Janet shook her head. "Manhattan would be a major upgrade for him, but he'd have to get rid of another chief elsewhere to get moved—because the Hamptons can afford to go without a chief and use a network of captains."

"I'm thinking about making you do detective work with Perkins and Nilman when I don't need you, and you three whiners will like it," I announced.

"I can't tell if we're being rewarded or punished," she admitted.

"Both," I promised. "As you'll get bored if I don't give you something to do, bump heads with Tiffany and put together as much intel for me as you can, aware we'll see the information in the investigation. Tiffany, no spicing up the evidence, no making it sound cooler with embellishments, and for fuck's sake, no collecting misdemeanors."

Tiffany tossed her head back and laughed. "I'll let you off the hook just this once, Sam. I think we've all had enough excitement for one day."

No kidding.

BAILEY

THE GRASSY PLAINS made way for desert. An endless sea of sand stretched out before me, and the sun blazed overhead. A yellow haze filled the sky, as though it burned. The heat embraced me, and I picked up the pace. The sand and gently rolling dunes gave way to hard-packed ground, which in turn rose into craggy hills. A hole in the stone led underground, and my magic illuminated the way.

"Oh, that's clever," Anubis said.

I snorted, having forgotten the divine accompanied me. "How clever?"

"Technically, all planes of existence meet at nexus points. If there wasn't a connection point, we couldn't teleport. View it as a hall with many doors, except the nexus is just a place of energy. And light. I suppose a little light from your world would reach this one at one of those points, but you would have to wait for dawn to return without the help of additional magic." Anubis grunted. "I think."

"You think?"

"It didn't occur to me you might have magic enough to use the nexus. I didn't think to check. I made some assumptions based on what I know of your lineage."

"It nice to know even di-vine mess up." I swished my tail, lowered my head, and delved into the cave. "This world weird."

"The universe is a weird place, yes. But an interesting place. A world without amusing little beings like you would be rather dull."

"I have question."

"Ask."

"If I have four par-rents, why only know two?"

"We divines aren't the brightest at times—and I don't think it occurred to either one of them that a possession could lead to them having children. I doubt it even occurred to them to check if they had produced a child. And even if they had thought to check, they would assume the child was of human nature. Divine doesn't mean we're infallible. We have to have the presence of mind to look into the past—or the future. It's much easier to look into the past than it is the future. It's usually not worth the hassle."

"But you do look into future?" I asked.

"Of course. As I said, we're not infallible, and we're as curious as humans at times. And for those of us who have mortal children, we're more inclined to put in the effort. Mostly. But I would suggest you not judge your divine parents harshly. They truly didn't know of your existence."

"How you know?"

"I asked."

I blinked, halted, and swung my head around to face him, yelping as I banged my horn into the stone. "You ask? How ask? Why ask? When ask?"

"Are you going to ask who I asked and where I asked, too?"

"Okay. Who ask, where ask?"

"You're supposed to guess who they are," Anubis complained.

"Com-plain, com-plain, com-plain. You tell me to ask questions."

"Samuel deserves every last bit of trouble you give him," Anubis muttered. "I asked recently, shortly after you went on your trip with your friend but before I joined you here."

I considered his answer, and as that was a rather short period of time, especially for a divine, I resumed my hike into the passage leading underground, following the pink, shimmering trail of light. "That fair. Why ask?"

"I wanted to prepare them for the marvel that is your existence. Even the divine need some warning about things like this. Your father, in particular, has a healthy sense of curiosity. Your mother is less curious, but she will wallow in guilt for inadvertently abandoning you. It was as much for their benefit as for yours. I'm benevolent like that. At times."

"Are you good god or bad god?"

"I'm both. I'm more neutral than anything else. My wife is typically considered a good divine unless provoked. She's a protector. Technically, I am as well, but not in the way people think."

I considered him and his role in Egyptian lore. "You

protect the natural order of death. You preserve death. Ensure those who die, die as fated?"

"That's a rather good way of looking at it. I help maintain order among the dead until they are renewed into life. Death is not as permanent as most like to think, though some do opt to remain dead—or have not earned their way back into the light. It's complicated."

"Life is." The natural passage widened to a massive staircase of carved stone, and the paintings I associated with Egyptian tombs decorated the walls. A faint, golden light illuminated the way, and I took care with my steps so I wouldn't tumble head over hoof into the depths. "I part Egyptian? In truth?"

"In truth. Your children will have their fair share of Egyptian in them, too."

"They better not walk funny."

Anubis snorted. "I see you're comfortable with the idea of having children."

"Want *all* the children. I get two for Christmas! Children are for hugging and loving, and they be the best children." I pranced and swished my tail. "I fight for them in match!"

"You're married to an incubus, Bailey. You can have as many children as you want whenever you want."

I halted, tripped over my own hooves, and rolled to a halt. I landed on my back, snorting at having made an idiot out of myself. "No ask Quinn yet," I confessed.

"You could always surprise him."

"Can't, he cheat. No babies unless ask. Me too coward to ask." I rolled back to my hooves and shook out my fur. "You no tell soul I fall down steps because we talk kids."

"If you don't want to ask him, you can ask one of us to take care of the matter."

I pricked my ears forward. "Be present to Quinn? Surprise?"

"I can confirm he is almost as child-focused as you are and would be very pleasantly surprised."

I pranced on the steps, careful to keep from falling again. "Please? Please? All children!"

"You're going to need to open a nursery at the station if you have all the children, Bailey."

"There day-care next door. Good place. Cops use often. They good place, pro-tec-ted."

"You have an entire family of divines who would be happy to babysit for you as needed."

"That sound scary."

Anubis laughed. "You're wiser than you look."

"Don't want kids tied to chair for ex-po-sure therapy."

"We didn't exactly tie Samuel down. We just didn't let him go home until he became accustomed to us is all. It wasn't that bad for him. Truly. He was just heavily sheltered until his mother felt he was ready to handle the insanity. If your children are exposed from birth, our insanity will be their normality. You must admit, Bailey. Little about you is normal."

"My poor babies."

"Somehow, I think they'll be just fine. I recommend you ask either the angel or the Devil for help with your scheme. Both can trick our little Samuel into behavior conducive for the development of little ones. I recommend you set a fixed number of children per pregnancy, else you may be surprised."

I lifted a hoof and revealed a single claw. "This many."

On second thought, if we only had one, they would be severely outnumbered by the adopted children. I revealed a second claw. "This many. That make even number of children. Only this many. You make sure those pesky divines know this. And those pesky others, too. This your job."

"Only you would boss a divine around and expect results," Anubis complained. "In this case, you're getting what you want, but don't expect that in the future."

"If you say so," I replied, picking up my pace and following my trail so I could make my way back to Quinn.

QUINN

I FOUND nothing of use within the main dome of the mining complex, but the auxiliary buildings proved to be a treasure trove of death, destruction, and treachery. Three vats, the kind I recognized as suitable for the mass production of gorgon dust, were filled with a smoking dark fluid.

Within them, I expected to find the bodies of gorgons. In time, the fluid would turn gray, and as it dried, it would become a chalky dust. A little magic from a live gorgon—or the right chemicals—would finish the process and transform the residual organic matter into a virus capable of transforming a human into a gorgon—one capable of infecting other humans with the virus that would strip victims of their humanity.

The only good news was that none of the vats had turned gray yet; until the color changed, until they reeked of gorgon, the developing dust couldn't hurt anyone.

Sighing, I trotted through the remaining buildings before returning to the broken fence. "Tiffany, please call Marshal Clemmends. Notify him I've found three vats suitable for the production of gorgon dust. The batches aren't complete yet, but we're going to need more napalm."

Tiffany's brows rose. "More? How many tankers are on the way?"

"Not enough to coat this entire mine, and I don't know if the pit has any decaying gorgons in it, either." I sighed. "It's a pity we're in a dry state. This would be much more convenient if we had a lot of water on hand."

"I'll call him. Are you contaminated?"

"No. I would shift if I were." I flattened my ears at my unfortunate tendency to shapeshift when exposed to any significant gorgon magics. "The dust is in development, and I don't know if the heat from the napalm will finish the batch, so also request a secondary containment shield. There's a lot of potential dust in there."

Janet stared at me, her eyes narrowing. "Do you think this is related to the 120 Wall Street event?"

"Anything is possible at this point, but I don't think Winfield became involved until later. My feeling for him was he was out for revenge over what happened at Wall Street. It does make me think Audrey was involved; she'd been involved with a live batch of dust when she kidnapped Bailey. And she'd tried to infect her brother with dust, too. Is there someone else behind the dust production? That I can't tell you. But hopefully this will be the end of it."

Janet nodded. "That makes sense. It does make me worried Morriston is involved, however. He would've known you married Bailey and that she had been a major player at 120 Wall Street. If he *is* angling for your job, Winfield would be an ideal accomplice."

"We could just be creating conspiracy theories, too," I muttered.

"That's also true.

"What about the rabies incidents?" Tiffany asked.

"That's a good question." I considered the various options, marveling how anyone would treat life as though it were cheap and readily replaced. "It really depends on what the motive is. Unless there is a mass outbreak, it's easy to treat humans. It's much harder to treat gorgons. Maybe someone's out to trim the numbers of both species? If gorgons are easily infected with rabies, humans can be infected with gorgon dust, a large-scale epidemic could be triggered in a very short period of time. That would leave humans naturally resistant to the gorgon virus as the sole survivors. The cream of the crop, so to speak."

"That theory is disturbingly sound but ambitious. Neutralizer does mess with gorgon biology," Tiffany stated. "So it's harder to cure because the neutralizer isn't as effective on gorgons. Correct? But it can work; your children are evidence of that. Glass coffins *can* work on gorgons."

"Along with divine intervention. The question is this: which divine helped the children?" I shrugged. "I'll ask some of my relatives if they can shine some light on this. My grandfathers have meddled some. The rabies shouldn't be an issue moving forward, from my understanding of the situation. I hate not knowing."

"Your job must drive you insane," Tiffany muttered, shaking her head. "I'll call that asshole, but I'm expecting special treatment from you in the future."

I snorted flame, amused over what I knew would happen over the holidays. "An arrangement can be made."

"See, Janet? This is how you handle police chiefs. You demand bribes to do unpleasant work."

"I get a paycheck. Apparently, that's the only bribe required for me to do unpleasant work."

Whinnying a laugh, I spun around and resumed my search of the complex, hoping I wouldn't find anything else.

I had enough trouble to last a lifetime. Maybe once Bailey returned, I'd be better equipped to handle additional trouble. Then again, Bailey brought extra trouble wherever she went.

You make trouble for fun.

BAILEY

THE TRAIL LED deep underground to a cave filled with floating crystals that shed golden light. The warmth of the afternoon sun flooded the place. My magic guided me to a crystal nearby.

"Welcome to a nexus," Anubis announced. "The last time I was here, there weren't any crystals, just balls of light. I suppose change comes to even us."

I peered at the crystal wrapped in my sparkling magic. "This lead to Earth?"

"Yes."

"You make trouble for fun," I accused. "I wait until sunrise near Quinn? Then ride sunlight?"

"Sunny would make it easier for you—and allow you to return faster. Or you could use that pretty bracelet of yours to forge a connection with little Samuel. Either would work.

My grandson was properly forged into a conduit for your use."

I regarded the divine with narrowed eyes. "Forged? That sound painful."

"The Devil decided to involve himself and may have exposed little Samuel to copious amounts of hellfire while he was a cindercorn. Add a little angelic magic in the form of your bracelet, and you can home in on him. I am disappointed I didn't think of such a trick myself. I merely acquired Sunny for you and made certain she could reach you no matter where you went—and provide a way back to Earth. She'll be here soon."

"My puppy? Here? Soon?"

"It took her a while to give the Devil the slip. He is rather persistent and wants you to use his magic rather than mine."

Divines. I could trust them to be competitive idiots.

Anubis barked a laugh. "Indeed."

Damned mind-reading divines.

"That, too."

A howl drew my attention to the stairwell leading back to the surface, and several moments later, a golden wolf barreled down the stairs. She crashed into Anubis, bounced off, and plowed into my legs. The animal's tail beat against me, and she yipped her excitement. I lowered my head and sniffed the animal, who didn't seem like much of a puppy to me; she came up to my belly at the shoulders.

"She'll be more of a puppy back on the mortal coil," Anubis promised. "She's in her prime here."

"What I do with her?"

"Sunny, shine," Anubis ordered.

The wolf sat, lifted her head, and barked once. Then her

fur began to glow with a golden light, and she radiated warmth.

"That it? I use this light?"

"Visualize who you want to go to, and her light will shine there. But note that this only works between here and the mortal coil. Some limitations can't be circumvented. This is one of them. One-way street."

"So I can go to Quinn?"

"Yes."

"And nothing bad happen?"

"You'll startle him, I'm sure."

I liked the sound of that. "We go now?"

"You can go now if you'd like. Give it a try. I'll nudge you along if you need help."

I scoffed at the thought of needing help to ride a beam of sunlight, even when the sunlight radiated from my puppy. "Okay. Sunny come, too?"

"She'll follow you. Your magic will leave a trail she can ride, much like you ride sunlight."

"You coolest puppy ever," I announced, nuzzling the wolf.

Of all the magic I'd ever done in my life, concentrating on Quinn came easily.

In all ways, he was the center of my universe, even when I refused to admit it and struggled with the basics, including telling him just how much I loved him.

Words were never enough.

QUINN

IN THE THREE hours it took the tankers and mages to arrive at the mine, I found little evidence of use, although I did find a laptop, several wallets, blood samples, and the frozen body of a gray wolf encased in plastic.

I dragged everything to the pile of evidence to be checked over and taken away for examination. When a CDC representative in a hazmat suit approached, I pointed at the stash. "This is everything of potential importance I found that probably isn't contaminated with gorgon dust. Check for gorgon dust and rabies, please."

The representative nodded, turned on his scanner, and went to work.

The evidence showed no signs of contamination from gorgon dust, but the scanner squealed when he tested for rabies. The wolf proved the primary source of the virus, but it also contaminated the other material.

"Is the wolf virus the same as on the wallets? I tried to avoid cross contamination, but I'm somewhat limited right now." I eyed the wolf body, wondering why the gorgons had kept such a thing so close to their hive. Had the wolf been brought in before or after the hive had been infected with rabies? The presence of rabies on the rest of the evidence indicated the hive had been wiped out by the illness.

I wondered if John Winfield was the idiot with aspirations to become a god. The ampoule of ambrosia implied he was the kind crazy enough to wield the divine essence as a weapon—or as a tool to become divine.

No matter how I turned the situation over in my mind, I couldn't figure out how the pieces fit together.

The CDC rep fiddled with the settings on the scanner and held it over the pile of evidence. It squealed and began to beep. "There are four distinctive strains of the rabies virus present."

"Is that device sensitive enough to determine if any of those strains have the capacity to be airborne?"

"Rabies is bad enough without the risk of it becoming airborne," the representative complained, but he fiddled with the device again. "One virus sample is still alive, but I have no way of knowing if it might be airborne."

"Seal everything and treat it like it's airborne. Just in case. Make certain no gorgons are exposed to the virus."

"Such as yourself?"

I snorted flame. "Do you think the virus will survive exposure to napalm?"

"No. I don't."

"I'll be fine. But you can have me dunked in neutralizer if it makes you feel better. No glass coffins, though. My wife will rampage if you put me anywhere near one of those."

"We could distract her for the three hour session. Or have her go in for a run, too. She just loves glass coffins."

I considered the rep. "You know Bailey?"

"I teleported from Washington, sir. I'm one of her trainers."

I flattened my ears. "Bomb trainer?"

He laughed. "I'm Roberto Dascurne. I'm not one of the bomb techs. I'm specialized in infectious diseases, and I've worked with her on immunity tests."

I relaxed. "How'd she do? She threw a party when her last batch of evaluations was finished."

"Great. I've figured out what causes her immune system to crash."

I lifted my head. "You have? What is it?"

"When she's overexposed to neutralizer, one of her

genetic markers switches from on to off; the marker is the one responsible for the production of antibodies. When this marker is off, the antibodies she currently has cease to function. It's the same basic idea of how angels can become infected with human diseases at will—and purge them at will. They flip this specific marker on and off at will. Bailey isn't capable of switching the marker on and off at will. Neutralizer is essentially a form of solidified magic."

"But she doesn't have any angelic blood."

"No, but she has a great deal of divine DNA. The ability of angels is divine in nature. But, now that I have a good idea of what's causing it, it's an easy fix."

"What do you mean? How is it an easy fix?"

"If her immune system fails, just give her an injection of ambrosia. That will turn the gene marker back on and reboot her immune system. Her immune system will then purge everything from her body. Hey, can you do me a favor?"

"What favor?"

"Convince Bailey to let us do a rabies test on her. The next time she finds a rabid puppy in a dumpster, don't start treatments right away. Give it a week. After we can confirm infection, we'd like to flip the gene off for twenty-four hours and then flip it back on. We want to see if she'll purge the virus like angels do."

The CDC needed to employ Tiffany full-time. She would be right at home with the crackpots who wanted to do research on my wife. "Write up a full report of all issues you expect, pitch it to Bailey. If I have to adopt another rabid dog or cat because of this, the CDC will be responsible for helping me find a bigger house. And the CDC will provide a trainer for exotic animals so we can both be licensed."

"I heard about the ocelot." Roberto nudged the wolf's corpse. "This is useful, as we do have that small pack of rabid wolves; if this virus sample matches their strain, we might have a good lead on the investigation. One of the wolves might be a suitable animal for your adoption."

"Why?"

"She likes humans too much. She's not a good release candidate."

"What are the odds she could become a wolf ambassador for the general public?"

"Pretty high."

I sighed. "I'll talk with one of my dog trainers, and we'll see if we can work with the wolf. Send word along the line we'll take responsibility for the wolf if there isn't a better placement for her elsewhere."

"Excellent. I'll let you know, and I'll send trainers for wolves and large felines in the next few weeks so you can be fully licensed. In the meantime, I'll have temporary permits issued for you."

"Call me after we get this mess dealt with. Best time would be in early January. What's the ETA on the tankers being ready to flood this place out?"

"Give me half an hour to get this evidence contained and into our truck, then we'll need twenty minutes to get the water tankers converted and start pumping. Try to avoid eating too much napalm, Chief Quinn. However amusing it is to watch a unicorn get drunk on flammable materials, you will not appreciate the hangover tomorrow."

"If my wife shows up, all bets are off."

"The last thing anyone needs is two cindercorns hopped up on napalm."

I whinnied my laughter. "Then tell the CDC to get on

finding reliable ways to light this blend of napalm. If you could do that reliably, you wouldn't be in this situation right now."

"I would've asked for a phoenix feather, but the last time we went that route, we got the whole damned birds, and that's even worse than drunk cindercorns."

"Well, maybe the next time my wife requests napalm, you'll listen. When she has to get creative, she gets really creative."

"Trust me, we know. We've learned our lesson. I wish you the very best of luck containing her in the future. You're going to need it."

BAILEY

UNLIKE WHEN I hitched a lift on a sunbeam, time distorted. I supposed distance factored into it; light only traveled so fast, and I had no way of judging how far of a gap I had to cross to travel between the divine realm and the mortal coil.

I disliked the darkness, but I looked forward to seeing Quinn.

Had I been thinking, I would've realized life rarely went my way. Instead of my usual, somewhat graceful landings, I popped into existence and crashed directly onto my target. I squealed, Quinn crashed to the ground beneath me, and had he been human or been a gorgon-incubus doohickey, I would've crushed him.

The peppery spice of napalm filled my nose, and after a stunned moment, I realized the gel-like fluid surrounded us.

"So nice of you to drop in," my husband muttered. "Could you please get off?"

"Oops." I rolled off him, splashed into the napalm, and scrambled to my hooves. Then I licked napalm off my husband's nose. He tasted even better when drenched with the sparkly gel. "Best present!"

Quinn groaned and rolled to his hooves, and the napalm dripped from his coat. "Welcome home. Enjoy your trip?"

A flash of golden light drew my attention, and a moment later, Sunny landed on my back. "Yes! Look! Puppy."

Quinn reached over, seized Sunny by the scruff of her neck, and waded through the napalm in the direction of a bright light. I realized someone had set up a spotlight near several large tankers, which were hard at work flooding the area with my favorite treat. I trailed behind Quinn, prancing in the gel while he delivered my puppy to Tiffany.

"Please make sure there's no napalm in her coat," Quinn said, releasing my puppy once certain Tiffany had a good hold on her. "Thank you."

Tiffany held my puppy in one arm and waved at me. "Nice entrance, Bailey."

"Nice? I squish Quinn," I wailed.

"He handled it with grace. He hasn't been completely squished. He's only slightly tenderized. Right, Sam?"

"I'm fine, Bailey. You startled me. We have to light up some napalm now. You can rub my back later as penance for landing on me."

Quinn's recommended 'punishment' caught my attention, and I regarded him with a hungry look. "Will need babysitter. Will take long time to rub back."

"I'm sure I can coerce one of my relatives to watch the kids for a while."

"Good. Good." I lifted my head and pranced in place. "Janet! Janet!"

Janet saluted me. "Go get that napalm lit so we can go home sometime this year."

"You stay for wedding," I declared. "There be one, even if have to take over Vay-gus."

Janet laughed. "Just get me home sometime this year, please. Also, I'd like to see you take over Vegas. Sounds like fun."

"Yes, can do. You have pets? Need pets watched? Home watched? Quinn? Did you take care of Janet's home?"

"I don't have any pets, and my house should be fine. The door was locked, and I have an alarm system. Don't worry, Bailey. Really."

I relaxed and nuzzled Quinn. "When we make fire?"

My husband chuckled and nipped my shoulder. "As soon as the containment field goes up. It won't be much longer. Let's go get into position so we can get to work as soon as they're ready."

I bolted for the dome, skidded to a halt in the napalm, and pranced while waiting for Quinn to catch up. "Hurry, hurry, hurry."

He laughed and joined me, rewarding me with another nuzzle and a nip. "Patience, Bailey. You'll get to play with napalm soon enough."

QUINN

BAILEY'S common sense and dignity dribbled out of her pretty equine ears, and she rolled in the napalm, kicked her hooves, and played like a child on a sugar high. What amused me most was that she didn't eat more than a bite or two before she abandoned all pretenses of maturity to romp and play in the gel.

I took a nibble here and there to see what all the fuss was about, but beyond the napalm having a warm, peppery bite, I didn't see the appeal.

I supposed her heritage played some part in it functioning somewhat like pixie dust for her. Her reaction did remind me a lot of how many reacted to the shimmering powder most used to improve their moods—if taken to the extremes.

Bailey flopped onto her back and wormed through the gel, and I stared in a mix of awe, amusement, and confusion at her antics. I hadn't even known cindercorns could, with enough work, slither across the ground on their backs.

My life had become so strange since Bailey had stormed into it. I took another bite of napalm just in case I hadn't consumed enough to turn me into a hyperactive menace.

Nothing happened beyond adding to the warmth in my belly. I expected that warmth would become stronger fire once the containment shield went up. I figured if I could survive hellfire, the ignited napalm wouldn't bother me.

I just needed to make sure I stayed out of Bailey's way while she freaked out. Unlike the incident at 120 Wall Street, I wasn't concerned about the mine crushing her; most of the buildings only had one or two stories, and it would take a lot more than some steel to slow my wife down.

Just to be on the safe side, I'd stay out in the open and leave the building demolition to her.

She'd have fun, and I'd have fun watching her have fun.

Not long after Bailey had decided walking was too much

effort and slithering was more up her alley, the containment shield snapped into place, and the barrier gleamed in the colors of the rainbow, illuminating the entirety of the mine complex.

"Showtime, Bailey." I nudged her with a hoof. "We need to light the napalm now."

"Napalm!" my wife purred, and she snuggled with the gel. "Yummy, delicious napalm."

I wanted to be the one she snuggled with, damn it. "Bailey. We have to light it on fire."

"Soon," she replied, and I got the feeling she used soon in the same way my divine relatives used the word: if left to her own devices, she'd leave me waiting for a few years first.

Great. I'd have to figure out how to light it myself. "How did you light it in New York?"

For a moment, I thought she wasn't going to answer me, as she started chowing down on her favorite treat. "Run fast, make fire."

At the rate of her napalm consumption, the CDC would need to bring in a few extra tankers to make up for her gluttony.

My poor wife. She'd have a record-breaking hangover in the morning.

I had no idea if I could run fast and make sufficient fire to light up the napalm, but I'd give it a shot. If I couldn't do it, I'd find some way to goad my drunk cindercorn wife into helping out. Shaking my head over the insanity, I pawed at the gel, snorted flame, and took off at a canter. Napalm splashed into my fur, and as soon as I hit full speed, my fur ignited.

Unlike hellfire, the napalm tickled more than it hurt. With a little experimentation, I discovered the faster I ran, the faster the napalm ignited. The thick gel resisted my efforts, but once patches of it burned without my interference, it began to spread.

Snorting flame helped, too.

The first time I passed my wife, she didn't even notice I'd turned her lake of napalm into flame. When she finally figured out I would take her treat away through burning it off, she surged to her hooves, charged a few paces in my direction, and snorted her displeasure.

"Bad Quinn! No burn!"

I skidded to a halt and snorted fire at her. "Yes, burn."

"No."

"Yes."

She closed the distance between us, reared, and stomped her hooves into the napalm. "Can't eat if you burn."

I longed to smack my forehead at the insanity. "Bailey."

"Not my napalm," she whined, and as I'd married a cindercorn with the general maturity level of a toddler given copious amounts of sugar, she rolled into the flaming gel. "Mine!"

If I loved her much more, my heart really would burst in my chest. "You're ridiculous."

She wormed her way to me and somehow managed to wrap herself around my forelegs. "You mine, too."

That was something. "Yes, I am. But I still have to light the napalm on fire."

"Mean!"

I regarded the gel, which had begun to burn merrily and spread. "I'm so cruel and mean. You'll just have to punish me after we get to our hotel."

"Promise?"

"The faster you ignite all this napalm, the faster we get to the hotel so you can properly punish me."

Bailey lurched to her hooves and galloped away, and the few times she slowed, probably long enough to catch her breath, she bucked and whinnied. I couldn't tell if the napalm had short-circuited her brain, or if she was that excited to take me to a hotel.

Either worked for me, and bemused, I watched my wife turn into a fiery psychopath hellbent on destruction.

TWENTY-TWO

Jerk husband.

BAILEY

NAPALM DID wonderful but terrible things to me, but unlike 120 Wall Street, I didn't become tangled in any debris. Unfortunately, to keep me somewhat contained, Quinn sat on me. He sat on me with his fat unicorn ass, and he refused to budge. Biting, clawing, and even poking him with my horn won me exactly nothing. If anything, my attempts to escape amused him.

Evil, evil Quinn.

"You devil," I hissed, snapping my teeth at him. "Eat flesh from bones!"

"If you want a steak, I hear there are some really good steakhouses in Vegas, but you'll have to wait until lunch." Quinn chuckled and bumped his nose against mine with no fear of me or my sharp, pointy teeth. "Bite me again. It tickles nicely."

Jerk husband. I struggled beneath him, and since he'd asked so nicely, I chomped on his shoulder. "Up! Up! You fat."

"If I let you up, you will go rampage some more. The napalm is burned out, and they're about to soak the place down. If I let you up, you'll dig under the nearest pile of debris trying to avoid the water."

"No water. Water *bad*."

"We need to be detoxed, Bailey."

"No. No. We die if we get wet."

"We're not going to die. We're just going to be cold and miserable for twenty minutes. Then we can shift back to human, get dressed, and go to our hotel. You can punish me extra for making you get wet."

"You just want to be pun-ished. It's not a pun-ish-ment if you like." I sighed. "No fair."

"Yes," he replied, and he nuzzled my neck. "And if you're cold and tired when we get in, I'll tuck you in and take care of you. I'll enjoy it immensely."

"You just enjoy not having to work for a few weeks."

"That, too. I was going to plan a wedding ceremony, but I think my relatives may have gone overboard, mutinied, and taken over."

"More time for us in hotel. Get good baby-sitter. We get children during day. Then we evict with relatives for night and have in morning," I suggested. "We need plenty of time at night. We spend Christmas here?"

"Christmas here is the plan. We'll have to sort our hotel situation out—assuming it wasn't sorted out for us."

"Your family nuts."

"Your family might be even nuttier than my family," he replied.

"Anubis wouldn't tell me who! He try make me play twenty questions. I suck at game. He suck. Stupid."

"It'll be all right. If you don't figure it out on your own, you'll find out soon enough. Do you think you're going to be scandalized when you see the showgirls?"

"After brassault, no. Show-girl boobs covered. Not covered at strip place. Not want see naked boobs. Seen too many naked boobs. Covered boobs okay."

"I'll only take you to a strip club if you ask me to really nicely."

"But why? Why go? We go hotel and do strip there. Better time."

Quinn laughed so hard he rolled off me. Before I could do more than stand, the shield overhead thrummed and a cold rain fell. I sighed, bowing my head as my coat steamed and began to cool. "This no fair. Now wet."

"It'll be okay," Quinn promised. "You'll see."

QUINN

ACCORDING TO MY WIFE, if she spent five more minutes as a sopping wet unicorn, she would surely die, the world might end, and there would never be fire anywhere on Earth ever again. The more absurd her claims became, the harder I laughed. I didn't enjoy taking a neutralizer bath, but I dealt with it. As soon as the deluge came to an end and the shield dropped, I trotted to the fence, where Tiffany offered me a change of clothes.

"Your grandfather brought your suitcase and my husband over."

Poor Perkins. "And how is your husband?"

"He threw up on your grandfather. And then he threw up on your uncle. Were you aware the Devil is your uncle? Your grandfather and your uncle are bickering. I expected that, but they're bickering in a surprisingly friendly fashion. I'm not sure how one can be your grandfather and the other can be your uncle, though."

"As a matter of fact, yes. I'm aware. The Devil is technically my great uncle, but he prefers uncle. I'm wise enough to give the Devil what he wants without a fight. Is Arthur all right?" Perkins throwing up on my relatives hadn't been part of any plan, but it would keep the bickering divine busybodies occupied while I got changed and coaxed Bailey into shapeshifting back to human.

"He'll be all right. It'll be an hour or two until his stomach settles, so expect some whining."

Whining I could handle. I could even handle vomit, but I'd much rather let my relatives handle any vomiting. Taking my clothes in my teeth, I trotted over to the tankers, and squeezed between them so I wouldn't give the crews a show.

Bailey would appreciate my jeans and t-shirt, as she loved when I dressed down almost as much as when I was in my uniform.

Stretching to work out the kinks from transforming, I strolled back to Tiffany. "That's much better. Thank you. So, how is Arthur really? Please tell me the vomiting has stopped."

"Stop being a worrywart. He'll be fine. One of the CDC reps is taking care of him, and the Devil and your grandfather are arguing over who could teleport him better. I think Arthur's allergic to teleportation magic."

"Wouldn't he break out in hives if he's allergic?"

"Maybe intolerant. Who knows? Honestly, I may have upset your relatives."

I stared at her. "How?"

"I asked why couldn't they teleport my husband without getting him sick. Bailey can. I mean, he still turns green, but he can handle her catching a sunbeam fairly okay now. He doesn't throw up. Not like this."

"Poor Arthur." I caught Tiffany in a hug and patted her back. "Thank you for taking care of Bailey."

While embracing her, I concentrated, searching for the markers of a fertile woman. To my amusement, I could sense that a few of my pesky relatives had taken a turn ensuring she was no longer barren.

I couldn't wait until she figured out she'd been played by my entire family.

Tiffany hugged me back. "Any time. You do need to make sure you let her get some more rest, but it'll be better now that you're on the same shift with her. You've both been stressed thanks to not being able to see each other enough."

"Quinn," my wife whined, and she wormed her way across the torched ground.

Tiffany covered her mouth with her hands. "She's not even trying to walk, Sam. She's slithering. On her back while waving her hooves in the air."

"I noticed. She was doing that in the napalm, too. She didn't want me to light it up, either. And I had to goad her into doing her share of the work."

"I'm cold, Quinn," Bailey complained, wiggling her way over until she wrapped her impressive bulk around my legs. "I'm wet."

"Well, if you shift back to human, you'll only be wet, and you'll only be wet because you're making me wet." I bent over and scratched under her chin. "I can't take you to the hotel if you're still a unicorn."

"Can, too. Drag behind truck. No care. Too tired."

"I promise it took a lot more energy to slither over here than it would've taken you to walk."

"No logic. Bad. Logic bad."

"I'm going to make my grandfather help you shift if you don't do it on your own."

"But it hurts," my wife complained. "No want more hurty."

Poor Bailey. I smiled at her, crouched, and scratched behind her ears. "Hungover already?"

"No fair."

"I can get you the hangover medication once we're in Vegas, and I'll pamper you all you want. It'll be easier on you if you shift yourself."

"Can grandfather cure hangovers?"

"He probably won't. He's the kind to let us suffer for our indulgences."

"Indulged much. Deserve hangover."

"Do you have Bailey's clothes, Tiffany?"

"And a nice, warm blanket so she won't put on a show shifting for everyone." Tiffany left long enough to bring a silvery thermal blanket and a pile of folded clothes. "Janet's out like a light in the ambulance, by the way. She's fine, but she must have been pretty tired before she got petrified. They were doing a check, and she decided to fall asleep on them. Since she's your cop, they want you to decide if she's going to the hospital."

"She is, and she's getting a rabies treatment."

Tiffany set Bailey's clothes down and handed me the blanket. "I'll let them know while you get her to shift."

I waited for Tiffany to get out of earshot before draping the blanket over my shivering wife. "Time to shift, Bailey. I'll warm you up properly at the hotel. I will go make my grandfather force you to shift if you won't do it on your own. I don't want you getting sick."

She whined about my terrible, cruel ways, but a shiver ran through her body as she cooperated. I held the blanket ready while her unicorn form dissolved, and she reversed back to human. I covered her up with the thermal blanket, tucking it in around her before gathering her clothes and helping her get changed.

The sneezes warned me the neutralizer bath hadn't done her any favors, but with my grandfather nearby and CDC reps underfoot, I figured if she got sick, *someone* would be able to deal with it. Once she finished dressing, I scooped her up, ignoring her tired protests.

Tiffany met me halfway to the tankers, and she snickered. "She's not a doll, Sam. She can probably walk."

"I'm walking for her." The complaining I expected didn't come, and when I checked on my wife, I discovered she'd taken a page out of Janet's book. "Do you think someone asleep can walk? I'm not sure I should put this to the test, Tiffany."

Tiffany peeked at my wife, laughed, and shook her head. "Okay. I'm an idiot. She did run across half the damned country looking for Janet. I'd say she's earned a nap." She pointed near the tankers. "Your family is over there with Arthur. Someone is bringing a vehicle for us. They're taking Janet to the hospital now."

"Good. I'll get Bailey settled at our hotel and then go see her and take care of the paperwork."

"Someone from the FBI is taking care of the paperwork."

My brows rose at that. "Really?"

"You'll be questioned at the hotel."

"Did they saddle you with coordination work?"

"I got tired of the various offices bickering. It was less of a saddling and more of a hostile takeover." Tiffany grinned and waved for me to follow her. "Arthur's over here. He'll be happy to see you're intact. He was worried he would have to try to figure out how to get two drunk unicorns under control while feeling like he might die."

"Why would he think I'd be drunk?"

"You were a unicorn with ready access to napalm. Why else?"

"Well, it's safe to say I don't react the same way to napalm as Bailey does."

"That's a shame. You would've had the time of your life if you did."

I snorted. "And the worst hangover of my life, too."

"That's true. Bailey's okay?"

I considered my wife, who slept quietly in my arms. "I'm assuming so."

"Maybe you should ask those pesky divines just to be sure. She had one hell of a run today and a lot of excitement." To make it clear she wasn't accepting a no from me, Tiffany placed her hands on my back and pushed. "That way, Sam."

"You're excitable." I went along with her wishes and strolled towards where she claimed my relatives waited. "What's gotten you riled up?"

"We have rooms at the Venetian, I'm starving, and I want to sleep. Your grandfather already checked us all in. There's a room for you and Bailey, a suite for the kids and a babysitter nearby so you can have some privacy, a room for Arthur and I, and some of your relatives also have rooms. It's going to be a madhouse."

"How did they get so many rooms on such short notice?"

"I guess Vegas at Christmas isn't all that popular?" Tiffany gave me another push. "You're slow. Hurry up. I'm hungry, Sam."

I shook my head at the woman but did as she asked.

BAILEY SLEPT LIKE THE DEAD, which did a good job of worrying me even more than when Winfield had shot her with ambrosia—or when she'd scared a few years off my life at 120 Wall Street. I worried so much that Tiffany and Arthur ganged up on me and stuffed a chill pill down my throat while Beauty and Sylvester laughed at my misfortunes.

Then, because children were truly a source of pure evil, they crawled into bed with Bailey and left no space for me.

Bailey hadn't even woken up, and she already had both whelps wrapped around her finger. I wondered if she'd even get to fight, as the children would ultimately decide their fate. Judging from appearances, our little family had already grown by two without us having to lift a finger.

I wanted to join them, but unlike my wife and the kids, I had work to do despite being so tired I wasn't against the idea of sleeping on the floor.

The Devil took pity on me and brought me coffee. "At least the new medication is much kinder to you. You're mostly coherent."

"Mostly. Did you have a good time tormenting your brother?"

"He is delightfully miffed I'm poking my nose in the family business. He's also miffed he's been fully exposed. Your parents are on their way. After seeing your friend's reaction to teleportation, it was decided the rest of the family could fly in like civilized beings rather than sick ones. Your friend is fine. He's enjoying certain amusements with his wife."

"She's going to be pregnant by the end of the day, isn't she?"

"No, no. She's being blocked until Christmas so her body has a chance to adapt to increased hormone production. Your grandfather handled healing—and creating—the appropriate bits. I'm handling the hormonal therapy. She has no idea what's going on, although she's enjoying some of the benefits of devilish meddling."

"I don't want to know."

"You're too much like my brother," the Devil complained, and he flopped onto the couch. "Your menagerie is at the vet for paperwork so they can come to the hotel. The hotel agreed to them staying if the CDC provided documentation on them. So, expect them to arrive later this afternoon. Your schedule will be open until Christmas, when you and your bride will be expected to attend your wedding. Most of the arrangements are being handled. My wife got bored, so she wanted to help."

I foresaw disaster. "Most of them are being handled?"

"We need to know if you want anyone in particular to be invited."

"Beyond the family? Not really. If I invite one person

from the station, I have to invite all people from the station, and I'm not sure we can fit that many cops here."

"It could be done. It would also be possible to charter a flight to bring them here and send them home the next day."

"That would be a very, very large wedding. Where would we hold it?"

"At the canals. The hotel has already consented to having the ceremony in the hotel proper. Dinner will be at the steakhouse, and we've managed to reserve the entire restaurant after their normal closing hours. That will give you time for your match for the gorgon whelps, which will be held at the pools for easy cleaning. To appease the hotel, it will be a demonstration match, so there will be guests observing." The Devil chuckled. "That means bloodshed must be kept at a minimum. Mostly, you'll be strutting your stuff while your wife shows off her immunities. The hotel will allow guests to be petrified if they sign a waiver and pay for the supplies required to reverse their petrification."

Yep. My official wedding would be even more of a disaster than the courthouse fiasco. "How many laws will we be breaking in one ceremony?"

"Disappointingly, none. Well, maybe one."

"Maybe one?"

"There's the issue of your in-laws."

"Which in-laws?"

"The ones I'll be hosting at a later time."

I wrinkled my nose. "Them. If they don't show up, I'm all right with this. They'll just upset Bailey."

"I have reason to believe it would be very therapeutic for her to speak her mind on their poor life choices."

When the Devil said something like that, I worried. "You've been peeking, haven't you."

"Of course. It's a trivial matter in the grand scheme of things, and it's close enough in the future to be of little consequence."

I doubted I would ever understand the divine. "Just tell them if they show up, they will be able to remove Bailey permanently from their life. Then give them plane tickets and pay for lodging because they're greedy assholes who would never spend a cent on their own daughter. I'll even pay for it myself."

"I will send you a bill. I presume you wish for their tickets to be for the most uncomfortable flight I can manage?"

"Tolerable seats. I'll leave their torture for the afterlife."

The Devil chuckled. "Excellent. That's all I need. For the next few days, worry about your wife and children. We'll take care of the rest."

"Do we have to do clothing fittings?"

"My wife has already handled that. She's rather skilled at judging clothing sizes."

Someone knocked at the door, and I opened it to discover a handful of cops, an FBI agent with a badge held up, and Roberto. The CDC rep waved.

"What can I do for you gentlemen?"

"We need to ask you some questions about the kidnapping of your police officer."

"And that's my cue to leave," the Devil announced before disappearing in a flash of silvery light along with the faintest hint of brimstone.

I shook my head at my uncle's antics. "Please come in, but we'll need to keep it quiet. The kids and wife are sleeping."

"Still?" Roberto asked. "She's been out since last night."

"She ran across half the continent, and the children have been displaced enough they're worn out. I've been promised, repeatedly, she's fine and I should stop worrying."

"And you've been given medication to help with that," he replied in a wry tone. "We'll need to question your wife when she's awake." Roberto grimaced. "Unfortunately, we'll also need to question the young gorgons. They are the kids in your care, correct?"

"They are. I haven't confirmed with them yet that their father will not be coming home," I replied, careful to keep my voice soft. "That is something I'll be handling this week. We don't know what happened to him, do we?"

"Not definitively, but we have had reports of wiped out gorgon hives in several states along with individual males without hives. He could easily be any one of those. All of the bodies were incinerated to prevent the production of gorgon dust. We will do our best to avoid that specific subject with them, but we do need to know as much as we can about their home life prior to the death of their hive mothers and their father."

"Were you able to get a confirmation they were treated with a glass coffin?"

"Yes. We also have records of the father paying a substantial fee for the assistance of an angel. The angel's identity is unknown to us, however. They aren't required to identify themselves unless they choose to. The angel did the work for a reduced fee, however. This was noted in the file."

"He probably didn't have the money for the full fee after the glass coffin treatments." My heart ached for Beauty and Sylvester. "I'll tell you everything I know about the situation. Perhaps I'll know enough to limit how much they'll have to discuss."

"It's worth a try," Roberto replied.

Everyone filed into the suite, and I was grateful I'd somehow gotten a suite with an actual bedroom so we wouldn't disturb Bailey and the children. I sat on the floor to prevent a discussion of who would be left standing, leaning against the wall and making myself as comfortable as I could.

Drawing a deep breath, I began from the moment I'd met Bailey and told them everything I knew of my ex-wife's plans, Bailey's interactions with John Winfield, and the 120 Wall Street incident.

TWENTY-THREE

That wasn't quite right.

BAILEY

I WOKE up with more snakes than I could count in my face, and none of them were my husband's crimson-hooded cobras. The snakes were a great deal smaller than Quinn's, and I realized they were attached to two young whelps. I couldn't figure out how I'd gone from a mine to a posh bedroom, but I didn't mind having two children treating me like a pillow.

I did, however, mind the lack of Quinn nearby to snuggle with. I also minded the headache piercing through my eyeballs to dig into my brain with a sharp, pointy stick.

Napalm hated me.

Stupid, delicious, yummy napalm.

To make matters worse, I needed to go to the bathroom, and I had no idea how to escape the clutches of two sleeping gorgon children without waking them.

"Quinn," I whined, well aware if my husband was in hearing range, he'd show up.

He hated when I whined.

Sure enough, my husband showed up, and he smiled at me. "I have your medication in the other room, and I'll order you something for breakfast."

"You are the best husband." That was close to telling him I loved him, right? I needed to figure out why my mouth hated spitting out those three important words. I could do it even with a headache. I just had to concentrate. "I love you, but I need to pee."

Crap. That wasn't quite right. I'd accomplished the important part and would give myself a gold star for effort later, but I'd gone and messed it up by blurting too much.

Quinn laughed, approached the bed, and rubbed the little girl's shoulder. "Beauty, you need to get up, little one. Bailey needs to use the bathroom."

Like me, the little girl whined, but she turned and latched onto Quinn, which gave me enough space to scoot away from the little boy.

Unlike his sister, he was having nothing to do with my escape, and he tightened his grip. His snakes stirred, and they nuzzled my cheek.

I couldn't do it. I couldn't dislodge the little boy. I stared at Quinn with wide eyes.

My husband dared to laugh at me, shifted Beauty to one arm, and worked his arm around Sylvester. "All right, Sylvester. You need to come with me so Bailey can wake up. She's not feeling well. You can take a bubble bath as soon as she's done using the bathroom."

Both children seemed to be fans of bubble baths, as they both clung to Quinn and woke up enough to stare at him with wide eyes. At first, I thought they were hopeful, but then Beauty's lip began to tremble.

"She's going to be fine, Beauty. She's just really tired from helping a friend, and she ate something that upset her tummy. She'll feel better after she takes some medication and has breakfast. You two need breakfast, too."

I crawled out of bed, and while I meant to stand and walk like a normal, functional adult, I smacked into the carpet.

Quinn chuckled and nudged me with his foot. "I love you, too, my beautiful, but you need to get yourself together. It's your turn to go through hours of questioning to make sure the FBI and CDC can do their work."

I groaned, gave up all pretenses of being a mature adult, and crawled to the bathroom, which fortunately wasn't far. "If I'm not out in twenty minutes, I fell asleep."

"I would offer you coffee, but you'd be upset because your coffee is so much better. There's tea."

"I don't want minty grass. I want coffee." I made it to the bathroom door, used the frame to get to my feet, and leveled a glare at my husband. "I'll accept bad coffee, but there better be coffee."

"If you make it through your shower without falling asleep, I'll provide coffee."

My husband's ultimatums didn't need any work, and after glowering at him, I slipped into the bathroom and began the tedious process of restoring myself to base functionality. During my shower, I discovered I'd been nipped by at least fifteen snakes, and one of the biting assholes had been Francisco, as he liked trying to poke heart-shaped patterns into me with his teeth.

It would take days for my cleavage to recover from Francisco's perverted attempt at art.

"Quinn, did you have to?" I complained loud enough to be heard over the shower.

As I hadn't locked the door, Quinn cracked it open and poked his head inside the bathroom. "What have I done now?"

"Fransisco bit a heart into me again."

With a smile that did a good job of convincing me I should invite him into the shower, he replied, "The children were upset after I put you to bed, and it was easier to calm them while shifted. He got ideas while I was distracted. I'd be sorry, but you were restless, and his nips seemed to calm you down, so once I saw what he was doing, I let him get away with it. Then the others joined in because they were jealous."

"The physical requirements for this to happen are disturbing. Your head must have been on my stomach." I pointed at my chest, where Francisco had left his mark. "Right in the cleavage, you!"

"I may have used you as a pillow while telling the kids a story."

Damn it, I couldn't even get mad over that. "Let me guess. The scaly bastards snuck up my shirt to complete their fiendish plans to mark my person."

"Francisco started it. I would be sorry, but it's a really nice heart, and you look lovely."

"If you're trying to be invited into the shower, it's working. You should come join me. You can wash my back."

And every other part of me.

Quinn laughed. "The children will be staying with my parents tonight, so you'll have to wait until then. My parents begged, and the children seemed interested because they want to have a big family of people to coddle them. It'll help them adapt to staying with humans—and my grandparents can reverse accidental petrifications. Hurry up so I can get you fed and get your medication into you."

"But I want you to join me in the shower."

"And I want to join you in the shower, but I have a bunch of law enforcement officers in the other room, and they're keeping an eye on the children. Once they're done with their questioning session, we have wedding planning issues to discuss, and then we get to spend until Christmas indulging in each other, seeing the sights, and playing with the children."

"Can we go straight to the indulging?"

His smile truly did unfair things to me. "I'm afraid not, my beautiful. You're all right? If Francisco's bites are bothering you, I'll scold him later."

"I'll scold him later, thank you. And cuddle him. But it looks like most everyone needs to be scolded. Did they all have to take a turn nipping?"

"The one on your shoulder was from Beauty. Her brother startled her, and she nipped. I scolded her only as much as necessary, but make sure you keep that in mind when we're out; they're both young enough still they nip defensively."

"It's a good thing I'm immune to snake venom."

"It really is. You'd be frothing at the mouth otherwise. Are you feeling any better?"

"I'm feeling like I'm alone in this shower."

"I'll take a shower with you later," he promised, backing out of the bathroom. "I've ordered breakfast for you and the kids, and it should be here soon."

I took that as a hint I needed to hurry up or risk losing my breakfast to a pair of hungry kids. I blitzed through the rest of my shower, piled my hair in a towel on top of my head, and changed into a pair of my favorite jeans, which would torment Quinn until he managed to get me out of them.

It would be a long day for both of us.

The hotel room's living room had turned into an investigation site with papers scattered on every available surface. Despite Quinn's claim the children were present, I couldn't spot them. "Where did my babies go?"

"Kidnapped by my parents. You get three breakfasts because my parents have decided they will be rampaging through Vegas and exploring the city. My grandparents went with them."

"Which grandparents?"

"All of them."

"That's too many grandparents." I shook my head and wondered how I'd even eat one breakfast. I glanced at the various law enforcement officers, and I pointed at the CDC representative responsible for a few too many torture sessions. "Fiend!"

Roberto laughed. "Good afternoon, Bailey. How are you feeling?"

"It is not afternoon. Quinn said he had breakfast for me. Three of them. Breakfasts happen before noon."

Quinn laughed, stepped around the various piles of paperwork, picked me up by my waist, and set me in front of the couch. "Make the woman some space so she can eat. And breakfast happened after noon because I called the front desk and asked really nicely for breakfast. I really wasn't expecting my parents to take the kids, so you really do have three breakfasts to choose from."

"Why choose?" I asked, plopping down on the couch between Roberto and an older man in a suit, likely some form of FBI goon ready to make my life miserable. "Bring the orange drink thing that makes the hangover go away, put coffee in reach, leave food. When the morning ritual has been completed, you may talk to me."

Quinn chuckled but obeyed, and I attacked the glass of orange-flavored liquid that would bring relief within minutes. Once I chugged it so it could work its magic on me, I went for the coffee to restore my base ability to function.

My choices of breakfast included pancakes, waffles, bacon, sausage, hash browns, more pancakes, and an entire jar of maple syrup for my enjoyment. It wasn't just maple syrup, it was the real stuff, the kind I drooled over in the grocery store but usually refused to pay horrendous amounts of money to buy for myself.

I made it through three pancakes and a stack of bacon before my stomach informed me I was no longer at immediate risk of starving to death. "Okay. You can talk to me now, but if you want me to talk without food in my mouth, you have to wait a while."

Quinn moved enough files so he could sit on the floor on the other side of the coffee table. "I filled everyone in on what I knew about Audrey, but they need you to fill in some blanks."

"We missed blanks from the first investigation?"

"Apparently."

Huh. I hadn't thought that was possible. I'd essentially crucified my husband on the cross of his sexiness factor, not that he'd seemed too upset over my blabbing about his prowess. "What did we miss?"

"Who she might have been in league with."

"Beyond that incubus, I don't know if she was in league with anyone," I confessed. "Or if she was, I wasn't aware of it."

"That's what I said, but they think we may have missed something. Well, we did. Who gave Audrey the gorgon dust that infected her with the gorgon virus?"

"I am still having trouble thinking of gorgons as being infected with a virus," Roberto admitted. "It's not usually on the CDC's radar to worry about gorgons infecting humans."

Quinn scowled. "Because it's not typically a contagious disease. Not really. Most gorgons are a natural species. Gorgon dust is basically a toxin that can change someone into a gorgon—and if the infection is potent enough, it can be spread. As a general rule, gorgons shun the manufacturing of dust. It involves too much sacrifice—or murdered victims. Or the bodies of a loved one. I'm concerned over what I saw at that mine."

"There were a lot of gorgon bodies," I whispered. "And a child."

"And they were likely going to be converted into dust. In a way, I regret you torched that gorgon. I would have enjoyed peeling information out of him."

"Peeling?" I asked with wide eyes.

"I would have used your potato peeler, the one I picked up at the restaurant store because you saw the demonstration of it tearing through a pineapple."

"Not my peeler!" I wrinkled my nose. "I hid the rusty one you wanted to get rid of under the sink because I couldn't bear to throw it away. You could use that one."

"Alas, we can't peel information out of the bastard, so we'll have to be satisfied with thinking about it."

I considered our conversation. "We're not good people sometimes, Sam."

My husband smiled at my use of his first name. "I know,

but he got off lightly. He deserved a far worse death than you gave him."

"So, I killed someone who might have been important."

"He would have tried to kill Janet. You made the right choice. You made the right choice killing Winfield, too. He definitely would have tried to kill Janet. And the only reason you weren't killed is because of your heritage. You took an entire ampoule of ambrosia."

I marveled at my husband's neutral tone. "Did someone give you a chill pill? Because you are way too chill for this discussion."

He sighed. "Yes."

"You're not a zombie." I spent a moment admiring him. "You're very pretty."

He chuckled. "I'm certainly glad you think so."

Roberto cleared his throat. "While I know we're interrupting what's supposed to be the start of your vacation, it's critical we figure out how this happened in the first place."

I chomped on a piece of bacon, sighed, and shrugged. "It's obvious that John Winfield got involved because he wanted to get revenge on me and Janet. I didn't take sufficient care with his fragile male ego. He also disliked having to answer to Janet, a woman. He was a sexist, unprofessional pig. He deserved to be pancaked by an angry unicorn."

To make it clear I had zero cares that I'd killed the piece of shit, I stabbed my last pancake with my fork, twisted the utensil, and dunked it into a puddle of maple syrup. I took my time with chewing, too.

My husband raised a brow. "That's disturbing for even you, Bailey."

"What we don't know is when Audrey may have gotten into contact with John Winfield. This could be relevant," the

FBI goon beside me stated. I considered asking him for his name, but I opted against it. If he wanted me to know—or care—who he was, he'd tell me. Until then, I'd do my part, answer his questions, and hope he left so I could attend to more important matters, mainly my husband.

"Why could it be relevant?" I asked when no one spoke and the silence began to bug me.

"He may have used his connections within the police department to get information on your whereabouts, which ultimately may have led to your kidnapping. In fact, I'm speculating that there may be something to the connection to Chief Morriston, as only the cops directly working with a chief, or other chiefs, would have any reliable data on where a police chief is going. Chief Quinn, your position would have been monitored, and it would have been very easy to determine where you would have taken your wife the night she was kidnapped. You have a preference for that hotel, and it's noted in your file."

Quinn's expression turned neutral, which I recognized as his anger beginning to bubble to the surface. "Winfield wouldn't have had access to that information, but Morriston would have."

"Correct. And if you were distracted with a situation dealing with your wife, you would have been in a position to be ousted from your position—or transferred due to poor work performance. Unfortunately, your work performance wasn't hampered due to your accrued paid vacation time and sick leave. Even police chiefs have allowances for family emergencies, and the kidnapping of your wife certainly counts. This is where things become complicated. If Chief Morriston was involved with your kidnapping, it counts as the assault and interference of a government employee *and* it would also be considered a deliberate attempt to interfere with law enforcement. The punishment for this is severe in the state of New York. Chief Morriston's rank would make the punishment even more severe."

"Do I want to know what an FBI agent considers to be a severe punishment?"

"A complete stripping of all of his memories and a complete rehabilitation as a civilian. If possible, his magical abilities would also be stripped. Chiefs have a great deal of power, but with power comes responsibility. There's too much potential for corruption."

"Absolute power corrupts absolutely," I muttered. "Realistically, what is the probability of this Chief Morriston fellow being involved?"

"Higher than we like. So, have you ever met him before?"

I glanced at Quinn. "Have I?"

"I have no idea."

I looked the man in the eyes and said, "I have no idea. What does he look like?"

The agent reached across the table, picked up a stack of folders, and flipped through until he located a photograph, which he held out so I could see.

The unfortunately familiar face of one of my father's friends stared back at me, and I wrinkled my nose. "Oh. Asshole. Yeah. Pimple Pecker. He's one of my father's friends."

My husband's brows shot up. "Pimple Pecker?"

"He's in love with his own pecker and needs to invest in a skin treatment plan. What do you want? I was like five when I came up with it. I thought I was clever at the time. Anyway, he's an asshole, and it's definitely safe to say we have a non-functional relationship. The last time I saw him,

I was sixteen, he grabbed my ass, and I would've kicked him in the shins if my father hadn't been glaring at me at the time."

"He grabbed your ass?" my husband asked, his tone dangerously soft.

Crap. I gulped, my eyes widening. "Well, uh. Yes. He's a dick. And he thinks with his dick. And I may have said some unfortunate things. You know how I am, Sam. I can't help it!"

"Whatever you said, it wasn't sufficiently harsh," Quinn snarled, and he hopped to his feet, walked across the room, and picked up a phone from the computer desk. He dialed a number, and after a pause, he said, "Grandfather, I need you to verify the truth about a situation."

He hung up, and the archangel popped into existence in a flash of golden light.

"I was wondering how long it would take you to ask for me," he said.

I made a ward against evil. "Archangels are extra assholes, and as I have a child named Sylvester, you need a new name."

"You can call me Sariel, as that cat is out of the bag now." The archangel glared at his grandson. "I can't believe you brought my brother into this."

"I didn't, not exactly."

"He really didn't. He bargained with a *lesser* devil." I wrinkled my nose.

Quinn sighed. "You're never going to let that go, are you? It's part of our job, Bailey. If a devil gets into trouble on the mortal coil, they can bargain their way out of traditional punishments. The favor I did was only partially work related; I prevented it from becoming a major incident, so he owed me a direct bargain *and* something that would help law enforcement in general. So when that devil couldn't pay back the bargain, the Devil did, and as it was to help recover Janet, it fit the requirements."

Sariel grumbled, and I almost expected the archangel to start cursing. "It annoys me that you speak the truth. He's going to be absolutely insufferable. And I heard about Easter, you little punk."

Quinn grinned. "You're always telling me I should be more open with the family. I am."

"You're enjoying this way too much."

I realized why the archangel was so grumpy, and I pointed and laughed at him. "You like your brother, and you have to admit it, because you're an archangel and you can't lie about it. Sucker."

The archangel sighed. "This is payback for when I chased you around that arena isn't it?"

It was now. "Yep."

"All right. What did you need verified?"

My husband looked me in the eyes and asked, "Bailey, is it true that Chief Morriston grabbed your ass when you were a minor?"

"If sixteen counts as a minor, yes. He copped a feel of my breasts when I was fifteen, too. It was an 'accident' in the swimming pool." I wrinkled my nose. "Honestly, I didn't even remember it until I saw that ass wipe's picture. He just managed to piss me off."

"She speaks the truth."

My husband's calm expression cracked, his cheek twitching. "Sexual assault of a minor is enough to lose him his rank, and if he found out I had married Bailey, she might have been inclined to talk about the situation—which would give him sufficient motive to have her targeted. If Audrey went to Winfield after the 120 Wall Street incident, and

Winfield went to Morriston for additional information on Bailey, then he could be complicit in her kidnapping. He knew if she spoke up, he could lose his job."

The FBI agent grunted. "And the statute of limitations doesn't apply in assault cases of a minor because of the nature of the crime. Sariel's confirmation of the incident would be sufficient to start a case on his character. Or lack thereof. Bailey, please forgive me for having to ask this, but did the assaults escalate?"

"No," my husband and I said at the same time.

I grabbed an unused napkin and flung it at him. "Not a single word out of you. I wasn't raped. Groped, yes. But not raped. And he always did it when my asshole parents were close enough to keep my mouth shut because they trusted him over me. And hated me. Still hate me," I said with a shrug. "I really completely forgot about it. I think there's a psychological term for that, isn't there?"

"Psychological repression or thought suppression," Roberto announced. "It depends on if you were doing it unconsciously or not. Thought suppression is when you deliberately forget about the event to dodge the trauma. Sariel? Can you tell which category she falls into? Either would be evidence of sufficient trauma to warrant pursuing in court."

"I won't prod into my granddaughter's memories without her permission."

I waved my hand. "Prod away, Sariel. I have nothing to hide."

Quinn stared at me with wide eyes, his mouth hanging open.

"What?"

The archangel stood before me, leaned over the coffee

table, and unwound the towel from my head and ran his fingers through my hair, brushing away the tangles. "You're a master at hiding, Bailey, but my grandson loves you because of it. He's just surprised you're so open about this. He expected you to retreat into your shell. You've grown a lot in the past few months. I will be gentle, but you may remember things you wish you had forgotten."

"If this will help resolve this, do what needs done. I can handle it."

"It's possible that once upon a time, you couldn't. And if it's discovered your parents were complicit in these assaults…"

If I hadn't been aware of my grandfather's true nature, his icy tone would've terrified me. "The Devil said there was a special place in hell for them."

"There is. But how special, I suspect I will find out. You are free to say no, but would you like me to evaluate your childhood? If anything, you will know I understand. You'll be able to move out of their shadow." Sariel stretched his wings, and bands of green and gold colored his feathers. "I may rethink my intention to have them at your wedding as guests dependent on what I see. I try not to prod too much into the past."

"It sucks, you'll probably be scarred for life, and it's a good thing you don't have a head, as I really don't want to see your expression."

"It will be an unhappy one."

"Yeah, that's why I don't want to see it," I admitted. "It's easier when I can't see the pity."

"You are too strong a woman to pity, Bailey, even if you can't see that for yourself." Sariel tucked my hair behind my ears. "You are less likely to remember much if you keep your eyes open. It's one of those funny things about human minds. It will feel as though I'm tickling the inside of your head. I apologize for that, but it's inevitable."

"Are you going to talk about it or just do it?" I asked, debating if I wanted to torment the archangel by undressing my spouse with my eyes while he poked around in my head.

Then again, I didn't like sharing. At all. When it came to Quinn, I was happily jealous and greedy. Selfish, even.

The archangel chuckled. "That you are."

"In case you weren't sure, gentlemen, angels are assholes. It's a truth of the universe."

While I mostly focused on my husband, I was aware of the FBI agent gaping at me. "You just called an archangel an asshole."

"If he had a head and tilted it to the side really far, he might be convinced I actually like him," I replied. "I could even be talked into confessing I love him despite him being an angel."

Quinn laughed. "I'm proud of you. You said it without looking like you swallowed a toad. If you don't run to the bathroom this time, I'll be forced to reward you appropriately later."

Over the past few months, he'd done an excellent job of training me into doing what he wanted using his body as an irresistible bribe. "I love you. Please reward me appropriately later."

The archangel chuckled. As warned, the inside of my head tickled, but I ignored his poking and prodding in favor of my husband. His smile promised the best kind of trouble in my future.

"All right. I'm done," Sariel announced.

I blinked. "That's it?"

"My grandson is a most excellent distraction. You were so focused on him you couldn't have cared less about what I was looking for in your memories."

"I'm so proud of you, Mr. Archangel. You're not nearly as stuffy and formal as usual. If you had a head, I would make Quinn find you a cookie." I sighed, and aware I couldn't afford to dodge the truth, I asked, "What did you find?"

"About what I expected having met those humans. They have earned their special place in my brother's keeping. I'm in no mood to be merciful on their souls."

"Abuse?" Quinn clenched his hands, and after several deep breaths, he relaxed.

Even a month ago, I'd instinctively flinched when he balled his hands into a fist. The first time he'd done it around me, I'd frightened both of us with my reaction.

"Yes. And Chief Morriston's behavior was worse than she remembers, and I can verify all incidents and draw up the accusations per mortal laws. I can also verify the presence of psychological scarring, and I will file the appropriate mortal paperwork required to bar her from taking the stand. I will have the truth of my words verified by another archangel *and* my brother, using my viewing of her memory as evidence."

I blinked. "You can do that?"

"Angels may always opt to take on the burden of witnessing on behalf of a mortal. But it requires what I did to you, a complete exposing of your memories and soul. Not everyone is as open as you."

"Me? Open? Have you met me?" I pointed at myself, and then I pointed at my husband. "You should hear some of the shit I say to him because I'm nervous."

"That is different, although I find it rather amusing how

often you lie to try to hide just how much you adore my grandson."

"It's his fault!"

"Yes, it is. It is a good thing that he, on an instinctual level, is aware of when you're fibbing. It doesn't hurt he's learned to speak your language, which involves a great deal of flailing, babbling, and running to the bathroom to hide when you've blurted some form of affection in a public space."

"Has everyone heard about that?" I complained.

Quinn grinned. "I thought it was adorable, honestly. I don't mind when you blurt things because you have no idea how to handle how much I love you. I know the truth."

"All right. So my parents were assholes, and they're friends with an asshole who may have been out to get rid of me. Something I'm entirely used to, for the record. On a scale of one to ten, Sariel, how much of an asshole were my parents to me? Outside of the bullshit I can't seem to forget no matter how hard I try?"

"Those things you cannot forget are defining moments, little granddaughter. To take them from you would be to change you completely. Some things may be best left undisturbed. I see no need to force you to relive such painful things."

"Psychological repression?" Roberto asked.

"Yes. To force her to remember these events would be traumatic for no good cause. Unfortunately, that sort of abuse is not well defined under mortal law. Mortal punishments would not fit the crimes they've committed, and she does not need money tainted with their sin. No, I believe I have a better thought on how to deal with them."

My brows rose at that. "How?"

"I'll let my brother and his devils deal with them. And *He* would never welcome such filth into *His* heaven. *He* is not as forgiving a father as some might believe. Mercy is only for those who are capable of mercy. They reap what they have sown, and they had no mercy for you, and will find no mercy at *His* hands because of that."

I wondered what the archangel had found in my memories to anger him so much.

"You will never know," he promised. "The little you remember now is all that you will ever remember, for I have taken that burden upon my shoulders."

I couldn't understand why, and tears burned my eyes, but I fought against them.

Sariel patted my cheek. "You already understand why, Bailey. Did you not welcome those little children into your heart for no reason other than because someone needed to love them? I can, so I did. I will be in New York for a while so that justice might one day be served."

The archangel disappeared in a flash of golden light.

I lifted my chin, refusing to bow beneath the onslaught of emotions roiling within me. No matter how hard I thought about it, one question rose above all others. "Do you really think Morriston would have been involved with this just to make sure I disappeared? Could so much of this have happened because of what he'd done when I'd been a teenager?"

My husband heaved a sigh. "I don't think so. I know so. Cops aren't infallible, Bailey. My station weeds out the bad seeds early; I can't abide by those types nearby. I sense them like a hot poker against my skin. And once I'm aware of them, it's my nature to discover their sins. Justice for all is the oath I swore, not justice for only those who are rich enough, white enough, magical enough, vanilla enough, or what have you. For all. Even if it means I discover one of my cops beats his wife and I must stand trial against him for learning the truth. Or if it means I have to answer a call because a cop's wife called another cop fearing for her life, knowing it would get back to me so I might help her and her children. We have a hard job, and some forget why we do as we do. And sometimes, it's a matter of absolute power corrupting absolutely. We aren't perfect."

"You are," I whispered.

Quinn shook his head. "No, I'm not. It took me a long time to learn what those odd feelings meant. People have suffered because of my ignorance. I do my best. But I'm not perfect. I have no doubt that there are men in the world who would do anything to protect the power they have—or reach for more of it because they're unhappy with where they are in their lives. Someone who is friends with the Gardeners isn't someone who would be satisfied with what he has. And you would have been a threat to that. Targeting Janet makes sense if his goal was to get rid of you. You would put everything, especially your life, on the line to protect her. And you did."

I had. "They just didn't know it's useless to target me with ambrosia."

"Let's just say I'm rather happy you're ridiculously durable."

I was. "What happens now? What other questions do you need to ask us? What can we do to determine if he's guilty?"

The FBI agent shook his head. "While we do need to get to the bottom of this, the archangel has all of the evidence we need to move forward with the case. We have sufficient ties to file charges with what we have. We need to build a case from this, we need to get more information on the gorgon dust and rabies cases, but I'm confident in saying we have enough evidence to prove this whole mess is somehow connected. With luck, we'll be able to piece together how and why. Sam if you remember anything, call me."

"What about me?" I demanded.

The FBI agent grinned at me. "You heard the archangel. He's taken that burden from you. I look forward to grilling an archangel. It's not every day I get to be a dick to a divine and he has to put up with it. I'm considering it a Christmas present."

I changed my mind about not caring who the FBI agent was, and I thrust out my hand. "Hi. I'm Bailey, and I think we should be friends."

"Chuck Levenger. You'll be seeing a lot of me, although you'll dodge the questioning sessions. You'll just have to deal with us questioning your husband."

"I'm counting that as a Christmas present."

He shot me a salute. "Excellent. This changes how we're going to move forward with this investigation. Honestly, I'm expecting this to be a bunch of dead ends, but we're better off than we were a few days ago. We'll be in touch, but I doubt we'll make much progress over the holidays, outside of filing charges and preliminary hearings. The holidays will delay things. Unfortunately, due to the nature of the charges, I expect Chief Morriston will be released on bail."

Quinn stiffened. "What if he runs?"

Everyone else in the room sighed, and Chuck held his hands up in a gesture of hopeless surrender. "I'll be recommending to the judge to deny bail, but I'm not going to hold my breath. But, stranger things have happened, and our side will have two archangels *and* the Devil verifying the truth of the situation. Maybe justice will be served quicker than I think—and without a fight."

My husband lifted his hand and rubbed the bridge of his nose before pinching it. "This sounds like a disaster in the making."

"If he's wise, he'll run and disappear, never to be seen again. If he gets out on bail and decides to run. If he is never seen again, I can live with that, you can live with that, and most importantly, your wife can live with that."

I could? I thought about it, and upon reflection, realized he was right. I could live with the man running off and never surfacing or bothering me again. "It wouldn't bother me very much," I admitted. "I wouldn't be happy about knowing an asshole is out there that might target some other teen, but if he cleans up his act and acts like an angel for fear of having his memory wiped and his magic taken, that's punishment enough, right?"

My husband didn't look convinced, but I'd figured him out better since we'd been married.

He'd never be convinced everything would work out unless there was no longer even a shadow of a doubt he'd secured my safety. I got to my feet, circled the table, and took up residence on his lap, grabbing hold of his wrists and wrapping his arms around me. "That's punishment enough, Sam."

"If you're certain," he conceded with a sigh.

"I'm certain."

TWENTY-FOUR

She pointed at the Devil. "He's wearing
a Santa hat."

QUINN

I SPENT a glorious week and a half exploring Las Vegas with Bailey, the children, and our menagerie of animals. At night, the instant one of my relatives retrieved the children and the pets, I did all the little things I hadn't been able to do in New York. I took Bailey out to dinner. Whenever a show caught her eye, I got tickets so we could see it. We went to the aquarium. I even managed to wrangle a helicopter flight over the Grand Canyon with a sunset dinner and champagne.

She soaked everything in, and much like a flower finally given enough sunlight to thrive, she bloomed. Her joy became even more intoxicating than alcohol, and I almost regretted I hadn't been fired like Chief Morriston likely desired.

Such days would be few and far between in our future, but they would happen.

Somehow, between the kids, between our work, and between everything, I'd see to it.

I'd show her that the future was something to cherish and look forward to. I'd turn the world upside down to make it happen for her, even if it took me our entire lifetimes to accomplish it.

True to the Devil's word, we didn't have to do much to plan our wedding, although I hit a snarl I wasn't sure I could overcome.

Bailey wanted to fight for the kids as she'd been taught, determined to prove she'd do anything to be worthy of being a mother, even suffer through the flames of hell. She refused to be a mistake in their young lives.

The children weren't interested in a fight. They'd already made their decision. It'd only taken a look for them to fall in love with her. Bailey hadn't even needed a look.

She'd only needed to know there were children who needed her.

Some things were meant to be. I'd have a harder time of it than Bailey, but it was a battle I'd face with a smile. Bailey was, from that very first look, their mother.

It'd take time for them to truly accept me as their father. In time, I would teach them their little hearts had enough room for me along with the memory of their true father, who'd paid the ultimate price for their sake. I still hoped I could lay his ghost to rest so they could have closure, but I already knew the truth. I wouldn't.

Angels couldn't lie. Well, angels could lie, but they'd cease being an angel the instant they spoke a falsehood.

Christmas morning rolled around, and the two children lost their minds from the instant they woke up until presents, an obscene number of them, arrived by archangel.

The Devil played Santa, something so absurd Bailey almost made herself sick laughing. I'd barely saved her from losing her breakfast by slapping my hand over her mouth and forcing her to breathe from her nose instead of swallowing air.

Patting her back resulted in a belch so epic my entire family stopped and stared at her.

"Oops," she whispered before hiccuping. She pointed at the Devil. "He's wearing a Santa hat. How can you expect me to not laugh?"

It wasn't until I focused on her to make certain she wasn't about to lose her breakfast again, that I realized we'd been played just like Perkins had asked for me to play his wife for Christmas.

I considered the likely culprits and picked the Devil as the one most likely to screw around with my evening ritual of preventing any unexpected additions to our family.

"Oops," he said with an evil smirk.

I turned an accusing eye on my grandfather, one of the few beings alive capable of potentially stopping the Devil from following through with his trickery.

"Did you really think I'd tell him no to that?" the archangel replied.

"What are you talking about?" Bailey asked, staring at me with wide eyes.

I surrendered, not that I'd intended to put up much of a fight. Smiling, I dropped a gentle kiss on her lips. "Merry Christmas, my beautiful. They're just busybodies."

I'd have to hit them and thank them later. I'd also have to thank them for doing the heavy lifting with Tiffany, who like my wife, was a little warmer than the day before to my senses. Well, compared to Bailey, quite a bit warmer.

It took some concentrating, but someone had taken my thoughts about quadruplets seriously, and I hoped they wouldn't kill me in nine months.

I shot the Devil a look and hoped he'd read my mind and be willing to negotiate on ensuring all four of the little ones made it into the world without incident.

"What about me?" my grandfather complained. "I'm just as useful as he is."

My wife laughed, and she grinned at Tiffany, who was snuggled up with her husband while basking in the glow of excited children and pets playing with their new toys. "The problem with sharing space with divines is they can read minds, and they just won't share what's so funny."

"Ain't that the honest truth," Tiffany replied. "Enjoy it while it lasts. We have a few hours before we have to get dressed and prepare for the wedding. Your idiot husband flew the entire damned station in."

I loved being Bailey's idiot husband, and I grinned at the annoyed scientist. "Yes."

My wife sighed and used my lap as my chair, a situation I rather enjoyed. "Today is going to be long but good."

Yes, it would be.

BAILEY

AN HOUR before I was scheduled to have a proper wedding ceremony while in a pretty white dress that belonged more on a supermodel than on me, I came to the conclusion my deadbeat parents wouldn't be making an appearance. I couldn't tell if I was relieved or annoyed I wouldn't be able to tear strips out of their flesh with the power of my words alone.

It would've been a memorable affair, but when I thought about it, I decided I didn't want my husband to have to face those assholes again unless necessary.

"They're not coming because I uninvited them," a deep, rumbling but warm voice stated behind me.

I about jumped out of my skin, as I thought I'd been alone in the suite while Tiffany had gone off to wrangle her dress with the Devil's help. I would've found that a great deal more worrisome, except the Devil had assured me he walked the straight and narrow as he valued his family jewels, which belonged to his wife and only his wife.

I'd learned a very valuable lesson: I feared the Devil's wife far more than I feared the Devil, and I hadn't even met her yet.

I turned to discover a golden-skinned man with sun-bright hair and molten yellow eyes favoring me with a smile. I'd met enough divines to recognize one, although I had no idea who he was or why he'd popped in for a visit. "I think you may have just scared a few years off my life."

His chuckles reminded me of rolling thunder. "You'll recover."

I considered his statement, weighed the advantages and disadvantages of them not attending, and ultimately nodded my approval. "Thank you for uninviting them. It would have been a pity if I'd lost my new shoes up their asses. Fortunately, I do have one shoe per asshole, but I would have to spend the rest of the night barefoot." I lifted the hem of my long, white dress to show off the pretty white heels, which would have inflicted glorious damage if I did get an opportunity to wield them like a weapon.

"More importantly than uninviting them, I made it clear if they ever brought any more distress to you in your entire lifetime, they would enjoy the company of a vengeful mummy until the End of Days, be it on this Earth or in the pits of hell. I may have informed them I would be rather pleased to escort them to hell myself to ensure they did not get lost on the way."

"I have no idea who you are, but you have earned some major wedding day points," I announced.

"I am a quarter contributor to your existence, something I regretfully did not know of until quite recently. I would have come sooner, but you were enjoying your time with your soul mate, and I was unwilling to interrupt your time of peace."

"I'm upgrading you to half contributor, as I've no interest in acknowledging the assholes beyond a general willingness to insert my shoes up their asses." While a silly enough declaration, I already liked the golden-skinned divine.

He didn't seem to mind my foul mouth and readiness to indulge in violence.

"However much I am displeased with their cruelties, you cannot erase them."

I snorted and waved my hand. "They're not worth my time, and I will. They got an honorable mention on my birth certificate. That's more than they deserve."

"You get that from your mother's side of the family," he announced with so much certainty I laughed.

"That's the unicorn side of the family?"

"That is correct."

"The unicorn side of this family is badass. I breathe fire."

"The fire breathing tendencies come from my side of the family."

I thought about that, considering what I knew about Egyptian mythology. "That would make you Ra or one of the incarnations of Ra. Amun-Ra? Ra-Ra the Sun God?"

"Ra-Ra the Sun God?" The divine covered his mouth with a hand and cleared his throat. "Ra. Amun-Ra is a later merging and not my original self. Humans added that in later. They do strange things like that. As you've likely guessed, I am, indeed, a sun god."

"The next time you decide to participate in nookie while possessing some human, I recommend you do a thorough background check on the humans you and your lover select."

"I will endeavor to keep that in mind."

"It's true, then? You had no idea I existed?"

"Had I, you would have discovered yourself taken from your mortal parents and put into a more appropriate care." Ra's expression darkened. "I have been warned I may not hasten their escort to their eternal torment."

"Christmas is a bit mandatory in the Quinn household, and so is that Easter one, apparently. Turns out *He* is Sam's great grandfather or something like that. His lineage is confusing on a good day."

"You are correct. I suppose that element of his lineage is suitable for you."

I blinked at that. "Is this what they mean when discussing potentially overprotective parents?

"Approximately."

I giggled. "He's mine so you have to accept him, and he's really good with kids."

"That also factored into my evaluation of his character. You require a nurturing hand."

Obviously, I would have my work cut out for me in the

formality department. Then again, I was impressed Ra spoke English in the first place.

"It is a benefit of divinity. We can speak all languages as needed."

"I hope you're not expecting me to learn Egyptian. I have enough trouble with English."

Ra chuckled. "I think you will be fine. There's the matter of your mother I wanted to discuss with you before your ceremony."

"Is she coming?"

"She is, but the moon is waning, so it is very difficult for her to manifest. She will be present, but she cannot create a form for herself. This is why we often meet as we do. A possession is easier when the moon is not at its peak. A price of companionship."

"That's okay. I'll meet her one day, right?"

"The next full moon," he replied with a smile. "It will even rise during the day, so we can meet with you, your husband, and your children. We would be pleased to share our time together on this Earth as we can."

While aware Sariel had taken some of my memories, I remained certain neither of my human parents would have ever considered willingly doing something that would cost them anything. Sacrifice, beyond mine, wasn't in their nature. Given an opportunity, they would've discarded me, a reality I loathed to think about.

Instead of spending his few, cherished moments with my mother, they would spend it with me instead.

I wasn't sure what to say or do, so I stared at him with wide eyes.

Ra simply smiled, reached out, and brushed my cheek with

the back of his hand. "It is not a sacrifice or a burden on either of us. It is a privilege and honor. You were not the result of a passing fancy, despite our not knowing of you sooner. We did not expect such a gift—we did not even hold hope of receiving such a gift. If it was so easy for the divine to have children, our offspring would have long since taken over the world. No, Bailey. While we have failed as parents, you are a creation of love. We look forward to teaching you that. While we cannot necessarily be with you at all times because of our natures, we can visit as often as you like. Just not together."

"What is my mother's name?"

"Menily. She will be an invisible presence for your ceremony today, but if you would have me, I would walk you to your groom as is the tradition of your people. In time, I will teach you the tradition of my people, and Menily will teach you the tradition of her people. Then, we will teach you the traditions of those who came before us. It will take a long time." Ra sounded rather pleased by that.

As always, I made a mess getting to where I meant to go, but every time life tried to kick me in the face, I somehow found myself looking directly at some bright new future filled with possibilities.

"Do you think I'll be able to talk Quinn—er, Sam—into renewing our vows every year according to old traditions? That seems interesting. He has a very odd lineage. You'd have to spend a long time teaching us the particulars of those traditions."

"I believe all you would have to do was ask and tell him you love him so much you want to reaffirm your vows. It is a show of dedication and faith. It will please him greatly."

It would. "Think he'll be cranky with me when he finds

out that I conspired with a divine about having a kid for Christmas?"

Ra chuckled. "Did you think you could pull such a trick without him realizing? He already knows. He is on the verge of bursting from joy."

As was I. "Do you think I'll still get to fight the gorgon?"

"Absolutely not. Your fight is cancelled on account of pregnancy, and I will utilize every trick in my arsenal to ensure that is so."

I pouted. "But it's only been a few hours!"

"You have already won that war. Your new children do not wish you to suffer for them, for they have suffered enough. They have chosen you as much as you have chosen them. Allow them this moment of peace. I am certain, once your children are born, your grandfather would be pleased to indulge your need to prove your mettle against him. That, I am afraid, is a tendency you inherited from me. We do like to rule over all we see, and he is a gorgon you have not yet conquered."

Damn it, I really couldn't argue with him. As I liked the compromise on finally getting my fight with Archambault Quinn, I surrendered. "That annoys me, but fine. Generally, I think we're going to get along just fine, old man. But I do have a request."

"Ask."

"Every last one of my kids gets a cool puppy like Sunny or Blizzard, and I don't care if you have to beg Anubis for help. All of my children need a badass puppy." To make it clear I meant business, I glared at Ra. "And I don't care if I got Blizzard out of a dumpster. He's a badass puppy."

My father laughed. "It shall be done, but I think, rather than wolves or mundane canines cured of infectious diseases, I shall partner each with an animal best suited for their spirits. For all you are a unicorn, you have a wolf's heart, and you live for your pack. That is why you have Sunny. Some of your children will be born to fly."

"Wait. *Some?*"

Ra smiled. "Did you really think you would stop after two?"

Oh, well. When I was honest with myself, I wanted nothing more and wouldn't change a thing.

Double Trouble is the next book in the Magical Romantic Comedy (with a body count) series. These stories, with the exception of Burn, Baby, Burn (sequel to Playing with Fire,) can be read in any order.

DEAR READER,

Thank you for reading Bailey & Quinn's second novel. I can already hear you asking about the wedding.

About that.

In time, you shall enjoy the wedding, as it will be the opening of their next adventure. And yes, those of you who love your fire-breathing unicorns, there will be a next adventure. (The Flame Game releases in October 2020.)

~The Furred & Frond Management on behalf of RJ Blain

About R.J. Blain

RJ BLAIN suffers from a Moleskine journal obsession, a pen fixation, and a terrible tendency to pun without warning.

When she isn't playing pretend, she likes to think she's a cartographer and a sumi-e painter.

In her spare time, she daydreams about being a spy. Should that fail, her contingency plan involves tying her best of enemies to spinning wheels and quoting James Bond villains until she is satisfied.

RJ also writes as Susan Copperfield, Bernadette Franklin, Audrey Greene, G.P. Robbins, and Lilith Daniels. Visit RJ and her pets (the Management) at thesneakykittycritic.com.

FOLLOW RJ & HER ALTER EGOS ON BOOKBUB:
RJ BLAIN
SUSAN COPPERFIELD
BERNADETTE FRANKLIN
G.P. ROBBINS

AUDREY GREENE
LILITH DANIELS